THE
PAINTED
BOY

BOOKS BY CHARLES DE LINT

The Riddle of the Wren
Moonheart: A Romance
The Harp of the Grey Rose
Mulengro: A Romany Tale
Yarrow: An Autumn Tale
Jack, the Giant Killer
Greenmantle
Wolf Moon
Svaha
The Valley of Thunder
Drink Down the Moon
Ghostwood
Angel of Darkness (as Samuel M. Key)
The Dreaming Place
The Little Country
From a Whisper to a Scream (as Samuel M. Key)
Spiritwalk
Dreams Underfoot (collection)
Into the Green
I'll Be Watching You (as Samuel M. Key)
The Wild Wood
Memory and Dream
The Ivory and the Horn (collection)
Jack of Kinrowan
Trader

CHARLES DE LINT

THE
PAINTED
BOY

VIKING
An Imprint of Penguin Group (USA) Inc.

VIKING
Published by Penguin Group
Penguin Group (USA) Inc., 345 Hudson Street, New York, New York 10014, U.S.A.
Penguin Group (Canada), 90 Eglinton Avenue East, Suite 700, Toronto, Ontario,
Canada M4P 2Y3 (a division of Pearson Penguin Canada Inc.)
Penguin Books Ltd., 80 Strand, London WC2R 0RL, England
Penguin Ireland, 25 St. Stephen's Green, Dublin 2, Ireland
(a division of Penguin Books Ltd.)
Penguin Group (Australia), 250 Camberwell Road, Camberwell, Victoria 3124, Australia
(a division of Pearson Australia Group Pty Ltd.)
Penguin Books India Pvt Ltd., 11 Community Centre, Panchsheel Park,
New Delhi – 110 017, India
Penguin Group (NZ), 67 Apollo Drive, Rosedale, North Shore 0632, New Zealand
(a division of Pearson New Zealand Ltd.)
Penguin Books (South Africa) (Pty) Ltd, 24 Sturdee Avenue, Rosebank,
Johannesburg 2196, South Africa

Penguin Books Ltd., Registered Offices: 80 Strand, London WC2R 0RL, England

First published in the United States in 2010 by Viking, a member of Penguin Group (USA) Inc.

10   9   8   7   6   5   4   3   2   1

LIBRARY OF CONGRESS CATALOGING-IN-PUBLICATION DATA IS AVAILABLE
ISBN: 978-0-670-01191-9

Printed in U.S.A.   Set in Stempel Garamond   Book design by Jim Hoover

FOR KIN & PENNY

THE
PAINTED
BOY

THE DRAGON GARDEN,
CHICAGO CHINATOWN, 2003

Jade that is not chiseled cannot become a gem.

—CHINESE PROVERB

THE BOY HAD finally fallen asleep.

Standing at the side of his bed, Susan Li pulled the cover down and studied the dragon tattoo that was not a tattoo. It took up most of her eleven-year-old son's back, a complicated pattern of golds and yellows with black outlines, the image bearing a disturbing similarity to the logo of the restaurant downstairs.

He'd always been a brave boy, never flinching over cuts and scrapes, but he'd cried in misery for hours at the pain of the image forming on his skin.

The family crest.

The family curse was what Susan called it.

She had three other children. She'd agonized over each of them until they reached puberty, then given thanks to the spirits of her ancestors that the child had been spared. Three times lucky.

But not this time.

"<Is he sleeping?>" a voice said in Mandarin.

She turned to see her own mother standing in the doorway.

"You don't have some magic to tell you that?" she asked.

Paupau frowned at the double insult—the tone of her daughter's voice and being addressed in their adopted language rather than Mandarin—but then her features smoothed.

"<I was only making conversation, daughter,>" she said.

Susan nodded. She wanted to rail at the older woman, but she knew it wasn't Paupau's fault. This was something that lay deep in the family's blood. It went back for generations.

"I thought my children would be free of the curse," she said. "That it would skip my children's generation as it did my own."

"<It's not a curse—you know that, daughter. It's a responsibility. And a great honor.>"

"<I could do without such honors,>" Susan said, finally switching to Mandarin.

It was impossible to read Paupau's expression.

"<I know,>" she told her daughter. "<But the duty lies in our blood. We can no more deny it than we can pluck the moon from the sky and wear it as a brooch.>"

"<What do I tell him when he wakes?>" Susan said. "<How do I explain this to him?>"

Paupau's gaze went to the sleeping boy.

"<That will be my burden,>" she finally said.

-1-

SANTO DEL VADO VIEJO, MARCH 2008

Fortune seldom repeats; troubles never occur alone.

—CHINESE PROVERB

ROSALIE BROUGHT a plate of beans and rice out to La Maravilla's back patio. Setting the plate on a table, she got a glass of water from a pitcher by the door, then settled gratefully into a chair. She'd been on her feet since early this morning and she'd be here until late tonight, working a double shift because her cousin Ines had asked her to cover for her.

For a long moment she simply savored being able to relax in the quiet. She took the elastic out of her hair and redid her ponytail. She pulled the chair on the opposite side of the table closer with the toe of her running shoe, then stretched her legs out on it.

It was midafternoon of another hot day and she had the patio to herself. The *touristas* preferred the air-conditioning inside, and in comparison the two-tiered patio was not only hot, but also shabby. It sported a motley array of plastic patio furniture, worn by use and discolored by weather. A fence of saguaro ribs ran along either side of the patio to the wall at the back; scraggly cacti grew in rock garden beds that followed the fences. More saguaro ribs served as a half roof over this part of the patio. Two large mesquite trees shaded the upper tier and were home to dozens of wrens and sparrows that would swoop down to snatch dropped tortilla chips. A low adobe wall separated the patio from the dusty alley behind.

The birds were bold, the tiny lizards shyer. But if you sat quietly enough, they would come out from between the saguaro ribs or rest on the wide top of the wall soaking up the sun.

Rosalie moved her plate closer and reached for her fork, but before she could take a bite, she heard the sound of rapid footsteps in the alley. A moment later, a dark-haired Chinese boy wearing a small backpack vaulted over the wall. He saw her, put a finger to his lips, then scrambled up into one of the mesquites with all the agility of a monkey.

While she was still registering his sudden appearance, she heard more footsteps. A moment later, two of the local gangbangers were staring at her from the other side of the wall. She didn't know their names, but she knew they ran with the Presidio Kings. The heavier of the two pointed at her with a muscled arm covered in tattoos. He had a crown tattooed on his forehead with devil's horns on either side. His companion had a knife scar down one side of his face.

"Yo," he said. "You there. You see a Chink go by?"

Rosalie had no reason to protect the boy hiding in the tree, but like most people in the neighborhood, she hated the swaggering gangbangers.

She shook her head.

"I find you've been lying to me," the man said, "and I'll come back and mess up that pretty little face of yours."

The threat made her angry, but she kept her temper in check. Confronting him would only make things worse.

She lowered her feet to the ground to make it easier to move if she had to retreat into the restaurant.

"I'm not lying," she said. "No one went by."

And it was the truth. The boy hadn't gone by. He'd climbed up into the tree.

The gangbanger held her gaze for a long moment, then he grinned. He blew her a kiss and the pair moved off down the alley. Rosalie raised her middle finger to their backs, but she stayed where she was until her pulse slowed a little. She waited a few moments longer before she went up the steps and crossed the upper patio to lean over the wall. She looked in the direction the men had gone, then the other just to be safe, before she quietly called up into the tree.

"They're gone," she said. "You can come down now."

He was just as agile in his descent, but whereas before she didn't doubt it was panic that had gotten him up the tree so quickly, now she was sure he was just showing off. He dropped the last few feet, landing lightly, and they stood there looking at each other.

He wasn't hard to look at, Rosalie thought. He seemed about seventeen—her own age—with the soft jet-black hair that you couldn't get out of a bottle, only from your genes. His eyes were so dark they almost seemed black, and he was sinewy rather than scrawny, as she'd thought from her earlier glance. His well-worn jeans were a boot cut, though he was wearing running shoes. His white T-shirt had no logo and could stand a wash. He had a gray hooded jersey tied around his waist.

"Thanks," he said.

She nodded.

"So, what did you do to piss off the Kings?" she asked.

"The Kings?" he repeated. "What, are those guys in a band or something?"

"Try gang. They were members of the Presidio Kings and seriously, you don't want to mess with them."

He held up a hand to stop her.

"I swear I have no idea what they wanted from me," he said.

"Then why were they chasing you?"

"I don't know. I got into town on the ten o'clock bus. When I got off the bus I noticed these guys—you know, the baggy pants, shaved heads, all the tattoos on their faces and everything."

She gave him a surprised look. "You saw the Kings at the bus station? That's weird."

"Why?"

"Because that's 66 Bandas turf."

"I didn't mean it was the same guys who were chasing me," he said. "They were just, you know, similar." He gave her a puzzled look. "Is it all gangs around here?"

She shrugged. "There's, like, two worlds," she said, interlacing her fingers and holding them up. "The world most people see and then the one that belongs to the *bandas*—the gangs. They don't really mix—lots of people don't know much more about the *bandas* than what they read in the paper—but if you pay any kind of attention, you can see them both. Here in the barrios, we don't really get a choice. They're always around and all you can do is try to keep out of their way."

"I wish I'd talked to you before I got off the bus."

"So, what did you do to get onto the 66ers' radar?"

"Nothing." He paused, then added, "Well, I talked to a cop."

She rolled her eyes. "Nice move."

"What? I was just asking him directions to some Chinese restaurants."

"You don't like Mexican food?"

"I love Mexican food. I was looking for a job. I went to this one a couple of blocks south of the bus station called the something Gardens—"

"Shanghai."

"Right. The Shanghai Gardens. The cook there said he'd heard the Imperial down here in Barrio Histórico was looking for help. When I stepped out of the restaurant, those guys were waiting for me and told me to hand over my knapsack. I got away from them and—"

"You got away from *two* different gangs?"

He shrugged. "As soon as I saw them, I recognized them from the bus depot, so I just took off. I'm a fast runner. But here's the funny thing. When I was crossing that bridge over the San Pedro . . ." His voice trailed off and he gave her a puzzled smile. "Why exactly do you have a huge dry riverbed in the middle of the city?"

"It's only dry until it rains in the mountains. Then it's a torrent that's so strong it can easily wash a car away. Some years it even overflows its banks."

"Really?"

She nodded. "So, you were crossing the bridge . . . ?"

"Yeah, and those guys were hot behind me, but when I got halfway across, they just stopped and stood there watching me run to the other side."

"That's because this side of the river is Kings' turf."

"The point is I've got no idea why those first guys were after me. And then, as soon as I started walking away from the bridge, I picked up the two you just saw and took off through the alleys to try to lose them."

"They must have seen the 66ers chasing you and wanted to know why."

"*I* wouldn't mind knowing why."

"Maybe they think you're a drug courier."

"A *what*?"

"You know. You're going into a Chinese restaurant, which could be a front for the Triads."

He shook his head. "Right, and we make our meat dishes with cats and dogs that we catch in the alleys."

She pulled a face. "I didn't mean it that way. But you hear people talking about it at school—how Asian gangs are supposed to be trying to muscle in on the *bandas'* turf."

"Asian street gangs are a far cry from the Triads. That's like comparing cockroaches to wolves."

"I wouldn't know."

"Well," he said, "I'm not Triad and all I'm carrying is a change of clothes. No drugs. No secret agendas."

"I believe you."

Rosalie leaned over the wall again to check that the alley was still clear.

"Are you hungry?" she asked.

"Sure, but—"

"C'mon. I was just having a late lunch. You can join me if you like."

She headed back to the lower part of the patio and he trailed along behind her.

"I'm Rosalie," she said as she indicated he take one of the chairs at the table where she'd been sitting. "What's your name?"

"Jay Li."

"Like Bruce Lee," she said, and faked a few kung fu moves.

He smiled. "No. My name's spelled L-I. And I don't really know those kinds of martial arts."

"Me neither."

"I can tell."

"Be nice, or you don't get any lunch. Rice and beans okay?"

"Anything'd be great."

She went into the kitchen and quickly made him a fat burrito. She put it on a plate with some tortilla chips and a little container of salsa.

"<Somebody's hungry.>"

She looked up to see her uncle leaning against the door that led to the restaurant. He had sideburns, his dark hair slicked back in a look that had been popular back in the fifties. Peeking out from under the rolled-up sleeves of his white shirt were faded *bandas* tattoos.

"<It's for a friend,>" she said, speaking Spanish as he had.

Her uncle looked past her to where he could see Jay through the window.

"<Does Ramon know you have this friend?>" he asked, smiling.

"<He's a *friend* friend. And I didn't even know he might be one until I met him a few moments ago.>"

Her uncle shook his head.

"<Still taking in strays,>" he said. "<You need to be careful, Rosalita. Not everyone is as good a person as you are.>"

She ducked her head in embarrassment.

"<I have a good feeling about him,>" she said. "<And a couple of the Kings were chasing him, so that makes him okay in my book.>"

Her uncle's features darkened. "<Those bastards—>"

"<It's okay,>" she said. "<They didn't cause any trouble. They were just being assholes, yelling at me from the alley before they took off.>"

"<Where was your new friend?>"

"<Hiding up in a mesquite he'd climbed. I swear he's part monkey, he got up there so fast.>"

Her uncle laughed, but then his features grew serious again.

"<What do they want with him, Rosalita?>" he asked.

"<I don't know. He—his name's Jay. He doesn't know, either.>"

Her uncle looked out the window again, then shrugged.

"<Just be careful,>" he said.

"<I will, Tío.>"

He shook his head as he walked back into the main part of the restaurant. "<You and your strays . . .>"

It was true, Rosalie thought. She couldn't resist them.

From the foundling cats and dogs that lived in and around her trailer at the back of her uncle's yard to the kids at school whom the other kids picked on.

But someone had to take care of those who couldn't take care of themselves.

Not that Jay didn't look capable of looking after himself, she thought as she brought the plate out to him. But everyone could use a kind word or a helping hand sometimes.

"Wow," he said as she set it in front of him. "This is a feast."

"You haven't eaten for awhile?"

"Just truck-stop food when the bus stopped."

She poured him a glass of water and slid it across the table.

"So, why do you want a job in a Chinese restaurant?" she asked.

He started to answer, but his mouth was too full.

"I grew up working in one," he said when he'd swallowed, "and it's pretty much the only thing I'm good at. Besides—apparently—getting into trouble."

She regarded him thoughtfully for a moment.

"Have you ever tried working in another kind of restaurant?" she asked.

He shook his head. "I've only ever worked in my parents' place, but I know the business from the ground up. I've been a dishwasher, busboy, waiter, and cook. I know how to clean up, order supplies, make the food, and work the cash." He took another, smaller bite from the burrito. "I need to get a job. And find out where the Y is so I've got a place to sleep tonight."

Rosalie nodded. "So are you on March break, or have you already finished school?"

"You mean like an accelerated program?"

"I guess."

He smiled. "Just because I'm Asian doesn't mean I'm an academic whiz. Maybe it's in my genes, because I've got a brother who's a doctor, and a sister who's a lawyer, and another sister who's the CEO of an NGO helping kids in Africa. But it never took with me. I'm a dropout."

"Were your parents disappointed?"

"You'd think. But Paupau told them—"

He broke off at her puzzled look. "Sorry. That's my grandmother on my mother's side. She's kind of like Marlon Brando in *The Godfather*. Everybody in the family—heck, everybody in the neighborhood—defers to her. Anyway, she told my parents that this was something I was supposed to do, so I left with their blessing."

"I don't get it. What are you supposed to do?"

He shrugged. "Who knows? She just told me to go someplace that feels right and then I'd figure it out."

"And your parents were really okay with your doing this?"

"Not really. I don't even know that I am. But you don't

argue with Paupau. She has a lot of strange ideas, but like I said, everybody pretty much does what she says. So I stuck my finger on a map and it came up Santo del Vado Viejo—which I've got to tell you, I'd never heard of before—and here I am." He smiled. "And who knows, maybe those guys chasing me and me hiding out in your tree is all part of some bigger plan."

"You don't believe that," she said.

"Paupau says there are no coincidences, there is only the fate that you must follow."

"But you're—" She hesitated, then plunged on. "You're just a kid like me. You should be going to school, hanging with your friends, enjoying your March break . . ."

"Which would beat being chased by a bunch of tattooed guys who want to kick my head in. I can't argue with that. So what about you? What's your story?"

He took another bite from his burrito and gave her an expectant look.

"There's nothing much to tell," she said. "I go to school. I work here in my uncle's restaurant. I hang out with my friends."

"And stay out of trouble."

"Usually, yes." She studied him for a moment before adding, "You know, my uncle's looking for a cook. Maybe he'll give you the job if I ask him."

"I don't know anything about preparing Mexican food."

"You can learn. It's not hard."

"I don't want to impose."

"It's cool," she said. "Really. Unless you really *have* to work in a Chinese restaurant."

"It's not that. It's just . . . I've got this letter of recommendation that Paupau said I should show any prospective employer. I don't know what it says, but I guess that's why the guy at the Shanghai Gardens was so helpful."

"You don't know what it says?"

He shook his head. "It's in Chinese. I know, I know. But I was born in Chicago, not in Hong Kong or the mainland. I can speak Mandarin, but I can't read it. Everyone in my family speaks Cantonese except for Paupau and my mother. Anyway, the point is your uncle wouldn't be able to read it, either."

"Tío Sandro makes his own decisions about who he thinks'll fit in here." She smiled. "And since I'm putting in a good word for you, I know the job's yours if you want it."

"I don't know what to say."

"And until you can get a place of your own, you can sleep on my couch."

He raised his eyebrows in surprise.

"Are you this nice to all strangers?" he asked.

"I just like helping people."

"And I totally appreciate it."

"Oh, and before you get any ideas," she said, "I've got a boyfriend."

"'S cool. I've got a girlfriend."

There was a laugh in his dark eyes that made her ask, "What's her name?"

"I don't know. I haven't met her yet."

"Has that line ever worked for you?" she asked.

"What? You don't believe in romance and true love? That somewhere out there is the one person who's going to make you complete?"

"Is this more of your grandmother's wisdom?"

"Nope, this is all my own."

She shook her head. "Life's not a pop song, it's a rap song. And around here, it's a *narcocorrido*."

"Say what?"

"Do you know what *corridos* are?"

"Some kind of Mexican music?"

She nodded. "They're part of the *norteño* tradition and usually have a polka beat. In the old days they would tell the stories of the Mexican 'Robin Hood' bandits like Malverde—'the generous bandit' who stole from the rich and then shared his loot with the poor. There's even a song about how at the end of his life, he got one of his own friends to turn him in so that his people would benefit from the reward money."

"Cool."

"If it's true."

"But now . . . ?" Jay said.

"Now bands sing *narcocorridos* praising the murderers

and drug lords who rule the *bandas*. It's weird, but in Spanish the word for band and gang are the same, and now these stupid kids are showing us why."

"But it's just like rap, isn't it? Most of the people who make it and listen to it aren't actually drug lords going around shooting people."

"No, here it's the *bandas* that get shot. A group'll sing a song in praise of one of the drug lords and members of a rival gang will shoot them for it."

"And is everyone like that around here?"

"No, of course not. But it still cuts close to home. My friend Anna's brother was killed in a drive-by a couple of years ago. My cousin José is in prison. The *bandas* are everywhere. Even my uncle ran with a gang when he was a kid, but he got out of *la vida loca* before he hurt himself or anyone else."

"Lucky."

Rosalie shook her head. "No, smart. And brave. It's hard to turn your back on your friends the way he had to. Because they're like your family. So he understands why José was running with the Kings, but it still breaks his heart that his only son's in jail."

Jay glanced where the gangbangers had been earlier.

"Maybe I picked the wrong place to move," he said.

"Oh, no. I'm making it sound horrible. There are lots of good people here, too. And there's lots of other kinds of music, and all kinds of arts and street fairs and festivals.

We have the mountains and the desert. I wouldn't want to live anywhere else."

He smiled. "Well, I'm here now, so I might as well get a taste of it."

"Do you want me to talk to my uncle? I'm working another shift tonight. You could help out and when it's slow I'll show you the ropes."

He plucked at his T-shirt. "I'm kind of grubby."

"Oh, right. You should have a shower and clean up first. I'll see if Anna's free to run you over to my place."

"Is this the Anna whose brother was killed?"

She nodded.

"I don't want to impose on her, either."

"Are you kidding? She's out of school, too, and is probably dying to do something. If you leave her alone, all she does is sit in her room and play her guitar."

"Yeah, but I don't know her and she doesn't know me . . ."

"Don't worry about it. All you need to know is that she's one of my best friends and plays in a band with my boyfriend, Ramon. You'll like her—she's cute."

"Great. I'll make such a good first impression on her all grubby like this."

"You made a good first impression on me."

He studied her for a moment with that solemn, dark-eyed gaze of his. Then he shrugged.

"And I have no idea how or why," he said.

"Maybe I just like the way you climb into a tree."

"Right."

She smiled. "Finish your burrito. I'm going to talk to Tío and then call Anna to come pick you up."

"Do you always get your own way?" he asked as she got up from the table.

Rosalie smiled. "Only when I'm right," she said.

Then she disappeared into the restaurant.

Jay finished his burrito, washing it down with half a glass of water. He hadn't thought the salsa was too hot while he was eating, but the spices had crept up on him. Setting the glass down, he got up and walked to the back wall of the patio. When he was satisfied that the gangbangers weren't still lurking around, he returned to the table to enjoy the quiet and warmth of the patio while he waited for Rosalie to return.

She reminded him of his sisters—not pushy, just very sure of herself—and it made him feel a little more at home in a place that was so different from where he'd grown up. When he caught the bus two days ago in Chicago, there'd still been snow on the ground. There'd been a *lot* of snow because they'd been having a brutal winter. But as the bus took him south, the snow had slowly disappeared, the temperatures rose, and then he was here, in this strange city in the middle of a landscape that seemed to be made up of nothing more than rocks and dirt.

He remembered Paupau nodding sagely when he told her where he was going, as though it was what she'd expected. As though she was familiar with his destination and it was exactly the place he was supposed to go. But now that he was here, he wasn't so sure. It seemed so much more intimidating than it had in the guidebook he'd been reading on the bus trip south.

Rosalie was right. He *was* just a kid still. He should be enjoying the March break and anticipating his return to classes. Except he didn't care much for school—or at least it didn't care much for him. Teachers, his fellow students— they all sensed the secret he carried but couldn't share. He doubted they would put it in so many words, but they knew there was something different about him and kept him at arm's length.

Maybe it was for the best that he had chosen a place so far away. The city and surrounding desert felt completely alien to him, but maybe alien was good. For one thing, he couldn't remember the last time he'd met someone his own age who didn't immediately tense up around him.

He noticed a tiny lizard making its way up the wall of saguaro ribs. It appeared to notice him at the same time because it froze in place—the lizard version of invisibility.

"What do you think, little brother?" he asked it. "Is Paupau a wise teacher, or just a crazy old lady?"

"Who are you talking to?"

Rosalie had returned. She stood in the doorway with a tall, well-muscled man standing behind her. His black hair was slicked back from his forehead and his skin was dark against his white shirt. Faded tattoos patterned his forearms. His face was impassive.

Jay started to point at the lizard, but it had taken his momentary distraction to vanish back in between the saguaro ribs.

"Myself, apparently," he said.

Rosalie's eyebrows lifted.

"My niece tells me you're looking for a job," the man said.

Jay stood up and came around the table.

"Yes, sir," he said. "I've got plenty of restaurant experience—just none of it with Mexican food."

"That can be learned. Do you take drugs?"

"No, sir."

"Are you a member of any gang?"

"No, sir."

The man studied him intently as he fired his questions. Then he asked the kicker:

"Do you have honorable intentions toward my niece?"

"Tío!" Rosalie protested.

Jay regarded him with surprise. He glanced at Rosalie before he answered.

"She's way out of my class, sir," he said. "And besides, I hear she already has a boyfriend."

Rosalie's uncle finally smiled.

"Good answer," he said. He offered his hand. "I'm Sandro Hernandez."

"But everybody just calls him Tío," Rosalie put in.

"I'm James Li," Jay said as he shook his new employer's hand, "and everybody calls me Jay. Thanks for this opportunity."

"You've got work papers?" Tío asked.

"I was born here. I've got my Social Security card."

"Great. We'll get the paperwork sorted out later. Rosalie says you can start training tonight?"

"As soon as I get cleaned up."

"I've already called Anna," Rosalie said. "She's on her way."

Rosalie had to get back to work, so she left Jay to wait for Anna in the dusty alley. He didn't have time to really start to worry about the gangbangers before a vintage turquoise-and-white Valiant pulled up. The driver rolled down her window and smiled.

"Well, look at you," she said. "All inscrutable and handsome."

Jay had to laugh. Rosalie was right. Anna *was* cute. Full-lipped and dark-eyed, black hair streaked with red, big jangly earrings. Her dark skin stood out against a cream T-shirt giving a shout-out to some Mexican band he'd never heard of. If Rosalie was a classic beauty, Anna was the wild girl you'd see sitting in the back of class, tapping her foot to some rhythm only she could hear. He could tell she was the girl who didn't wait to be asked to join anything—she made her own plans and did the asking.

"Cool car," he told her.

"I know—isn't it? My brother got it fixed up for me for my sixteenth birthday. He did most of the work on it himself."

"Nice to have that kind of talent."

Something changed in her face.

"Be nicer if he'd stuck to it instead of jacking cars for the Kings. Maybe the asshole'd still be alive."

There was a moment of awkward silence, then Jay nodded. "Rosalie said something about . . . um . . ."

Anna sighed. "Sorry. I've got this love/hate thing going with my memories of him." She gave him a too-bright smile. "So, are you getting in?"

"If you're sure it's not too much of a bother."

"If it was, would I be here? Don't be shy."

He went around to the passenger's side and opened the door.

"You want to drive?" she asked as he slid in.

Jay shook his head. "I don't even have my license. But I'm excellent at grabbing a subway or bus."

"Then it looks like I'm driving."

She was good company, chatting and laughing like they were old friends. The first thing she asked as they pulled away was what he had on his MP3 player. When he named a few of the bands, she nodded her approval and he felt like he'd passed some kind of test. He was glad he had because Rosalie wasn't just right about her being cute. She was also right about him liking her.

What wasn't to like?

Too bad it couldn't go anywhere. He didn't flatter himself that her flirting was anything but just the way she was—friendly and fun. Even if she did become more interested, nothing could happen. Not with the secrets he carried.

"Rosalie says you're in a band," he said. "What are you called?"

"We're Malo Malo." She pulled a face. "Yeah, I know. 'Bad Bad.' It kind of sucks. But Ramon—"

She glanced at him.

"Rosalie's boyfriend," he said.

"Yeah. It's Ramon's band—I mean, he started it—so he got to pick the name."

"What kind of music do you play?"

"We do some rap, some rock, all mixed up with the barrio flava—you know? Well, here we are."

They were only a few long blocks from the restaurant when Anna turned the Valiant down a dirt alley and pulled up along a chain-link fence. There was a low adobe house facing the street with a long silver trailer at the other end of the yard. Both had blue trim around the doors and windows. In between was a big expanse of dirt. Mesquite and palo verde trees grew at the back of the yard, shading the trailer, and there was a two-armed saguaro cactus by the house that stood almost thirty feet tall. Dried grasses and clusters of prickly pear followed the line of the fence.

And then there were the dogs. Jay counted eight. They were mongrels of all sizes, from something he thought was a terrier mix to a big, long-legged mastiff. The rest were various combinations of shepherd, lab, and some kind of yellow dog that he couldn't place.

"I could've walked here, easy," he said, turning back to Anna.

She shook her head. "Not with the Kings looking for you. You wouldn't have gotten half a block. What do they want with you, anyway?"

"Haven't a clue."

She gave him a look.

"Seriously," he said. He nodded toward the yard, adding, "What's with all the dogs?"

"Oh, that's our Rosie for you. We call her Our Lady of the Barrio because she's always taking in strays. She finds homes for most of them, but there's always a bunch hanging around." She smiled. "That goes for people, too. She puts in time at the soup kitchen and homeless shelter and takes all kinds of loser kids at school under her wing."

"I hope I'm not too much of a loser."

Anna gave him a light punch on the shoulder. "I'm kidding. But Rosie's pretty much a freakin' saint, no lie. I don't know how she juggles it all and still keeps up her grades. How're you with dogs?" she added as they got out of the car.

"I'm cool."

Anna opened the gate and the pack came running. Anna stepped forward, like she was going to calm them down, but they all stopped within a few yards and sat in the dirt, staring at them. No, Jay realized. Staring at *him*.

"That's weird," Anna said.

"What is?"

"Well, usually they're all over visitors, yapping and carrying on."

She gave Jay a puzzled look.

He shrugged. "I'm good with animals. We understand each other."

She looked back at the dogs, a little frown furrowing her brow.

"Obviously," she finally said and led the way to the trailer.

Jay paused at the door even though Anna had already gone in. She turned to look at him.

"What's the holdup?" she asked.

"Nothing. It's just . . ."

He didn't know what to say. He felt the presence of some kind of protective barrier keeping him out as effectively as if Anna had closed the door in his face. It took him a moment to realize it was the blue paint on the door and door frame. It seemed to vibrate when he looked at it closely and gave off a spicy scent that attracted him as much as it repelled.

"We have this, um, superstition in my family," he finally said. "About blue trim on doors."

Anna raised her eyebrows.

"It's just," he went on, "we think it's bad luck to go in unless someone actually invites us in."

"You're shitting me. What are you, a vampire?"

"Walking around in the day?"

"Okay," she said, "I'll give you that. But do you know why so many houses in this part of the country have blue on the windowsills and doors?"

He shook his head.

"It's to keep out the evil spirits." She waited a moment, then added, "Are you trying to tell me you're an evil spirit?"

He laughed. "Hardly. And who says the spirits have to be evil?"

"What would be the point of keeping out good spirits?"

"I suppose you're right."

"So, are you coming in, or what?"

"Are you inviting me?"

She rolled her eyes. "Come in, come in, already. You're one weird dude, you know that?"

"So I've been told."

But as soon as she spoke the words, he could cross the invisible barrier. He dropped his knapsack by the door and looked around. The trailer wasn't much on the outside, but inside it felt bigger than he thought it would and it was tidy. The furniture was all mismatched thrift store finds, but Rosalie obviously had a good eye and managed to bring harmony into what might have been chaos.

"And here come the cats," Anna said.

Jay turned to see a gray tabby and a slinky black cat coming down a short hall. They stopped when they saw him, hissed, and fled to the room at the far end.

"Good with animals?" Anna asked.

"Not so much with cats, I guess."

"The shower's through there," Anna said, pointing to a door down the narrow hall. "She keeps her spare towels on the shelves behind the door. Use whatever you need."

"Thanks."

"I'll go play with the dogs. Unless you need me to invite you into the bathroom before you can use the shower."

He smiled. "No, I'm good."

He waited until the door closed behind her before he went into the bedroom. Staying in the doorway, he knelt down on the carpet. The two cats were under the bed. A third, a striped orange-and-white tom, glared at him from the windowsill.

"Okay, tiger brothers," he said. "Can we have a truce

here? I promise not to hurt you or Rosalie. I'm just staying for a couple of days and then I'll be out of your lives again. What do you say?"

The cat on the sill continued to ignore him, but the gray tabby came out from under the bed. It sat and regarded Jay for a long moment, then began to groom itself. The second one emerged as well and jumped onto the bed. They weren't friendly, but at least they appeared to be willing to keep the peace while he was here.

"Thanks, guys," Jay said.

He stood back up and went into the bathroom.

It felt great to be clean again. He let the water pour down, relaxing under its spray until he started thinking about the gangbangers who'd been chasing him. There were gangs in Chicago. Crips and Bloods, the Latin Kings. The Chinese and Vietnamese kids had their gangs, too. But it wasn't hard to stay out of their way. Jay had always found it easy to stay off anyone's radar. Like the little lizards back at La Maravilla's patio, he just faded into the background. It was only when he spent time with people who didn't know his secret that they usually got uncomfortable.

But here he seemed to be the focus of everybody's attention. The gangbangers. Rosalie. Anna.

He turned off the shower and toweled himself dry.

He liked both girls, but the gangbangers worried him.

Maybe they were the reason Paupau thought he should be here, but this whole gang business seemed much too big for him to deal with.

"We can't protect everything," Paupau told him once, "so we must make our choices count."

She kept the peace in Chinatown, but it wasn't through confrontation. He wasn't entirely sure how she did it.

A finger on a map had brought him here, but now that he was here, he had no idea what to do next. One of Paupau's proverbs popped into his head:

To know the road ahead, ask those coming back.

It was sensible advice, except how did you know who'd already gone ahead, and who was to say they would even be coming back?

He sighed and went to get dressed, then realized he'd left his knapsack by the door. He wrapped the towel around his waist and poked his head out to check. Good. Anna was still outside. He went and got the knapsack and was on his way back to the bathroom when the front door suddenly opened. He tried to turn around, but he was too late.

"Are you about done?" Anna was saying as she came in, then her eyes went wide. "Holy crap! That is some serious ink."

The dragon image took up most of his back, a complex pattern of swirling golds and yellows, the dragon outlined in black: limbs, head, horns, tail. The detail was so intricate that you could almost think you saw each individual scale.

The head lay across his shoulder blades with the curling tail disappearing under the towel at the small of his back. It had grown in size as he'd grown, always taking up the same space on his back.

This was the secret he couldn't share.

When he was eleven, it would have brought Children's Services in to investigate, because what kind of parents would tattoo their child like this? Keeping it hidden meant he couldn't go to gym, couldn't go swimming, couldn't get naked with a girl—though that had been more his frustration than anything his parents or Paupau would have sympathized with.

Six years of keeping it hidden like he had some kind of stupid, secret identity—can we say Dragon Boy, anybody?— and now, because he'd let down his guard for just a moment, all the alienation he'd had to suffer was for nothing.

Oddly, the only thing he felt was relief.

"It's not a tattoo," Jay found himself saying before he could stop himself.

"Yeah, right. And I'm so brown-skinned only because I take the sun so well."

"No . . . I mean . . ." Jay let the words trail off.

"So what are you? Some kind of painted boy?"

Jay didn't know what to say.

"That is so freaky," Anna went on, then her eyes narrowed. "You're not one of those ninja Yakuza guys, are you? Because I saw a movie about them."

Jay shook his head. "Yakuza and ninjas aren't the same thing, and they're both Japanese. I'm Chinese."

"So it's some kind of Chinese gang thing. That's why the *bandas* are after you, isn't it? You're part of the Asian invasion into their turf."

"How do you even know about that kind of thing?" he asked.

She shrugged. "You have to be informed. How else do you know who to avoid?"

When she put it like that, he understood. It had been the same back in Chicago. But here the necessary knowledge didn't appear to just let you survive high school. Here, apparently, you lived or died by it. Literally.

"Well, I'm not in a gang," he said, "and it's not a gang tattoo. It's an image of a dragon, nothing less, nothing more."

Anna studied him for a long moment.

"I don't know why," she finally said, "but I find myself wanting to believe you."

"That's good, because I'm telling you the truth. All I am is another kid—just like you."

When Anna grinned, he knew that she was going to let it go. For now, anyway.

"I'm no kid," she shot back with some of her earlier friendliness. "I'm a rock goddess. Or I could maybe be if we can ever get this band off the ground. We've got a zillion MySpace friends but it's still hard to get a decent gig."

Jay imagined her onstage. If she played half as good as she looked, she was probably right.

"I should get dressed," he said.

"Don't feel like you have to on my account."

He raised his eyebrows, but she only smiled and waved him off to the bathroom.

Don't get too excited, he thought when he closed the door behind him. She was only flirting—like she had when they first met. Though now he could sense a reserve that he was pretty sure hadn't been there earlier. Or maybe he just hadn't noticed. Rosalie, he realized, was naturally cheerful, but Anna had to work at it. There could be any reason for the melancholy under her jokes and flirting—from distrusting a stranger to having to deal with the loss of her brother on an ongoing basis—but this wasn't the time, nor was it his place, to talk to her about it.

Everybody had secrets—some bigger than others. Like the image of a dragon he carried on his skin.

He considered asking her not to tell anyone else about it, but that would only feed her suspicions. Besides, he was seventeen now. Lots of kids his age had tattoos. It was no big deal, unless he made a big deal out of it.

He dressed quickly, stowed his dirty clothes in his knapsack until he could get to a Laundromat, and rejoined Anna in the living room.

"All set?" she asked.

He nodded. He dropped his knapsack by the door again

and followed her outside where the dogs were waiting quietly—almost in deference—for them. For him.

It was a weird feeling, and one he hadn't experienced before.

It was one of those nights at La Maravilla. The middle of the week, but between the steady flow of *touristas* and their own regulars, they'd been nonstop busy ever since five. They had to close the patio because with every inside table occupied, they didn't have the staff to deal with the overflow.

Jay waited on tables with Rosalie because Tío had no time to show him around the kitchen where he and the dishwasher Paco dealt with the steady stream of meals going out and dirty plates coming back in. It wasn't until almost ten o'clock that Tío was able to leave the kitchen and lean on the counter beside where Rosalie was making out a bill.

"<He's good,>" Tío said, motioning to where Jay was cleaning a table.

"<I know. He puts everybody immediately at ease and he hasn't screwed up one order.>" She looked over at her uncle. "<You should hear his Spanish—you'd think he grew up in the barrio.>"

"<Heh. Full of surprises.>"

"<And he's making great tips—we both have. The first

time he came back with a bill, he gave me everything. I told him the tips were his and he gave me a surprised look. He told me that back home, they just put all the tips in a jar and then divided them equally at the end of the night so that the people in the back got their fair share.">

"<I like him more all the time.>"

"<Me too.>"

Working with Jay had made the night go quickly. He always had some little joke or funny observation that he'd share as they passed each other, going from table to kitchen and back again.

Tío pushed away from the bar and stretched.

"<Well,>" he said before he went back into the kitchen, "<if he turns out to be a lousy cook, we've found the perfect waiter.>"

Anna came back around eleven when they were getting ready to close up. She sat on a stool by the bar, drying the glasses that Rosalie washed, her body turned so that she could watch Jay as he cleaned tables.

"I think you like him," Rosalie said.

"I do, but . . ."

"He asked me if you have a boyfriend."

"Really?"

Rosalie nodded. She could see that Anna liked the idea, but she could also tell that something was bothering her.

"Okay," she said. "I know that look. What's up?"

"I don't know that I *want* to like him."

"If that's supposed to make sense to me, I have to tell you that it doesn't."

Anna sighed. "What do we really know about him?"

"This from the girl who's always telling people not to judge anything unless you know something about it?"

"This is different," Anna said. "*He's* different."

"You mean because he's Chinese?"

"God, no. It's just . . . did you know that he's got this tattoo of a dragon that covers his whole back?"

"How would I know that?" Rosalie gave her friend a considering look, then added, "How do *you* know that?"

Anna waved a hand. "I just happened to come into the trailer when he was getting clean clothes out of his backpack, and there he was wearing nothing but a towel. It doesn't matter. The point is, you know who has ink like that, right?"

Rosalie shook her head.

"Come on, girl. The Asian gangs are all into dragon tattoos."

Disappointment rose in Rosalie. "You think he's in a gang?"

"I don't know. But you know how they say at school that they're trying to move in, and then there's the fact that the *bandas* are all interested in him. So he could be a spy. He says he isn't—a spy or in a gang. But that's not the weirdest thing. When I first asked him about the dragon, he said it wasn't a tattoo. I may only have my brother's name inked on my shoulder—so I'm no expert—but I know a tattoo when I see one."

Rosalie looked over at Jay. He was now putting chairs up on the tables.

"He doesn't look like the kind of kid that'd have a big tattoo," she said.

"Well, he does. And then there's how he had to be invited into your trailer like some kind of vampire."

"What do you mean?"

"He wouldn't go in until I invited him."

"That's weird."

"Tell me about it," Anna said. "And I haven't even told you the whole business with your dogs."

She turned back to Anna, her pulse quickening. "What happened with the dogs?"

"Nothing happened to them. It's the way they were around him. No barking and trying to jump up. Nothing. I didn't have to say a word to them. They just all sat in a half circle, looking at him, like he was their pack leader or a saint or something."

"Even Oswaldo?"

That was her mastiff who wasn't mean, just enthusiastic, but because of his size most people couldn't tell the difference when he came charging across the yard toward them.

"*All* of them," Anna said. "The cats were different. They

hated him, though now that I think of it, they didn't seem so hissy when I came back into the trailer to see if he was done with his shower."

"And were hoping to catch him naked."

Anna gave her a light punch on the arm.

Rosalie grinned, but changed the subject. "So what does it all mean?"

"I have no idea. I just know I'm spending the night with you and I'm going to have a baseball bat under my side of the bed in case he tries something funny."

"Don't you think you're overreacting?"

"You weren't there, Rosie. It was all really weird."

"Okay. But you don't have to come over. I'll bring Oswaldo into my bedroom tonight."

"Weren't you listening to me?" Anna said. "The dogs treat him like he's a saint."

"Oh, come on."

Anna crossed her heart with a finger. "I swear."

Rosalie realized that her friend was completely serious.

"Fine," she said. "You know you're always welcome. But this better not be an excuse to go crawling into his bed in the middle of the night."

She danced back before Anna could punch her again, but Anna didn't move.

"I just want to talk to him," she said. "I want him to tell us who he is."

When the restaurant was all cleaned up and ready for the next day's business, Rosalie grabbed a stuffed garbage bag by the kitchen door.

"I can get that," Jay said, starting to get up from his chair.

But Rosalie waved him off. She took the bag out to the alley and dropped it into the Dumpster, lowering the lid carefully so that it wouldn't clang when it closed. She started back, but a voice stopped her.

"Hey, homegirl."

"Who . . . ?"

Then Rosalie saw her under the security light of the building across from the alley, lounging against the side of her old Buick four-door. Maria Sanchez. Once upon a time they'd been best friends. But then Maria got jumped in with the Kings to become one of their Presidio Queens. Her hair was in cornrows and she wore baggy black cargo pants and a tight white T under a brown hoodie. The only sign of her gang colors was the red-and-green handkerchief tied around her right wrist.

"Hey, Maria," she said. "What's up?"

Maria shrugged. "You know. This and that."

"What are you doing here?"

"Heh. That still feels weird to me."

"What does?" Rosalie asked.

"You asking me what I'm doing here. Time was, you'd want to know why I *wasn't* hanging with you."

"That was your choice, not mine."

"Yeah, so you keep telling me. But other girls from our old crowd still hang with me and I don't see them wearing any colors."

"Maybe because the *bandas* didn't kill their mother."

"*Bandas* didn't kill your mother," Maria said. "Meth freaks did."

Rosalie shrugged. What was the difference? One was as bad as the other, and her mother was still dead.

"Anyway," Maria went on, "I just came by to give you a heads-up."

"About what?"

"Your China Boy. Maybe Tío's old ties can keep the Kings away from your family, but Cruz knows you lied to him and there's always some wannabes hanging around who might get the idea that doing you some hurt would let them get in good with him."

"Cruz is the guy with the crown tattooed on his fore-head?"

Maria nodded.

Maybe she'd have to start bringing Oswaldo in to work for protection, Rosalie thought. Too bad Jay *didn't* know kung fu.

"What do the Kings want with him?" Rosalie asked. "He's just some kid from Chicago."

"It's not about the Kings," Maria told her. "Word is Flores wants to see him."

Rosalie felt a little sick. Amada Flores was everything that was wrong with the barrios. He was one of the Mexican drug lords who'd set up shop in Santo del Vado Viejo. Violence followed in his wake.

"But *why*?"

"Like I said, I don't have a clue. But you know how it works. Flores isn't going to give a shit about any agreement Tío has with the *bandas*. Somebody's going to be collecting your homeboy, and I'm guessing probably sooner than later."

"Why are you telling me this?"

Maria pushed away from her car.

"You turned your back on me," she said. "I didn't turn my back on you."

She got into her car before Rosalie could respond. It started up with a coughing backfire. Rosalie watched its taillights until the Buick turned out of the alley, then stood there for a long time after it was gone. She knew she should tell Tío, but she also knew what his response would be: Jay would be out on the street before she could finish passing on Maria's message.

Maybe it would be better that way, considering everything Anna had told her. She didn't owe Jay anything. But she liked him. And then there was the fact that he was alone here.

Anna was right.

She *was* a soft touch.

So she'd tell Tío. But first she'd let Jay tell his side of the story.

It was a good plan—or at least it seemed that way until they all left the restaurant. As Paco said good-bye and wandered off down the alley heading for home, Rosalie saw a couple of girls standing across the alley under the security light where Maria's Buick had been. The pair wore the red-and-green colors of the Kings openly. One of them made some signs with her hands, then the two of them laughed and disappeared into the darkness.

"What did she say?" Rosalie asked Tío. "I know those were gang signs."

Tío's face had gone dark with contained anger.

"She signed 'Your ass is ours, bitch,'" he said. His gaze went to her. "Is there something going on that I should know about, Rosalita?"

"It's not like you think."

"I don't know what to think," Tío said. He looked from her to Anna and Jay. "Unless there's more to the story about what happened on the patio this afternoon with you and Jay and the gangbangers."

"There is," Rosalie had to tell him, "but I didn't know it then."

"There is?" Jay said, clearly surprised.

Rosalie ignored him, keeping her attention on her uncle.

"But we shouldn't talk about it here," she said. "Let's wait till we get home."

Tío nodded. "But then you'll tell me everything."

"Everything I know."

Normally they would have walked the few blocks home, but since Anna was here with her car, they all rode with her. The short trip passed in silence. When the dogs gathered around the gate to greet them, Rosalie could see what Anna had meant. There was no raucous barking, no jumping up for attention. The pack sat quietly, their focus on Jay as he got out of the car.

Tío hadn't been part of Rosalie and Anna's conversation back at the restaurant, but he couldn't ignore the dogs' uncharacteristic behavior. He stopped, his hand on the gate, his gaze tracking from the dogs to where Jay stood.

"What . . . ?" he began.

But Rosalie gave him a little push on the back. She'd been scanning the long dirt alley for any sign of the Kings. With the constant warring between the *bandas*, it wasn't impossible that the four of them might suddenly become the target of a drive-by.

"I know it's weird," she said. "But let's get inside."

Tío nodded. He opened the gate and led the way into the adobe house. When they were in the living room, he waved them all to chairs. But once they were sitting, he continued to stand. He looked from Rosalie to Jay.

"Now who's going to tell me what's going on?" he asked.

His voice was mild, but they all caught his contained anger. Rosalie felt terrible. He'd worked so hard to build up the business and divorce himself from his *bandas* past. Now here she'd brought the danger right to them. Saying she hadn't known didn't make her feel any less guilty.

"I told you the truth about this afternoon," she said. "Two of the Kings came looking for Jay while he was hiding in a tree above their heads. He says he doesn't know why and I didn't until I talked to Maria when I was taking out the garbage."

"Maria Sanchez?" Anna asked. "I thought you two weren't talking, not since she got jumped in by the Kings."

"We haven't been. But she was waiting for me in the alley. She said she came to warn me."

"Do you even trust her? I mean, why would she do that?"

Rosalie sighed. "She said that just because I'd turned my back on her, it didn't mean that she'd turned hers on me."

"What did she *tell* you?" Tío asked.

"That it's not just the Kings looking for Jay—it's all the *bandas*. Apparently Flores wants to see him."

Anna gasped. Tío sat down on a chair across from where the three of them sat in a row on couch. His shoulders slumped.

"Who's this Flores?" Jay asked.

"Amada Flores." Rosalie told him. "Styles himself as a local businessman. He owns a pool hall on Presidio. But the truth is he's one of the Mexican drug lords who use Santo del Vado Viejo as their base of operations on this side of the border. They call him 'El Tigre.'"

She watched Jay's eyes widen, then he gave a slow nod.

"Of course, they would," he said.

"So you do know something!"

"I don't know anything," Jay said. "But there's a long-standing hostility between dragons and tigers."

"I don't understand," Rosalie said.

"It means he *is* in a gang," Anna said. "He's got that big dragon tattoo on his back."

Tío leaned forward. "Maybe you should tell us what you do know."

Jay could only shake his head. "If I knew anything useful, believe me I would."

"Well, it seems to me," Tío said, "that you have two choices here. You can walk away, and we can only hope the trouble will follow you. Or you can tell us what you do know. Maybe we can help."

"You wouldn't believe me."

"Try us," Rosalie said.

Jay gave another slow nod.

"Paupau—my grandmother," he added for Tío's and Anna's sake. "She says the root of the hostility between dragons and tigers is because they're on opposite sides of the zodiac."

The other three looked at him with blank bewilderment.

"Maybe you should go back to the beginning," Tío said.

Rosalie and Anna nodded in agreement.

"The beginning," Jay repeated. "The beginning of dragons, or how I found out that I was one?"

There was a long moment of silence, then Tío cleared his throat.

"Start with your own story," he said.

Jay nodded. He looked up at the ceiling, unable, Rosalie thought, or unwilling to meet their gazes.

"There are five tribes of dragons," he finally said. "I was born to the yellow."

"So the Chinese gangs don't have an initiation?" Anna asked. "You're *born* into a gang?"

"They're not gangs," Jay said.

"But—"

"Let him tell it his own way," Tío said.

Anna nodded. "Sure, it's just . . . never mind." She made a motion like she was zipping her mouth shut. "I'm listening."

"The four other dragon tribes," Jay went on, "are each connected to one of the four directions—east, west, north, and south—but the yellow dragons are solitary. Our place is in the center. In the old days, we protected the emperor, but there is no emperor anymore, so now we have to choose a place or a people to look after. If the spirits of our ancestors approve of our choice, and we prove worthy, we're given the full mantle of our tribe, not simply an image on our skin."

Anna looked as if she wanted to say something, but when Jay paused, she pretended to zip her mouth again and shook her head.

Jay stood up. He pulled off his shirt and let them look for a long moment before he put it back on. Instead of returning to the couch where Rosalie and Anna were sitting, he stood by the cold hearth so that he could face them all.

"It's not a tattoo," he said. "It appeared on my skin when I was eleven years old, marking me as one who's supposed to take on the responsibilities of the yellow dragon's heritage. This is something that passes down through families, but not everyone is chosen."

Anna couldn't contain herself. "Appeared?" she said. "It just *appeared*?"

"It wasn't a painless process," Jay said. "It took a whole day, but yes, it just appeared."

Rosalie glanced at Anna, then returned her attention to Jay. She tried to school her features, but she was sure that her face showed the same disbelief as the others'.

"What do you mean by the full mantle of your tribe?" she asked.

Jay gave her an embarrassed look. "We become dragons."

"You mean it's like getting jumped in by a gang? I know—it's not a gang. But basically you get to call yourself a dragon then, right?"

Jay shook his head. "No, we *become* dragons."

"What, *literally*?"

"Oh, come *on*," Anna said. "That's—"

"Impossible," Jay agreed. "Don't you think I know how it sounds? But my grandmother Paupau is always talking about the shape-shifters that live unknown among us— animal people who walk around in human skins. Some are here to help mankind, others are monsters. I've never seen one myself, but you should see the way people act around her. Even the tongs give her respect. She's supposed to be a dragon and my guide."

"So we're supposed to believe you can turn into a dragon?" Anna said.

Jay shook his head. "So far as I know, I can't. You wanted to know what I know. Well, this is what I know. Or it's what I've been told."

"But if you prove yourself worthy you become a dragon?"

"I guess. I don't know."

"And Flores is *actually* a tiger?"

"Look, I know what it sounds like. I can't explain the things that Paupau's told me over the years. All I know for sure is that the dragon image just appeared on my back when I was eleven, but everything else? That there are monsters and secret animal people living among us? That I've got this duty to find a people in need and protect them? It sounds just as crazy to me. When I'm with my grandmother, it all seems to make sense. But as I stand here trying to explain this to you guys . . ."

He tried again. "I got a fever. I thought I had the flu. But it hurt so much, and then I woke up with that thing on my back, and Paupau started training me to be ready to accept the responsibilities of my heritage. But I've never seen a dragon, except when I look in the mirror at my back. I've never seen Paupau's image and I've *sure* never seen her turn into a dragon."

There was an uncomfortable silence.

"The dragon *really* just appeared on your back?" Rosalie finally asked.

Jay gave a weary nod. He didn't look like a crazy person. He just looked like a kid, as confused as they were.

"Yeah," he said. "It really did."

Rosalie took a breath. She knew what Anna and Tío would think, but she had to play the devil's advocate.

"So then," she said, "couldn't the other stuff maybe be true, too?"

"Jesus!" Anna broke in before Jay could answer. "Would you get real?"

Rosalie gave her a shove, but Anna ignored her.

"So," Anna asked Jay, "do you have any other superpowers besides being able to make tattoos just appear out of thin air? And by the way, I'd really like a rose, here on my ankle."

She stretched a leg out in front of him.

"I don't *have* any superpowers!"

"Okay, okay."

Another uncomfortable silence fell. Rosalie wished Tío would say something, but he seemed far away, deep in thought.

"Where did you learn to speak Spanish?" she asked, just to talk about something normal for a moment. "Because your accent makes you sound like you grew up around here."

Jay gave her a surprised look. "I don't speak Spanish."

Tío and the girls exchanged puzzled looks.

"<But you speak it fluently,>" Tío said, switching to Spanish. "<We heard you talking to the locals in the restaurant.>"

"<I wish I did,>" Jay told him, "<but I'm crap at languages. I . . .>"

His voice trailed off and he put a hand to his mouth, his eyes widening in surprise.

"Jesus," he said softly. "What's happening to me?"

Tío got up. Crossing to where Jay stood, he laid a hand on the boy's shoulder.

"It's okay," he said. "You didn't remember you could speak Spanish, but some part of you did, and it just kicked in automatically."

"I guess . . ."

He squeezed Jay's shoulder, then steered him back to a chair.

"I can't explain the tattoo," Tío said, "But as for these other things that your grandmother told you . . . I mean no insult by this, Jay, but you could have been brainwashed. It's what happens here with the *bandas*. The young men and women are taught the lies of gang life by our culture and from seeing the gangbangers every day on the street and in their schools. They have money and girls and cars. They party and everyone walks carefully around them. What child—unsure of his future, perhaps unhappy in his home—would not yearn for that kind of acceptance?

"I know this because I was one of the boys brainwashed by the music and what I saw on the street—the high life that the gangbangers seemed to live.

"But what you don't see until it's too late is the reality of the violence. The beatings and killings. How, even in this so-called family, there are the haves and the have-nots. You do what the lieutenants tell you, or you will suffer. You'll steal for them. You'll fight your rivals and kill them if need be. You'll do jail time and find that the gangs are even stronger inside than they are out on the street.

"But you will do what you're told, because if you don't, the next victim will be you. You will be the boy found dead in some gully, or shot down in a drive-by."

Rosalie shivered. Tío rarely talked so personally about the *bandas*. She knew he'd been a gangbanger. She knew he'd been to jail. But now it seemed to have been only yesterday, not years ago. Her heart went out to him.

"But why?" Jay said. "Why would Paupau fill my head with lies?"

"I can't answer that. Only she can."

Jay gave a slow nod. He lifted his head and met Tío's gaze.

"It would be easier to believe that," he said. "Horrible, but easier, because it would mean that the world could make sense again and I wouldn't be a freak. But what if they're not lies? Neither she nor my family has anything to gain by putting a huge tattoo on my back and then filling my head with weird stories and training me for six years."

"As I said," Tío told him, "I don't have the answer for that."

"I know one way to find out," Jay said. "I can go see the tiger and find out what he wants with me."

"No!" both Rosalie and her uncle said at the same time.

"You can't simply have a conversation with a man such as El Tigre," Tío went on. "He has no moral compass. He could kill you with less thought than we would have before stepping on a bug."

"He's right," Rosalie said. "It's too dangerous for you to just go to him."

"But what else can I do?" Jay asked. "It's either that, or I put all of you in danger. I don't learn anything about myself. I don't find out why I'm here."

Tío shook his head. "Please wait. I still have some

contacts in *la vida loca*. Let me see if I can find out what Flores wants from you."

Anna nodded. "Yeah. We can hang tough for a day or so."

"But why should you have to? I brought this trouble to you. It's my responsibility to fix it."

"Let Tío ask around first," Rosalie said.

Jay gave a reluctant nod.

"So," he said, "what time do we start work tomorrow?"

Tío shrugged. "Around ten. We only do breakfast on the weekends."

- 2 -

He who asks is a fool for five minutes.
But he who does not ask remains a fool
forever.

— *CHINESE PROVERB*

JAY WOKE UP early the next morning. He lay
there in the bed in Tío's spare room, staring up at the ceiling, listening to the strange sounds the local birds made.
Anna had pointed some of them out to him yesterday—
Gambel's quail and doves and this punky little black-and-
gray bird with a Mohawk crest and a name he still couldn't
pronounce, but he could see in his head because Rosalie had
written it down for him: phainopepla.

He'd been dreaming about Paupau, remembering one
of her talks. This had been the one about responsibility.
How people like the two of them didn't let others do the
hard things. They took responsibility and went out and got
it done themselves.

So he knew what he was supposed to do, but he lay there a little longer, wishing, and not for the first time, that he could have been born into a normal family. The rest of them—his parents, his sisters, his brother—they all looked normal. They couldn't do the kinds of things that Paupau said she could and he would do. But they still listened to her like she was some old Chinese lady mash-up of the Dalai Lama and the Godfather.

Not that he didn't love them. Not that he didn't love Paupau. But he just wished she had told him what he was supposed to do with his life instead of filling him with old stories and vague promises that made him both eager and uneasy.

Still, if he didn't know what to do with his life, he knew what to do with his morning.

After washing up and dressing, he went online using Tío's old, clunky computer. He found a map of the area, fixed the names of the main streets in his head, then left a note on the kitchen table:

Running a few errands. See you at the restaurant.

He went out the front door, avoiding the backyard with its strange pack of too-attentive dogs. The morning air still held the cool of the evening and he could hear doves in the palo verde trees at the front of the house. When he got as far as the corner, he stopped for a moment just to take it all in. Standing on these dusty streets with their adobe houses and cacti and dirt gardens, it was hard to believe he'd been fighting his way through some three feet of snow a few days ago.

And what was up with Rosalie's dogs, anyway? he wondered, looking back at Tío's house.

Old Mrs. Chen back home had a pair of Yorkshire terriers that were never shy about letting him know just how little they liked him. The two of them drove him crazy, yapping and straining at their leashes whenever he met them on the street, but that was almost better than Rosalie's dogs, who simply stood there staring at him like he was about to lay down some great doggie wisdom.

He hadn't even talked to Rosalie's dogs the way he had to her cats. That was showing respect, as Paupau would say, so he'd done it, feeling stupid the whole time, though oddly enough, it had worked. Considering he'd never done it before, he was surprised that it actually had.

All these things together . . .

The dogs, the cats, suddenly being able to speak Spanish like a native.

Some drug lord sending out his tattooed gangbangers after him.

That made even less sense, but at least there was an easy way to find out the answer:

All he had to do was go see the tiger.

According to Anna and the Hernandez family, he was being an idiot, but Paupau had told him that when one arrived in a new city, it was good manners—not to mention, expedient—to introduce oneself to the local powers that be. She didn't mean the mayor and city council, or even the police department. Instead, she'd talk about how every neighborhood had a person, or persons, who were the heart—the *soul*—of its streets and alleys. They weren't always necessarily recognized as such, but they were there all the same. Those who people looked to with respect and sometimes even a little fear.

Which, he supposed, described Paupau herself as much as any drug lord.

Was he an idiot? Supposedly, all Flores had to do was take a dislike to him and he could have him killed.

Last night, he'd agreed with the others. He'd gone to sleep in Tío's guest room with the expectation that it was best to let Tío try to ask around in his own safer way. The problem was, thanks to dreaming about Paupau, this morning he'd woken up not with confidence but with the sure knowledge that presenting himself to Flores was the right thing to do.

After a few moments, he set off again. Wearing his hoodie up so that he just looked like one more barrio kid, he got to Camino Presidio after only a few false turns. A quick look around told him that there was no pool hall in sight, so he asked directions from a man waiting at a nearby bus stop.

"<There's El Conquistador,>" he said, pointing south. "<It's open twenty-four hours, but it's a long walk. Other-

wise, the closest place is Pinky's, but it's a few blocks east from Presidio on Forty-Second, not on Presidio itself.>"

"<That's okay,>" Jay told him. "<I don't mind the walk. I'm enjoying the weather.>" At the man's puzzled look, he added, "<I'm from Chicago. We still have three feet of snow there.>"

"Ai-yi-yi."

"<And El Conquistador is the only one on Camino Presidio?>" Jay asked.

The man nodded. He looked as though he had more to say, but then his bus pulled up with a hiss of brakes.

"Thanks!" Jay called to the man.

The man turned back to look at him from the top step of the bus.

"<Be careful,>" he said. "<That can be a rough place, even this early in the day.>"

Then he was inside and the doors closed behind him.

Jay watched the bus leave, then set off for the pool hall.

El Conquistador looked as rough as the man had suggested it might. The adobe walls were flaking a sunwashed, pale green paint, and the windows were grimed with dust. The tall saguaro standing at the edge of the building had patches of unhealthy yellow. Around its base, the weeds and prickly pear were a long-dead brown. Up and down the street, and in a gravel parking lot beside the pool hall, low riders and chopped bikes were parked.

But that was only the outside of the building. Inside was where the real danger would lie.

Jay wasn't afraid the way he knew he should be. He'd woken with a confidence he couldn't explain away simply from having dreamed of Paupau, a confidence that stayed with him now. Perhaps it was because he knew that the gang members Flores had surrounded himself with weren't the danger. They didn't need to be.

Not with Flores there.

El Tigre.

In the spirit realms, Paupau said, the big cats were the mortal enemies of the dragon clans. Sometimes that enmity carried over into the physical realms. But enemies didn't need to fight one another, Paupau had also said. If they did, the world would be wracked with even more wars than it already was.

It was only eight thirty when Jay crossed the street to the pool hall, but he still expected El Tigre to be inside. Sure, it wasn't exactly the best time of day to go talk to a drug lord. If you believed the stereotypes found in videos and movies, Flores should still be in bed, or only just getting to bed after a long night of partying and doing business. He wouldn't be in this pool hall at this hour of the morning, hanging out with his gangbangers.

But Paupau had been available to anyone who needed to see her, night or day—it was part of her responsibility to her clan. No one made an appointment. She simply *knew* when they were coming and would be waiting for them before they were able to ring the bell to her apartment or enter the restaurant where she held court in a corner booth.

So El Tigre would be here. If he wasn't, then he wasn't a spiritual force. He was just a gangster with a provocative nickname. Considering that possibility, Jay felt the muscles in his shoulders tense uncomfortably when he put his hand on the door.

There were over a dozen people in the pool hall and they all turned to him when he stepped inside. Jay had expected the gangbangers to be Mexican, and most of them were, but there were also a couple of blacks, a white, and even a guy who looked East Indian. They all had gang tattoos on their forearms—some also had them on their necks and faces—and they wore their red-and-green *bandas* colors: scarves around their wrists or on their heads or dangling from a back pocket. Red or green T-shirts. Red or green baggy pants. Though most of them looked to be in their late teens or early twenties, there were also three adults.

There was the fat guy sitting behind the counter at the back of the room who was obviously the owner or manager, and a lean, handsome man playing pool who stood up from the shot he'd been about to take. They were both Mexican. The third was an attractive Native woman who sat at a corner table by herself, her dusty tooled-leather cowboy boots propped up on a second chair. She wore a choker with a large turquoise stone and a straw cowboy hat that hid her eyes until she tilted her head to study him.

A funny thing happened when Jay looked at the woman and the man by the pool table.

Over the years, Paupau had often told him various parables and what Buddhists called jataka stories—the kind that you were supposed to contemplate until you gained some small flash of enlightenment. But she had little practical advice. Direct questions were always answered with evasions. His supposed heritage—this spiritual burden and gift of the Yellow Dragon Clan—was something that could only be approached from the side, she claimed, never directly. He would learn what he needed only when he needed to know it. Until then, he had to trust that this would be the case.

For instance, once she told him that they shared the world with many other spiritual beings whose strengths were rooted in various animal clans. That as he went out into the world, he would meet them and immediately know them, as they would know him.

"How will I recognize them?" he'd asked.

"How could you not?" was her unhelpful reply.

He hadn't understood then, but he did now. Looking at the man by the pool table and the beautiful woman with her straw hat and cowboy boots, he felt an odd *ping* in his mind—as though a bell had sounded, but its tone was made up of colors rather than sound—and he knew that they were more than what they seemed.

"You sure you're in the right place, kid?" the fat man behind the counter asked.

Jay blinked. He realized he'd spaced out.

"I'm here to see Mr. Flores," Jay said. "I've heard he's looking for me."

Jay pushed back his hoodie as he spoke. Two of the gangbangers started to move forward.

"Wait," the man by the pool table said.

His voice was quiet, but it snapped like a whip. The gangbangers stopped in their tracks.

"I'm Flores," he said to Jay. "What makes you think I'm looking for you?"

Jay shrugged. Now that he knew that Flores was more than the gangster he pretended to be—just as Paupau was more than an old lady sitting in a back booth at the Dragon Garden back home—the tension left his shoulders.

"How could I not know?" he asked.

He was pleased with his response—it was the way Paupau would have answered. But then he saw El Tigre's eyes narrow in angry suspicion and he realized he shouldn't be getting cocky.

He held his hands out in front of him, palms up.

"I'm new in town," he said. "I just thought it would be polite to meet you. I mean you no harm."

One of the gangbangers snickered. Flores didn't look at him. He just said, "Shut up," and continued to study Jay.

"Who sent you?" he finally asked.

"Nobody. My grandmother thought I should do some

traveling, so I closed my eyes and stuck my finger on a map. Santo del Vado Viejo is what came up."

Flores nodded as though this made perfect sense.

"Boss," another of the gangbangers said when Flores continued to stand by the pool table, cue in hand, all his attention focused on Jay. "You want us to take this kid out back and—"

Flores turned on the man. "Didn't I tell you all to shut up?"

"Yeah, but—"

"Get out," Flores told him. He waved his free hand to take in the rest of the room. "All of you get out of here."

From the angry looks the gangbangers shot his way as they filed out, Jay knew the smart thing to do was just stay where he was. He tried not to let the weight of El Tigre's gaze worry at his nerves, but it was hard. Moment by moment he could feel the tension return to his neck and shoulders.

"So no one sent you?" Flores said when the last of the gangbangers had filed out.

"No, sir."

"And when you say you mean me no harm," Flores went on, "do I have your word on that? That you won't bring your weight, or the weight of your clan, down upon me?"

Jay started to respond, but something in the other man's careful phrasing made him stop and think first.

"Yes, sir," he said finally. "So long as you can guarantee a similar safety for me and, uh, those under my protection."

He hoped he'd said that right. Apparently he had, because Flores nodded and he seemed to relax.

"But we're only talking a deliberate attack, right?" he said. His phrasing lost some of its formality. "Because these *bandas*, they're still just kids. They get into fistfights and crap like that."

"Um . . ."

"But no weapons," Flores said. "I get that. Nobody gets hurt for real on either side."

When he fell silent, Jay felt he was supposed to say something.

"Right," he said. "Well, I should get going."

Flores nodded. "I'll put the word out. You ass'll be as safe here as it was in—where did you say you were from?"

This felt like a trick question that for some reason it was important he not answer.

"I didn't," Jay said.

"That's right, you didn't. But you got here on a bus from Chicago."

Jay shrugged.

"Yeah, I know. That doesn't mean anything. I appreciate your stopping by, kid. You can tell the boys to come back in on your way out."

He turned away from Jay and went back to lining up his shot on the pool table. Jay glanced from him to the man behind the counter, the woman at the corner table. The fat man ignored him but the woman winked at him before she looked away.

What was that supposed to mean? Jay wondered as he made his way outside.

His shoulders tensed again when he stepped out onto the street where the gangbangers were hanging around, smoking cigarettes. Their dark gazes turned on him as one.

"Uh, Mr. Flores said that you can go back in," Jay said.

He walked quickly away before any of them could respond, going back the way he'd come. He felt a prickle at the nape of his neck as he made his way up the street, but kept himself from turning around to make sure they weren't following. When someone suddenly fell in beside him, he thought his heart would stop. He stumbled, but the newcomer caught his arm before he could fall. He looked up to see that it was the woman from the pool hall.

"Jesus!" he cried. "Where did you come from?"

The *ping* of familiarity he'd felt before went through him again, but this time, with her hand on his arm, it was like a static charge. The woman smiled and let go. Like Paupau, she was a lot stronger than you'd think from looking at her.

"Seriously," he said. "How'd you get here so fast?"

She ignored his question.

"That was a very interesting conversation you had back there," she said.

"Did Mr. Flores send you after me?"

"Flores does his best to ignore my existence," she said.

"But I saw you back in the pool hall."

She nodded. "I do what I can to annoy him."

"I don't understand."

"You don't have to." She looked him over, starting from his feet, until her gaze reached his eyes. "So," she went on, "it looks like you worked out a truce."

"I guess. I just don't want any trouble."

"Nobody does." She paused and smiled. "Well, that's not true. I know people who thrive on trouble. But I understand what you're saying. You just want to get along."

Jay nodded.

"But what if you can't? What will you do if he breaks your truce?"

"I don't know. Do you think he will?"

"Hard to say. It depends what's most profitable. Let's just hope Flores doesn't figure out that you're here without backup or much experience." At Jay's surprised look, she added, "Oh, come on. You and I both know there won't be some 'wrath of the dragon clans'"—she made quote marks in the air with her fingers—"coming down on him. You're here to see how you can fend on your own. This is like some Chinese version of a spirit quest for you, isn't it? To see if you're actually worth the mantle of your clan."

"How can you know that?"

She shrugged. "I've heard how it works with your people. Go back far enough and I figure you'll find we're kin."

"Yeah, right."

"I didn't say the bloodlines run close. But the scales you can hear whispering against each other in your mind? I hear them, too."

Jay just looked at her.

"I know what you're wondering," she went on. "Where does she align? East, west? North, south? Well, it's different here than it was in China. Here the four directions belong to the thunders—the big mysteries—and the animal clans belong only to themselves. But we recognize some clans as kin, and we can make alliances, same as anybody else."

"Is that what you're doing?" Jay asked. "Making an alliance with me?"

She gave him another shrug. "Maybe I'm just being friendly."

Sure, Jay thought. Tall, gorgeous Native American women were always looking to make friends with some kid like him.

"So what's the deal with you and Flores?" he asked. "Do you have an alliance with him, too?"

Her eyes flashed and she spat in the dirt between them.

"I'll give you that one," she said in a tight voice, "because you don't know any better. But don't bring it up again."

"Look," Jay told her. "I don't know you and I don't know him. I don't care what is or isn't going on between you because it's none of my business. I only came by because I want to be left alone."

He turned to go, but she caught his arm with that strong grip of hers. When he stopped, she let her hand drop.

Jay had to make an effort not to reach up and rub his arm.

"We're not enemies," the woman said.

"Yeah, but are we friends? Like I said, I don't know you and I'd just as soon not get involved in whatever's going down between you and Flores."

"Except isn't that exactly why you're here? The yellow dragons—isn't your whole thing about making places safe, fixing what's wrong?"

"I don't know why I'm here."

She nodded. "Okay. Play it that way. But let me know if you change your mind."

Why did everybody think he was so much more than what he was?

"How would I get hold of you?" he asked. "I don't even know your name."

"And I don't know yours."

"I'm Jay Li."

She shook her head. "That's not your *name*," she said. "That's just what you go by."

"Excuse me, but isn't that what a name is?"

"Not in the clans."

"I don't have a clan name."

"My point, exactly. You're too young to have one. And I'm too old to be giving mine away to just anybody."

"So when you say I should let you know if I change my mind . . ."

She laughed. "Don't worry. If you do, I'll know."

"But—"

"Later, Jay Li."

Maybe he blinked. Maybe he had a momentary sensory lapse. But one moment she was standing right in front of him, the next she was half a block away. She lifted her hand, turned, and stepped between a pair of buildings. Then she was lost from sight.

Jay stood where she'd left him, staring down the street to where she'd disappeared. He couldn't help but feel that he must have dreamed the whole encounter. Never mind all the things Paupau had told him. Never mind the growing list of strange—sometimes impossible—things that he'd already experienced since the bus let him out in Santo del Vado Viejo yesterday.

The dogs' odd behavior?

Suddenly being able to speak Spanish?

They were nothing compared to what he felt now.

He remembered what she'd said:

The scales you can hear whispering against each other in your mind? I hear them, too.

After everything else—the dragon on his back, Paupau's endless training stories that left him more confused than prepared—that was the one thing he couldn't escape. He hadn't told the Hernandezes and Anna about it last night, because how do you begin to explain the constant sound and feel of some enormous scaled being shifting inside you?

But the woman knew.

She seemed to know exactly who he was and why he was here, even when he didn't.

This is like some Chinese version of a spirit quest for you, isn't it? To see if you're actually worth the mantle of your clan.

What did she expect, that he'd put El Tigre in prison and clean up the barrio? That some kid could accomplish what the whole police department couldn't, just because he had a dragon on his back and his grandmother told him stories about these heroic men and women who were both human and dragon and went around standing up to injustice?

The yellow dragons—isn't your whole thing about making places safe, fixing what's wrong?

His encounter with the woman left him feeling more troubled than talking to Flores had. El Tigre was only an opponent—why, Jay couldn't begin to figure out—but they'd worked out a truce even if it didn't make sense why a man like him would listen to, or care about, a kid.

But the woman . . . talking to her made the whole world feel wrong. Like the dirt underfoot was suddenly spongy. That here in the middle of this desert, he was standing underwater.

He needed a couple of deep breaths to steady himself, standing there swaying on the sidewalk. But finally the world settled down again. Everything felt normal, except for the whisper of scales rubbing against scales that he heard somewhere deep in his mind.

Though that was beginning to seem normal now, too.

Or at least familiar.

"You did *what*?" Rosalie said when Jay got back to Tío's house.

"Yeah," Anna added. "Do you have a death wish or something?"

Tío had already gone ahead to the restaurant by the time Jay returned, but the girls were sitting on the back patio, gossiping over coffee. He supposed that he should have expected this reaction.

"I don't have a death wish," Jay told them as he sat on the low wall dividing the patio from the backyard. "I just want to be left alone, and I figured the best way to make that happen was to go talk to him. So I did, and now it's all cleared up."

Rosalie shook her head. "*How* can it all be cleared up? What did he want from you? What did you say to him?"

Jay looked over his shoulder. The dogs had all gathered nearby, sitting on their haunches, watching him. He was going to have to try talking to them, he thought, as he turned back to the girls.

"I still don't know for sure what he wanted," he said. "I get the feeling that he thought I was some kind of threat to him."

"Yeah, right," Anna said.

Jay smiled. "That's what I thought, too. But it was weird, right from the moment I first went through the door of the place."

He moved from the wall to the table where they were sitting. Pulling up a chair, he leaned his arms on the table and told them everything—even how he'd had that strange *ping* of recognition when he saw Flores and the woman.

"You're saying she just disappeared?" Anna said when he was done.

Jay shook his head. "I don't think so. She's just, like, really fast or something."

"It all sounds so bizarre," Anna said.

"Welcome to my life."

"Can you trust him?" Rosalie asked. "Flores? I mean, he's just some gangster, right? How can he be trusted?"

"I know," Jay said. "That woman sure didn't trust him. I don't even know that I do. But I want to if it means I can get the chance to have a normal life."

"But she thinks you were—what? Sent here to clean up the barrio?"

Anna snorted. "Good luck with that."

"Right," Jay said. "It's stupid to expect that of a kid."

"Except," Rosalie said, "if you've got these special powers . . ."

Anna laughed, then using a deep, mock-serious voice, she quoted from the *Spider-Man* movies, "'With great power comes great responsibility.' As if," she added in her own voice.

"And I don't have any powers," Jay said.

The girls both looked at him.

"Okay, so I've got some weird things going on. But I'm not Superman. I'm not even Spider-Man."

"But what if the woman's right?" Rosalie said. "She seems to think you're here on some kind of spirit quest to, you know, awaken this dragon thing in you."

"You guys are taking this way more seriously than I do," Jay said, "and I'm the one who's been living with a dragon on his back and Paupau's stories for the last six years."

Anna shook her head. "Don't look at me, cowboy. I need more proof than I've seen so far. We only have it on your word that you didn't know Spanish before you got here, and that the tattoo just showed up on your back one day."

"It's not a tattoo."

She waved a hand. "The jury's still out on that. But Our Lady of the Barrio here is way too trusting."

"I'm a good judge of character," Rosalie said.

Anna laughed.

"Well, you're my friend, aren't you?"

They locked eyes for a moment, then Anna nodded.

"That's true," she said. She turned to Jay. "Don't get me wrong. I like you. I even sort of believe you—or at least I believe that you believe. But I'm not sure I trust you."

"What's that supposed to mean?"

She shrugged. "I don't know. I just have this weird feeling that we'll put all this faith in you, and then you'll turn around and break our hearts."

"I wouldn't do that."

"And I believe that, too," Anna said. "Or at least that you wouldn't do it on purpose."

"I just want an ordinary life," Jay said. "Can't we pretend that none of this weird stuff ever happened and start over? I'm just the new guy from out of town who's started working at the restaurant."

"I can do that," Rosalie said.

"So trusting," Anna said.

"Anna . . ."

"Okay, okay. I can try, but . . ." She pointed a finger at Jay. "Don't make us regret this. I may look like some sweet rocker chick, but don't think I can't seriously mess you up, because I can."

"Fierce," Rosalie said.

"Better than trusting."

"Sometimes."

Anna nodded. "Sometimes," she agreed.

When they both turned to Jay he held his hands palms out in front of himself.

"I'll be good," he said. "Honest."

Anna grinned. "I do like a boy who knows his place."

- 3 -

If the roots are not removed during weeding, the weeds will grow again when the winds of spring blow.

— CHINESE PROVERB

AS THE NEXT couple of weeks went by, Rosalie found it easier than she thought to put aside the mystery that was James Li. It wasn't that she didn't think about it from time to time—mostly when she was lying awake waiting for sleep—but he was just so . . . normal. He was a hard worker, a good learner—his peach salsa was to die for—and an easy person to be around, both in the restaurant and out. He got along well with all her friends—even her cousin Ines, who was notoriously picky about whom she liked. Ramon, who never had a lot of time for anyone who wasn't a music junkie, planned to take Jay hiking in the desert.

He fit in so well she almost forgot that Jay hadn't always spoken Spanish. That the image on his back had appeared overnight. That the dogs had treated him with such strange reverence at first, although now they simply jumped all over him like any of her friends.

If only Tío and Anna had been able to just let the mysteries go as well.

But inevitably Tío would take her aside and start in on some repetition of the conversation they'd been having ever since he learned about Jay's visit to the pool hall.

"<But think, Rosalita,>" he'd say. "<If Jay was really sent here to clean up the barrios, if kids didn't have to grow up with no future except for jail or a drive-by . . .>"

"<People would still have to make a choice, just as we did. And besides, maybe it's not like that at all. Maybe it's like he wants it to be, that his grandmother sent him here so that he could have the chance for a normal life instead of how he had to live back in Chicago. Don't forget, he's just a kid.>"

"<Who has something that makes El Tigre worried enough to cut a deal with him.>"

"<I know. But we don't know why, and we have to respect Jay's wishes in this. Maybe he'll change his mind, but until he does . . .>"

Tío would nod. "<Sure. Maybe.>"

With Anna, it wasn't as much what she said as what she didn't. It was clear that Jay wanted to be more than friends, but Anna would joke and flirt with him, pretending to be completely oblivious to what he was really trying to tell her.

Rosalie knew better. She knew that Anna was actually charmed by his attempts, but she was freaked about his past. About what he might be. She wasn't sure that any of it was true, but what if it was?

Since there wasn't anything more Rosalie could do, she talked to Jay about how hopeless he was at furthering his own cause instead. That was when she found out that not only had he never slept with a girl, he'd never actually been on a date.

"You can't be serious," she said.

The two of them were sitting in lawn chairs in front of her trailer one night after work. She had school the next day, but she was still wound up from the evening shift. The dogs lay sprawled in the dirt around them. There was no moon, but the stars were so bright in the clear sky that not even the light pollution from downtown was able to dim them.

"How can you never have been on a date?" she asked.

He shrugged. "For the same reason that I didn't take gym or do any sports."

He jerked a thumb over his shoulder at the dragon on his back.

"Okay, that's just weird," she said. "What were your parents thinking?"

"It wasn't my parents. It was Paupau."

"Didn't she realize how it would make you a magnet at school? The guy who ignores girls. And I know the girls would have talked about it because they had to have been interested in you. At least they sure would have been in my school."

"Better that than their finding out the real reason I was different."

"You don't believe that."

He shook his head. "But Paupau did—you'd have to meet her to understand how you just don't argue with her. When you try, it's like you're not even speaking."

"She sounds horrible."

"No," Jay said. "It's just a different culture. And then there's that whole dragon business."

Rosalie nodded. "Godfather meets the Grinch."

Jay laughed.

"I'm sorry," Rosalie went on, "but how could she not know that all these things would guarantee that you couldn't have a normal life?"

"She knew. I think she felt bad about it, too. But the way she sees it, I *can't* have a normal life. Not with what I'm supposed to have sleeping inside me."

"Well, what about the other people in your family that were dragons? What did they do?"

"She never talked about them except in vague terms. And remember, I've never even *seen* the dragon on her back.

Maybe Tío is right. Maybe it's all some weird scam."

"But what would be the point?"

Jay sighed. "I have no idea."

They didn't say anything for a while. Rosalie patted Oswaldo. As the oldest and most dominant of her little pack, the big dog always had the place of honor next to her. Jay stared up into the starry sky.

"Can you really feel it inside you?" Rosalie asked. "This dragon thing?"

Jay took so long to answer that she didn't think he was going to.

"Yeah, I do," he finally said. "I hear the whisper of its scales and . . . I feel something under my skin—like there's something enormous sleeping inside me and if it ever wakes up, it'll burst right out of me." He smiled. "I feel like a puddle that's hiding an ocean under its surface. An ocean that's huge and . . . unfathomable. And really scary."

"That's so creepy."

He nodded. "And the thing is, I can't figure out if it's real, or only my imagination. You know, because I've been brainwashed into believing it's there."

"Tío didn't mean anything by that."

"We both know that's not true," Jay said. "And just because something's horrible, that doesn't mean it isn't also true."

"You shouldn't have to suspect your own family."

"I know. And I don't, I guess. But I think about it every

once in a while. What makes me believe that I haven't been brainwashed into believing all of this is how El Tigre really wanted to cut a deal with me. Why would he do that if I was just an ordinary kid? And then there was the woman who came up to me after I left the pool hall. I can either believe there's this big conspiracy that includes my family and people I can't imagine them knowing, or . . . you know."

"You've got a dragon sleeping inside you."

He nodded.

"Which seems just as impossible," she said.

"If not more." He sighed. "And that's why I want a break. Why I want to pretend I'm just this kid from Chicago who's working in your uncle's restaurant and maybe making a few friends."

"You're doing that."

"I know." He smiled. "And it feels really good. It'd feel even better if Anna didn't see a lunatic every time she looked at me."

"She makes up her own mind about things," Rosalie said, "so you never know. She could still come around."

"You really think so?"

Rosalie shrugged.

"So how far is it to the desert?" Jay asked.

He was obviously as ready as she was to change the subject.

Rosalie made a lazy wave with her hand. "This is all the desert."

"You know what I mean."

Rosalie nodded and smiled. "We're right on the edge of town here." She pointed east. "The national park is about a mile or so in that direction. If you follow our street, you'll find a trailhead right where it ends."

"That close . . ."

"Closer," Rosalie told him. "We might have put down a layer of adobe and concrete and steel, but the desert's right there underneath it all. Sleeping. Dreaming. Dangerous, if you don't treat it with respect."

"Like my dragon."

Rosalie hesitated for a moment, then gave a slow nod.

"I guess so," she said. "I guess you could say it's just like your dragon."

"Maybe that's why I'm here. Maybe I'm supposed to learn something from the desert. Though it's funny. Paupau says that the dragon clans are born from the sea and we usually live near some large body of water, like she does in Chicago."

A chill ran through Rosalie—not of fear, but of recognition, though recognition of what, she couldn't say.

"This was all ocean once," she said. "The old people say you can still see the ghosts of mermaids in the dry washes when it rains." She gave Jay a thin smile. "Maybe that's not just some BS story like I always thought it was."

"Really? This was all an ocean?"

Rosalie nodded. "When Ramon takes you out into the

desert on Sunday, ask him about it. He knows places where you can see shells and fish that are imprinted right into the rock."

"I'd like to see that."

"You know," Rosalie went on, "you should think of keeping a journal. My teacher Ms. Baca says that putting your thoughts down on paper is a great way of figuring out what's going in your head. Writing it down makes it easer to see the connections or something like that." She grinned. "Or you could start a blog."

"I don't have a computer."

"Tío would let you use his. Or you could use the ones at the library."

Jay shook his head. "No, it's too public. I might as well start an Internet support group for people who think they might be dragons."

Rosalie laughed. "I wonder who'd join?"

"I don't think I'd want to know."

"Well, if you want to try the journal route, I've got some extra school notebooks."

"Sure, why not. So long as no one else but me has to read it."

- 4 -

JAY

I feel kind of weird writing in the notebook that Rosalie gave me. At first I thought I'd wait for something interesting to happen, but my life's fallen into such a routine that I realized I could end up waiting forever. That wouldn't be such a bad thing, because who needs interesting times? They're just another way of saying "trouble." Me, I like the normal.

But Rosalie keeps asking me how the journal's going, if it's helping me figure things out. I don't want to lie to her, but I don't like disappointing her. She means well. She thinks it'll help, and maybe she's right—or she would have been right, except the dragon's not really a problem anymore. Sure, it never goes away, but I'm happier here in Santo del Vado Viejo than I can ever remember being—even back when I was still just a kid, before the dragon showed up on my back.

It's not that I don't love my family, or Chicago. I miss everything about home except for the weather—even my sister Julie's teasing and Paupau's lectures. I like the narrow streets of Chinatown, busy and full of life from early in the morning to late at night—I felt safe in all the noise and bustle. But here I'm free. My life is normal. Maybe things got off to a bad start the first day—what with the *bandas* chasing me and all—but since then I've finally been able to see what it's like to live an ordinary life.

Mostly. There are still a few too many "so you're a dragon" conversations with Tío and Rosalie. Though I've got to say I prefer that to the way Anna studiously ignores it.

I know. I'm whining about how I just want to forget the dragon, then I'm whining because Anna does exactly that. But it's different with her. She doesn't want to talk about it because I think she'd rather just pretend the whole thing didn't exist. I'm not sure if she believes in it or not, but either way it kind of scares her. I see it in her eyes. I'm either nuts or I'm dangerous.

Don't get me wrong. It's not like she's unfriendly or anything. But she also makes sure that we're never alone. It's never just the two of us, and how do you talk about this kind of thing in a crowd?

Maybe I'll surprise her one day and just blurt out how I feel in front of everybody.

I don't know. Girls are just a total mystery to me.

I didn't lie to Rosalie about how I've never gone out with a girl. It's the sad truth. I'm like any other guy. I obsess over them all the time. The problem is that I've always had to do it from a distance. Now that I don't have Paupau looking over my shoulder—grilling me about some girl I'd been seen talking to at school, or whatever—I could hook up with anybody and nobody could say different. But the only girl I want to be with in Santo del Vado Viejo is Anna.

Maybe the real problem is that I'm just not cool enough to be her boyfriend. Rosalie's taken me to some band rehearsals and now I've also seen Malo Malo onstage. Let me tell you, Anna really *is* a total rock goddess, while I'm just a guy who's never going to be much more than a cook from Chicago's Chinatown.

The band plays this weird mix of garage rock, surf guitar, rap, and mariachi music. I've never run into anything like it before. A lot of the songs feel instantly recognizable and hooky, but they're still fresh, while some of them are so unexpected that it just makes you grin because they all come together so perfectly. And while you just want to dance—especially to the instrumentals—it's not all party time, either. A few songs are updated versions of those traditional *corridos* that Rosalie told me about, but most of them are ones that Ramon has written about the border problems and growing up in the barrio. Some of those are justifiably angry, and some just break your heart.

They're seriously good. Ramon plays trumpet and guitar and does all the lead vocals. There's Margarita on drums, Luis on bass. Gilbert plays both keyboards and trumpet, and sometimes a whole horn section on those keys of his. Hector's on the turntable. But good as they are, Anna just blows them out of the water. She's sexy as hell up there, but she's not using it, she doesn't even need it, the way she can play. I've never heard sounds like she gets out of her Les Paul, and she's all over the stage, even while she's cutting loose with some blistering lead.

But I'm not crazy about her just because she's hot. I mean, it doesn't hurt, but there's something else there for me . . . some, I don't know, connection, though I guess that's what everybody thinks about the person up onstage that sends their pulse into double time.

I'm not the only guy standing there, mouth open and totally in love. I look at some of them just oozing cool, and I think about me, and I know I don't have a chance. But I'm not ready to give up just yet. Like the *I Ching* says, "Perseverance furthers. It furthers one to have somewhere to go." Or as my dad puts it: "You can't win if you don't play," though he was talking about lottery tickets.

Rosalie asked how the writing's going again tonight and I was able to tell her "fine." She gave me a kind of a look, but what? I'm going to show her what I've written? Like that's going to happen. I feel weird enough blathering all over those pages the way I do without actually showing them to somebody else.

El Tigre was true to his word—the *bandas* have left me alone. I'm not saying they've suddenly started to like me or anything. Whenever I see one of them on the street they give me what Tío calls a "thousand-yard stare." He says it's a prison term, but I know what it means. It's this cold, hard look, full of hate and promising trouble. So long as all they do is stare, I don't care.

But it reminds me again of how different it is here from at home. It's not like there weren't gangs. The Latin Kings started up in Chicago and we had some in our school. You'd pass them in the halls—colors hidden, but we all knew who they were, and as long as we stayed out of their business, they stayed out of ours.

The *bandas* here in Santo del Vado Viejo have been on my case since I first stepped off the bus. Who knows what would have happened if I hadn't gone and talked to El Tigre? But I made the deal, and they're honoring it. So I try to ignore them the best I can.

The only strange thing is, when they do give me that look, I don't feel nervous. I feel angry instead, and I'm not a guy who walks around being angry, especially not with losers like the *bandas*. But it happens, and when it does, I can almost feel something big shifting inside me. And that sound I'm always hearing—the rustle of scales against each other—grows momentarily louder.

I know. It doesn't make a lot of sense. But it's real. I experience it. And it's not a pleasant feeling.

I was going to find my own place, but Tío insisted that I take his spare bedroom for as long as I want. He won't even let me pay rent. He says with José in prison and Ines living on her own he's got plenty of room, and considers it incentive for me to stay on at La Maravilla. We both know he can't afford to pay me more than he does, but if I don't have rent expenses, it's that much more in my pocket and he thinks there's less chance that I'll pack up and leave at the first opportunity.

I thought he was overselling my usefulness, but I've got to say I was surprised with how easily I got into it.

"You're a natural," he told me two days after I'd started learning to make the dishes on La Maravilla's menu. "I've never seen anyone pick it up so fast."

I wanted to just take the compliment, but I had to be honest.

"I've been doing this since I was nine years old," I told him, "helping out at my parents' restaurant."

He shook his head. "No, it's not only the experience.

You have a real gift in the kitchen, just like my mother did." He grinned. "She could make a beautiful meal out of nothing more than dirt and weeds."

"Yum."

He pretended to take offense but then grinned and gave me a light tap on the shoulder with his fist.

I almost don't want to like Rosalie's boyfriend Ramon. He looks like all the seriously cool guys back at my old school with his Latino good looks, the long, black hair tied back in a ponytail, the big dark eyes that the girls would be endlessly texting about. You look at him, and you just know he could have any girl he wanted—though to Ramon's credit he sees only Rosalie.

When he's onstage, he's all fire and charisma and ten feet tall. Really. He's so much bigger than life. Offstage, he's soft-spoken but he's got a quick smile, and man, does he know a lot about everything. Music. Books. History. The desert.

And let's face it: Sure, he's cool, but he's so damn nice. When you're talking to him, unlike most people, he's totally paying attention, not thinking about what he's going to say next. You can't not want to be his best friend, though you know you've got to earn it.

Last night he stayed over in Rosalie's trailer like he does most weekends. This morning I wake to find him at the foot of my bed and realize what roused me is him tapping the end of the footboard with his shoe. I look at the window and it's still dark outside.

"What time is it?" I mumble.

"Morning," he says in a cheerful voice. "But it's supposed to get really hot today so I thought we should make an early start."

"This isn't morning," I tell him. "This is just cruel."

He laughs and taps the footboard again.

"I've got coffee waiting for you," he says, and leaves the room.

Turns out he's as good at making coffee as he is at everything else. I warm up some tamales I brought home last night. By the time we're done eating, have shouldered backpacks that are filled with water bottles and energy bars, and head out the door, the sun's starting to come up. We leave Tío's house and walk toward the pink sky that's haloing the peaks of the distant mountains.

I knew the desert started up just at the end of the block. That's where Tío's street, Calle Esmeralda, meets Redondo Drive, and it's where the Vulture Ridge trailhead begins, one of a dozen or so trailheads from which you can go hiking into the southern part of Hierro Madera National Park. But in the two weeks I've been here, I never once walked down to even just have a look. I figured there wasn't much to see.

Besides, I'm a city kid. We were always too busy with

the restaurant to go for Sunday drives. Sitting on Tío's patio, and lying in my bed at night, I can hear the coyotes, and that's about as close as I ever got to the desert. But now, standing here at the trailhead with Ramon, I'm stunned by its beauty.

For one thing, there are wildflowers everywhere. Ramon names them—pink fairy dusters, yellow brittlebush, red desert globemallow, and Indian paintbrush—until it just sounds like a poem he's reciting. Even the cacti have flowers. When I seem surprised, he says, "Why shouldn't they? Their ancestor was the rose, which is why she's the Mother of the Desert."

Like I said, he knows a lot about everything.

The trail starts easily enough. It's a gentle slope going up into the foothills. But then it starts winding back and forth on itself and the incline gets steeper and steeper. We stop once in a while to catch our breath and take in the view—though I think Ramon does it more for my sake than his. He's in great shape. But under Paupau's tutelage, I've practiced endless breathing techniques and special exercises for flexibility and strength, and I have no trouble keeping up. When Ramon realizes this, we don't stop unless there's a particularly spectacular view, like the one of the city spread out in the valley below us before we take the trail to Vulture Ridge on the other side of the mountain.

At one point a pair of red-tailed hawks rides an updraft near the trail's edge. Ramon grins and lifts a hand to them.

"<Hey there, uncles!>" he calls to them.

I smile and give them a wave, too. I get the *ping* inside my head that tells me they're more than the birds they seem to be.

"Paupau—my grandmother," I tell him, "likes to think that we're all brothers and sisters—animals, birds, people."

"Makes sense to me," he says. "Out here it's aunts and uncles, though you hear the animal people called 'cousins.'"

My gaze goes to the hawks, distant now.

"But those birds—" I begin.

"Wouldn't be animal people," Ramon says. "I mean, they're probably not born with enough cousin blood in them. They'd be part of a . . . I'm not sure what to call them. There's this group of men—Yaqui and Kikimi, some Mexicans—who drink mescal tea and meditate until they can slip their human bodies and rise up on hawk wings. We call them *mescaleros*—or just the uncles."

"So you can sense the difference between regular people and . . . um, animal people?"

He shakes his head. "No. Though everybody's supposed to have some faint trace of the old animal blood in them."

"Then how did you know those hawks were . . . what did you call them?"

"*Mescaleros.* And I didn't. I just give that greeting to any red-tailed hawk I see out here in the desert." He grins and adds, "Don't look so disappointed. Look around you. The world's still full of magic."

We've come off the mountain as we were talking and are walking along a ridge about the width of a country road. The ground drops suddenly on either side and the view is stunning. On the right, the Hierro Maderas march into the distant horizon. On the left, the valley holding Santo del Vado Viejo is spread out like a Navajo blanket displaying jewelry.

I stand there for a long moment, mesmerized by the view. I have never in my life seen anything like this. We're so high up that turkey buzzards are circling below us. I think of sharks, drifting deep under the ocean's surface, then remember what Rosalie told me. I turn to Ramon.

"Rosalie says this was all an ocean once," I say.

Ramon nods his head. "That was long, long ago." His voice is no more than a thoughtful murmur. "But I'll tell you, sometimes when I'm walking down there in the desert, I think I hear waves and the songs of the fossilized fish, slowed down by the weight of stone and dirt and time, but an echo's still there." He shoots me a quick look before he adds, "Once when I was hiking up a dry wash south of the city, I swear I saw the ghost of a giant longfin dace swimming away from me."

Then he laughs. "You must think I'm a complete space cadet."

"No, I think it's cool."

He lifts an eyebrow.

"Seriously," I tell him. "Like I said, my grandmother's always saying how everything's connected. All of us on this world. And the past and the present, too."

"That's what the Kikimi say, too. They don't have words for 'past' or 'future' or 'now.' According to them, it all happens at the same time."

"You mentioned them before. Who are they?"

"The local Natives. They got relocated to a rez north of where we are right now, but they used to live all along the banks of the San Pedro."

"Which is a river with no water."

Ramon smiles. "Wait till the rainy season. It runs so high then that we often get some serious flooding."

"That's what Rosalie told me."

"Stick around long enough," he says, "and you'll see." He hefts his backpack and swings it onto his shoulders. "We should get a move on. You're going to love this next view, but it'll still take us a while to get up to it."

He points to a peak that doesn't seem so far away, but I've already learned how deceptive distance can be. It looks like it's maybe a fifteen-minute hike, so that means it'll probably take a couple of hours.

"You coming?" Ramon asks.

I realize I've been daydreaming. Giving him a quick nod, I trot over to fall in step with him as we follow the contour of the ridge to where the land starts to rise again.

"I can see Rosie's pretty fond of you," he says after we've been climbing for awhile.

"We're just friends," I tell him. "Really."

He laughs. "I know that. Rosie and me, we're tight. I don't have any worries there." He waits a moment, looking away to the horizon before turning back to me. "But I get the sense she's . . . disappointed in you."

I sigh.

"You don't want to talk about it, that's cool," he says.

"It's not that. It's just . . . she thinks I can get rid of El Tigre. That I can get rid of all the *bandas*."

His eyebrows go up in surprise, but all he says is, "Can you?"

"No. I don't know. It's hard to explain."

He waits, but while I like him, I'm not about to start talking about dragons.

"Well," he says when he realizes I'm not going to continue. "You ever decide to give it a shot, you can count me in. I hate those freaks."

See, that's the way he is. That's what makes him so cool. Something comes up and he just makes the decision. He does the right thing without having to think about it. I wish I could be like that, but I don't even have the first clue about what the right thing is that I should be doing.

We walk awhile longer in silence until finally I have to ask: "Aren't you even curious how a kid is supposed to be able to shut down a gangster and all his *bandas*? Because I sure am."

Ramon shakes his head. "If Rosie thinks you can do it, then I do, too. I'm guessing you're just not ready yet."

"How are you supposed to get ready for something like that?"

"Beats me. I'm just a musician—what the hell do I know?"

It's a couple of hours later before we reach the vantage point that Ramon wanted to show me. The air feels thin up here, but it's so damn clean it doesn't matter. I can't remember ever tasting air this clean. We're on the very top of the sky, away from all the pollution and crap, and every breath I take feels like it's purifying me. And the view . . . if the view from the ridge was something, this one's almost impossible to take in. We have the mountain at our back, while in front of us, its brothers and sisters spread off into the horizon, tall and majestic, with a sky above that's so big it doesn't have an end.

"Isn't this the most beautiful thing you've ever seen?" Ramon asks.

I stand there mesmerized. He's right. It's totally amazing. But the most beautiful thing I've ever seen? There's another picture in my head, but I'm not about to tell Ramon what it is.

"Okay, give," he says. "I can tell you don't agree. Tell me one thing you'd rather be looking at."

I shake my head.

"No, this pretty much beats any view I've ever seen before," I tell him.

"Except for . . ."

"Give it a rest," I say with a smile.

"Nope. Not until you tell me. Because if you know something better than this, I want to go see it."

"You're going to think it's stupid."

"No, I won't."

I sigh. "Okay. How about every time I look at Anna?"

I can't look at him. It's worse when he laughs. But then he punches me on the shoulder and I know he's not laughing at me. He's not laughing *with* me—because I'm not laughing—but at least he's not laughing at me.

"If you feel that way," he says, "why don't you do something about it? Ask her out, man."

"No. She's totally not into me that way. It's . . ." I hesitate, then give a mental shrug. "It's got to do with this whole business of how I'm supposed to be able to take down the *bandas* and clean everything up."

He gives a slow nod. "I can see how she'd want that. You know her brother was killed by the *bandas*, right? She'd want to see them go down more than any of us."

"It's not that she thinks I can do it," I tell him. "It's that she thinks it's all bullshit. Or if it's not bullshit, then it freaks her out."

"What are you talking about?"

"It's . . . I don't . . . oh, hell."

I sit down on a rock. The landscape frees me. Staring out at the vast display of the mountains, I can tell him the whole thing. About Paupau, the mark of the dragon appearing on my back, what happened when I first got here, meeting with El Tigre, everything.

He sits down beside me and doesn't interrupt.

"Is that why Anna calls you the Painted Boy?" he says when I'm done.

"Yeah, it's really ha-ha."

He gets more serious. "So you don't think you're ready?"

"Ready? I wouldn't know where to start." I study him for a moment before I add, "How come you believe me?"

"I didn't say that I did."

"But you're not calling me out on it."

He shrugs. "What would be the point? I know there's weird crap in the world." He smiles. "You know, like the *mescaleros* and the ghosts of long-dead fish. But whether I believe it or I don't, that doesn't change the fact that you've got to deal with it."

Like I said, how can you not want a guy like this for a friend?

"So there's that," he goes on, "and I can't do anything about it, but Anna . . . come on, man. Have you told her how you feel?"

"I never get the chance. She always makes sure we're in a big group where I can't even start."

He laughs. "Yeah, I can see her doing that."

"And besides, just look at her. She's way too cool for a guy like me."

"Bullshit. Yeah, she's all glam onstage, but that's not who she is. Or it's only part of who she is."

"Maybe. But when she *is* on that stage . . ."

"Let me tell you," he says. "She's serious about the music and she's no showboat. She listens to what's happening around her and serves the song. Sure, when it's her turn to step up for a solo she lets it all out, but that doesn't make her too cool or special—not the way you're thinking."

He stops for a moment, then goes on, "Let me put it another way. People think we're special up there on the stage, but we're the same as everyone else. What makes us different is only that we get up there and play out our dreams. Do you get what I'm saying?"

"I guess. . . ."

"Because if your dream is to be the damn best car mechanic or plumber, and you work at it every day, then you're special, too."

"Easy to say."

He shakes his head. "I'm serious, man. You have the balls to follow your dreams and you're living the beautiful life."

"Which makes me . . ."

He laughs. "Well, I don't know about all this dragon crap, but you're one damn fine cook."

I don't say anything, but he won't let it go.

"And that means," he says, "that you're cool enough for her. But you've got to tell her how you feel. You can't write the movie in your head and then get pissed off because she's not following the script. Or maybe she's following it too well, considering you already wrote the bummer ending."

"You make it sound easy."

He shakes his head. "Laying your heart out there is never easy, man. Doesn't matter if it's getting up onstage or telling somebody how you feel. Maybe you're going to blow it. Maybe you're going to get hurt. But you can't not try. What the hell kind of way is that to live?"

"Safe," I say.

"Unhappy," he corrects me.

I nod. "Okay. I get it."

"So maybe she'll shoot you down," he says, "and you're still going to be bummed. But maybe you'll hit the jackpot."

"How's that?"

"Maybe she'll say, 'Sure, let's do something together.'"

"Maybe," I say and we leave it at that.

The rest of the day we just talk about how it was growing up—me in Chinatown, him in the barrio—and he tells me about the land. What the plants are called, what they're good for. The wildlife. Names the birds we see. I saw a lot of this stuff in the little guidebook I read on the bus coming down, but seeing it up close makes it real like a book never could.

By the time we get back to Tío's house I'm glowing from both a bit too much sun and the great time I had. That night I sleep deeply and dream I'm back in those mountains, but this time I'm like one of the *mescaleros* that Ramon was telling me about. I'm riding the winds high in the thin, cool air, sailing effortlessly above the peaks. When I wake, I can't remember if my wings were a hawk's or a dragon's.

After that Sunday with Ramon, I take to going out for walks in the neighborhood after work. I like the quiet and the night air, and there's not much else to do that late, anyway. I'd call my parents, but because of the time difference I can only do it from the restaurant just before we start serving dinner. Otherwise they're fast asleep. Tío's usually busy working on the restaurant's books, making up the deposit, putting together his food orders. Ines is friendly enough, but she's got a whole other life that only seems to start when the restaurant closes, and she doesn't come by the house much. The clubs she goes to don't get happening until around midnight, and that's not my scene. Not that she's ever asked me to tag along or anything.

As for Rosalie, if it's a night off, she spends the evening with Ramon after she's done her homework. If she's been in the restaurant that night, she usually hits the books in her trailer.

"I can't believe you don't miss school," she said to me once.

"I can't believe you like it."

She shook her head. "In five or ten years, when you get tired of working in a restaurant, you'll regret not having your diploma to fall back on. Graduates get the good jobs."

"In five or ten years," I told her, "I could be a dragon for real, doing whatever the hell it is that dragons do. Then whether or not I have a diploma won't matter, will it?"

We've only known each other for a couple of weeks, but it's already an old argument.

So she's got her boyfriend and her studying. Sometimes I hang with them. Sometimes Rosalie and I go to band rehearsals. Sometimes I sit with Tío on the patio and get him to tell me stories of how things used to be in the barrio. But mostly it's just me and the desert night.

With Tío's house so close to the national park, all I have to do is walk that long block and I'm at the parking lot by the trailhead. Even sitting on the front porch, I can hear the coyotes. But I like walking along Redondo Drive, which borders the park. I can smell the creosote and dust; the sky is huge above me and filled with stars. Sometimes I catch glimpses of javelinas rooting around in the prickly pear.

The third or fourth time I take a late night walk, I bring the dogs with me. I already walk them sometimes before work. Rosalie just shakes her head because I can take them all off leash and even she can only do that with maybe half of them. She's got a few rescues that are really skittish and liable to snap—or so she says. She talks about how they've been mistreated and they need to regain their trust of people, but they're cool with me. All of them are. They just flow around me, marking cacti and clumps of dead weeds, checking everything for smells. But they stay close and come as soon as I call them. We've got an understanding, I guess.

So I'm a little surprised and freaked out when they take off on me just after midnight one night. I'm even more worried when I see the figure they've spotted down the street ahead of us. I yell at the dogs and chase after them, but they don't listen. The dogs herd what I see is just a kid up against a chain-link fence, then they pen her there in a half circle of bared teeth and fierce growls.

"I'm sorry, I'm sorry!" I cry to the kid as I catch up. I pull dogs away so that I can get to the girl. "Go on, get out of here," I tell them. "Jeez, Oswaldo, what're you thinking?" To the girl I quickly add, "They won't hurt you. I won't let them hurt you."

I repeat the words in Spanish.

I'm so pissed off at myself. Why did I have to get so cocky, thinking I could control the dogs just because I'm supposed to have some kind of stupid dragon blood? Rosalie warned me that a few of them aren't properly socialized yet. I've never had a dog in my life, but suddenly I know better? This girl could have been seriously hurt.

She's maybe fourteen or fifteen, barefoot, in raggedy pink cotton trousers and a lime green T-shirt that hangs down to her knees. Her hair's a mix of light and dark brown tangles, streaked with blond. Her eyes are large and seem almost luminous in the dark.

I find it odd that she doesn't seem scared. That she's out here on her own so late at night.

Odder still is the little *ping* of recognition that tells me she's from one of the animal clans. Except that can't be right. I mean, she's really just a kid.

"I know they won't hurt me," she says. She's got a lower voice than I expected. "Not with you here to protect me."

Trusting much? I think.

But the dogs are no longer paying attention to her. My pulse starts to slow down and I guess everything's okay. No harm done. But no more midnight rambles with the dogs, that's for sure. It's not fair to anyone we might run across. I mean, this poor girl . . .

"I'm really sorry about them scaring you like that," I say, feeling the need to keep apologizing.

"I wasn't scared."

So now I'm wondering what kind of drugs she's using. But I go on. "They've never done that before."

She shrugs. "It's just their nature."

She's way too calm about this.

"You're out kind of late," I say.

She nods. "But it's so nice late at night. I mean, look at the stars. Just *look* at them!"

She twirls in a circle as she speaks, her fingers pointing straight up at the night sky. I know just what she means—

it's one of the reasons I like to go walking this late—but I'm not some little kid who should have been in bed hours ago. And she's definitely got to be stoned.

"Where do you live?" I ask.

She gives a vague wave of her hand toward the east.

"Let me walk you home," I say.

"It's a long way."

Maybe in her mind it is, but I know there are only a few houses between here and the trailhead, so it can't be that far. And I'm sure not leaving her out here on her own. I start down the street and she falls in step beside me. The dogs range ahead, except for a little Jack Russell/toy poodle mix named Pepito who growls at the girl until I shoo him away.

"What's your name?" I ask.

"Lupita."

"I'm Jay," I tell her.

She grins. "I know that. Everybody knows about you."

"What do you mean?"

"You know, how you're all dragony and everything."

I stop in my tracks. "Who told you that?"

Lupita's got a big smile. "Why would someone have to tell me? Ai-yi-yi! If you don't want people to know you're a dragon you shouldn't walk around the way you do, all big and rumbly, with a fire in your belly."

"I don't know what you're talking about."

"Oh, you're so cute. Are you still going to walk me home?"

She seems to shimmer under the streetlights. For a moment I think I see small antlers poking up from the tangle of her hair, long droopy rabbit's ears hanging down on either side of her face. I remember the little inner *ping* I felt when I first saw her. Then the antlers and droopy ears are gone.

"What do you mean by 'everybody'?" I ask. "Who's this 'everybody' that knows about me?"

She shrugs. "Oh, you know. All the cousins."

I give a slow nod. "And you're one, too."

"Well, duh."

"How old are you really?"

She cocks her head. "What do you mean by 'really'?"

"Well, you look fourteen or fifteen—in, um, human years."

"Oh, that," she says. "We always look young to the five-fingered beings when we change over."

"By 'we' do you mean all the cousins?"

"I don't know about all the cousins," she says, "but that's how it works with the jackalope clan."

"Jackalopes aren't real," I tell her. "Even I know that. They're just this joke that somebody started—some taxidermist putting deer horns on a jackrabbit."

She pulls a face. "That's gross." She pokes me with her finger. "Does this feel real?"

And then she does it some more—poke, poke—after which she pouts, crosses her arms across her chest, and turns away.

"I'm sorry," I say. "I didn't mean to be insulting. This is—all of this is just really new to me."

She looks at me over her shoulder.

"Are you really sorry?" she asks.

"Really."

"How big is your sorry?"

"I don't know what you mean."

She's turned fully around now. "Is it as big as a house? As a mountain? As the moon, moon, moon?"

She does another one of her twirls, arms held straight out. Pepito gives a sharp bark.

"Oh, be quiet," I tell him.

"That doesn't sound like you're very sorry."

I point at the dog. "I was talking to Pepito."

"I think you're bossy."

I sigh. "I'm not. It's just that it's late and I don't want to wake people up."

"Why not? It's a beautiful night. I love the night, don't you? Or are you like the snake and lizard cousins who are always looking for some stretch of sunlight to loll about in?"

She keeps twirling as she speaks but now she stops and looks at me, hands on her hips, waiting for an answer.

"I like the night," I assure her.

"I knew you did. I've seen you out walking before. We have so much in common, don't you think? Except you're not very good at saying you're sorry and I am. If I was sorry about something, I'd be as sorry as the whole wide world."

"That's exactly how sorry I am," I say, falling into the spirit of things. "I'm as sorry as the whole world and the sky above it, too."

"Oh, good." She takes my hand. "Well, come on and I'll show you where I live."

She leads me to the trailhead. I've never actually gone into the park at night, preferring to walk along the edge so that the dogs don't go running wild. They're always wanting to go in and I have to call them back, but tonight they settle down in the dirt, as though this is something I'm supposed to do on my own.

I pause to look back at them. "Don't get into trouble. And don't chase *anybody*!"

"Bossy, bossy," Lupita says with a laugh, and tugs on my hand.

As she pulls me along, I keep catching glimpses of those small deer horns and the long floppy jackrabbit ears. I suppose the weirdest thing is that I don't find them strange anymore.

I'm a little nervous at first. We're moving quickly and I'm thinking of Ramon's warnings about being careful of the cacti—some of the thorns have barbed ends, and I don't relish the idea of having to pull them out one by one. But Lupita is sure-footed, steering us easily on a weaving path in between the saguaro and cholla and prickly pear, and I realize that my night sight is much better than I thought, because I can see almost as clearly as if it were day.

It takes us half the time to get into the foothills that it did when I was last here with Ramon. Instead of following the trail, Lupita leads me up a ravine that soon turns into a small canyon. There isn't as much vegetation in here. It's mostly just a jumble of sand and rock with dead weeds and small trees I can't name growing along and up the sides. Soon the red stone walls tower above us. Lupita lets go of my hand and starts up this vague winding ghost of a trail that I can barely make out even with my night sight.

"Aren't you coming?" she asks when she realizes I'm still standing on the canyon floor.

"Coming to where?"

"Up here with me. You'll like where we're going."

"Come on, Lupita. It's the middle of the night."

"I know. Isn't it great?"

"I don't know. . . ."

"Oh, pooh! What kind of a dragon are you?"

"The kind that should know better," I mutter.

But I start up the faint trail. She darts ahead, nimble as a bighorn, laughter trailing behind her. Eventually I catch up and join her on an enormous slab of rock that sticks out of the side of the mountain. We're hundreds of feet above the desert, which stretches away from the mountain for as far as the eye can see.

It takes me a few moments to realize what's missing.

"Where's the city?" I ask. "Shouldn't Santo del Vado Viejo be out there?"

She shakes her head. "We've kind of taken a step sideways. This is what the world looks like without all that concrete and metal."

"I don't understand."

She laces her fingers together. Wiggling the fingers of one hand, she says, "This is the world where we met." Then she wriggles the fingers of the other hand. "And this is where we are now. They kind of take up the same space except they don't. It's simple when you think about it."

This is one more thing that Paupau never told me about, but I'm tired of being the gawking tourist, so I just nod like I get it.

"And this . . . is this where you live?" I ask.

I'm astonished by the view, how the desert spreads out under the huge velvet expanse of sky thick with stars. So it's got that totally going for it. But after that? We're still just standing on this slab of rock sticking out of a cliff.

She laughs. "Of course not, silly. I live with some deer cousins in a trailer not far from where you do."

"But you said—"

She does that finger-poke thing again. "Oh, you. You take everything so seriously. You can still walk me home. But first we needed to see this. Isn't it grander than grand?"

She gets up and starts to dance. I try to grab her. If she

falls, it's a long way down. But she slips out of my reach. I hold my breath as she pirouettes right to the edge, then back. She sinks gracefully into a cross-legged position directly in front of me, takes my hand and pulls me down.

"Don't dragons dance?" she asks.

"I don't know many dragons. Just Paupau—my grandmother—and I've never seen her dance."

"Well, that would be just sad—if you couldn't dance, I mean."

"I guess."

I catch the glimpse of deer antlers and long ears again—here, then gone.

"Can I ask you something?" I say.

"Anything. Fire away."

"I keep thinking I see little horns poking up out of your hair and sometimes your ears are long and droopy like a . . . um . . ."

"Jackrabbit?"

I nod. "Anyway, I was wondering . . . why do I see that—I am seeing it, right? And these little horns . . ."

She nods. "It's just easier to see deeper when we're in this in-between place."

"Deeper."

"Mmm."

"What do you see when you look at me?"

She laughs. "Well, you're cute—is that what you wanted to hear?"

"No. Can you see the dragon?"

She nods again. "Sort of. There's this . . . big shadowy shape inside you—or I suppose it's more like the *idea* of something really big, curled up and sleeping in your chest. It's confusing, because it fits right there in your chest, but at the same time I can also tell that it's really like the size of a mountain or something."

"I wonder how I'm supposed to wake it up."

She gets this alarmed look and grabs my arm.

"No, no, no," she says. "You shouldn't do that!"

"Why not? Everybody seems to think I'm here on some kind of spirit quest to get in touch with my inner dragon, or prove myself to him or to the clan or *something*."

"Well," she says, "there's other ways to do that. You could start by accepting that your animal spirit isn't separate from you. It's as much a part of you as your arm or your leg. It's just one of the things that makes you who you are. Being a dragon, you can't shift shape because you don't want the dragon rampaging around and wrecking everything in sight—apparently that's what happens when cousins first wear their dragon shape, I don't know why. Or at least it does with the feathered serpents down south. But you can still get in touch with its essence and draw on its power to—you know—do stuff."

"What kind of stuff?"

She shrugs. "Cousin stuff. You know, see things as they really are, step in between the worlds. Be faster and stronger. Heal more quickly. Live longer. All kinds of good things."

"You make it sound like being a superhero."

"Maybe those stories started with us." She pauses and cocks her head. "Who says you're on a spirit quest?"

I tell her about how Paupau sent me away from Chicago, what the strange woman told me outside the pool hall, what Rosalie and Anna and Tío made of it all. How cool Ramon is, though I'm not sure he really believes I'm telling the truth.

"What did the woman look like?" Lupita asks, then just says, "Hmm," when I describe her.

"What?" I say. "Do you know her?"

"Maybe. She sounds like one of the rattlesnake twins, either Ramona or Rita."

"Is that good or bad?"

"Depends on how you like your poison," she says.

"What's that supposed to mean?"

"Nothing. You just don't want to get on the bad side of either of them is all. You probably met Rita. I don't go down around South Presidio much—too many *bandas*— but I've heard she's been hanging around there. I wonder why she's trying to recruit you."

"You and me both."

She nods. "I understand exactly why you don't want to be involved—all it does is make enemies and cause more trouble."

"I guess. But if I thought I really could help . . ."

I'm thinking of Anna's brother, Rosalie's mother, and all the others who have died.

"But we're not players," Lupita says. "We're not the movers and the shakers—well, at least I'm not. You can go all dragony, but why would you want to because then it'd be all—'Look out! It's Japanese monster night!'"

"If it's that dangerous," I say, "why would Paupau just send me off to figure this all out on my own? You'd think she'd want me to stick close, or that she'd at least warn me."

"She never told you that waking your dragon could be dangerous?"

"Not the way you're telling me. But I guess that explains why El Tigre wanted to work out a truce with me. He must have figured that otherwise I could just stomp him and his whole neighborhood. Except why would he think I'd risk the lives of all the innocent people who live in the area?"

"Guys like him don't worry about other people. They only go by what *they'd* do."

"You'd have to be crazy. And I think the dragon clans are crazy, too, if they just let people like me walk around trying to figure it out on their own."

"Oh, somebody's probably paying attention," Lupita says. "If it's anything like the way it works with the feathered serpents, there's some kind of fail-safe built in. Down there the old clan members show up en masse and shut the rogue down."

"When you say shut down . . ."

"I mean they kill him."

"Wonderful."

"Oh, don't be such a worrywart. All you have to do is make sure you don't get really mad about anything."

"How am I supposed to do that?"

"Well, we could go tease the javelina boys. That's always fun."

"Maybe so," I tell her. "But right now I just want to collect the dogs and go home. I've got a lot to think about."

And a phone call to make, I add to myself.

Lupita takes me back to the trailhead where the dogs are waiting, and we walk her home. On the way back to Tío's, I call Paupau. I don't care how late it is.

But of course, all she does is turn my questions into Zen riddles that I'm supposed to figure out on my own or the answers won't have any worth. I begin the conversation full of righteous indignation and end it as ignorant as when I got on the bus in Chicago in the first place.

I spend some time with Lupita almost every night after that. I usually take the dogs for a short ramble after work; by the time we return, Lupita's waiting in front of Tío's house and we walk down to the trailhead. Sometimes we walk in the desert here, sometimes she takes me to that in-between place where the desert is the same but there's no trace of civilization. We talk long into the night and kick up dust underfoot. Sometimes I swear I can hear the tide of the ancient seas that were once here.

And a funny thing happens. The more time I spend with her, the more comfortable I get with being able to talk about my secret. She's not like the other friends I've made here in Santo del Vado Viejo. Maybe it's because she's not entirely human.

Anna doesn't want to know about it, and I haven't been alone with Ramon since our hike. Rosalie and Tío, God bless them, really think I should be using whatever it is that I've got to take down El Tigre and clean up the barrio, so, pressure much? But Lupita is just easygoing and matter-of-fact about the whole thing. There are no Zen riddles. No unanswered questions. If I ask her something and she knows the answer, she just tells me; if she doesn't know, she says so. Sometimes she asks one of the other cousins and tells me what they said the next time we meet. Sometimes we just don't figure it out.

But if Lupita takes the mystery out of one part of the equation, she puts it back through just being who she is. She looks like an ordinary girl—like the little kid I first thought she was—but then I'll catch a glimpse of the small three-tined antlers poking up through her tangled hair, or the droop of her hare ears, like long braids.

And while we talk about everyday things—what bands we like, or how building a wall between properties doesn't do a whole lot to promote friendly interchange—our conversations can just as easily be about things that ordinary people would never talk about.

Like the other day. We're sitting on a limestone outcrop and she's kicking her heels against the stone while trying to explain how being a jackalope makes it hard to get respect from some of the other cousins.

"Because I'm not a dragon," she says. "I'm not like a unicorn, or the *cadejos*, either, with all kinds of cool stories floating around about me. Jackalopes are just a joke."

"I don't think you're a joke."

"That's nice of you to say, except that's exactly what you thought jackalopes were when we first met."

"I didn't know any better."

"Like that's an excuse."

"What's a kad-ey-ho?" I ask to change the subject.

"It's kind of a rainbow-colored dog with cloven hooves. They're born in the heart of a volcano."

I smile. "Really."

"Really."

"That's very cool."

She sighs. "You see what I mean?"

"That doesn't mean you're not cool, too."

"Except I'm not *cadejo* cool."

"Yeah, but—"

"Or even dragon cool."

"If dragons are so cool," I say, "why does it take a jacka-lope to show them how to relax?"

Lupita grins and taps her fist against my shoulder.

"That's because we're very relaxing cousins to be around," she says.

She lies back on the stone. After a moment, I do, too, and we're quiet, staring up into the night sky that goes on just a few light-years beyond forever.

Paupau can talk all she wants about clan responsibilities and nebulous dragon gifts, but sometimes all a guy wants to do is chill out with a friend and not have to think about anything.

- 5 -

Even those who work to prevent something can be hurt or damaged by it.
—CHINESE PROVERB

IT HAD BEEN a long day for Rosalie. She took care of her menagerie of cats and dogs, then headed off to school, where she tutored some kids during lunch. After school, Ramon picked her up so they could help at the local soup kitchen until it was time for Rosalie's shift at La Maravilla. It was a slow night, so she got most of her homework done in the moments she could snatch between orders. Now, back home, she'd just finished the last of it and could finally spend a little downtime with Ramon.

They were sitting on the front porch when Jay came outside. He'd taken the dogs for a walk, then gone to take a shower. Rosalie was looking across the street when Jay opened the front door, and she blinked in surprise when a small figure sitting by the curb rose to her feet. Rosalie could have sworn there hadn't been anyone there a moment ago. The girl gave Jay an enthusiastic wave.

"So who's your new girlfriend?" Rosalie asked.

"Yeah, and what happened to Anna?" Ramon added.

"Anna's not interested in me," Jay said.

"That's not true," Rosalie said. "She just confused about stuff."

"The big question," Ramon said, "is did you ask her out yet?"

Jay shook his head.

Ramon held his hands out in front of him. "So you don't know for sure."

"Maybe not," Jay said. "But it seems pretty obvious to me."

"You shouldn't have given up on her," Rosalie said. "You just needed to give her a little more time to get used to all of . . . you know."

"I haven't given up. I'm just trying not to think about it."

Rosalie nodded. Her gaze went to the girl waiting for Jay across the street. "Your new girlfriend seems a little young," she said.

"Lupita's not my girlfriend. She's a cousin."

"I didn't know you had relatives in the area," Rosalie said.

"She's not that kind of cousin," he told her.

"I don't get it."

He smiled. "Ask your boyfriend what I mean." He lifted a hand. "I've got to run."

Rosalie watched the two of them head off down Calle Esmeralda toward the trailhead. Jay seemed positively sedate next to his companion. The girl skipped around him, sometimes walking backward so that she could face him, then twirling around in dizzying pirouettes.

When they were too far away to make out clearly, Rosalie turned to Ramon.

"What did he mean by that?" she asked.

"You know the uncles?"

"The ones always sitting around drinking mescal tea to get high?"

He shrugged. "That's one way of looking at it. Another might be that they're freeing their spirit so that they become hawks and fly out over the desert."

Rosalie was used to what she thought of as Ramon's poetic flights of fancy. She supposed it was why he was such a good songwriter.

"So another word for your *mescaleros* is 'cousins'?" she said.

"No, the cousins aren't shape changers—they're the animal people."

"What's the difference?"

"The animal people were here even before the Yaqui, or

the Kikimi, or any of the Pueblo peoples. They aren't men who can become animals, or animals who can become men. They're both animals and men at the same time. In fact, sometimes they walk around like a mash-up of both. Men with coyote or deer heads—that kind of thing."

Rosalie couldn't hide her disbelief.

"I'm just telling you what the stories say," Ramon said. "I've never met one myself."

"And Jay's new girlfriend is one of them?"

Ramon smiled. "You're so ready to deny the possibility, but you still believe that Jay has a dragon sleeping inside him."

"I'm not sure I believe that's true, either—or at least not literally. But there's something weird going on. You know he says he never learned Spanish?"

Ramon nodded.

"And yet he speaks it fluently—with the same accent as everybody else living down here. But we had some tourists in from Mexico City and I heard his accent just shift to theirs. I've even heard him talk to customers in German and Japanese, but he doesn't even know he's doing it. It's like whatever language somebody uses, that's what he answers in."

"Maybe he's one of those savants," Ramon said. "You know, with Asperger's or something."

Rosalie smiled. "Could be. He's smart all right. But then . . ."

"There's his dragon."

Rosalie nodded. "If it's real . . ." She shook her head. "I think that's part of the reason Anna's so confused. With my mama and Paulo getting killed, she can't imagine anyone having the chance to get rid of the *bandas* and not taking it."

"And do you feel the same way?"

"Kind of, I have to admit." She sighed. "If Jay's dragon power is real, then it's frustrating and scary. And if it's not, well, why would he lie about it? Is he delusional?"

"Confusing."

"Like I said."

Ramon took her hand. "There's nothing we can do about it, you know that. It's not something we can fix."

"I know. I wouldn't even know how it should be fixed. And I totally get how Anna feels. Because if such a thing is real, then what else is?"

"Like the uncles turning into hawks."

Rosalie smiled. "I guess. But I was thinking more along the lines of, what *can* we trust to be real?"

"You, me. The street in front of us. Your uncle's house. They're all real." He squeezed her fingers. "But mostly you and me."

Rosalie leaned her head against his shoulder. He always managed to say the right thing. It didn't make matters any clearer, but she felt better all the same.

Lupita had never figured out how to make herself look older—it was a trick, she explained, that some cousins had and some didn't. She didn't, so she was stuck looking as young as she had when she'd first taken human form. She was probably older than anyone who'd be at the show Malo Malo was playing the following weekend, but she didn't want to go, even though it was all-ages.

"I don't like being treated like a little kid," she had said.

"But you're going for the music," Jay argued, "and you love to dance. Who cares about the other people?"

She shook her head. "I'll just listen from outside."

The night of the show, Jay looked for Lupita when he arrived with Rosalie, but he couldn't spot her.

"Are you coming?" Rosalie asked.

Jay joined her in the line to get his hand stamped. They were on the guest list so they didn't have to pay, but they still only got red stamps, which meant they couldn't order alcohol.

"Who were you looking for out there?" Rosalie asked.

"Nobody. I was just wondering if I knew anyone."

He didn't tell her about Lupita because it was just too complicated. And besides that, the truth was he sort of liked having something here in Santo del Vado Viejo that he'd found on his own.

As if to bring the point home, Rosalie laughed and said, "Like you know so many people."

"Hey, I'm getting there. Didn't Paco say he was coming?"

"Paco always says he's coming, but he never shows up. Haven't you figured that out yet?"

What Jay had figured out was that Paco smoked way too much weed, taking every chance he could when he wasn't washing dishes to go out in the alley and toke up.

"I guess I should have," he said. "But I think he'd really like the band."

"I think a lot more people would, if they only gave them a chance. But I'm biased."

Jay shook his head. "No, they're really good."

"And you're biased, too."

Jay laughed. "Maybe a little."

The hall was quickly filling up with people, from young teens to those in their twenties. Though he recognized some of the *bandas*, Jay didn't spot any gang colors, which made sense; they wouldn't have been allowed in if they were wearing them. There were lots of skeleton T-shirts, all kinds of variations on the gangly dancing Day of the Dead skeletons that were the band's logo. Rosalie told him that they were called *catrin*, and based on the art of José Guadalupe Posada.

Most popular was the official Malo Malo merch: black T-shirts showing ribcage bones on the back and front, or long black scarves printed with a twisting line of vertebrae. Some people wore plastic skull masks, while more than a few had actually painted the skull image on their faces. It gave the crowd an eerie look.

The opening band was nothing special, and people talked through most of their set. Jay felt a little sorry for them, but he was as guilty as anyone else, chatting with Rosalie and her friends at the back of the hall. Then finally after a short break, it was time for Malo Malo.

Jay pushed to the front of the stage with the others as the intro for the first song began, kick drum and bass combining in a steady heartbeat rhythm that you could feel deep in your chest. Ramon said it was the band's way of "tuning the audience." Jay hadn't understood what he'd meant until he went to his first show and found his pulse adjusting to, and then keeping time with, the beat.

Hector began a scratching counter rhythm on his turntable, sounding like chickens pecking in a yard, then suddenly a spot came on to capture Ramon and Gilbert at the front of the stage, sharing a mic. They started with a flourish on their trumpets and played some jaunty mariachi tune until Gilbert backed away, switching to long, slow notes, while Ramon started rapping the story of how the band came together.

The spots weren't on Anna yet, but her guitar could be heard weaving a delicate harmony to Gilbert's trumpet. The band hit the chorus with everybody singing, then the music stopped for a moment before it came roaring back in double time, the trumpets high and sharp. The spotlight touched Anna just as she broke into a killer guitar break that sounded like speed-metal flamenco.

When Ramon started the next verse, strobing lights washed the crowd and they pumped their fists as he sang of everybody needing to find a place for themselves in the world. The pogoing audience flickered in the strobes, the skeleton images rapidly appearing and disappearing, and then a funny thing happened.

At first Jay didn't realize what was going on when a desert landscape appeared in between the strobe flashes. He was dancing in the hall, then in the desert, then in the hall, the switches keeping time to the lights. And it wasn't only visual. Sound stuttered between the silence of the impossible landscape and the pounding throb of the band's music. He could smell the clean night air of the desert against the hot, sweaty crowd by the stage. The desert was cool and dry, the hall steamy.

He stumbled and might have lost his balance, but the jostling press of the crowd kept him on his feet. Then he stood motionless, eyes wide, trying to understand what was happening. A wave of panic tightened his chest until he suddenly understood:

The music and lights were breaking down the barrier between this world and the in-between place.

Ever since Lupita had brought him there he'd been trying to return on his own. It was simple when he was with her, a sideways shift, but he couldn't seem to manage to cross over without her.

"You can't think about it," Lupita tried to explain. "You have to relax and just do it. Then when you make the step across, do it like you're expecting it to work, not like you're hoping it will."

He tried it now, just told himself that he was in that desert, and the strobing effect stopped. He stood in the dirt, a vault of stars above him, his ears ringing from the music a world away.

Then he allowed himself to return and he was back in the thick of the dancers, the lights still strobing, nobody apparently having noticed either his disappearance or his sudden reappearance. He threw back his head and laughed.

He'd never tried any drugs—Paupau had drilled that into him: It was too dangerous with the dragon sleeping inside—but he thought this was what it must be like, as though the world was bigger than you thought it was, making you feel tall and a little reckless.

Anna took another solo, playing louder and twice as fast. Her head was tilted back, hair flowing, fingers dancing on her guitar neck as she spun like a dervish across the stage. Jay grinned, thinking she was the very picture of the rock goddess.

The crowd went wild and never quieted down until the third and last encore.

Later, everybody on the guest list helped tear down the equipment and lights, or made themselves useful in other ways. Jay found himself at the merch table with Margarita and Hector, bagging T-shirts and CDs. Jay liked them both, though he didn't know either well. Hector, tall and rangy with his long dark hair in a ponytail, was shy offstage. Margarita looked tiny next to him—a short, dark bundle of energy. She had so many friends that Jay'd never had the chance to just hang with her on her own.

They were doing a brisk business until a guy Jay recognized as a local gangbanger stepped up to the table. The King's crown symbol was tattooed on the back of either hand. Another tattoo made it look as though he had a strand of barbed wire wrapped around his neck.

Jay knew he was one to talk, with the image of a dragon taking up his entire back, but the gangbanger's tattoos left him with an unpleasant feeling—even the one of Our Lady of Guadalupe on his forearm. But that was probably the point.

As the gangbanger leaned on the merch table, bringing his face in close to Hector's, a few more Kings pushed through the line to stand behind him.

"You got all these barrio songs," the gangbanger said, "talking about making good, getting the girls, and collecting the ching ching."

Hector nodded. "Yeah, I guess we do."

"So when are you going to write a song about the real success story we got happening down here?"

"What're you talking about?"

The guy looked at his fellow gang members, eyebrows raised as if to ask, "Can you believe this guy?" then turned back to Hector.

"I'm talking about El Tigre, man," he said.

The other *bandas* nodded in agreement.

"Word," one of them said.

"Yo, you tell 'em, Alambra."

"Yeah," Alambra went on. "You're singing about Malverde and all these other banditos been dead a hundred years. It's time you tell some new stories, man."

"We write the stories we want to write," Hector said.

"Yeah? So maybe you should want to write one about El Tigre. We'll make sure it gets lots of play."

Jay remembered the day he met Rosalie and her telling him how the gangbangers would sometimes take young bands in under their wing. They'd give them support, make sure their music got played, and provide all the dope and partying anybody might want. But the downside was that you were in their pocket. You played the music they wanted you to play, where they wanted you to play it, and if they decided they didn't like you anymore, you could end up beaten or dead.

The sweet deal could turn bad before you knew it.

So he wasn't surprised at Hector's reluctance to even talk to the gangbanger.

"It's not like that," Hector was saying.

"You can't write about our main man?" Alambra asked. "Why can't you give us a rockin' *narcocorrido* about El Tigre? Put that Malo Malo spin on it, man."

"Because we don't write about shit," Margarita said before Hector could answer.

Alambra didn't even look at her as he said, "Shut up, bitch. Was I talking to you?"

Margarita stood up from behind the table.

"You need to leave," she said. She pointed at Alambra. "You and all your asshole loser friends. Don't make me call security."

It was like dropping a pebble into a pool, Jay thought. A stillness arose on the heels of her words, expanding from where she stood and spreading throughout the hall. Ramon and the others who were still on the stage turned to look in the direction of the merch table. Hector and Jay started to stand up. Alambra's gaze slowly found Margarita's face.

Jay was so mesmerized by the dark anger flooding the gangbanger's features that he never saw the knife appear. He wasn't even aware that anyone was in danger until Alambra's arm shot across the table and he buried the blade in Margarita's chest.

"*No!*" he heard Anna scream from the stage.

Cries of shock and alarm rose up all around them.

Alambra pulled the knife free and blood flowered on Margarita's T-shirt.

Margarita's eyes went wide from shock. Her mouth opened, but no sound came out and her legs gave way. As she began to crumple, Hector lunged for her.

"Who's the piece of shit now, bitch?" Alambra asked.

Margarita slumped in Hector's arms. Her blood was all over him now, too. Jay clenched his fists, so tightly his nails dug half-moons into his palms. He turned back to find the gangbanger grinning, and the controlled calm he'd developed from years of training with Paupau disappeared as though it had never been.

He didn't fight it. Instead, he let that enormous *something* he always felt shifting inside him grow, rising up to fill not only himself, but the entire hall. No—it was more like *he* was filling the hall, because as the secret behemoth grew inside him, he merged with it. He could feel the weight of enormous wings on his shoulders pushing against the roof high above. His lungs were hot with raging coals and fire. There was a roaring in his ears, like a long continuous rumble of immediate thunder.

The fire, when it burst from his mouth, could have erupted from a flamethrower: an awful, blistering tongue of heat that enveloped the gangbanger. Jay stomped his enormous hind foot—ten times the size of an elephant's—and the ground shook, the building trembled. He stomped again, claiming his victory over his foe and marking his territory. Cracks streaked up the walls. Dust and plaster flaked and fell. A second blast of flame and the gangbanger was briefly outlined before he was entirely consumed and collapsed into ash.

Jubilant with the death of his enemy, the monster that held Jay stomped its hind foot a third time. More dust and plaster fell. The cracks widened. The roof supports began to groan.

But then the part of the behemoth that was Jay realized what he had done.

The building was collapsing.

A building full of people.

The band, his friends, the staff, the members of the audience that hadn't left yet—

A panicked fear for their safety gave him the strength of will he might not otherwise have been able to muster. Using all those years of training, he focused and fought to contain the beast until he finally had it under control.

Barely.

"*Out!*" he cried. To his ears, his voice was the thunderous roar of the dragon. "*Everybody out!*"

He let his wings expand until they pressed up against every portion of the roof. He held the structure up, straining under its massive weight, as the people fled. The giant shape he held was starting to falter—the dragon returning to its slumber in his chest—and he didn't know how long he could keep the building from collapsing.

But he couldn't let them die.

He wouldn't.

Not Rosalie and Anna.

Not any of them.

He didn't care about the gangbanger, but Margarita was already one too many.

Rosalie was up on the stage, coiling guitar and microphone cords with Anna, when the commotion began at the merch table. She looked over just in time to see Margarita rise to her feet, yelling something at a guy that she recognized as one of the local gangbangers, a guy they called Alambra. She didn't actually see Margarita get stabbed, but she immediately knew something bad was happening when Alambra pulled back from the table and the front of Margarita's T-shirt went red. Anna shouted something from beside her and the two of them ran for the end of the stage.

And that's when things got really weird.

She saw Jay raise his arms, all his attention focused on Margarita's assailant, and felt a sudden pressure in the air as though a thunderstorm had come up out of nowhere. The small hairs on her arms rose up and her skin prickled. Jay opened his mouth—impossibly wide, it seemed—and Alambra twitched as though something had struck him. She knew he was considered a real tough guy—so she was surprised when his eyes went wide with shock and fear.

What was going on?

Jay stamped his foot on the floor and Rosalie could swear she felt reverberations shake the stage where she was standing. A second stomp on the floor and Rosalie saw cracks running across the floor and up the walls. Plaster dust floated down from the ceiling. And then . . . and then . . .

Alambra was briefly outlined as though he stood in the middle of a blazing inferno before he went black, then gray, then . . . the only way to describe it was that he seemed to disintegrate. He turned to ashes.

Rosalie's heart pumped far too fast. What she'd just seen was impossible.

"What the f—?" she heard Anna start to say.

But a rumbling roar shook the hall. Rosalie could see the cracks expanding on the walls, reaching up and criss-crossing the ceiling. More dust and plaster fell down on the crowd.

"*Out!*" a voice that was like a deep roar cried. "*Everybody out!*"

It took Rosalie a moment to realize that it had come from Jay.

Move, she told herself.

The building was going to come down around them.

"Come on!" she yelled at Anna.

But Anna was already heading back to where the band had left their gear.

"Anna!" she called after her. "We need to get out of here."

The exits were choked with people pushing and shoving in a panic to get out. She hoped no one would get hurt in the press.

"Screw that!" Anna said. "I'm not leaving without my guitars."

Rosalie ran over to where the rest of the band was frantically grabbing what gear they could. She picked up a couple of trumpets, then herded Anna and the others to the exit at the back of the stage. Before she went down the stairs, she looked back to see Jay standing alone, arms still raised, back bent as though he thought he was supporting the whole weight of the building.

"Rosalie!" Ramon called.

She turned away. "But Jay—"

She wanted to drag him out, but she had the uneasy feeling that maybe it was true. Maybe he *was* all that was keeping the building up. She knew Ramon wouldn't leave without her, so finally she ran down the stairs.

The air was cleaner outside, away from the falling dust and grit. People were milling around everywhere and she could hear sirens in the distance.

Come on, Jay, she thought. Everybody else is out. You don't need to stay any longer.

She put the trumpets down on the ground and was about to start back for the building, when Ramon stopped her.

The building collapsed.

It fell in on itself with a thunderous roar, sending up plumes of dust and dirt. All that was left in the silence that followed was a heap of rubble inside of what remained of the walls.

Rosalie stared in horror.

Oh, Jay . . .

In The Dragon Garden restaurant in Chicago's Chinatown, Katharine Xú looked up from the newspaper on the table in front of her. The restaurant wasn't busy, but what had caught her attention had nothing to do with the handful of remaining customers. She gazed into some far distance that only she could see. Emotions flitted across her usually stoic features. Worry. Disappointment. Anger. Sorrow.

She stood abruptly from her table and headed for the front door.

"Paupau?" her daughter called from behind the counter where she was working on the day's receipts. "Is everything all right?"

Paupau's only response was to give Susan a distracted wave, then she was out the door.

She had no time for conversation. She had somewhere else she needed to be.

In the alley behind a soup kitchen in New York City, a small white woman with dark brown hair and violet eyes was sharing a cigarette with an old black man. They were sitting on the back stoop of the building, talking about nothing in particular—the strange weather this summer, a blues riff that sounded like the clatter of a subway car—when the woman broke off in midsentence and stood up.

"Sorry, Jake," she said, "but I have to go."

She strode off down the alleyway and was around the corner and lost from sight before her companion even had a chance to ask what was the matter.

In a dojo in San Francisco, a Japanese man was running his kendo class through a series of exercises when he suddenly stopped, wooden sword held high in the air above his head. He seemed far away in his mind for a long moment before he finally lowered the sword and looked at his class.

"My apologies," he said. "But I must leave."

He walked across the dojo, laid his sword on a table by the door, and then went out the door.

In a garage on North Lamar Boulevard in Austin, Texas, a tall black man stood up from the Harley he was working on. He pushed his dreads back over his shoulders.

"Crap," he said. "I was really looking forward to a burrito when I was done with this."

A dark-haired woman lifted her head from under the hood of a vintage T-Bird to look at him.

"What's up?" she asked.

"Business," he said. He cleaned the grease from his hands on a rag. "Bad business."

"You need a hand with it?"

She'd known him long enough to know not to ask what kind of business.

He shook his head. "But thanks for the offer. I'll see you in a couple of days."

And just like that he was out the door, walking into the bright sunlight that beat down on the pavement of the garage's parking lot. A moment later his long legs had taken him out of her sight.

Jay hadn't thought he could hold out as long as he already had. It seemed impossible that he could even be doing it—some kid supporting this whole freaking building all on his own—but even as it was dropping back into its slumber, the dragon lent him strength, and to keep the beast under control he'd found reserves of willpower he didn't think he had. He supposed he could thank Paupau now for the years of intense training designed to keep him strong and focus his will. Things like standing on one leg for hours, or hanging from the chin-up bar until he thought his arms would fall off. "It's good to build up stamina," she'd say when he complained, "for a human as well as a dragon."

But nothing could have prepared him for this, because the dragon was almost asleep again, the building was taking forever to clear, and it was all he could do to stop the roof from crashing down.

He was trembling from head to foot by the time everybody was out, but finally they were all safe and he didn't have to bear the enormous weight anymore. Except then the realization suddenly hit him. He was so screwed.

How was *he* supposed to get out?

Who was going to hold up the building until he made it to safety?

No, scratch that. Never mind getting out. Who was going to hold the building up *right now*? Because he was losing his grip on it.

He tried to wake the dragon again, but the rage that had come from seeing Margarita die was gone. There was only fear left, and that didn't seem to be enough. His brain was blank. Anything that might have helped—from what he'd learned having the dragon waken, to his studies with Paupau—was gone. There was only the crack of the rafters overhead. The thunder of the building collapsing.

He stared up, stunned, until he remembered the other thing he'd learned today.

Just before the roof crashed into the floor, he shifted to Lupita's in-between place.

The silence was absolute after the roar of the collapsing building. He stared up and drank in a dark desert sky, rich with stars. And free of falling debris.

He let out a breath he hadn't been aware of holding and slowly walked in the direction of where the parking lot would be in the world he'd just left behind. When he judged he'd gone far enough, he shifted back. The quiet of the desert was immediately swallowed by pandemonium. People shouting and talking. Sirens approaching.

Jay stared at the wreckage of what had once been a music hall. Part of him was numb. Part was horrified. He'd just killed one of the gangbangers, fried him to a crisp with hardly a thought. He'd just pulled down this enormous building, almost killing everyone inside. But another part of him thought that making the gangbanger pay for killing Margarita was the coolest thing ever. And he'd come through in the end, hadn't he? He'd saved everyone. He really *was* some kind of kick-ass superhero.

He heard someone behind him, footsteps crunching in the dirt, and turned to see Anna, her face streaked with grime and tears. He thought she'd be freaked by what had happened, but she only looked angry.

"You did this," she said.

It was a statement, not a question.

"I guess I did."

She slammed her palms against his chest and he staggered back.

"You did this," she repeated. "But you couldn't do it before Margarita got killed?"

"It's not like that. Before tonight, I didn't know I could really—"

She cut him off. "Bullshit. You told us all about the dragons and crap."

"But I had no idea how to—"

"You could have gone and shut them down—all those goddamn posing *bandas*—but no, you had to wait to make some big statement with it, didn't you?"

"What are you talking ab—"

She slammed her palms into his chest again, hard enough to make him stagger back.

"Margarita's dead! Don't you get it? She didn't have some magic power to protect her. She was just our friend, a kid who played in our band, and now she's *dead*!"

Over her shoulder, Jay saw Rosalie approaching with Ramon and the other band members. They walked like zombies, dejected and stunned, carrying the few instruments they'd been able to grab before they'd fled the building. Behind them, Hector knelt beside a blanket-draped body.

Here he was thinking he was so cool, that Anna was going to be impressed. But their friend was dead. Murdered.

"I . . . I . . ." he tried, but he couldn't find the words.

"You could have stopped it before."

Jay shook his head. "I didn't know that guy was going to—"

"Not now. Back when you went to see El Tigre. Instead you just made some kind of deal with him and now Margarita's dead."

"That deal was supposed to—"

"You make me sick. I hope I never have to see you again."

"Anna," he tried again, but she was already gone.

He could see Rosalie a step or two ahead of the others. He couldn't read her expression, but still he didn't know how he could face her. It was going to be the same as with Anna. All of them were going to feel the same.

Maybe he *should* have done something before. Instead of making the deal, maybe he should have tried to wake the dragon instead, smashed the crap out of the *bandas'* pool hall with all of them in it. Then Margarita wouldn't be dead.

"Jay," Rosalie began.

But he shook his head. He couldn't stay to hear it. There was no place for him here.

Before Rosalie could reach him, before Anna could shove him again, he stepped away to the in-between place, its calming desert. He sank to his knees, too weak to stand.

He'd wrecked everything. He'd messed up and people had died because of it. Not as many as might have, but he was no hero for saving them. Not when he'd created the danger in the first place.

The image of Anna's face—the tears streaming down her cheeks, the anger in her eyes—wouldn't go away. He sat up and hugged his knees, rocking back and forth.

What was he going to *do*?

Rosalie stood with her mouth agape, staring at the place where Jay had been. She'd thought she'd seen the gang-banger turn to ash and vanish before the building came down, but even with everybody talking about it, she hadn't really believed it. He had to have just disappeared into the crowd while everybody was looking at Margarita and Hector. But even if it had happened, how could Jay be responsible? Even if he *could* turn into a dragon, there'd been no dragon. Just Jay standing there with his arms spread wide.

But this . . .

"Mother of God," Gilbert said, and crossed himself.

"What . . . how did . . . ?" Rosalie couldn't seem to make her mouth work properly.

"It was magic," Ramon said.

Rosalie glanced at him. She heard in his voice the shock and wonder that she and Gilbert were feeling, but there was also the satisfaction of finally having something confirmed. The only one of them who didn't seem surprised was Anna. She just looked pissed.

"Did you see?" she said. "He's like some kind of freaking superhero, but he still couldn't take the time to save Margarita."

"What are you talking about?" Gilbert said. "What happened to Jay?"

"He took off on us," Anna said. "What else would you expect from a guy like him?"

Rosalie wanted to protest, but just then someone came over to say that the police wanted to speak to them.

"Wait up," Ramon said. "Nobody saw anything, okay? Not unless you want to spend the rest of the night talking to some cop who could give a shit about a couple more dead Mexican kids."

"Why should we protect Jay?" Anna demanded.

Rosalie could see that she still wanted to hit something.

"I'm not saying you should," Ramon told her. "But tell me. What did you see him do in there?"

"He—well, the gangbanger—oh crap, I don't know. But you all saw him just disappear in front of us, right? So he must've had something to do with what happened in the hall."

"We don't know that."

"How about this," Anna said. "He let Margarita die. Why should we cover for him?"

Ramon shook his head. "We're not doing that. I want to protect *us*—all of us that are still here. If we tell them what some of us saw, or thought we saw, they're going to think we're high and be all over us for drugs and who knows what kind of crap. We could even get locked up for psychiatric evaluation. Do you want that?"

"No, it's just—"

"We wouldn't even be able to go to Margarita's funeral."

Anna thought it over. "Fine, I get the picture."

Ramon looked at the others. "Everybody else okay with this?" Silence. "Okay, let's go talk to the cops."

It was easier and harder than Rosalie had expected. Easier because the police simply took their statements at face value, but harder because this was Margarita they were talking about. *Their* Margarita. Not some stranger, but their drummer and friend.

When they were finally done, Ramon, Rosalie, and Anna found themselves still standing in the parking lot, staring at the ruined music hall. Everyone else had gone home except for the police and the fire department, and a handful of rubberneckers, hanging on in case something else happened. Ramon draped an arm over each of their shoulders.

"Let me take you guys home," he said.

Anna shook her head. "I want to go to the hospital or the morgue . . . or wherever they took Margarita."

"You know we can't do that."

"Then what *can* we do?"

"We can go home."

"You can stay with me," Rosalie said.

"What if Jay's there?"

Rosalie sighed. "I know it's easier to believe that this was his fault—that he knew all about what he could do—but I really don't believe that he did."

"Margarita's still dead."

"I know. It's horrible but—"

"The *bandas* killed her. Like they killed my brother . . ."

Rosalie nodded. "I know. My mother's dead because of them, too."

"God, I hate living like this."

Ramon drew them both in close. Anna wept into his shoulder while Rosalie stroked her hair.

"I'll go talk to Margarita's parents," Ramon said when Anna finally pulled away and stepped back. She rubbed at her eyes with the sleeve of her hoodie. "Better they hear it from one of us than from the *policía*."

He drove the girls back home and walked them to the door. Tío was waiting up so, once Ramon left, the two girls camped out in his living room. Over the cocoa Tío made them, they told him what had happened.

It was late before Tío finally let Rosalie chase him off to bed with her argument that he had a restaurant to open in the morning, and later still before Anna eventually fell asleep on the sofa. It was only then that Rosalie was able to deal with her own grief. Somehow, she'd managed to keep the flood of numbed shock and sorrow at bay while dealing with the police, taking care of Anna, talking to Tío. Now it washed over her like storm waters rushing through a dry riverbed. She cried for Margarita, for Margarita's parents, for all of them. For the gifted life cut too short. For the friend she'd lost. For a world in which such things not only happened, but were all too common.

But while her tears exhausted her, she wasn't able to fall asleep the way Anna had. She lay on her half of the big sofa and closed her eyes, trying not to think, but that just made her think more. After a while she got up and stood in the door of Jay's room.

Enough time had passed that she had begun to question what she'd seen in the parking lot: Jay standing there, present one moment, gone the next. People didn't just disappear—well, not into thin air the way it had seemed that he had. People disappeared all the time, but they either walked away from their lives, or someone took them.

So which was it with Jay?

When she looked around the room, there wasn't much of his personality visible. The furnishings were all Tío's, as were the posters on the wall, most advertising local galleries. But she saw his backpack lying in the corner by the dresser. His MP3 player was plugged into the wall socket, charging. Crossing the room, she opened the top drawer of the dresser. Jay's few clothes were all still there, all neatly folded. She was about to close the drawer again when she saw the corner of the notebook she'd given him peeking out from under his T-shirts.

She hesitated a moment, then pulled it out. Sitting on the bed, she looked around again. It was hard to tell that anyone lived here, which also made it hard to tell if Jay had simply abandoned his few things or was planning to come back. The flimsy notebook felt heavy in her hand. She wasn't sure she was actually planning to read it. Then she glimpsed her own name in the first paragraph and the next thing she knew, she was deep into what he'd written.

It was strange, reading about things she had experienced herself only to see them now from a different point of view. The change in Jay as the journal continued was disconcerting, too. He went from the kid she'd met a few weeks ago—not really sure what he wanted out of life, easy and fun to be around, crushing on Anna—to someone so full of—

Anna would say bullshit.

But Rosalie thought it was maybe more like potential. Big, weird, mysterious potential.

She tried to convince herself it had to be a story he was writing. But she knew it wasn't. She'd probably always known that it wasn't, that it was all real—the dragon, the magic, *everything*.

"But how can it be?" she said aloud, the words startled out of her mouth.

She looked to the doorway. She half expected someone to be standing there, shocked that she'd be invading Jay's privacy. Truth was, she was shocked herself; guilty, too. But these things she'd been reading . . .

She fell back on the bed and let the journal drop as she stared up at the ceiling. She was so tired. Too tired to get up and go to her own bed.

In the end, she fell asleep where she lay.

The destruction of the dance hall brought out half the neighborhood. Whether or not they'd actually seen anything, they were all happy to talk to the various news reporters who vied to get reactions from people on the street.

Five-fingered beings weren't the only ones drawn to the

wreckage. Cousins stood around the parking lot in human form, exchanging their own stories.

"Oh, man, you should have seen it," Miguelito told his crew.

They stood bunched in a group just beyond the spotlights of the television cameras and the lights of the police cars, a group of javelina boys, thin as rakes with spiked hair, baggy pants, and oversized sweatshirts.

"He just filled the whole hall," Miguelito went on, "this huge freakin' dragon, bright as gold. He didn't need no bling—he *was* bling. He just opened that big dragon mouth of his and *fried* Alambra."

Dino, the youngest of the gang, had stayed inside with Miguelito.

"It's true," he said.

Carlos elbowed Rico. "And you had us come out for a smoke."

Rico shrugged. "Hey, what can I say?"

"I heard the dragon just turned him to dust," Javier said. He'd been outside with the others.

Miguelito shook his head. "No way. He turned him to *ash*."

Carlos sighed. "Aw, man. That's so awesome. Why couldn't I have seen it?"

They all started talking at once.

"Word."

"Totally."

"So sick, man."

Dino poked Miguelito in the shoulder.

"Look," he said, and pointed across the parking lot.

The boys all turned to see.

"Holy crap," Carlos said.

They didn't need their enhanced night vision to pierce the shadows where the foursome stood.

An old Chinese woman. A hot little white woman. And two scary dudes, one black, the other Asian.

At least that's what any five-fingered being would see. The javelina boys saw four dragons, auras of their great golden shapes rising behind them to fill the sky.

Rico shivered. "Oh, man. What are *they* doing here?"

"Looks like they're arguing," Carlos said.

Miguelito nodded. "Totally intense."

"You know what this is like?" Javier said.

The others all turned to him.

"It's what they say about the feathered serpents down south," he said. "They watch to make sure no one gets too cocky. I'll bet they're here to check out the damage."

Miguelito nodded again. "And maybe lay down some of their own damage on our dragon."

Because that was how the javelina boys saw it. The dragon that had fried Alambra was one of their own. He'd taken down a King, just like that. The freaking Presidio Kings ruled the barrio and everybody had to stay out of their way, five-fingered beings *and* cousins. But their dragon, he hadn't taken any gangbanger crap. He'd just fired up some righteous dragon retribution.

Javier gave Miguelito a push. "You've gotta tell them, man. Tell them our dragon had cause. Alambra knifed that girl—isn't that what you said?"

"Yeah, but—"

"You've got to set them straight. You know how it goes with the feathered serpents. They figure someone's gone a little loco and . . . " He mimed cutting his throat his throat. "They just shut him down. That's why those dragons are here."

"I can't just walk up to a bunch of big cousins like that and tell them what's what. Man, they might fry *me*."

"No, it's on you," Rico said and the others all nodded in agreement. "We'll have your back, man."

The others didn't look as happy about that, but they all nodded again.

So Miguelito hitched up his pants and set off across the parking lot, his homeboys trailing behind him. He licked his lips as he got closer. Man, he was dry. Then one of the dragons noticed them and all four turned.

When they got close enough to talk, Miguelito stepped out in front of the gang. He tried to meet their gazes, but he couldn't lift his own from where it was locked on the ground at his feet.

"Uh . . ."

"What's up with you boys?"

Miguelito stole a quick glance up. The black man had spoken. Miguelito cleared his throat and tried again.

"Excuse us for the . . . um . . . interruption," he managed.

He glanced up again and the white woman was smiling.

"Don't be afraid," she said. "Do you have something to tell us?"

Miguelito nodded. "I was inside when it happened, you know? I saw everything."

"Well," she said, "we think we've figured out what happened, but I'd like to hear what you saw."

So he told them about Alambra killing Malo Malo's drummer and how the dragon took him down. He grew more confident when he saw they were actually listening and probably not going to fry him. He went on to tell them about how the building started to fall apart—"I guess that dragon forgot he was inside when he got so big"—and how the dragon had held up the building until everybody got out and it finally came crashing down.

"And the dragon?" the Chinese woman asked. "Where did he go?"

Miguelito shook his head. "He didn't go anywhere. He was still inside when the building came down."

She glanced at the music hall. When she looked back, Miguelito could see the worry in her eyes.

"You all saw this?" the Asian man asked, looking to the rest of the gang.

They all shook their heads except for little Dino.

"Oh—only me—sir," he said. "I—I saw it, too."

"He's not in there now," the black man said. "I don't sense him anywhere."

The white woman nodded. "He must have crossed over to the other side."

"Yeah," the black man said. "I'm guessing he banked his dragonfire when he crossed, which is why we didn't notice him when we came in. We're never going to find him until he wakes it up again."

"I don't need to hear anymore," the Asian man said. "Sounds like the boy got a little carried away, but then he took back control and did what had to be done."

The black man nodded. "I sure don't see any evidence that we've got a rogue."

The javelina boys stood listening to all of this with big eyes. What a story they had to tell now.

As though just remembering that they were still there, the Chinese woman turned to them again.

"Thank you for your help," she said.

It was an obvious dismissal and the javelina boys quickly took the hint.

"I'm going to stay on and look for him," they heard the Chinese woman say as they walked away.

"Don't be too hard on him," the other woman said.

"I will be as hard as I need to be."

Then the boys were out of range and could hear no more. But once they were a safe distance away, they watched the dragons vanish, one by one, all except for the Chinese woman, who turned and walked away into the crowd.

The night, Miguelito thought, felt a lot smaller when they were gone.

"Damn," Carlo said. "That was totally awesome."

The others all nodded in silent agreement.

Rosalie woke up after only a few hours of sleep because there was someone at the front door.

Tío will get that, she thought, but she knew he wouldn't. Tío could sleep with a whole mariachi band playing around his bed.

When the doorbell rang a second time, she forced herself to go see who it was. Anna started to sit up when she came into the living room.

"What . . . ?" Anna began, rubbing at her eyes.

Rosalie shook her head. "It's nothing. Just go back to sleep."

"Can't," Anna mumbled, but she was asleep again as soon as her head touched the pillow.

When Rosalie opened the door and found a short Chinese woman standing on the porch, she knew exactly who it was.

Jay's grandmother didn't look nearly as formidable as Jay had made her out to be, but maybe that was because Rosalie had grown up around gangbangers and wasn't easily intimidated. Seeing her standing here just awoke Rosalie's anger. The way this woman had treated her grandson bordered on the criminal. He hadn't been allowed girlfriends— not any friends at all, from things he'd said. He hadn't been allowed gym, or track, or any kind of sports, only a strict regime of endless exercise sessions under this old woman's watchful eye, which, in the end, hadn't provided him with anything useful.

With that kind of life, it was amazing that Jay could still be the guy they'd all grown so fond of these past few weeks.

"You must be Paupau," she said.

The woman didn't appear surprised to be recognized. Maybe she thought it was her due.

"I'm here to see my grandson," she told Rosalie.

"He's not in."

"Can you tell me where I might find him?"

Rosalie thought about what she'd read in Jay's journal, what could happen to him now that he'd let the dragon get out of control. She knew why his grandmother was here.

"No," she said.

Paupau studied her for a moment before she asked, "Because you don't know where he is, or you don't want to tell me?"

"Both. Good-bye."

She started to close the door, but Paupau put her hand on it and the door became impossible to move. The old woman was stronger than she looked, but then she had a dragon hidden inside her, too.

"Let me speak to your parents," Paupau said.

"I don't have parents."

"Everyone has parents, child."

"Unless they're dead or they abandoned their family."

"I'm sorry," Paupau said. "I had no idea—"

Rosalie shook her head. "Don't lie. How could someone like you feel sympathy?"

"Now why would you say that?" Paupau asked.

Although her voice was mild, there was a hardness in her eyes. But Rosalie had grown up in the barrio. She still wasn't impressed.

"I know how you treated Jay as a kid," she said. "I guess it's different in Chicago, but around here we'd call that abuse."

"You have no idea what you're talking about."

Rosalie shook her head. "Except I do. Let's start with tattooing a dragon on his back when he's what? Eleven years old?"

"That dragon—"

"Is a symbol of the dragon that lives inside him and it just 'spontaneously appeared.' Yeah, yeah. I know that. But it wouldn't have happened if you weren't in the picture. And then you went on to steal his childhood from him and all you gave him in return was the chance to kill himself and everybody around him if he wasn't a hundred percent careful every moment of his life."

"You are treading on dangerous ground, girl."

"Why? Are you going to bring my uncle's house tumbling down on my head with a stomp of your own dragony foot?"

The hardness in Paupau's eyes flashed with anger.

"Your rudeness is inexcusable," she said. "You need to—"

But Rosalie cut her off. "No, *you* need to go away. We have our own problems here and we don't need someone like you around to add to them. So, dragon lady, why don't you move your hand, get off my porch, and go back to Chicago where you can intimidate people, because it's not going to work here."

Rosalie met the old lady's gaze without flinching. Finally Paupau nodded.

"He needs my help," she said before Rosalie could close the door, "and I will find him. Wherever he is in this world, I will find him."

Rosalie thought of Jay vanishing in the middle of the parking lot last night.

"Good luck with that," she said.

She leaned her back against the closed door, anticipating she didn't know what. Another knock? Maybe a repeat of what had happened last night, except this time the cracks would appear in Tío's ceiling and it was his house that would come tumbling down.

"Who was at the door?"

She looked up to see Tío coming out of his bedroom.

"Jay's creepy grandmother," she said. "But I think she's gone now."

Tío frowned. "You weren't rude, were you? Why didn't you at least invite her in?"

Rosalie rolled her eyes. "Considering the things she did to her own grandkid, you'd actually want her in your house?"

"No, you're right. Did she say what she wanted?"

Rosalie shook her head. "Just that she was wanted to talk to Jay."

"Strange." He looked to the kitchen. "You didn't put the coffee on?"

"I just got up to answer the door."

She continued to lean against it as she watched Tío head for the kitchen. Paupau hadn't said what she wanted, but she'd already known from reading Jay's journal. What was it that his friend Lupita had told him?

If it's anything like the way it works with the feathered serpents, there's some kind of fail-safe built in. Down there the old clan members show up en masse and shut the rogue down.

That was what Paupau was doing here. She'd come to shut Jay down.

To kill him, Rosalie supposed. Her own grandson.

And she'd thought the *bandas* were heartless.

Rita squatted in the shade of a mesquite tree, a still figure in a straw cowboy hat and dark clothes. She was a long way from the *bandas'* pool room, but she appeared as comfortable in her current surroundings as she had been in a corner booth watching Jay and El Tigre take each other's measure.

She'd been drawn here last night after sensing the dragon rearing up inside the boy—a great golden shape that lifted above him, blinking into awareness and tall enough, it seemed, to brush the stars. It had stayed awake long enough to kill one of El Tigre's gangbangers and then bring down the music hall, but by the time she'd arrived, it was already gone. She was tempted to follow Jay when he disappeared into *el entre*, then realized she could find him there whenever she wished. Instead, she decided to await the arrival of what his actions would bring.

Across the parking lot she could see the ruin of the dance hall. Yellow police tape cordoned off the area, but that hadn't stopped the endless parade of onlookers. As the night faded and the dawn crept over the horizon, she'd remained under the mesquite, motionless and unnoticed by all: gawkers and media, police and firemen, and even a handful of beings like herself, who weren't strictly human.

Rita lifted her head when one of the latter reappeared at the far edge of the parking lot. She had the appearance of an old Chinese woman, but Rita could see the dragon curled up inside her as clearly now as she had last night. She tracked the woman's progress until she was standing by the yellow tape. Though power radiated from her like

light from the sun, the onlookers on either side of her gave
no indication that they felt it. But Rita did. Around the
cousins, that potent an aura was impossible to ignore.

Rita watched her for a few moments longer, waiting to
see if any of the old woman's earlier companions would re-
join her. When the woman remained by herself, Rita finally
stood up and crossed the parking lot herself.

Paupau was deep in thought, staring through the ruin of
the building on the other side of the flimsy tape barrier,
when a woman spoke.

"<This must be something new for you,>" the newcomer said in flawless Mandarin.

Paupau turned slowly and regarded the Indian woman—
or at least what appeared to be an Indian woman; she
might be Mexican—but Paupau could smell an old snake
tribe in the deeps of the stranger's blood.

"<What must be?>" she asked.

The woman shrugged. "<Well, everybody knows
how you old dragons like to get your own way. I saw
the bunch of you looking to take down the kid who just
woke to his power, but then you had to walk away empty-
handed.>"

Paupau's eyes narrowed. "<You were spying—>"

"<Merely observing. But now I'm curious. The others obviously decided that there was no cause for alarm,

but you're still hunting the boy—your own grandson, no less.>"

"<A man died here. His life taken by a dragon of my clan.>"

Rita shook her head. "He wasn't a man," she said, switching to English. "He was a piece of crap that got what it deserved."

"James still needs to explain"—she made a motion with her hand that took in the ruined dance hall—"all of this."

"You dragons have a funny way of bringing up your young. You might consider adding a little hands-on knowledge and kindness into the mix."

"How is any of this your business?"

"It's not. But I like the kid and I'd hate to see him have to turn on you to protect himself."

"I can protect myself," Paupau said, "but I thank you for your concern for an elderly stranger."

Rita laughed. "You've got that all mixed up. I don't care what happens to you, dragon lady. I just don't want to have to see the boy live with the guilt of having had to defend himself against his own grandmother."

Paupau remained silent for a long moment.

"Regardless of what you would like," she said finally, "I will still find my grandson. And he will still explain what he has done here."

"Then let me help you with that," Rita said. "The boy's dragon woke when his friend was murdered. Before he got

it back under control, he'd killed the murderer and inad-
vertently weakened the structure of the dance hall. When
he realized what he'd done, he used the dragon to hold up
the building until everyone had escaped, then he let the
whole thing fall in on itself. But I'm sure you and the other
dragons already figured that out or they'd still be hanging
around here with you."

"Yes, we are quite capable of reading sign. And we spoke
to those who witnessed the event."

"So now your compadres are gone and you should be,
too."

"You are treading on thin ground, snake woman."

"Why? Are you going to turn *dragon* on me now?
That's a nice example to set for your grandson. But then,
you haven't really given him anything clear to work with,
have you? You just sent him out into the world on his own
and if he makes it, fine. If he doesn't, you and your friends
step in to deal with him and clear up the mess. It's all 'better
luck next time.'"

"How we do our business is not your concern."

"Oh, but it is," Rita told her. "You're on my turf now
and I say neither you nor your business are welcome here."

"And you are so powerful you can force me to leave."

Rita shook her head. "No, but what makes you think
I'm alone here?"

Paupau hadn't been paying attention. If she had, she would
have sensed their approach, smelled the animal clans hidden

behind their human faces. She could see them now. She didn't know how many cousins, from how many clans, were standing amid their human counterparts. But there were many. And where the humans were staring at the ruin of the dance hall, talking to each other, these others stood with a cousin's stillness, their attention only on the snake woman and herself.

She turned back to Rita. "I am of the Yellow Dragon Clan, snake woman. You will need more than this small army to force me away against my will."

Rita smiled. "They're not here to fight you. They're here to see if you're going to be their new protector. The one they have has served them well, but she grows old now."

Paupau knew who Rita meant. She had caught the scent as soon as she'd arrived in Santo del Vado Viejo.

"You think a dragon would do a lizard's job?" she said, unable to keep the condescension from her voice.

Rita's eyes narrowed. "Señora Elena is the matriarch of an old and revered Gila clan. Speak of her with respect."

"Because she does such a fine job of upholding her responsibilities."

"At least she doesn't let her pride hide her limitations from herself."

Paupau bit back an angry retort. This snake woman was as bad as the child in the house where her grandson had been boarding. Brash, rude, and unhelpful. Their disrespect brought out the worst in her. But she would rise above it.

"How is any of this my concern?" she asked, keeping her voice mild.

"It's not. That's why you need to go. Both you and I know you're too old a dragon to take a place like this under your wing."

And then Paupau understood.

"You mean to have James accept the responsibility," she said.

"Not exactly—or at least not yet. But I think he could work out if you leave him alone."

Paupau gave a slow nod. "So that is why the fates sent him here."

"Say what?"

But Paupau didn't bother to explain. All she said was, "I give you my approval."

"Wasn't asking for it, dragon lady. I just want you to go away."

"And I will do so," Paupau said. "But I will be keeping watch on the situation. If it gets out of hand again, James's fate will not be up to me, but to the council as a whole."

"Yeah, well, we'll climb that cactus when we have to."

Paupau gave the snake woman a short brusque bow, then turned and walked away, back straight.

Do me proud, James, she thought as she crossed the parking lot.

She knew she was hard on her grandson, but she had to be. Dragons held far too much power to be allowed to run wild. But they also had to learn to wield the responsibility on their own, because in the end, they protected a place alone. She could only pray that James didn't draw the council's attention again. The snake woman had no idea how much worry this night had brought to her.

- 6 -

Not only can water float a boat, it can sink it also.

— CHINESE PROVERB

THE VISIT FROM Jay's grandmother was only the first intrusion into what Rosalie thought should be the privacy of their grief. Not long afterward, a detective called reminding them to come down to the station to read and sign the statements they'd made last night. Ramon drove Rosalie and Anna to the police station, but when they were done, reporters were waiting outside. A sympathetic police officer took them out the back way. The press wasn't as easy to avoid at the wake that evening.

At one point the band members gathered by a side door to get a break from the crowd inside the funeral home.

They weren't there long when a reporter approached. He made the mistake of shoving his microphone in Anna's face and asking her reaction to what had happened at their gig last night.

"If you don't get the hell out of here," she told him, "you're going to be eating that mic."

The reporter smiled like she'd made a joke. The smile disappeared when she lunged at him. The reporter almost fell down dodging her. Hector and Rosalie both had to hold her back.

"You'd better go, man," Hector told him. "She gets like this and it's all we can do to hang on."

The reporter beat a hasty retreat.

It wasn't till later that night, when Anna had been dropped off at home and Tío was still at the restaurant, that Rosalie was able to sit with Ramon on the porch and talk to him about Jay's journal. At first, Ramon was reluctant to read the notebook himself.

"Please," Rosalie told him. "I know it's invading his privacy, but it seems to explain a lot and I really need to talk to someone about what's in there."

So Ramon had a look while Rosalie hovered at his shoulder, trying hard not to be impatient for him to be done. After a while, she managed to settle down and look out into the desert night while he read. She studied the shadows across the street, wondering if Lupita was hidden there, watching them right now. Or maybe Jay was.

It was all so impossible, but she'd seen him disappear in the parking lot, vanishing right in front of her. You couldn't fake that.

When Ramon finally closed the notebook, she gave him an expectant look. He smiled.

"So what was it that you wanted to talk about?" he asked.

She punched him in the shoulder. "Oh, you! Everything. Did you *read* what's in there?"

"You want to know if it's true?"

She nodded.

"I can't say. The hike we took is. The conversations aren't word-for-word the way I remember them, but it's still pretty much what we were talking about. But the rest of it . . . " He shrugged.

"Come on," she said. "After what we saw in the parking lot . . . how can it not be true?"

"Just because one impossible thing is true doesn't mean they all are."

She frowned at him. "But you're the one who's always talking about the spirits of the desert and everything."

He gave her another smile. "I didn't say I don't believe what he wrote."

She raised her fist but he caught it before she could punch him again.

"We have to be reasonable here," he said.

"Nothing about this has anything to do with reason.

That's what I'm trying to figure out. There's got to be something we can do to find Jay and help him."

"I don't think so," Ramon said. "It's amazing and wonderful to find out for sure that the world's so much bigger than we thought it was a few days ago. And we can think and wonder about it all we want. But our part's done. Stuff like dragons and animal spirits don't have a whole lot to do with our lives here. It's like a storm passed through the barrio and now we have to pick up where we were before it hit. But the magic's not ours. We got to see it, but now it's gone."

"Jay's our friend," Rosalie said. "We can't just pretend he never happened."

"No, but we were only a part of his life for a moment. He . . . all this stuff has just moved on."

"But—"

"And it's dangerous," Ramon said. "Look what happened to Margarita."

"That wasn't Jay's doing."

"No, but we could have all died in what followed, and that *was* Jay's doing."

Rosalie shook her head. "I'm not giving up on him just because it's scary. I've found ways to work around the danger of living here, and I'll find a way to work around what's going on with Jay, too."

She gave him a fierce look and he had to smile.

"I kind of thought you'd say that," he said.

"Then why were you arguing with me?"

"I wanted to make sure you knew exactly what you were getting into."

"That's a big part of the problem," she said. "We don't have any idea, really. Where do we even start?"

"We can try looking for Lupita."

"Right. We'll walk around in the desert and call her name."

"Maybe the uncles can help us."

"I'm not drinking mescal tea to have visions," she said.

Ramon shook his head and smiled. "I was thinking more of just talking to them."

A big crowd gathered in San Miguel Cemetery for Margarita's funeral. Family and friends, kids from school, fans wearing Malo Malo scarves, holding flowers and pictures of Margarita. Rosalie stood behind Margarita's family along with the band and their friends. Everyone wore black. She wondered what life was like for kids who didn't grow up in the barrio, kids who hadn't been to as many funerals as she had in her seventeen years. Mama and Paulo. Kids from school who had the bad luck to get caught up in *bandas* business. Neighbors in the barrio who were in the wrong place at the wrong time.

There were too many dead.

She'd worn this black dress too many times.

There were a couple of news vans parked outside the cemetery. Occasionally, sunlight winked on the lens of a camera, but no one tried to intrude. Considering the dark looks Anna kept giving the camera crews, they'd be smart to move on before the funeral was over.

Rosalie looked away, returning her attention to the service. She had trouble focusing on Father Ramirez's words, but the tone of his voice was soothing and she took what comfort she could from it.

Given the circumstances, the day was obscenely beautiful. Clear blue skies, the sun bright, but it wasn't too hot. It was Margarita's favorite kind of day. The kind of day when she would try to get everybody to skip school and go out into the desert. Oh, how Rosalie wished she were here now, leaning over to whisper in her ear, "This is way too depressing. Let's go visit the cacti."

Rosalie's gaze lifted past the priest to where the Hierro Madera Mountains rose up from the eastern horizon. But then something closer at hand caught her attention.

Standing a hundred yards away, half-hidden by the tall cross rising above a grave, was a familiar figure. Jay stood with his arms wrapped around himself, his hoodie hanging low over his eyes. She didn't know how anyone else would feel about him being here, but her heart lifted to see that he was safe and cared enough to pay his respects.

Beside her, Ramon could tell that something had distracted her, but before she could point Jay out, he vanished.

It was just like the other night in the parking lot. One moment he was standing there by the cross, the next he was gone.

Ramon leaned closer until his mouth was by her ear. "What is it?"

"Nothing. I'll tell you later."

After the service, Margarita's father came over to them. He pressed Ramon's hand.

"<You always looked out for my little girl,>" he said.

Ramon ducked his head, his gaze on the ground. "<Not well enough.>"

"<There was nothing you could have done, Ramon. I don't blame you for what happened. But I have something to ask of you.>"

Ramon raised his gaze. "<Anything, Señor Vargas.>"

"<Promise me that you will not seek to avenge her.>"

"<I . . .>"

Rosalie gave them a sharp look. She'd never even considered that any of the band members might want more vengeance than Alambra's death. Why would they? They weren't gangbangers. That wasn't the way they lived their lives, spinning in circles of violence. But she could see from Ramon's face that he'd been considering it.

How could he have kept it from her? *How* had he kept it from her?

"<Promise me, Ramon,>" Margarita's father said.

"<But, Señor Vargas—>"

"<Do you not think I know how you feel? My own heart cries out for vengeance. But if we do this thing, they will win. Do you understand me? They will win and Margarita will no longer be a victim of their violence. Instead, she will have become a cause of further heartbreak and pain. To the mothers and fathers of the *bandas*, the gangbangers are still their children. I would not have her remembered in such a way.>"

"<But what can we *do*?>" Ramon asked.

"<We can pray.>"

Ramon sighed. He looked away from Señor Vargas, anywhere but at Rosalie.

"<Will you do this thing for my family?>" Margarita's father asked. "<For the memory of your friend? Will you let the violence end with her passing?>"

Finally, Ramon cleared his throat. "<I will.>"

But even Rosalie knew that when it came to the gangbangers the violence would never end.

She and Ramon stood silently as Señor Vargas returned to his family. They watched the group walk across the cemetery to the waiting cars.

"When were you going to tell me?" Rosalie asked.

"I don't know," Ramon said.

"You weren't going to tell me, were you?"

He finally turned to look at her. "I didn't know what I was going to do. Maybe nothing. But if I did figure a way I could get back at the Kings, I couldn't bring you into it."

He held up a hand before she could speak. "You have a large and forgiving heart, Rosie. How could I ever make you a part of anything like that?"

"I have no forgiveness for the *bandas*."

"No, you wouldn't. But you wouldn't strike against them, either."

There was nothing Rosalie could say because he was right.

"You agree with Anna, don't you?" she said instead. "You think Jay should have crushed the *bandas* when he had the chance. You think he should have killed them all."

"I believe that, when he went to meet El Tigre," Ramon said, "he didn't know how."

"But now?" Rosalie asked when he didn't go on.

"Let me put it this way. If the whole membership of the Kings had been inside the music hall when it collapsed and they'd all died . . . I wouldn't be unhappy. And if there was a button I could push that could still make that happen, I'd do it."

He looked away to the mountains and signed the shape of the cross, forehead to chest, shoulder to shoulder. Rosalie took his hand when he was done.

"Maybe I'm worse than you," she said, "because I think I'd do the same, but I wouldn't ask forgiveness for the evil thought."

Ramon sighed. "Oh, Rosie. What are we doing, living in this place?"

"I can't leave," she said. "This is my home. It was my

parents' home. If I abandon it to the *bandas*, then they will truly have won. I can't let that happen. I won't."

"I know, I know. But days like these are hard."

Rosalie nodded. She looked at the TV crews on the other side of the fence, filming people leaving the cemetery.

"Those vultures don't make it any easier," she said.

Ramon followed her gaze. "Let's hope none of them try to interview Anna again."

"Why are they even here? Who turns on their TVs to watch people grieving?"

"I think the reporters are hoping for more," Ramon said.

"More what?"

He shrugged. "You know. Drama. Like if the Kings showed up."

"Not even they'd be that stupid."

But then Rosalie caught sight of someone on the other side of the cemetery fence. At least she wasn't wearing gang colors.

"I take that back," she said. "I can see Maria—over there, past the TV van."

"What's she doing here?"

"I don't know. I'm going to go talk to her. Could you keep Anna busy?"

She didn't have to explain why. If Anna saw someone connected to the Kings here today, she'd go ballistic and the TV cameras would get all the dramatic footage they could want.

"Sure," Ramon said.

Rosalie waited until she saw that he'd caught up with Anna and the others. When she did start for the gates, she held back so that they'd go through well ahead of her. Once outside, she walked along the parked cars to where she'd seen Maria. She half expected her to have vanished—not quite the same way that Jay had, but gone all the same. Yet when she came around the side of the TV van, Maria was still there, leaning on the hood of her old beat-up Buick.

"What are you doing here?" she asked.

"Once upon a time," Maria said, "Margarita was my friend, too." She held up a hand before Rosalie could speak. "No, don't start in on how it was my choice. You have no idea why I hooked up with the Kings and you never bothered to ask. You just cut me off when the deal was done."

Rosalie took a steadying breath.

"Okay," she said. "So why did you join the Kings?"

Maria shook her head. "Now's not the time to get into that—not with Margarita fresh in the ground and the trouble that could be coming."

"What trouble?"

"Right now it's mostly between Flores and the Kings. Guys like Cruz and Switchblade—they're El Tigre's lieutenants," she added. "Anyway, they want payback for what happened to Alambra, but Flores says—"

"Wait a minute," Rosalie broke in. "Payment for what happened to *Alambra*? *He* killed Margarita."

"After she dissed the Kings."

"Oh, for God's sake."

"I'm not saying everybody agrees," Maria said. "I don't. And neither does Flores. He's already pissed off that Alambra broke the truce with your China Boy—which I've got to say, nobody can understand. What's so important about him?"

"Ask Alambra."

Maria gave a slow nod. "So it's true. He did use some kind of weird *brujería* on him."

Rosalie kept quiet.

"Okay," Maria said. "So maybe he's a player, and that's why El Tigre wants to keep the peace with him. But the Kings aren't happy. Flores told us that if he wasn't already dead, he would have killed Alambra himself. And the same goes for anybody else who wants to cause trouble for any of China Boy's allies. But I think maybe one of them's going to decide to take a run at El Tigre, and the way they'll do that is by going after one of you and forcing his hand."

"Why are you telling me all of this?" Rosalie asked.

"I don't want to go to another funeral for somebody I used to call a friend."

"You're not like them," Rosalie said. "Why don't you quit the gang?"

"It's not that easy."

"Tío did."

"Those were very different circumstances. The Kings owed him. But they own me."

"How can you say that? How can you live that kind of life?"

Maria shrugged. "Ask me again if we get through all of this. Maybe I'll feel like telling you then."

"But—"

"I have to go," Maria said, pushing away from the car. "I've been here too long as it is. If anyone saw me talking to you . . ."

Rosalie didn't argue. She got out of the way when Maria started the Buick. Standing there in the dirt by the cemetery fence, she watched Maria pull out onto Mission Street and drive away.

"I remember the day she came to school wearing the Kings' colors," Ramon said. "You just cut her off."

"What was I supposed to do? Overnight she became the enemy."

Ramon shrugged. "I don't know that it's ever as simple as that. We live every day with the *bandas* in our lives. We all have to find our own way to cope."

They were standing outside the Vargas house. The street was lined with cars. The mourners spilled out into the yard, talking in quiet voices, many of them smoking. The reporters were finally leaving them alone.

"I did ask her why she did it, you know," Rosalie said.

Ramon shook his head. "No, you confronted her. It's not the same thing."

Rosalie sighed. Ramon always kept her honest.

"It just took me by surprise," she said. "It took everybody by surprise. She was always so against the gangs."

"No surprise there, with her mother working for the probation department."

"And her dad being a teacher," Rosalie said. "I know. But then one day she's hanging out with us and the next morning she comes in wearing gang colors. How could I not freak out?"

"Nobody's blaming you, Rosie. Not with Tío and what happened to your mother and Paulo."

Rosalie nodded. "It felt like such a betrayal."

"I know." He put his arm around her shoulders. "And I know you, too. You probably still find yourself regretting the things you said to her."

God, that had been such a terrible morning. The things that had come spilling out of her mouth while Maria just stood there and took it . . .

"We were friends for so long," Rosalie said. "And I felt even worse when her family disowned her."

"Yeah, that was harsh."

Rosalie knew they should go inside the Vargases' house again but she couldn't seem to muster the energy.

"I saw Jay at the funeral," she said.

Ramon turned to look at her.

"He was by that big cross near the gates and kind of hiding inside his hoodie."

"I never saw him," Ramon said. "When did he leave?"

"As soon as I noticed him. Except he didn't walk away or anything. Instead, he just did that disappearing trick of his. Poof, he's gone."

"I wish Anna hadn't gone off on him," Ramon said.

"I know." She leaned her head against Ramon's shoulder. "But at least we know that he's okay."

Ramon let her chill for a few more minutes, then he straightened up and took her hand.

"We should go back inside," he said.

The next day Rosalie took another day off from school. She knew she was only delaying the inevitable, but with the funeral still so fresh in her mind it was hard to see the point. Why bother graduating when tomorrow you could be the next victim? She knew she'd see things differently in time—she'd been down this road before—but right now she could no more imagine sitting in class than she could joining one of the gangs herself.

After Tío went off to the restaurant, she took the dogs for a long walk, following Redondo Drive for a couple of miles along the perimeter of the park. The desert landscape seemed more dangerous than it ever had before she'd read Jay's journal. Was an invisible Lupita out there right now, watching her and the dogs go by?

It was like Ramon had said. The world was bigger than they'd ever thought it was. Or at least bigger than she'd ever thought it was.

When she finally got back home, she took a shower, collected Jay's journal, and walked over to Anna's. Half a block away she could hear the angry sound of an electric guitar. It got louder and louder the closer she approached. Standing on the street outside the Castillos', Rosalie was surprised that none of the neighbors had called in a complaint. But everybody would know the story of what had happened, and Rosalie could only hope they'd understand.

She waited until there was a pause in the music before she rang the bell. The only response was the guitar starting up again, louder and angrier than before. Rosalie tried the door. It wasn't locked, so she went in. By the time she was standing in Anna's doorway, she had her hands over her ears.

Anna stood facing the window. Rosalie called out, but she couldn't make herself heard. She waited another couple of moments, then walked over to the amplifier and pulled the power plug from the wall. The sudden silence felt almost as weird as the music had been.

Anna whipped around, but her mood softened when she saw who it was.

"I'm not going to school," she said.

"Yeah, me neither."

Anna's eyebrows went up.

"It's hard for me, too," Rosalie said. "Every time I walk down a hall I'm going to expect to see her, but she won't be there. She's never going to be there again. And everybody's going to want to talk about what happened and . . . I'm just not ready."

Anna nodded. She unstrapped her guitar and set it in its stand. For a long moment the two of them stood there, almost like strangers, then Anna crossed the room and they held each other for a long time. Neither of them cried.

"I don't know how much more of this I can take," Anna said.

She turned away and sat down on the small sofa across from her bed. Rosalie joined her. Anna laid her head on the fat-cushioned back and stared up at the ceiling.

"Every time somebody else dies," she went on, "it's like another piece of my heart gets torn away. It feels like I've got nothing left inside anymore."

"I know."

"How do you keep going on?"

Rosalie shook her head. "I don't know. I've got Ramon."

"He's like a rock."

"He's hurting, too."

"I know he is," Anna said. "Maybe more than any of us. I just meant the way he keeps it all together for everybody. That night it happened. At the wake. At the funeral."

"Did you know that he was planning some kind of payback against the Kings?"

Anna's eyes widened and she shook her head. "Oh, my God. Did you talk him out of it? I'd love to see those

sorry bastards taken down, but all that's going to do is leave
Ramon dead or in jail—which is the same as dead, because
the *bandas* in there will take him down."

"Margarita's father made him promise not to do anything."

"And did he promise?"

Rosalie nodded.

"Good." Anna waited a beat, then added, "Jay could
have stopped this from happening in the first place."

Rosalie didn't try to argue.

"That's why I'm here," she said. "Because you believe
that."

"What do you mean?"

"You need to read this," Rosalie said, handing her the
notebook.

"What is it?"

"Stuff Jay was writing before everything went to hell.
Kind of like a journal."

"I don't want to read it."

She tried to hand it back but Rosalie refused to take it.

"Humor me," Rosalie said.

Anna held the journal unopened on her lap. She tapped
the cover with a calloused fingertip.

"What are you doing with this, anyway?" she asked.
"It's not like you to go prying into people's private stuff."

"I'm trying to figure out what happened to him—where
he went. This explains a lot."

Anna shook her head. "I don't care. Jay's the last person I'd want to—"

"Are you going to read it, or do I have to tie you down and read it to you?"

"Don't you get it?" Anna said. "I don't—"

"Please."

Rosalie reached over and opened the journal. She flipped through the pages until she came to where Jay wrote about the hike the desert.

"Just read this part," she said. "It's about that Sunday he went with Ramon. I checked with Ramon and he says it's pretty much true."

She waited until she was sure that Anna was actually reading before she got up. She stood at the window looking down the alley behind the Castillos' house until she finally heard Anna close the journal. She waited a few moments longer, watching a stray cat unsuccessfully stalk a bird, before she finally turned around.

"Well?" she asked.

"People can write down anything they want," Anna said, her voice flat. "That doesn't mean it's true."

Rosalie noted that Anna didn't say anything about Jay's feelings for her, but she let that slide.

"I told you," she said. "Ramon said that's how their conversation went. So if that much is true . . ."

Rosalie let her voice trail off.

Anna sighed. She dropped the journal on the sofa and leaned her head against the headrest again.

"You think I overreacted," she said.

Rosalie shook her head. "You were working with what you knew."

"I overreacted."

"Maybe. But do you believe now that he didn't know he could do whatever it was he did?"

Anna sighed. "Probably."

"He really, really likes you," Rosalie said.

"Yeah. So I read. But considering what I said to him, I'm sure he doesn't now. And I wouldn't blame him."

"We don't know that."

Anna looked away.

"I really believe he's just some kid that's in way over his head," Rosalie said. "And now he's out there somewhere, all messed up, and he can't even come to us because he thinks we all hate him."

"I don't know how I feel."

"Bullshit. I think you held him at arm's length because you did like him and it scared you. What he might be scared you."

"But Margarita . . ."

Anna started to cry. Rosalie enfolded her in her arms, her own eyes welling up with tears.

"I know, Anna. I know. It—it's like Paulo and Mamá all over again . . ."

After a few moments, Anna pulled back. She got up to get a tissue and blew her nose. By the time she sat down with Rosalie once more, she'd regained her composure.

"So we need to find him," she said.

Rosalie didn't have to ask who. She just nodded.

"Ramon has some ideas," she said.

She'd been planning to tell Anna about seeing Maria Sanchez at the funeral, but decided that one small victory was enough for now. Anna had been way angrier than Rosalie when Maria hooked up with the Kings.

Instead, she talked about Ramon wanting to visit the *mescaleros*.

While she felt she could blow off school for one more day, Rosalie didn't feel right about leaving Tío in the lurch. So after she left Anna's, she returned home to feed the dogs, changed into a blouse and skirt, then went in to work.

Ines was already there. She might act like a wannabe with her fixation on clothes and partying and clubbing, but in her heart she was still a barrio girl and knew to do the right thing. She was here without complaint because she was needed, waiting tables and handling the register. Paco was doubling as busboy and dishwasher while Tío had taken over the kitchen. He looked very relieved to see her.

"How are you holding up?" Ines asked when Rosalie came behind the bar.

"It's hard."

Ines squeezed her shoulder. "Are you sure you're ready to be here?"

"Probably not. But I can't leave you guys on your own."

That wasn't something Rosalie would have shared with Tío—he would have sent her home. But Ines understood. She gave Rosalie's shoulder another squeeze, then split up the tables between them.

It wasn't until a couple of hours later that things got scary.

The restaurant was still two-thirds full when Amada Flores walked in. Alone. No bodyguards, no *bandas* in tow, nobody but himself.

Rosalie had never seen him in person before. He was much more handsome than news reports made him out to be, but he was a lot more frightening, too. Pictures could never capture the confident grace with which he moved, nor the feral power that crackled in his dark brown eyes. His smile was utterly charming. The eyes said he could kill you at any moment, for no reason, without remorse.

The entire restaurant went still. No one spoke. There was no clink of cutlery against plates. Ines was in the middle of changing a CD, so even the sound system was silent.

Rosalie realized that her hands were trembling. She clasped them together, but it didn't seem to help. She was still shaking inside.

The unnatural stillness brought Tío out of the kitchen, and that worried Rosalie more than any fears she might have for herself, Ines, or their customers. She saw the hardness settle over Tío's features, putting a dark look in his eyes that reminded her that once he'd been considered almost as dangerous as El Tigre was now.

"You're not welcome in this place," Tío said.

El Tigre's own cold gaze went icier still. But his voice was mild when he spoke. "You don't even know why I've come."

"I don't care. Get out of here."

"Be careful, old man. With one word I could have this little restaurant of yours come crashing down around your ears as easily as your cook destroyed the music hall."

Tío shot Rosalie a look and she shook her head. She had no idea how Flores had come to that conclusion, either.

"Then either do it or leave," Tío told the gangster.

Anger flashed in El Tigre's eyes, but he kept himself otherwise under control.

"You need to understand something here," he said, his voice still mild. "I know all about you doing Julio's time. How when you got out of jail, you wanted to get out of the life. You're a stand-up guy—you proved that by taking the fall—so Julio gave you his blessing. You're off-limits to the *bandas* and he even fronted you the money to open this place."

"Which I paid back, with interest."

"Whatever. Your problem right now is that Julio Garza doesn't run the Kings anymore. I run the Kings. I run all the *bandas* south of the San Pedro."

"Is there a point to all this old history?" Tío asked.

"Yeah. Keep shooting off your mouth, and I bring it all down. So give me a little respect, old man, and listen to what I have to say. I show you respect by coming here alone, my hands empty."

He held out his hands as he spoke.

Tío gave him a curt nod. "I'm listening."

"I'm here about the dragon," Flores said.

Tío's face remained blank.

"Your cook, Jay Li," Flores went on. "I need to get a message to him."

"We haven't seen him since . . . that night."

"I told you, I'm not playing—"

"And I'm telling you," Tío broke in, "he never came back. Not here, not to the house."

Flores took a moment to consider that. He studied Tío until he was finally satisfied that he was getting the truth.

"He needs to know," Flores said, "that the attack had nothing to do with the agreement he and I had. I knew nothing about what Alambra had done until it was too late. If the dragon hadn't killed that whore's son, I would have done it myself."

"Margarita Vargas is still dead," Tío said.

"And I take full responsibility for that. Tell him if you see him. Whatever we need to do to make things right again, I'm ready to talk to him."

He was scared of Jay, Rosalie thought. No, not scared—respectful. Which she would have thought strange if she hadn't seen how Alambra had died. But Flores was still a power to be reckoned with, and not only because the *bandas* were under his command. There was something about him, just as there was with Jay. She thought about how he was called the Tiger and wondered if perhaps it was more than just a name.

"I have my doubts that we'll see Jay again," Tío said. He went on as El Tigre began to interrupt. "But *if* I do, I will give him your message."

Flores nodded. "Do this and the arrangement you had with your old boss, Julio, can continue with me."

Before Tío could respond, Flores turned away and the door closed behind him. Tío stood there for a long moment. He looked around the restaurant and Rosalie knew just what he was feeling, how he hated that all this old *bandas* business had just come up in public. But the gazes of the customers were sympathetic and she didn't think any of them would talk about what they'd witnessed, if not for Tío's sake, then for fear of coming to the attention of El Tigre.

Tío's gaze swept across the restaurant one last time, then he went back into the kitchen. Rosalie started to follow, but Ines laid a hand on her arm.

"Let him be," she said. "He's embarrassed and mad, and that's never a good combination. Give him a chance to work through it."

Rosalie nodded. Though Ines and her father weren't

close, they knew each other well. And Ines was right. Tío always needed time to process the unexpected.

"So what's the story with Jay?" Ines wanted to know. "Flores seemed almost, I don't know how to put it . . ."

"Respectful?"

Ines nodded. "But he's just this kid from Chicago, right?"

"Pretty much."

"Except Flores is saying that Jay blew up the dance hall?"

Rosalie shook her head. "Jay didn't blow anything up. I was there."

"I wonder why Flores thinks he did?"

"Who can figure how a mind like his works?" Rosalie said.

The front door opened again, interrupting them. Rosalie braced herself against Flores's return, but it was just an older couple.

"I'll get this," she said.

She grabbed a couple of menus and went to greet the newcomers.

Both Anna and Ramon were waiting when Rosalie got home from the restaurant. They were around back on the patio with the dogs scattered all around them. Pepito was the first to notice her return. He barked and leaped from

Anna's lap and then the whole pack was jumping around Rosalie until she gave them the command to stand down. She fussed over them all, then made her way onto the patio and collapsed into a chair.

"You didn't tell me that Maria was at the funeral," Anna said.

Rosalie sighed and shot Ramon a look. He shrugged.

"It just came up," he said. "I didn't know it was supposed to be a secret."

"It's not. It's just . . ."

"You thought it would set me off," Anna said.

"I didn't know. But you were just starting to give Jay the benefit of the doubt and . . ."

"I get it," Anna said. "You thought I'd go postal on you." She sighed. "God, am I really such a schiz?"

"You're just intense," Ramon said. "And empathic. So when you're feeling other people's pain, you feel it intensely."

"Not to mention your own," Rosalie put in.

"I guess."

Anna sighed again, then noticed how Pepito was giving her a hopeful look. She patted her lap and he bounded up, curling into a contented ball.

"Why do you think Maria keeps giving you these warnings?" she said.

"I don't know. I don't get it, either."

"I don't get *her*," Anna said. "When you think how

she was before she joined the Kings and, God, her family. They're like the poster people for an anti-gang ad."

"We should still be careful," Ramon said. "We have to tell everybody to watch out."

"Maybe not," Rosalie said, and she told them about Amada Flores. "It sounds to me," she said, finishing up, "like Flores is pretty serious about sticking to this agreement of his."

"Big whoop," Anna said. "Look where that got Margarita."

They all fell silent. The dogs, sensing their unhappiness, grew restless.

"I talked to one of the uncles about Jay," Ramon said after a while.

Rosalie looked up, happy to have something else to think about.

"Does he know where we can find him?" she asked.

"Yes and no. I told him what we knew. When I got to the part where Jay just disappears he started talking about how there's another desert inside the one we can see—or maybe he said it's kind of a step sideways."

"Like in Jay's journal."

Ramon nodded. "He called it *el entre* and said that's where we need to go looking."

"How are we supposed to do that?" Anna asked, then she shook her head. "I can't believe I just said that. Now you've got me on the mystic dragon wagon."

"He told me that there are lots of ways," Ramon said.

"Meditation or mescal tea can open the door. Or we can go on a spirit quest."

Rosalie started shaking her head as soon as he mentioned the mescal tea.

"Or we can go into this desert," Ramon went on, "the one that we can access, and ask for help from the spirits."

"And they're just going to come to us," Anna said.

Ramon shrugged. "I'm only passing on what Alfredo told me. He says there are places where they tend to appear more often than usual. There's one he called Crow Canyon, but I couldn't figure out where he says it is. But another one's up in the mountains off the Vulture Ridge trail and I think I know the place he means."

"So let's go," Anna said.

She put Pepito down on the ground and stood up. The dogs all scrambled to their feet.

"It's past midnight," Rosalie said.

"So?"

Rosalie turned to Ramon. "The trail will be dangerous in the dark, won't it?"

He shook his head. "Not really—not with this moon. But that doesn't mean we shouldn't be careful. And we need to put together some gear. Water, energy bars, flashlights, ropes . . ."

"We're just going up the trail," Anna said.

"And you never know what you're going to run into out there," he told her. "C'mon, Anna. It's basic Desert 101."

Anna looked from him to Rosalie. "Okay, so we put

some gear together, and then we'll go, right?"

"Why can't this wait until tomorrow?" Rosalie asked.

"Because if I don't do something," Anna said, "I'm going to go out of my mind."

"That's not a long trip," Ramon told her, smiling.

Anna gave him a light tap on his shin with the toe of her shoe.

"Ow!"

"I think you need a more manly boyfriend," Anna told Rosalie.

Rosalie smiled and thought, as if. But she didn't say anything. She was happy to see Anna stepping outside of her anger and sorrow long enough to be teasing Ramon. And tired though she was, she completely understood Anna's need to be doing something.

"Let me get changed and leave a note for Tío," she said.

- 7 -

When the tree falls, the monkeys scatter.
— CHINESE PROVERB

- i -

IT WAS ALMOST dawn before Jay became aware of his surroundings. As soon as he did, his heart sank. He was still in the desert that existed sideways to the world where he'd woken the dragon and killed a man. He might want to think of that place as "the real world," but so far as he could tell, this other desert had just as much substance as the one he'd left behind.

He could feel the dirt under his knees. He could smell the desert all around him. His throat was scratchy and dry. He could hear quail and doves and the rustle of a snake as it moved through the dirt nearby.

No, this world was real. It was just a different kind of real.

He was stiff from the awkward position he'd slept in. As he stretched, arms overhead, he realized there was someone sitting a few feet away. Lupita. She grinned when she saw he was awake.

"I've never seen anyone sleep like that before," she said. "You know, on their knees with their face pressed against the dirt. Is that particular to dragons?"

He dropped his arms. "Not now. I'm not in the mood for jokes."

"That's usually the best time for a joke."

He shook his head again. "You have no idea what I've done."

"Sure, I do. I was up in the rafters watching the whole show and I really had to scramble when you brought the roof down. But you were right. They're a great band."

"Lupita, please . . ."

"Please, what? You're not going to go all morose on me now, are you?"

All Jay could do was look at her.

Lupita shrugged. "Well, it seems like you are."

"In case you don't remember, a friend died and I just killed someone."

"He deserved it."

"That's not the point. Whether he lived or died wasn't up to me to decide. And Anna was totally right. I could have stopped it all from happening in the first place. But no, I had to make some stupid bargain instead. I should have just knocked that pool hall down around their ears when I first got there. Then they would have known I was serious. Then they wouldn't have messed with any of us."

Lupita shook her head. "And you'd be no better than them. You took the high road. You didn't just lash out *before* they did something. That's how *they* do things."

"But if I had shown them I meant business, Margarita wouldn't be dead."

"You didn't kill her, Jay."

"Right."

"Your friend's death is awful—I get that," she said. "But look at what else happened: You got in touch with the dragon part of you and you didn't lose control."

"How can you say that? I almost killed everybody in the hall."

"*Almost*, but you didn't."

"I don't see how that makes much of a difference."

"Do you see a bunch of old dragons standing around, waiting to lay down their judgment on you?"

"No."

"That's because they came and checked out the ruin of the dance hall, decided you were cool, and then went back to whatever it is that dragons do. Sleeping with their faces pressed into the dirt, maybe."

"Ha-ha."

"I try," Lupita said, pretending not to hear his sarcasm.

Jay thought about what she'd said.

"They were really here?" he asked. "A bunch of dragons?"

Lupita nodded. "Everybody's talking about it. They showed up like they owned the place. They were in all shapes and colors. Big and small. Black and white and Asian. They had some big discussion, and then they left. Remember what I told you about the feathered serpents down south? Don't you think that if these dragons had thought you were a problem they'd have found you by now and shut you down?"

"I guess."

"And, anyway," Lupita said. "It's not up to you to deal with El Tigre. He's not your responsibility."

"But that's what dragons do. We protect."

She shook her head. "If you get rid of him, somebody else is just going to come along and take his place. Maybe somebody worse. At least El Tigre keeps most of his business out of the barrio."

"But the *bandas* make everybody miserable. Everybody's scared of them, and with good reason. Look what happened to Margarita."

"The only way you could make it better," Lupita said, "would be if you took charge. And that means you'd have to stay here. Not just for a week or a few months. You'd have to stay here forever, because as soon as you leave, someone else will be sniffing around to take El Tigre's place."

"I could do that," Jay said. "I could live here."

It would be a way for him to atone for what had happened to Margarita.

But Lupita shook her head as though she could read his mind.

"You can't do it out of duty," she said. "You have to do it out of love."

"Love? You mean I have to be in love with someone who lives here?"

Lupita gave a small laugh. "I'm not talking about how you feel about that cute guitar player you're all gaga about. I'm talking about the barrio. About the land under the barrio. The desert. You have to love this patch of the world with all its warts and blemishes."

"Oh."

"And you'd have to get Señora Elena's okay."

"Who's she?"

Lupita shook her head. "Ask Rita."

"You mean the woman from the pool hall?"

"What you're getting into is the business of the big cousins. It's not stuff anyone like me should be involved in."

"Why not?"

Lupita sighed. "Remember? Jackalope equals joke?"

"Not to me."

"That's sweet, but it doesn't change anything. If you want to know more, you really need to talk to someone like Rita."

"I don't know," Jay said. "She seems to have her own agenda."

"Everybody has their own agenda—that's the way the world works."

"Even you?"

She grinned. "Even me. Though mostly I'm about staying off everybody's radar and having fun. You remember fun, don't you?"

She gave him an expectant look, but Jay was too preoccupied with what she'd said about agendas. He supposed he must have one, too. He just wasn't sure what it was. Would staying here be something he did because it was what he wanted to do, or because it was a duty that Paupau had laid on him? He was the one who'd put his finger on the map to choose Santo del Vado Viejo, but she was the one who'd had him do it. To complete his training, she'd said. That made it sound temporary. But if he took on the responsibility of protecting this place, Lupita had already told him that he couldn't simply walk away later, because that would only make everything worse for those still living here.

And even if he did decide to become the protector of the southside barrios, who said he was good enough? He'd called up the dragon and killed a gangbanger, but he wasn't entirely sure how he'd done it, and Amada Flores was no common gangbanger. Jay knew that if he made the decision to stay, eventually he'd have a confrontation with Flores.

"God, I really have to think about this," he said.

"You should have some fun first," Lupita told him. "The best way to think about something is to not think about it. Then before you know it, the thing you need to figure out comes bubbling up from somewhere in the back of your head and you're all ready to go. But in the meantime, you're not sitting around all moody and unhappy. You'll never get that time back, you know."

Jay shook his head. "No, seriously. I have to work this out."

Lupita sighed. She studied him for a long moment, then abruptly stood up and vanished. Jay blinked. He didn't think he'd ever get used to that.

- *ii* -

JAY

I'm not sure how long it is—maybe fifteen minutes later—when Lupita reappears.

"Here," she says, and drops a school notebook onto my lap.

It looks just like the ones that Rosalie gave me back when my life was only mildly messed up. A pen is clipped to the front cover.

"Where'd you get this?" I ask.

"From your room. I couldn't find the one you'd already been writing in so I just grabbed a fresh one."

If she couldn't find the other one, that probably meant Rosalie had it. Which also meant she'd read it, looking for clues as to where I'd gone. Great. So now she knew the full depths of my obsessing about Anna. But I supposed that was the least of my worries. It wasn't like Anna was ever going to talk to me again. Probably none of them would after I'd let Margarita get killed.

Then I realize that Lupita had to go into Tío's house to get this.

"This was all you took, right?"

"Ay-yi-yi. Now you think I'm a thief!"

"No, of course not. I don't know what I think."

"I thought it would help," Lupita says. "Like when you wrote in it before. But now you're mad at me, aren't you?"

I shake my head. "No, I'm not mad," I tell her.

At least not in the angry sense, I add to myself, but there's always the possibility I'm going out of my mind.

"You're right," I add. "Writing things down did help me put it all in perspective. Thanks."

She pulls a burrito wrapped in waxed paper out of her pocket.

"Here, I brought you this, too," she says. "To give you the energy to think."

"Thanks."

I unwrap it and take a bite and my mouth explodes with spicy flavors. The filling might even beat Tío's, and that's saying something.

"This is really good," I tell her once I've swallowed. "Where did you get it?"

"I made it."

I lift my eyebrows.

"I'm not totally useless," she says.

"I didn't think you were. You just never struck me as the homemaker type."

"There's lots you don't know about me."

I nod. "There's lots I don't know about *me*."

She pokes me with her finger.

"Don't start brooding about that, too," she says. "Everybody's got a piece of the stranger inside them. It's what lets us surprise ourselves and keeps things interesting."

"Everybody doesn't have a dragon that could wake up and smash everything around them."

But she disagrees with me again.

"Everybody's got that, too," she says. "Their dragons aren't always so literal, but if they get out of control they can do all kinds of damage just the same."

"I suppose."

She grins. "Eat. Write. Work your way back to the dragon boy I used to know."

Then she gives me a jaunty wave and she's gone again.

"That doesn't surprise me anymore," I say to the empty place where she was a moment ago.

But I'm lying.

I finish the burrito and drink some of the water that Lupita also brought me. Then I find a piece of shade under a stand of palo verde and mesquite. With my back against the trunk of the mesquite, I open the journal and try to catch up.

I write for at least an hour, but it doesn't help. All the things that have happened in the past twenty-four hours or so have been about doing and surviving, and not so much about reflection. I read it over, trying to find something I can hold on to, something that has meaning, but it's not there.

What I need is a new perspective. I roll up the notebook and shove it in my pocket. Standing up, I get my bearings, then go up into the mountains along the trail that Ramon took me to, what seems like a lifetime ago.

The trail I'm following isn't the exact same one. It's not a hiking trail in this desert, and it doesn't take the same winding route up the mountainside, but there's still a kind of path I can follow, and it does seem to go in the same general direction. I don't know who made it. The Native people, maybe, or cousins. Or it could be a game trail, beaten down by the hooves of deer or bighorn sheep. I wouldn't know.

It takes me a few hours, but by mid-afternoon I'm finally at that lookout Ramon showed me. I drink the last of the water—I know I'm going to regret that later—and sit down on a big rock to take in the view.

I needed this. When I look out on the vast panorama— the sweep of the desert below the mountains, untainted by buildings and roads, no matter how small; the blue expanse of sky above without a single jet contrail—I really know I'm outside of everything. My problems seem small and insignificant, remote from this place, from me, from any-thing of importance.

I lean back until I'm stretched out on the rock, the back of my head on the rough stone. I stare up into the endless blue for a long time and I let it take me away. When I wake up, the day's gone and so is most of the night. The dawn pinks the distant horizon and I watch as the sun's light in-tensifies and slowly spreads across the landscape.

I realize I'm thirsty and that's when I notice the two water bottles and what must be another burrito. I look around.

"Lupita?"

I don't know when she was here, but she's not now.

I open one of the water bottles. I plan to just have a couple of sips but I drink almost two-thirds of it in one long gulp. Then I devour the burrito. It's cold, but it tastes amazing. This one's full of eggs and bacon with pieces of peppers and squash and that amazing array of spices. My mouth is still tingling long after I've finished eating. I wish Lupita were here so that I could thank her.

The sun's up over the horizon now. I get up and stretch, then sit down and pull out the notebook again. Rereading what I wrote yesterday doesn't make my choices any clearer.

I just don't know where to go from here.

No, that's not true. I know all my choices. I just don't know that I want to make any of them—especially not the one that I know is the right choice.

I could be the barrio's protector. That's already in me—hardwired into my genes, maybe, but it's still real. Except, do I really want to stay on in a place where I've already burned all my bridges? And whatever else I know or don't know, I'm sure that taking on this responsibility as a penance isn't how it should go. Even Lupita says I have to do it out of love. For the place itself—the dusty barrio and the land it stands on.

The problem is I'm not sure I can separate the two.

I need better advice—or at least another informed opinion. I remember what Rita said to me outside the pool hall. I'd asked her how I could get in touch with her, and she'd given me one of those enigmatic answers that Paupau treasures. Something along the lines of when I was ready to talk to her again, she'd know.

I close the notebook with the pen inside to hold my place. I look out at the desert.

"Okay, Rita," I say aloud. "If that's even your name. I'm ready to talk now."

"Talk is cheap," a voice says from behind me. "The real question is, can you walk the walk?"

Okay, I did call out to her, and whether I like it or not, I really am getting used to people popping in and out of sight. I can even do it myself. But when I hear that voice, I still just about jump out of my skin.

I turn around and there she is. She's still wearing her scuffed cowboy boots and her straw hat, its brim cocked low so I can't see her eyes. The piece of turquoise at her throat gleams in the bright sunlight.

"Why does everybody think I know more than I do?" I say.

She pushes the brim of her hat up and smiles, but I don't get a whole lot of comfort from that smile.

"I don't think that," she says. "Not anymore."

"What changed your mind?"

She shrugs. "This and that. What changed yours?"

I give her a confused look.

"About taking a stand," she says. "You were pretty set on keeping out of all of this the last time we talked."

"What makes you think I've changed my mind?"

"You called for me, didn't you?"

"So Rita *is* your name."

She gives me another shrug.

"If you haven't changed your mind," she says, "why did you call me?"

I look away from her. "I need to talk to somebody."

"And you called on me because we're so close?"

I don't have to look at her face to hear the smirk in her voice.

"I kind of already burned all my bridges with anybody else I could talk to," I tell her. "Except for Lupita."

"The jackalope girl."

"She's been a good friend."

"Easy," she says. "I'm not dissing her. Lupita's a good

kid." She waits a beat, then adds, "What about your grand-mother? Why aren't you talking to her?"

"How do you know my grandmother?"

"She came with a bunch of dragons to look at what you did last night. I talked to her this morning before she left town."

"I didn't know the two of you were friends."

She smiles. "I wouldn't call us friends. She doesn't seem to like me much, and I don't care about her one way or the other so long as she stays out of my way."

"Oh." Then I have to ask, "Was she mad at me?"

"Not particularly. Is that why you don't want to talk to her?"

"I guess."

I find it hard to imagine that Paupau would be so close and not try to find me. That she would come with a bunch of dragons to lay down judgment instead of asking me what happened.

Rita sits down on a nearby rock and tucks her legs up under herself.

"Okay," she says. "What do you need to talk about?"

I'm not sure where to start.

"I wish I could just be normal," I find myself saying instead.

"You don't really."

I start to protest, but her gaze locks on mine and I can't lie. It's true. Everybody wants to have something special about them and I'm not any different. But why did it have to be this?

"Still," she goes on, "if you need to feel normal, you could look at it this way: You're a normal whatever-you-are. I'd say you're the best whatever-you-are, but there's always room for improvement, right? Lord knows I could fix a thing or two about myself."

"So I'm a normal whatever-I-am," I say. "But what if the dragon wakes again only, next time, I can't control it?"

She gives me a funny look.

"You know that you and the dragon are one and the same, right?" she finally says. "It's not some big dangerous thing sleeping inside of you. It's part of who you are. It goes right down to your genes the way the rattlesnake is in me. You can't separate the one from the other."

It's my turn to just look at her. I don't really understand what she's saying. I mean, I understand, but it doesn't make sense. Paupau always talked about the dragons like they were these spirits that chose to live inside us. But then I remember Lupita telling me pretty much the same thing.

"Your grandmother never told you, did she?" Rita says.

I shake my head. She doesn't have to say the next thing: what else hasn't Paupau told me?

"So I shouldn't be worried about it?" I ask.

"Oh, I'd be cautious, darling. That's a big piece of power to have sitting there inside you. But the thing to remember is, you control it, just like you control where you walk or how far you throw a rock." She smiles. "You don't have conversations with your arm before you get it to do something, do you?"

"No . . ."

"But you know enough not to squeeze a raw egg too hard . . . unless you're making an omelet. It's the same thing. The dragon's just another part of you that you can choose to use, or not. Which brings me back to my first question. Are you ready to take a stand and get rid of El Tigre and his gangbangers?"

"I don't know what I can do besides waking up the dragon and burning them all like I did last night, and I don't think I'm ready for that."

"That's not exactly the optimum solution anyway," Rita tells me. "For a lot of reasons. I suppose it could happen—depending on how badly El Tigre wants to stay here—but before you even think about stepping up to deal with that little drama, you have to get Señora Elena on your side. Without her backing, you won't have the other cousins ready to stand behind you once El Tigre is gone."

"I have no idea what you're talking about."

"You know what cousins are?"

"Of course. And Lupita mentioned Señora Elena, but she said I had to ask you about her."

"She's comes from the old Gila monster clans—sort of Santo del Vado Viejo's version of you dragons. The cousins will back whoever she approves and if you've got them on your side, it'll be a lot easier to handle all of this without a lot of bloodshed."

"Why doesn't one of them do it? For that matter, why don't you?"

She shrugs. "One of the other cousins might be able to pull it off, but without the rep of something like one of the dragon clans behind them, they'd spend rest of their life here fighting off every other lowlife predator who might come along and want to take a shot at being in charge. Nobody wants that. But if a dragon was the big gun? Oh, yeah. That's a whole different story. Nobody wants to piss off a dragon by making a play for his turf. The smart wannabe is going to take a wide detour around this place and look for easier pickings."

"And what about you?"

She smiles. "I don't have those kind of ambitions."

"But you still want the barrio cleaned up."

"It's not just the barrio. The ugliness El Tigre brings with him bleeds all the way into *el entre*—this desert. Rosa made the land for us to cherish, not to piss away. You can't see El Tigre's influence here as easily as you can in the barrios, but it's still here. He's chasing away all the good spirits. Give it a few years and all those dark places in his heart will start manifesting here, and then we'll really be in trouble."

"Rosa . . . is that, like, some cousin name for God?"

"We don't believe in gods," she says. "Not when we know that Raven pulled the world out of that big old pot of his, and Rosa made a garden out of the desert."

I start to say something about how it isn't much of a garden, but that's the kind of thing I would have said before I left Chicago. Now I realize there's stuff growing everywhere. It's not a garden like we'd think of back home, but it's full of life and growing things all the same.

"Look," Rita goes on, "it was bad enough when it was just Julio running the *bandas*, but he was only a five-fingered being. How much trouble could he really cause us? He made the barrio an ugly place, sure, but his influence never crossed over here. El Tigre, he's a whole other assful of thorns."

"So I talk to Señora Elena," I say.

I'm trying to picture what she'll look like. What's a Gila monster, anyway? Some kind of lizard? But who says she'll look like one? I don't look like the dragon that Paupau tells me I carry and Rita says is a part of me. And she doesn't look like a rattlesnake, unless you look into her eyes and realize that she doesn't seem to blink. There's no room for a rattle in those tight jeans she's wearing, either. Yeah, I looked. What guy wouldn't?

"And then what?" I go on. "I have some kind of confrontation with El Tigre?"

"First worry about getting Señora Elena's approval," Rita says.

"Why? Will it be that hard?"

"Normally," she says, "a nice kid like you, with the

weight of the Yellow Dragon Clan behind him? You'd be a shoo-in. The problem is, El Tigre got her approval, too, and now she's not so trusting."

"She gave her approval to *him*?"

I'd assumed that he'd just shown up one day and taken over.

Rita shrugs. "He showed her a different face from the one we know now. He can be very charming."

"Yeah, like a viper—uh, no offense."

I spoke without thinking. It's easy to forget that while she looks like a beautiful Native American woman, she's from the snake clan. She holds me with a hard gaze for a long moment, then shrugs again.

"None taken," she says.

I know we should be getting ready to go see Señora Elena, but I can't stop thinking that Paupau could have strung me along the way Rita says she did. If it wasn't Paupau, I'd be mad, but come on, she's my grandmother. And it's hard not to want to win her approval. Back home, *everybody* walks carefully around her.

I still can't believe she didn't try to find me.

"She was really here?" I find myself saying. "My grand-mother?"

Rita nods. "But I wouldn't be getting all misty-eyed about it. She was strictly here on business. Dragon business."

"Yeah, she gets like that. Did she try to pull rank on you?"

"She's got no rank over me. The older dragons forget that they're not in China anymore—hell, these days half of them aren't even Asian. There are no more emperors and empires, and all they are is homeless protectors looking for a place that they can watch over in a land that doesn't care about them, or even believe they exist. What's hardest for them to get is that it's not all about them anymore. No one reveres them now just because they're dragons. Any respect they get, they have to earn.

"Mind you, some of them do get it. Others, like your grandmother—it's much easier for someone like her to pretend that nothing's changed and she's still at the top of the food chain."

"Well, I don't think that," I tell her, "but when I think of Paupau—my grandmother—and what the dragon did at the dance hall the other night—"

"What *you* did," she corrects me.

"Okay. What I did. I mean, there's a lot of power there."

Rita nods. "But the difference between this world and how it once was for the old dragons is that we're not afraid to gang up to take them down."

"Oh."

She laughs. "Don't look so worried. That wasn't a threat or a warning for you personally. Do you have any idea how long it takes a bunch of mixed-clan cousins to agree on anything? If the situation came up, you could be long gone before we reached a consensus on what to do."

"Why don't you deal with El Tigre in the same way you would with a dragon?"

"Weren't you listening? The cousins talk about it, but nobody can agree on how it should be done. Most of the time hardly anybody even bothers to show up for the discussion." She looks up at the sky, reading something I can't see. "We should get you over to Señora Elena's place. Are you ready?"

"No."

But I stand up and brush the dirt from my jeans.

I wasn't sure what kind of place Señora Elena would have. A cave in the mountains? A shack in the desert? A hacienda overlooking some hidden green valley?

Turns out she lives in the barrio, too, in an old adobe building just a few blocks from the trailer park where Lupita shares a double-wide with some deer cousins. A pretty Mexican girl around my age is sitting in a plastic lawn chair in front of the building, reading what looks like a school textbook. She seems familiar, but I can't place her. She also has a red-and-green scarf tied around her wrist. Kings' colors.

Rita stops as soon as we turn the corner.

"The girl's name is Maria," she says, "and don't worry about her being a gangbanger. Some of them still know enough to show respect to the old powers."

As soon as she says the girl's name I remember. She's got the kind of look that you don't quickly forget. Not exactly my style, but totally hot.

"She's the girl who used to be Rosalie's friend," I say.

Rita takes my comment for a question.

"How would I know?" she says. "Just go and tell her you're here to see Señora Elena and she'll show you inside."

I turn to her. "Aren't you coming with me?"

"There are a lot of places where I'm not exactly welcome," she says. "This is one of them."

"I don't understand."

"You don't have to. You either go talk to Señora Elena, or you don't. I'll see you around."

Then she steps away into that other desert, and I'm left on my own. I wish she hadn't taken off. For all of Rita's attitude, it feels like I have someone in my corner when she's around. I don't even know what I'm going to say to Señora Elena. But I suppose talking to her can't hurt. Maybe she can actually help me figure a few things out, though if she's anything like Paupau or Rita, I'm probably just going to end up feeling more confused.

I start down the quiet street and Maria looks up as I get closer. Her eyes go wide. I don't know how she recognizes me, but it's obvious she knows who I am. Or maybe it's just *what* I am. She stands up and holds the textbook against her chest. I can read the title. *Adventures in English Literature*. There's something so mundane about her being here, doing her homework, except knowing what she is, it all seems wrong.

"<We don't want any trouble here,>" she says in Spanish.

"<I'm not here to cause trouble. I just want to see Señora Elena.>"

"<She's got nothing to do with the *bandas*.>"

"<I know that.>"

"<Then why are you here?>"

"<I could ask you the same question. If she's not connected to the Kings, why are you sitting outside her place like you're her security guard? Did El Tigre put you up to this?>"

"<No.>"

"<So why *are* you here?>" I ask.

"<It's complicated.>"

"<Isn't everything?>"

She looks like she isn't going to tell me. There's no reason why she should, really. But then she shrugs.

"<I live here,>" she says. "<When my parents kicked me out of the house, Señora Elena took me in.>"

"<Did she know about the . . . you know . . .>"

I point to the scarf tied around her wrist.

Maria nods. "<Of course. She's old, not stupid. But she's different, too. She sees past the surface.>"

At first I'm not really sure what that means. But then I think about it. A gangbanger, sitting here doing her homework. Living with the old lady who's the spiritual heart of the barrio, which is about as far as you can get from the gangbanger mentality.

"<You don't really care for the *bandas*, do you?>" I say.

Her only answer is to spit in the dirt.

"<So why did you hook up with them in the first place?>" I have to ask.

She studies me for a long moment, then she nods toward the door.

"<You should talk to Señora Elena,>" she says. "<Like you came here to do.>"

I stand outside, held back by the blue trim on the door. When I look back at Maria she nods.

"<Oh, yeah,>" she says. "<I forgot. So long as we've got the spirit protection up, you guys need an official invitation.>

"<Unless it's a public place.>"

She shrugs. "<Like I care. Just go on in.>"

My eyes take a moment to adjust once I'm inside. I'm standing in a kitchen. The furnishing are simple, the colors muted except for some odd flourishes. A tablecloth with a bright Navajo pattern. A bright turquoise mug standing beside the sink.

"<She's in the next room,>" Maria says from behind me.

I cross the kitchen, hesitate in the doorway, then step through. Maria follows. It's like the kitchen in here, too, simple furnishings, everything in subdued desert colors. A foot-high Jesus hangs crucified on one wall. A portrait of

Our Lady of Guadalupe regards him from the opposite side of the room.

The light's dimmer in here and it takes me a moment to find Señora Elena sitting with her hands folded in her lap. I get that *ping* of recognition that she's more than what she seems. I also get the sense that she's been waiting for me.

Her house hadn't been what I expected, and neither was she. I pictured a small, thin woman, gray-haired, wrapped in a shawl—don't ask me why. From the way people have talked about her, I guess I thought she was all used up. But though she's not much taller than me, she's broad—face, shoulders, hips—and she has a glow about her as though she's filled with a barely contained light. Her skin is the dark hue of the local cousins—more Mexican brown than African—with thick black hair and a smooth complexion that belies her years. Her eyes are deep pools, so dark their brown is almost black.

All in all, she seems as formidable a woman as Paupau, so I'm not sure why she can't handle El Tigre. I know Paupau would shred Flores with a single hard stare. But I'm not here to critique how Señora Elena handles barrio business.

I give her a formal bow, bending from the waist, my gaze on the floor.

"<I am honored to meet you, mistress,>" I say to her in Mandarin, the ceremonial language of my clan. "<My name is James Li, of the Yellow Dragon Clan. I apologize

for intruding upon you unannounced like this, but I have great need of your advice.>"

I repeat what I've said in Spanish. When I lift my gaze to hers, I find her smiling.

"<Well, Maria,>" she says, looking over my shoulder. "<He's certainly polite enough, isn't he? That's what I like about these dragon clans.>"

I'm not sure if she's making fun of me, or if she's serious. Maria doesn't say anything. Señora Elena studies me for a moment, then waves me to a chair.

"<Sit,>" she says. She switches to English, her accent thick. "And tell me why you need the advice of an old woman who the world has left behind."

"You don't seem so old to me," I say as I sit down.

She wags a finger at me. "Manners I appreciate, but flattery is annoying. Now talk to me."

She's the kind of person who encourages intimacy just by being who she is, but I feel a little self-conscious around Maria. Even if she claims to hate the gangbangers, do I really want one of the Kings to know everything there is to know about me? Still, having come this far, it doesn't make much sense to back off now. I take a steadying breath, try to figure out where to start, then decide to just tell her the whole story, from when I first put my finger on the map, to how I came to be sitting here with her. The only thing I gloss over is how I feel about Anna. I also don't tell her that Rita brought me here.

There are a lot of places where I'm not exactly welcome, the snake woman had told me before she disappeared. *This is one of them.*

If there's bad blood between them, I can't see how mentioning her would help.

Señora Elena nods when I'm done. She smiles at me.

"So you've come to take my place," she says.

I quickly shake my head. "No, it's nothing like that. It's just I was told I should talk to you before I do anything."

She laughs. "You misunderstand. I'm happy to retire from this business of responsibility—a failing business, as I'm sure you've discovered. I still have the respect of my people, but I can't understand why. Everything I've held together over the past few hundred years has come unraveled."

I glance at Maria, wondering what's she making of all of this. But she's sitting in a chair with her knees pulled up to her chin, staring out the window as though she's not paying any attention to us.

"Because of El Tigre," I say.

She nods. "Flores is like a cancer, slowly eating away at the barrio, and we are helpless to stop him."

"I don't mean this to sound like more flattery," I say, "but I've been told you're very powerful. Why can't you do anything?"

"My strength comes from the land," she explains. "Not

simply this desert, but also the one that lies on the other side of the veil, *el entre*. What the locals might call fabled Aztlán, if they were able to see it. But Flores has been here long enough that he can draw on the same mysteries that I do. We are too evenly matched now, and any conflict between us will do more damage to the very thing I wish to protect."

"And he and I aren't?"

She shrugs. "It's different. You dragons are different. Your strengths come from within." She pauses, then adds, "As does a portion of El Tigre's powers, but he also taps into the very blood of the earth that lies under the barrio. He ignores the medicine wheel that underlies everything, taking what he wants but giving nothing back. The desert medicine is like a well, and our respect for it is the spring that replenishes it."

"So you're saying he's stronger?"

"Maybe yes, maybe no—it all depends on the will. Do you have the will?"

"I . . . I'm not sure . . ."

But I realize that what makes me unsure is not whether or not I'll try to do what I know I must—what I *need*—to do. It's whether or not I have any chance to pull it off. I look at Señora Elena and can see she knows exactly what's going through my head.

"So what will you do?" she asks.

"I don't know. What I'd like to do is get rid of El

Tigre and remove the weight of the *bandas* from this community."

Señora Elena gave a slow nod of her head. "I can certainly support that, but there's something you should remember. Cousins don't like bullies. They're not as concerned when it only affects the five-fingered beings— humans," she adds at my puzzled look.

I hold out my hands. I've heard this term before and it never quite makes sense.

"You wear the shape of a five-fingered being," she says, "but it's not your true shape, just as this is not mine."

Now I get it. I think.

"I don't like bullies of any kind," I tell her.

She shrugs. "What the five-fingered beings do among themselves doesn't concern cousins."

"But the gangbangers—"

"I know, I know," she says. "And not all cousins will ignore what the *bandas* do. But I tell you this so that you will understand that you can't simply step in and kill El Tigre. So far as most of the cousins are concerned, that would only be replacing one bully with another. They will not give you their support and without it, you won't be able to protect the barrio."

This is a lot like what Rita was telling me.

"I don't want to kill him," I say.

"He might not give you a choice."

I can't believe I'm having this conversation. Is this really what Paupau had in mind for me?

"You must understand something else," Señora Elena says. "The blood that runs under the skin of the desert can be a dark current. You have seen some of the dangers that the five-fingered beings present—the *bandas* with their guns and knives and drugs. But the world of the cousins can be dangerous, too. They are not all old women such as myself. You know the stories of the old gunslingers? How the young ones would test the speed of those who were already famous?"

"Sure."

"Even if you do everything right," she says, "some of them might still want to test you."

I shake my head. "I don't want to kill anybody. I'm not a killer."

"You killed a man two nights ago."

"I . . . that was in self-defense. Sort of."

Señora Elena shakes her head. "Be honest with yourself, if with no one else. You killed that man in retribution for what he had done."

I want to argue that I'm really not like that, but she's right. I feel terrible about having done it, but that's exactly why I killed him.

"I don't want to kill anybody else," I tell her. "He was a bad man, but it shouldn't have been up to me whether or he lived or died. I just . . . I just saw red . . ."

"But you will still take the chance and confront El Tigre."

I nod. "I can't let things go on the way they are."

Señora Elena smiles. "No, you could. But it's the mark of your worth that you won't. And that you can feel regret for causing the death of even such an evil man as the one you killed that night. You will do well in my place, my young dragon, and I give you my blessing."

She closes her eyes and we sit there in silence until I hear Maria get up from where she's been sitting behind me. She touches my shoulder.

"It's time to go now," she says.

I have a thousand more questions, I want to say. There's still so much I need to know.

Still, I get up and start to follow her out of the room. But before we can leave, Señora Elena speaks again.

"One more thing, young dragon."

I turn in the doorway.

"Be careful who you trust," she tells me. "Not everyone who offers you help means you well, especially among the cousins."

I never mentioned either Lupita or Rita by name and I don't know any other cousins besides El Tigre and Señora Elena herself.

"Anyone in particular?" I ask, trying to be cool about it.

What if she means Paupau? I think. And then I remember how Rita warned me about her as well.

But Señora Elena has already closed her eyes once more. Maria touches my arm. I hesitate a moment, then follow her into the kitchen.

Though I feel like we spent hours in that dark room, it's still early morning when we emerge from the house and step into the dusty alley. But the sun's higher in the sky than it was when I arrived. I blink in the bright light.

Maria turns to look at me.

"So it seems like you really are a good guy, China Boy," she says.

"I'm just a guy."

"With a dragon inside you."

I shrug. What am I supposed to say? I settle for, "You don't seem surprised by any of this."

Now it's her turn to shrug.

"I've lived with Elena for a couple of years now," she says. "I've seen buffalo men and crow boys. Deer girls and beings that walk like men but have the head of a coyote. I've seen the little lizard girls and roadrunner *brujos*, the javelina boys and the hawks that become men, or maybe it's the other way around. Maybe they're men who become hawks. All I know is it's a big world out here—bigger than most people realize—and sooner or later, most of it seems to drop by and visit Elena."

"I've only seen a jackalope girl and a woman who's supposed to also be a rattlesnake. Oh, and that other desert. *El entre*. What did Señora Elena call it?"

"Aztlán." She says the word with longing. "That I'd like to see."

"It's not much different from this world," I tell her.

"There's just no buildings or roads or people. There's nothing human."

"Like I said, that I'd like to see."

I almost say, "I could take you," but I don't know what the protocol is—or if there even are rules. Maybe that's a place only for cousins. Maybe something bad happens to humans like in the old fairy tales where somebody goes into fairyland for a day and a hundred years pass by in the world they left. What I do know is I didn't get that *ping* when I met Maria and I don't want to take the chance.

"You never did tell me how you ended up joining the *bandas*," I say instead.

She looks away.

"Look, I know you don't have to tell me anything," I say, "but it would really help me get a handle on how things work down here to know why someone like you, who obviously hates the gangs, still feels like she has to join up."

She continues to look away, but she says, "I did it to protect someone."

"I don't understand."

"The gangs are all about respect," she explains, turning back to me. "I don't mean they've got some kind of bullshit code of honor, because they'll break their word in a minute if it suits them and they think they won't get caught. It's about who's the toughest, who can take what they want without consequences." She taps her upper arm, but I don't really know what that's supposed to mean. "That's what they respect. The toughest, the meanest, the smartest. So when they have the chance to pull in somebody who's against everything they stand for, man, they'll jump at the chance."

I remember Rosalie telling me how Maria's mother worked for the probation department and her dad was a teacher. I can see how their daughter becoming a King would look good for the *bandas*. But when I say as much, Maria shakes her head.

"I made a good substitute, yeah, but I wasn't the one they had their eyes on."

I give her a blank look for a long moment and then it hits me.

"Rosalie," I say. "They were after Rosalie because it would totally devastate her uncle."

Maria nods. Then she pokes me in the chest, bunching up my T-shirt.

"You don't talk to *anybody* about this, China Boy. Not ever. *Comprende?* You do and I don't care how many dragons you've got living in your chest, I'll still come looking for you."

"But if Rosalie knew—"

"She can *never* know."

"Why not?"

"Come on, use your head. It'd kill her. After what happened to her mother and Anna's brother—and now

Margarita—it'd push her right over the edge. She'd go loco and who knows what she'd do? She'd probably try to go after the *bandas* on her own and get killed for her trouble."

"I guess. . . ."

Maria puts the palm of her hand on where she'd been poking me. She smooths my T-shirt.

"Besides," she says, "you're going to fix everything, right? There aren't going to be any more *bandas* once you're done with them. So she doesn't ever have to know."

"That's the plan," I tell her with more confidence than I actually feel.

She cocks her head and studies me for a long moment, reminding me of Lupita. Then she nods.

"You are so screwed, aren't you?" she says.

"Yeah, pretty much. But someone's got to do something, right?"

"You could walk away. This isn't your problem."

"I could, but I can't. It's . . . I guess it's hardwired into the dragon part of me to see it through."

"The dragon . . ." she repeats. "I see you cousins walking around like people so much that I keep forgetting what you really are."

I almost say, "I'd like to," but then I remember my conversation with Rita. She pulled the truth out of me. I don't really want to be normal. But why couldn't everything just be a little less complicated?

"Elena gave you the heads-up about cousins," Maria

goes on, "but there's something else you should keep in mind before you step into the war zone."

"What's that?"

"It's not just about Flores and the *bandas*. Santa del Vado Viejo's a prime route for the Mexican drug cartels. If you take out El Tigre, they're going to be looking to replace him."

Great. I hadn't even considered that.

"I don't think they normally get a guy like Flores," she said. "You know, a cousin. But they've got enough guns and crazy gangbangers that they don't really need anything more."

I give a slow nod.

"How do you even live in this world?" I ask.

"It was hard at first. I got beat up a lot and you don't want to know about how I got jumped in. But I toughened up quick. It was that or die. And now—"

I don't even see the flick knife appear in her hand, but suddenly it's there, the blade out and pointed right at me.

"Now they just think I'm a little loco," she says, "and they give me some space." The knife disappears as magically as it had appeared. "But you know how it is. Bottom line, when they say spit, I say how far."

"It must be hard—"

Her face goes dark. "Hard doesn't begin to cover it, China Boy."

"My name's Jay."

She nods. "Yeah, sorry. It's just that's what the 'bangers call you."

She looks away for a moment. When she turns back the dark hardness is gone.

"Margarita's funeral is today," she says. "They'll be interring her in San Miguel Cemetery."

And that's like a bucket of cold water in my face. Yeah, I don't want to be normal. But I don't want people dying around me, either.

"Are you going?" she asks.

I shake my head. "No one there wants to see me."

"No one wants to see me there, either, but I'm still going. I'll just stay in the background, play it low-key."

I shake my head again. "Look, thanks for all your help. I need to go figure out a few things."

"If I can do anything . . ."

"It's cool. I appreciate it, but this is something the dragon needs to—"

I break off, remembering one of the other things that Rita told me.

"I mean," I say, "I've got to work out how this is going to go down."

I hesitate a moment, then step away into the other desert. Into *el entre*. The Aztlán Maria wishes she could go to. I see her face as I leave and she doesn't even blink. She's probably seen people disappear a hundred times before.

I lied to Maria about the funeral. I do go to San Miguel Cemetery for the graveside part of the service. I stand half hidden by a tall cross near the front of the cemetery, too far away to hear what the priest is saying, but close enough that I can see how upset everybody is. I pick out Anna, standing stiff beside Rosalie. The other members of the band are there, too. Ramon. Luis. Hector and Gilbert. I see Margarita's family. Tío. A lot of people I don't know, though I recognize some of them from various Malo Malo gigs.

I think about Margarita as I watch the somber scene. She was so much fun, so full of life, but she didn't take crap from anybody. Which is what got her killed.

I start to feel angry all over again. Her death was so pointless. All the camera crews parked along the road like vultures don't help my mood. Maybe the dragon could toss their vans into a pile—how'd *that* be for some news? Then I realize Rosalie is looking in my direction, her eyes widening, and I know it's time to go.

I don't worry about anyone seeing me do this. Or maybe I don't care right now. I just step away into the other desert. Once I'm there—with the cemetery, the cars, the crowds all gone—I stand amid the cacti and mesquite, my hands opening and closing at my sides. Finally, I sit cross-legged in the dirt and tell myself to breathe slowly, to calm down.

At least here I won't hurt anyone.

That's when a small hand falls on my shoulder and gives me a squeeze. Before I have time to react, Lupita sits down in front of me, her knees touching mine.

"Rough day?" she says.

I wait for my pulse to slow down again before I answer.

"I've had better," I tell her. "Thanks for dropping off breakfast."

She waves it off.

"How'd you know where I was?"

She touches her nose. "Jackalope superpowers. I followed your scent."

"Nice trick."

She shrugs. "Little cousins like me might be a joke but we're not totally useless."

"I keep telling you—"

"Yeah, yeah. I know. And you're very sweet. But in the big scheme of things, I'm way way down on the list." She waits a beat, then asks, "So what's been happening?"

So I tell her about Rita and meeting Señora Elena and Maria.

"That was very brave of Maria," Lupita says.

I nod. Maria told me not to tell anyone, but who's Lupita going to tell?

"Why isn't Rita welcome at Elena's?" I ask.

"That's an old story," Lupita says. "The way I heard it, Señora Elena blames Rita for her brother Enrico's death. Supposedly, Rita filled his head up with how it was wrong that El Tigre was here and convinced him that he was much stronger because he had the weight of right on his side and, you know, he had the whole Gila monster thing going for him. But when Enrico went head-to-head with Flores—"

She breaks off as she realizes what she's saying.

"That's starting to sound familiar," I say.

Then I have a thought. I look around.

"Can she hear us?" I ask.

"Can who hear us?"

"Rita."

I feel nervous just saying her name.

"Why would she hear us?" Lupita asks.

"Well, when I wanted to talk to her, all I had to was say her name and poof, there she was."

"Did you just say her name, or did you call her?"

I give Lupita a confused look.

"I mean," she says, "did you put some intent into wanting to see her?"

I have to think about that for a moment.

"Yeah, I guess I did," I say. "That makes a difference?"

Lupita nods. "Sure it does. It's not like she's one of the big thunders living back up in the mountains who knows what's going on everywhere at the same time."

There's so much I don't know.

"So could I call you to me if I put intent into it?" I ask.

She smiles and shakes her head. "Little cousin, remember? We don't know those kinds of tricks."

"God, I don't know what to do."

Lupita doesn't say anything for a long moment. Then she sighs and gives me a sad smile.

"Yeah, you do," she says. "You just don't want to."

"Can you blame me?"

"Are you kidding? If it was me, I'd already be hiding out somewhere down in Mexico or Texas—anywhere far enough from here that still has some desert."

"Except I don't have that option because . . . you know . . ."

"It's what you need to do," she finishes.

I nod. "Pretty much."

Lupita hesitates for a moment, then she says, "Well, if I were you, I guess I'd start with going into the mountains and practicing."

"Practicing what?"

She smiles. "Being a dragon."

I just look at her for a long moment.

"You know," she goes on. "Out there you can get all big and scary and break stuff without anybody getting hurt."

"That's actually a pretty good idea."

"What?" she says. "Like I couldn't have one?"

"I don't know about the big and scary part of it," I go on as if she didn't say anything, "because the last time none of that happened. I was just me. But there was definitely breaking stuff involved. I really do need some practice."

"Which was my idea."

I smile. "Totally."

"And maybe you couldn't see it," she adds, "but I saw the dragon when you called it up in the dance hall and you definitely got big and scary."

"Really?"

She nods. "Yeah, you weren't all the way into its skin,

but I could see it filling the hall, pushing up against the ceiling."

"So maybe I could do this thing."

"I'm guessing you could do anything you wanted." She pauses at the look on my face, then grins. "Big cousin, you know?"

"I guess."

It's still hard to think of myself in that way.

"Let me know when you plan to go to El Tigre," she goes on.

"It'll be as soon as I can. Probably tomorrow morning, when the barrio's quiet and there isn't as much chance of people getting caught up in the crossfire."

"Good thinking."

I look at her, then I add, "You can't come. I don't want to see you hurt."

"I wouldn't go on my own."

"Yeah, but still . . ."

"Look," she says. "Little cousins like me, we're not very powerful, but there are a lot of us and we're stronger than regular people. Like Rita told you, when you get a bunch of us together we can be pretty formidable. And a lot of us hate El Tigre for how he's stolen the medicine from Señora Elena and for everything he's done to the barrio. Cousins are no safer there than five-fingered beings."

Remembering what Señora Elena told me, I give her a doubtful look.

"How many times do I have to say this?" Lupita says.

"We're not helpless. I'm going to put the word out and when you go face-to-face with him, we'll be there to bear witness and help out as much as we can. It won't hurt if the *bandas* see you show up with your own gang in tow."

"Yeah," I tell Lupita, "but Rita said it would be pretty impossible to get everyone on the same page. I don't want anybody else getting hurt. There's already been enough of that."

"Showing how strong we are is going to make sure that won't happen. Instead of them thinking they can just go after some kid and everything gets messy, it'll stay between you and El Tigre."

Where it could still get messy, I think. And then I start thinking about how different the cousins are from the human people I've befriended since I got to Santo del Vado Viejo—*thought* I'd befriended, since they didn't exactly stand up for me after what happened to Margarita and the gangbanger.

"People really have trouble with us, don't they?" I say.

"What do you mean?"

"Well, as soon as they find out what we are they just . . . you know . . ."

"You're talking about Anna."

I shrug. "Maybe. Partly. Mostly. I don't know."

"Is she your first?"

"First what? Girl I've obsessed over? Not really." I think about the girls at school back in Chicago. "She's the first I've actually talked to. You know, the first where there

was the possibility of something. Until she found out about
the dragon."

Lupita nods. "I've been there. It seems like there's always going to be people who don't handle it very well when
they find out about us. But you know, it's not really their
fault."

"How can you say that?"

"Well, it's not just the shock of finding out that we exist.
The very fact that we do changes how they come to see the
world."

"And people don't like change."

"Not most of them."

I remember what Rita said about Paupau.

"Some cousins are like that, too," I say.

I look away across the desert. Here on the other side
of the cemetery where they're laying Margarita into the
ground, I feel calmer. More sure of myself and what I now
know that I am. More comfortable with the cousins and
their hidden culture.

"Well," I say, "I don't know what the big deal is. I didn't
freak out when I found out about you."

She gives me a look.

"What?" I ask.

"Of course you didn't. You're a great big dragon, aren't
you?"

"Except I thought of myself as a normal kid. I didn't
know animal people were real, or that I was supposed to
take all those things Paupau told me literally."

Her look doesn't go away.

"And yet," she says, "as soon as you arrived here you were talking to little lizard cousins, and the cats and dogs in Rosalie's yard."

"How do you know that?"

She shrugs. "Word gets around."

"I was being polite."

"And what you're doing now is stalling," she says. "You need to either go practice the dragon stuff and get this done, or step away from it. Either way, I've got your back." She grins, adding, "Though getting away sounds like it'd be more fun. I know the place where the agave spirits hide their tequila. We could invite a bunch of cousins and have a party."

She gives me an expectant look, but she already knows my answer.

"Yeah," she says when I don't bother replying. "I get it. You have to do this thing. But it was worth a shot."

We both stand up.

"Be careful," she says.

"I will."

I haven't a clue what I'm going to do once I get into the mountains, but better I figure it out there on my own than when I'm standing in front of El Tigre.

"And we'll have your back," she says. "All you have to do is deal with El Tigre. We'll make sure the *bandas* don't step in."

I think of a gang of little cousins standing up to the gangbangers—a ragged collection of jackalopes, cactus wrens, lizards, scorpions, and other small animal people. The gangbangers would walk all over them. Except, maybe not. I'm not sure it's size that decides where a cousin fits on the scale of importance. Rita's a snake. She's not physically big in her animal shape, but apparently she's still a big deal.

I'm about to ask Lupita how it works, but then I realize that she's right—what I'm really doing is stalling. So I just thank her and turn to the mountains.

- *iii* -

Lupita watched him walk off into the desert, weaving in between the cacti and brush, getting smaller and smaller until finally he was swallowed by the vegetation and she couldn't see him anymore. She let out a deep sigh. Long after he was gone, she continued to stand there, listening to the birdsong in the cacti and mesquite. After a while she heard footsteps crunching in the dirt behind her. She didn't turn around, not even when Rita spoke.

"You did well, little cousin."

"Yeah, well, I feel like crap. He's my friend and I feel like I betrayed him."

"He's our only hope to fix this problem," Rita said. "Someone needed to give him that little extra push to get him to do the right thing."

"Maybe."

"And you were very convincing. The way you would go back and forth between sending him off and reinforcing the idea that he was the one who had to deal with Flores. You almost had me believing you thought he should just turn his back on all of this."

"I still half think he should."

Rita didn't reply. Lupita felt the weight of the other woman's unblinking gaze and sighed.

"Okay," she said. "So he needed to be convinced. But why did it have to be me?"

"Because right about now, you're the only one he really trusts."

"And see how great that's turned out for him."

"He doesn't ever have to find out."

"I'll still know," Lupita said.

Rita shrugged. "Get over it. And even if he does find out, he'll be glad you did it. In his heart, it's what he wants to do. You know that."

Did she? Lupita wondered.

She finally turned to Rita. "Tell me he's not going to end up dead like Enrico."

"Come on," Rita said. "He's a dragon. What can hurt him?"

"That's what you said about Gila monsters and look where it got Enrico."

"I thought Enrico was stronger than he turned out to be."

Lupita shook her head. "You don't see the start of a pattern here?"

"What else can we do?" Rita asked. "Do you really want things to go on the way they are now? It's not just humans who are getting killed in the crossfire of what the gangs are doing, and it's only going to get worse."

Lupita gave a reluctant nod. The number of cousins who'd died because of the *bandas* wasn't high, but it was rising. Javelina boys who'd "disrespected" gang colors. A deer girl run down in a car race out on the highway. Two old quail aunts, cut down for target practice.

"I know," she said. "But I like Jay, and I'm worried about him. He's so new to the dragon."

"Trust me," Rita said. "If I didn't believe he could handle it, I'd never let him go up against Flores."

Which was what she'd said about Enrico, Lupita thought again. But this time she held her tongue.

"Don't worry so much," Rita said. "I know he's strong. I just hope we don't need a repeat of what happened at the music hall for the dragon to get up to speed."

It took Lupita a moment to understand.

"You mean somebody might have to die for this to work?" she said.

Rita looked away to where Jay had walked off into the desert, her gaze ranging far, as though she could pierce the distance and see him.

"Somebody always ends up dying," she finally said.

There was a story that went around among the cousins about how the snake women like Rita and her sister, Ramona, could see into the future. If that was true, Lupita thought, what did Rita see? And for that matter, if it *was* true, why hadn't she foreseen Enrico's death? Or Margarita's?

Though maybe she had and she'd only kept quiet because it was all part of some plan of hers.

Ay-yi-yi, Lupita's head was starting to hurt. She wished she could roll back the weeks to the time before she'd met Jay. Back then, all she had to think about were things like teasing the javelina boys, racing with her jackrabbit cousins down the dry washes, or maybe playing chase with the hummingbird girls in the gardens of the five-fingered beings. But now . . .

No, she realized, that wasn't true. She was happy to have met Jay. She liked him, but more important, she knew she was better for knowing him. Being with him had woken something up inside her that she never knew she had. Issues and causes had always seemed like a waste of time and energy because who cared what a little cousin had to say about anything? Now she realized that helping other people lent weight to your life. At least it did to hers.

"It used to all be like this," Rita said.

Lupita looked up to see that Rita was still gazing out across the desert.

"What did?" she asked. "Do you mean the desert?"

Rita shrugged. "The desert. The spiritlands. The land on both sides of the border." She turned to look at Lupita. "Once—back in the days before the five-fingered beings came—there was no border. There was no difference between spirit and dream and the world Raven pulled out of that pot of his."

"You were there at the beginning?" Lupita asked.

Rita laughed. "I'm not that old, darling. But I was here when the humans first came, and I've watched them bleed the medicine right out of the world." She shook her head. "Year by year, they've pushed it across the border and now they stand around and scratch their heads, wondering where it's all gone."

"They're not all bad," Lupita said.

"And neither are all rainstorms. Some nourish the earth, and some tear it apart with their fury."

"But—"

"Oh, I know," Rita said. "We can't turn time back to the days that were, and Cody's showed us often enough what happens when we meddle with the fabric of the world. Remember the time he took the whole world of the five-fingered beings and rolled it up like a carpet?"

Lupita nodded. "I've heard the story."

"Well, it sure didn't work out like he thought it would," Rita said. "All he managed to do was split the world in two so that now we have their world *and* the spiritlands."

"I thought that was just a story."

"It is. But that doesn't mean it isn't true. You get to sharing Coyote tales and it all sounds like something you'd tell around a campfire."

"So that's what you meant about how it all used to be one."

Rita nodded. "We can walk between the two, but humans—well, they're a mix of those who don't even re-member the medicine, those who still yearn for it, and the very few who are like us and can cross back and forth."

"So what does any of that have to do with Jay taking down El Tigre?"

"Nothing. I was just remembering. But maybe indulging in a little bit of wishful thinking, too. I look at Flores and the *bandas* and I see in them all the things that are wrong with the world of the five-fingered beings. Get a yellow dragon in there running the show and maybe, just maybe, we could have one little corner of the world as close to the way it should be as we're going to get, all things considered."

"And if Jay fails?"

"Then I find somebody else. I'm not giving up on this."

"I'm going to get the cousins together," Lupita said. "For when he goes up against El Tigre."

"Yeah, well, good luck with that."

"Maybe we'll surprise you."

"I hope you do," Rita said.

Lupita searched the snake woman's face, but she couldn't read anything in her impassive features. Then she thought of something she'd meant to ask Rita earlier.

"Why did you want me to get Jay to go practice in those particular mountains?" she asked. "He could just as easily have done it here."

Rita smiled. "Because the thunders live there. With any luck, he'll run into one of them and then we'll see his dragon wake up for sure."

"You think old spirits like that would help him?"

"I don't know. Maybe they'll help him, maybe they'll take offense at him showing up in their territory and he'll have to defend himself. One way or the other, by the time he comes back, he's going to have learned how to access his dragon side. If he hasn't, Flores won't ever have to worry about him showing up."

"Why didn't you tell me that?"

"Would you have sent him if I had?"

Lupita glared at her. "You're going to pay for it if anything happens to him up there. I'll make sure you regret it."

"What's to regret?" Rita said. "Whatever happens, at least one of you little cousins has grown herself some backbone. That's a step in the right direction."

Then she stepped between the worlds, and Lupita was alone in the desert once more. There seemed to be a storm brewing up the mountains. She didn't see any lightning, and the grandfather thunders weren't rumbling yet. But even down here in the desert she could feel the pressure building.

She considered following Jay to warn him about the thunders, to tell him what Rita was up to and her own part in it. She was willing, now, to confess and take responsibility for what she'd done if it would save his life. But then she thought of El Tigre, of all the cousins who were being hurt and killed because of him and the *bandas*.

Maybe Rita was right. Lupita knew that Jay was determined to get Flores and the gangs out of the barrio. So if this was what it took . . .

Maybe he *would* thank her when it was all over.

She watched the dark skies for a little while longer, then stepped back into the world of the five-fingered beings.

There were cousins to gather. Jay said that he'd confront El Tigre as soon as he could. That meant tomorrow morning. She didn't have much time.

- *iv* -

Hours after Margarita's funeral when Maria still hadn't returned, Señora Elena went out into the alley behind her house. She looked up and down the dirt road. Her gaze finally settled on a small, gray-brown lizard sunning itself on the top leaf of a stand of prickly pear.

"<Have you seen that girl of mine, little cousin?>" Elena asked.

The lizard responded with a question of his own. "<Is it true what they say? That you've sent a dragon to rid us of El Tigre?>"

Cousins, Elena thought. Were there ever worse gossips?

"<There is a dragon,>" she said, "<and I believe he plans to confront Flores. But I didn't call him to me, and whatever he does, he does of his own free will.>"

The lizard's tongue flicked nervously. "<El Tigre will eat him whole and then spit out the bones, just as he did your—>" He paused, catching himself at the dark look in Elena's eye. "<Just as he's done to others.>"

He was probably right. And that made Elena wonder why she'd let Jay go so readily, without trying to talk him out of it, yet was still so angry with Rita for pushing Enrico to do the same thing. She didn't think it was only because Enrico had been family—her younger, headstrong brother who would never listen to her—though that was a large part of it.

"<Something must be done,>" Elena said. "<Someone must at least try.>"

"<You should call up the spirit of the land. Then you'd be stronger than him.>"

Elena shook her head. "<Once I could have. Maybe. But I waited too long, and Flores has slowly closed all the roads I know that lead to her.>"

"<And the dragon can open them?>"

Elena shook her head again. "<I don't think so. And how would he know to try?>"

"<You could have told him.>"

Elena shook her head a third time.

"<Why not?>" the lizard asked.

"<It would have given him false hope. This can only be settled with whatever strength he can muster from within himself.>"

"<Is this another one of your big-cousin rules?>"

"<What is that supposed to be mean?>"

The lizard shrugged. "<You're always talking about the right and the wrong way to do things.>"

"<I don't—>"

"<Not you, personally, señora. But you know how it is in all stories. Coyote says this, Raven says that. Don't kill the other cousins for fun. Respect the other cousins' territory. Take responsibility for everything you do. Don't break your word.>"

"<Those aren't rules,>" Elena told him. "<Most of that's just common sense, and knowing what's right and what's wrong. You get that from in here.>" She touched a hand to her chest. "<Not from anybody telling you.>"

"<I suppose.>"

"<Now, about Maria . . .>"

"<I heard some crow boys talking about her. They say she's sitting at the bus stop at the end of the block.>" The lizard nodded toward the west end of the alley.

"<What is she doing there?>"

"<I don't know. They were talking about her because she's been there for hours. She doesn't get on a bus. She doesn't do anything. She just sits there and stares at the ground.>"

Elena studied the lizard, but she didn't really see him. What he said made no sense. It was so unlike Maria.

The lizard shifted uncomfortably.

"<I'm just telling you what I heard,>" he said.

Elena sighed. "<Yes, of course. Thank you, little cousin.>"

Maria was where the lizard had told Elena she would be, sitting at the bus stop at the end of the block, elbows on her knees, eyes on the ground. There was nothing of interest there. A flattened water bottle. Cigarette butts. Candy wrappers and chip bags. Elena stood by the bench, waiting. When some time went by and Maria still didn't look up, Elena finally sat down beside her.

"I think I've been hanging around you and your friends too much," Maria said after a few moments.

"What do you mean?"

She shrugged. "I don't know. At first it was just that I could see your animal faces, even when you walk around like humans. But now . . ."

"Now?" Elena prompted.

"I'm getting premonitions."

Elena couldn't tell from the tone of Maria's voice whether the girl thought this was a good thing or a bad thing.

"What kind of premonitions?" she asked.

Maria turned to look at her. "That someone's going to die."

This was *brujería*, not cousin business, and Elena knew little about it. But she could see that Maria needed to talk about it.

"How do they come to you?" she asked. "When you're dreaming, or are they waking visions?"

"Neither. It's just this really strong feeling that I can't shake. I thought it might have been about Margarita, but she's gone now and the feeling hasn't gone away. If anything, it's gotten stronger. I'm worried that—you know . . ."

She looked away. Elena put her hand on Maria's arm.

"When it's my time to go on," she told Maria, "I'll be ready. I don't fear what comes next."

Maria nodded. "But you've lived a long and full life. I worry that it's about Rosalie, and she hasn't."

"Ah."

"I've already tried warning her a few times because I know the Kings are still gunning for her, but she doesn't seem to take me seriously. I don't know what else I can do."

"I would think," Elena said, "that you have already done much for your friend. Does she not appreciate the sacrifice you've already made?"

"She doesn't know. I've never told her."

"Why not?"

"It wasn't about her knowing. It was just about keeping her safe. If she ever found out, she'd get herself killed."

Elena was quiet for a long moment, then she squeezed Maria's arm.

"I have no words of comfort for you," she said. "I can only tell you that in the end, we do what we can and we can do no more. After that, events will take the paths that they choose."

Maria nodded. "I know. And the way things are going, we're long past comfort now."

She sighed and sat up, slouching against the backrest.

"Do you think Jay's actually going to go up against Flores?" she asked after a while.

Elena nodded.

"And does he have a chance?"

"Maybe yes, maybe no," Elena said.

"Yeah," Maria said. "That's kind of what I thought."

- *v* -

Rosalie never brought her dogs into the desert, not even at night when there was no one around. She knew Jay had been doing that, but when she walked them, she didn't. There was just too much trouble that the dogs could get into otherwise. They could turn into a real hunting pack, going after mule deer or a jackrabbit. Once that started, it was hard to stop them, and it would just cause too much trouble the next time she took them out in the barrio. And then there were the thorns they picked up brushing against the cacti. Working out the fishhook cholla barbs was a chore that neither she nor the dogs enjoyed.

Somehow those problems had never come up when they were out with Jay.

But Jay wasn't here, the dogs were at home tonight, and it was just the three of them on the trail, heading up into the mountains: Ramon in the lead, Rosalie following him, with Anna taking up the rear. They each carried a small pack filled with supplies: water, energy bars, flashlights, and small first aid kits. Ramon carried a rope and had a knife sheathed at his belt, but he'd also given each of the girls a compass and a map of the area into which they were heading.

"Why do we need these?" Anna asked as she took the map and compass from him.

"It's in case we get separated," Ramon explained.

"Except we're not going to get separated," Rosalie said.

Ramon nodded. "That's the plan. But the desert has a way of messing up plans. It's always better to go in prepared, instead of running into trouble and then wishing you'd been more cautious."

Rosalie was nervous, but once they were on the trail, she could feel herself relaxing. The moonlight was so bright that they had no trouble following the slow switchbacks up into the foothills. The saguaro towered high on all sides, casting deep shadows. Something about the giant cacti always brought a feeling of peace.

"It's all so beautiful in this light," she said.

Ahead of her, she saw Ramon's head bob in agreement. "The sacred beauty," he said. "That's what the *mescaleros* call the desert in the light of the full moon."

"I don't know about the beauty," Anna said. "This reminds me of the old days when we used to go out and party in the desert. Drink some beer, smoke a little moto."

"Yeah, a few years makes a big difference," Ramon agreed. "I guess we were all crazy back then, into the whole party scene. Hell, I even wanted to be a gangbanger."

"You?" Rosalie said.

She couldn't hide her surprise. But Anna took it in stride.

"I didn't know that," she said.

"There's lots we don't know about each other. Everybody's got a whole hidden world hiding there behind their eyes."

"But a gangbanger?" Rosalie said. "Why?"

Ramon shrugged. "When you're a little kid all you see is the low riders and how cool the *bandas* look. They're styling. Party all the time, pretty girls on their arms. What's not to like? You don't see the violence. You think of it as a way of *protecting* yourself against violence because you're part of a crew. Nobody's going to mess with you."

"And then?" Rosalie asked.

He shrugged. "You either stay stupid or you grow up and see it for the lie it is."

Anna laughed. "You sound like one of the pamphlets Mrs. Mercia keeps in her office."

"Doesn't mean they aren't true."

Anna was silent for a long moment and Rosalie knew she was thinking about her brother.

"Yeah," she finally said.

"How are we supposed to summon these desert spirits?" Rosalie asked, to change the subject.

Ramon glanced back at her. "Honestly, I have no idea. Alfredo only told me the best places to look. He said it would become clear once we were in the right place."

"That's helpful," Anna said. "I'm surprised he didn't tell you that we should get naked and dance in the moonlight."

"Like you wouldn't enjoy that," Rosalie said.

"Out here with cacti?" Anna said. "I don't think so. For me, Our Lady of the Barrio, it has to be the right time and right place, and this is neither. But I'd love to see *you* cut loose for a change."

"I'd do it if it could actually help Jay."

Anna grinned. "Oh, I'm sure you getting naked would be a big help. What do you think, Ramon?"

He turned his head, teeth flashing in the dark.

"I think you're a troublemaker," he said, "but it doesn't make me love you any less."

"Come on," Anna said. "I'm just trying to lighten the mood." She paused a moment, then added, "If it wasn't for me, we wouldn't even be out here looking for Jay."

"How do you figure that?"

"Well, according to Rosalie, I'm the one that drove him away."

"I didn't say that," Rosalie said. "I just . . . you know—"

"Wanted me to look past the end of my nose. I get it. I'm here, aren't I? But I have to tell you, I don't think we're going to find any spirits waiting for us. I mean, yeah, everything looks all mysterious and cool in the moonlight, but really. Helpful spirit guides showing up just because we need them? What are the odds?"

"I don't know," Ramon said. "The new boy in town likes you, but it turns out he's carrying around the spirit of some big old dragon inside him. What are the odds of that?"

"Okay, okay."

Anna stopped walking and raised her arms up to the sky. The other two turned to look at her.

"Oh great and mighty spirits of the desert," Anna cried out. "Please come to us. Show us how we can find and help our friend Jay."

While Rosalie knew Anna was only goofing off, she couldn't shake the unexpected feeling that something was listening—the cacti, the land underfoot, she wasn't sure what. But whatever it was, it made the hair at the nape of her neck stand up. Then, as Anna's voice echoed off into the desert, the world seemed to give a little shiver and Rosalie knew a moment of vertigo. She had long enough to notice that the moonlight suddenly seemed brighter before an unfamiliar voice spoke from directly beside her, saying, "Wow, is she always such a drama queen?"

Rosalie jumped, bumping hard into Ramon. The two of them would have gone tumbling into the cholla except that the stranger, moving more quickly than Rosalie would have thought possible, grabbed them each by an arm, pulling them back onto the trail.

Not only was the stranger quick, Rosalie thought, but she was strong, too. And then she realized who it was.

"Mother of God," Anna said at the same moment, her eyes going wide.

She made the sign of the cross.

Rosalie understood Anna's shock completely. It was Lupita. But a different Lupita from the young girl Rosalie had seen before. This one had long jackrabbit ears hanging down like a pair of braids, and pushing up out of her hair were two small deer antlers. But she was wearing the same kind of raggedy clothing—baggy black sweatpants and a tight pink sleeveless T-shirt.

Lupita regarded Anna, then turned back to Rosalie.

"She really is a total drama queen," Lupita said.

Rosalie had almost made the sign of the cross herself.

"You—you're Lupita," she said.

The girl nodded.

"Jay's . . . um . . . cousin."

"I'm a cousin, but not the way you're thinking."

"And you . . . you have antlers and . . ."

"Long ears," Lupita finished for her.

She flipped them coquettishly, to bring the point home.

Anna looked back and forth between them.

"You *know* this . . . this, uh . . . *spirit*?" she finally asked Rosalie.

Rosalie couldn't stop staring at the antlers and ears.

"Kind of," she said. "But she didn't look like this the last time I saw her."

"That's right," Ramon said. "She's the girl who was waiting for Jay in front of Tío's place the other night." He turned his attention to Lupita. "But looks are always deceiving when it comes to the animal people, isn't that right?"

Lupita gave him an amused look. "I'm not one of the big medicines, if that's what you mean. What you see is what you get."

"So you're just a kid," Ramon said.

"Except for the ears and the . . . you know . . ." Anna muttered from beside him.

Lupita nodded. "The way cousins count the years, sure, but what's that got to do with anything?"

"We need to speak to one of the desert spirits," Ramon said. "I guess what you call the big medicines."

Lupita's smile faded. "Ai-yi-yi. Do you think the thunders come at anyone's beck and call? And do you think you could actually have a conversation with one? That's like trying to have a conversation with a mountain or a lake."

"But—"

"What you need is a cousin," she said. "Like me." She flipped her ears again, then gave a knowing tap to one of her antlers. "Walking around as a five-fingered being. Flesh and bone. Because you're looking for Jay, right?"

Rosalie nodded. "Can you help us?"

"Sure. I could show you where he is, but you can't go to him right now. He's kind of busy."

"What's he doing?"

"Practicing how to be a dragon."

"Oh."

There was a moment's silence, broken by the hoot of an owl calling from its perch, high on the top of a saguaro.

"Why does he have to practice what he's already supposed to be?" Anna finally had to ask.

Lupita shrugged. "He's not very good at being a dragon and he needs to be, because he's going to go head-to-head with El Tigre."

The three teenagers exchanged looks.

"This is my fault, isn't it?" Anna said. "It's because of what I said to him in the parking lot the other night."

"Partly, sure," Lupita told her. "But you're not the whole story. He's also really upset about your friend being killed, and I guess he wishes now that he'd just shut the *bandas* down instead of going for any kind of peaceful negotiation."

"He can really do that?" Rosalie asked.

"What, shut them down?"

Rosalie nodded. Lupita looked away before answering.

"He's got mad skills," Lupita finally said. "No question

there. The problem is, I'm just not sure he really knows how to use them."

"What do you mean?" Rosalie said. "He brought down the whole music hall."

"Yeah, but he was really angry that night. This is something he has to be able to call up whenever he needs it, not only when he gets really pissed off about something. He needs to get it together, and he needs to do it fast, because if he can't show that he's the full, real yellow dragon deal when he goes up against El Tigre, Flores is going to slaughter him."

"So he has to kill El Tigre first?" Ramon asked.

Lupita nodded. "But according to Señora Elena—"

"Who?" Anna broke in to ask.

"She's—" Lupita began, then shook her head. "Never mind. It's too complicated to explain. All you need to know is that if Jay kills Flores, it'll make everything a waste of time."

"I don't get it," Anna said. "El Tigre will be gone. And if Jay can handle him, he can get rid of the gangs, too."

Lupita nodded. "Probably. But then every wannabe gangbanger boss will want to take a run at him."

"I don't understand."

"What he needs to do," Lupita explained, "is take control of things without being a bully about it. If he can pull that off, he'll have our support—all of the cousins, you know?—and there won't be any more *bandas* coming into town because none of us will let them get a foothold. It also means that none of the cousins will make a try for him, either."

"You make it sound like some old western movie," Ramon said.

"Why don't the, um, cousins—why don't they do that now?" Anna broke in.

"Cousins have trouble agreeing on pretty much everything," Lupita said.

"Then why would they support him?" Rosalie asked.

"Because if he does it right, he'll be *ours*. He'll be so rooted to the land—to this place—that to go against him would be like not breathing anymore, or cutting off your own hand."

"He'll be your spiritual leader," Ramon said.

Lupita nodded. "Exactly."

"But he's just a kid," Rosalie said.

"No," Lupita told her. "He's a yellow dragon."

"Not yet," Anna said. "You told us he was still practicing to be one."

Lupita gave her a considering look. Rosalie thought she saw a flicker of worry in the jackalope girl's eyes, there, then gone.

"Don't worry," Lupita said. "I have faith in him."

"But what if he kills El Tigre?" Rosalie had to ask. "What happens then?"

"Then he has to prove himself to every wannabe who

comes along and thinks they can do a better job."

"How can we help?" Rosalie asked.

Ramon nodded. "Is there anything we can do?"

"You could be more supportive," Lupita said.

She spoke to them all, but she looked directly at Anna.

"What do you expect me to do?" Anna asked.

"Oh, I'm not saying you have to pretend to be in love with him or anything, but you could be a little less harsh."

"Maybe I've been hard on him," Anna said, "but think about what it's been like for me. From what happened to my brother to—"

Lupita held up a hand to stop her.

"Don't need to know," the jackalope girl said. "Don't care. I'm just saying, if you want to help, dial back the heavy vibe." She paused, then added, "You could even apologize. Otherwise, the best you can do is just make yourself scarce until all of this blows over."

"But Jay—"

"Doesn't need the distraction that you are unless you're standing in his corner going, 'Yay, Jay!'"

"You don't—"

"Yeah, I know. Now I'm the one being harsh. But this is serious business. However it goes down, he can't afford to be distracted."

"So what *can* we do?" Rosalie asked.

"Seriously?"

"Of course, seriously."

"Come down to the pool hall when Jay goes up against El Tigre," Lupita said. "Show that you really do support him. I've been out talking to the cousins, but I don't know how many will actually come and we need a lot of bodies to be there. I want to fill the street if we can."

"What for?"

"As a show of force. And to stand up to the *bandas* while the big guns go at each other, mano a mano."

"We could do that," Ramon said. "We could put the word out that Malo Malo is playing a free gig. That'll bring out a few hundred people."

"We could play the gig for real," Anna put in. "In memory of Margarita."

"We'd need a drummer."

"Chaco Rios could fill in. With Margarita gone, he's the best drummer we have in town."

Ramon nodded. "And Billy's uncle has a couple of flatbed trucks at the junkyard. We set the gear up on them, power with generators, and then just roll in, ready to play."

"It all sounds good," Lupita told them. "Just make sure everybody stays out of Jay and El Tigre's way."

Ramon nodded.

"When's it all going down?" he asked.

"It looks like tomorrow morning, in front of El Conquistador. Jay just wants to get it over with."

Rosalie remembered the last time Jay had gone off to see Flores. He hadn't had the patience to wait then, either.

"We'll have to work fast to get it all organized," Ramon said.

"Then let me get you back to your world," Lupita told them.

"Our . . . *world*?" Anna said.

Lupita grinned. "Where did you think you were? Do you see any city lights? Do you hear any traffic?"

An echo of Rosalie's earlier vertigo returned. She steadied herself with a hand on Ramon's arm. She remembered thinking how bright the moon had gotten when Lupita appeared, but then the shock of the jackalope girl's appearance had swallowed her attention. She'd never looked around. When she did now, she saw it was true. The light pollution of Santo del Vado Viejo simply wasn't there. And the quiet around them was profound.

"Where—where are we?" she asked.

"We call it *el entre*," the jackalope girl told her. "It's the place in between your world and the spirit world."

"I don't understand. You brought us here? *Why* did you bring us here?"

Lupita pointed to the mountains behind them. When they turned to look, they saw flashes of light rising up behind the range.

"What's that?" Rosalie asked.

"Jay," Lupita told her. "Practicing."

"But—"

"When I first heard the three of you talking, you said

you were looking for Jay, so I brought you here, where he is."

"Can we go see him?" Rosalie asked.

"I'm thinking now is probably not a good idea. Let him stay focused on what he's doing." Lupita grinned then. She raised her arms theatrically high. "Here we go."

Another flash of vertigo hit Rosalie, here, then gone. This time she wasn't the only one affected.

"I think I'm going to hurl," Anna said.

"Sorry," Lupita told them. "Everybody has a different reaction to the transition." She waited a moment to make sure they were all right, then added, "Stay safe," and vanished.

"Okay," Anna said. "That's just creepy."

Rosalie turned away from the glow of Santo del Vado Viejo that filled the night sky to the east and looked toward the mountains. There were no lights flashing there now.

"Did all of that just happen?" she said. "For real?"

Ramon put his arm around her shoulder.

"Afraid so," he told her.

"It was so beautiful there. . . ."

Ramon nodded.

"Yeah, yeah," Anna said, "but right here and now, time's wasting. We've got a gig to get up and running."

- *vi* -

Lupita stood in *el entre* feeling guilty all over again. She hadn't wanted to put Jay's friends and the band's fans in danger, but she wasn't sure how many cousins she could actually gather and she kept going back to what Rita had said about maybe it would take somebody dying to bring out the dragon in Jay. She didn't want anybody to be hurt except for El Tigre, but if there were going to be casualties, better it be among the five-fingered beings than the cousins. The cousins had never asked humans to take over their land and push the medicine away.

She knew that wasn't the right way to look at it. What they had to do, cousins and five-fingered beings, was learn to get along. Except the five-fingered beings didn't even know that her people existed, and if they did, most of them would just try to find some way to use the cousins the way they used up everything else. So why should she worry about what might happen to any of them?

Because they weren't all like that.

She sighed. Oh, but it made her head hurt. Taking on responsibility was a lot harder than she'd ever thought it would be. Maybe that was why she'd avoided it for as long as she had.

She waited a little while to see if Rita was going to show up, then finally sat down to face the mountains. She watched the flashes of light that rose up from behind the ridges and hoped it really was Jay practicing. That it wasn't the thunders ganging up on a yellow dragon.

- *vii* -

Jay didn't know if he'd ever get used to how different it was in Santo del Vado Viejo. The climate was certainly part of it, but mostly, there was just so much space. There wasn't a building more than a few stories high anywhere, so the sky felt like it was right on top of you. In the barrios, the alleys running behind the houses were as wide as most Chicago streets. Get out past the city and it was all open desert. No matter where you went, you felt exposed.

That had been bad enough. *El entre* was worse. Knowing about the animal people, how someone like Rita could simply appear when you called her name, you couldn't help but think that you were constantly surrounded by invisible spirit presences. And here in *el entre* . . . the spiritlands . . . Aztlán . . . whatever this place was called . . . this was where all the spirits came from.

He kept looking around as he walked, thinking he'd caught movement out of the corner of his eye, but whenever he turned, there was nothing—there was *nobody*—there.

Finally, he forced himself to stop worrying about it. If there *were* spirits watching, let them. It wasn't like he could stop them.

It didn't take him as long to get up into the mountains as he thought it should have, but he wasn't surprised. Something about the place—the air, or maybe what Lupita called "medicine"—made it seem as though time moved faster, or sometimes slower—you could never tell which. There were evenings he'd gone rambling with Lupita for what felt like a week, but when he got back to Santo del Vado Viejo only a couple of hours had passed. Other times, he'd be here for no more than a few minutes and an hour would have gone by.

Once he was in the mountains, he followed a switchback until it finally led him out onto a long ridge. He was high up now—maybe a third of the distance to the peaks, which reared still taller into the sky above him. The ridge took him around the mountain where it opened up onto a small plateau. He stood there for a long time, taking in all the space and trying not to feel too small. Though maybe feeling small was a good thing. Maybe it would help him keep everything in perspective.

"So dragon," he said aloud. "Are you ready to wake up?"

There was no response, not even the shifting feel of scales deep in his mind. But he remembered what Rita had said:

You don't have conversations with your arm before you get it to do something, do you?

So he reached into his pocket and pulled out a short length of saguaro rib that he'd collected on his way into the mountains. He held it between his thumb and forefinger. Thinking of fire, he blew on the free end.

Nothing happened.

So where was the fiery dragon breath when you wanted it?

What he needed, he supposed, was to key into that moment in the music hall. Except how was he supposed to do that? He'd been so angry that night. And he shouldn't need anger. He wasn't the Incredible Hulk. Both Rita and Lupita had told him that the dragon was a part of him, not something he changed into.

You don't have conversations with your arm . . .

He tried again, this time just assuming that the piece of cactus would burst into flame.

Still nothing.

This was stupid. The dragon was real. He knew that. Everybody from Paupau to the gangbanger girl living with Señora Elena knew it. So why couldn't he set just one freakin' little twig on fire?

He glared at the cactus he held and blew again.

The rib burst into flame.

"Ow, ow!" he cried.

He dropped it, shaking his fingers to try to cool them down.

That *hurt*.

But it had worked.

Okay, that was cool, he thought as he sucked on his fingers. But then he remembered the gangbanger in the music hall, how Jay had burned him to a crisp after the gangbanger stabbed Margarita.

Doing that kind of damage . . . maybe it wasn't cool. But it was effective. Or at least it would be if he could learn how to call it up whenever he needed it.

His fingers still hurt. You'd think a dragon would be immune to his own flame. Still he had enough time to feel a small flicker of satisfaction that he'd actually done it before a slow clapping started up behind him. Jay didn't have to turn around to hear the mockery in the sound, but when he did, for a long moment he couldn't see anyone. Then he realized what he'd initially thought was nothing more than a jumbled spill of red rock actually had a man lounging on the top of it.

The stranger was dressed in jeans, a white T-shirt, and scuffed cowboy boots. His hair was as black as Jay's own, in a long braid that had fallen forward to hang down his chest. His eyes were dark and the *ping* his presence registered in Jay's head was deep and resonating.

Great, he thought. This was just what he needed. Some big-deal cousin to hang around and watch him make a fool of himself.

Self-consciously, he stuck his burned fingers in his pocket.

"Who are you?" he asked.

The man raised his eyebrows. "We don't throw names around as casually as the five-fingered beings do—or didn't anybody tell you that?"

Jay shrugged. Did nobody else get tired of all this so-called mystery about names?

"Like I care," he said. "A name's a name."

"And filled with medicine."

"Whatever. Do you have a reason for following me here?"

The man smiled. "I didn't follow you. I was already here. You just didn't notice me."

Jay supposed that was possible—if the man had been hiding behind the rocks. But he didn't quite buy it. You couldn't get much more out of the way than this plateau in the middle of *el entre*, so if the stranger wasn't here to spy on him, then why *was* he here?

Jay decided he didn't care about that, either.

"Well, I'm kind of busy here," he told the stranger.

"I can see that. Are you going to burn your own toes next?"

"Look, I—"

"Because it's all very entertaining. I've never seen a dragon burn himself before."

Jay swallowed a sharp retort. He had no idea what kind of cousin or spirit the stranger was, but he didn't need Lupita here to tell him this man was a big deal. Power crackled in the air and Jay realized there was no point in being rude. The last thing he needed right now was to make another enemy. And who knew? He might even gain himself an ally.

So he took a deep breath to steady himself before he bowed and offered the stranger the same formal greeting he'd given Señora Elena.

"<I am honored to meet you, sir,>" he said in Mandarin. "<My name is James Li, of the Yellow Dragon Clan. I apologize for any discomfort my rudeness might have caused you.>"

Before he could repeat what he'd said in Spanish, the stranger held up a hand.

"<Now there,>" he replied in flawless Mandarin, "<is the much-vaunted politeness of the yellow dragons you hear about in the old stories.>" He switched to English. "And it explains your casual attitude to the sharing of names."

"Sir?"

He shrugged. "You dragons can't be controlled by the use of your name. My people can't be, either, but that's mostly because we don't have names."

Jay couldn't stop himself from asking, "Then what do people call you?"

The stranger gave another shrug. "You can call me Abuelo, if you need to call me anything."

"Grandfather," Jay repeated.

It seemed like an odd choice. The stranger appeared to

be in his late twenties—old enough to have a son, but hardly old enough to be a grandfather already.

"You don't look very grandfatherly," Jay said.

"You don't look like much of a dragon."

"Half the time I'm not sure what I am."

"Ah. That explains it."

"Explains what?"

"How a dragon could burn himself." He paused and studied Jay for a long moment before adding, "It's not really fire, you know. You didn't really burn yourself."

"What are you talking about?" Jay held up his burned fingers. "Just look at . . ."

His voice trailed off because there was nothing there—the skin wasn't even red anymore. The blisters and pain were all gone. He'd been so distracted that he'd never noticed.

"Did you—what did you do? How did you make the burns go away?"

Abuelo shook his head. "I didn't do a thing. I didn't have to. Dragonfire doesn't burn like that."

"I saw a man burned to ash," Jay said. "*I* burned him to ash by breathing fire on him."

Abuelo gave him another considering look.

"Have you ever seen a man hit by lightning?" he asked. "And I don't mean a glancing blow. I'm talking about old-school fire-from-the-heavens lightning that can level a ponderosa pine sixty feet tall and leave nothing but ash."

Jay shook his head.

"That's what dragonfire can do. What it can't do is hurt the dragon who called it up."

"But I saw . . . I felt . . ."

"It was in your mind. You expected to burn your fingers, so you did. And you don't breathe dragonfire, though I suppose you can call it up that way. Most people find it easier to just throw it like this."

Abuelo flung out a fist as though he was throwing a ball. Jay wasn't sure he actually saw a trail of light, but he certainly saw the explosive flare in the sky above them.

He turned back to the stranger.

"Who *are* you?" he asked.

"Nobody."

Jay shook his head. "No, you're from one of the dragon clans." He remembered something Lupita had told him and added, "Are you a feathered serpent?"

Abuelo shook his head. "I tell you, I'm nobody. Once I lived in the world you come from, but that was a long time ago."

"What made you leave?" Jay asked.

Abuelo looked away for long enough that Jay wished he hadn't asked the question, but then the man sighed.

"Did you ever think you could make a difference?" he asked.

Jay nodded. He had—or at least other people had thought it for him. Anna and Rosalie and Tío. Rita and Lupita. Even Maria and Señora Elena. He just wasn't so sure he could do what they all expected of him.

"I did, too," Abuelo said. "I thought I could make the world a better place. I thought I had all the answers. But in the end I was as bad as Cody. Everything I touched went the wrong way."

"Cody?"

"You know the stories, how he brought death and illness and fire and who knows what else into the world."

Jay shook his head.

"They call him Coyote in the stories."

Jay remembered those, from Lupita.

"My mistakes weren't ever quite on the scale of Cody's," Abuelo went on, "but they still caused problems. People still got hurt. Finally, I had enough and I retreated to these mountains. It's good here. You can spend a whole day watching the sky change and nobody gets hurt."

Jay thought about what he was planning to do, this confrontation with El Tigre.

"What kinds of things did you try to do?" he asked.

Abuelo shrugged. "Oh, the usual. Mostly it boiled down to trying to get people to stop pissing on each other. But you can't change everybody's way of looking at the world. You can only change things if there's someone in charge who makes people do the right thing, but you know how it goes. The ones that want to be in charge shouldn't be, and the people who fall into the job, or get pushed into it . . . sooner or later they get corrupted. Or screw up. Or both."

"Crap."

"You said it."

"No," Jay told him. "I mean, yeah, what you're saying is probably true. I'm sure it's true. But it just means I'm really screwed."

Abuelo didn't say anything, but his eyebrows went up in a question. Jay hesitated for a moment, then went ahead and gave Abuelo the CliffsNotes version of his story.

Abuelo seemed to be a good listener, but when the story was done and he still didn't say anything, Jay began to wonder if he'd even been listening. Finally, the man stirred.

"So people are guilting you into doing this?" he said. "It's not something you think should be doing?"

"Yes, no. I don't know. It's all so confusing. I'm just a kid."

Abuelo smiled. "You kept saying that while you told me your story, but what does it mean?"

"That I'm too young to have to be making decisions like this."

"You're never too young to do the right thing," Abuelo said.

Jay nodded, but he had to ask, "Or too old? Because here you are."

Something flickered in the man's eyes, but then he shrugged.

"That's true," he said. "So I'm probably the last person you should listen to."

"I'm sorry," Jay told him. "That was rude of me. If

you have any advice for me, I'd really like to hear it."

Abuelo made another fist and tossed lightning into the sky above them once more. He turned back to Jay and gave him a thin smile.

"I suggest you should at least learn to control your fire," he said.

"Can you show me how?"

Abuelo nodded. He came down from the rocks, landing lightly on his feet. Standing, he was a little taller than Jay. He tapped a finger on Jay's chest, on his breastbone.

"We call this the heart of the medicine," he said.

"You mean my *qi*?"

"If that's the dragon name for it. But whatever you call it, everything comes from that place inside us. Our medicine. Our identity. Our understanding of how everything we are connects under, not only our skin, but under the skin of the world around us."

Paupau had told Jay as much. *Qi* was the life force, she said. When enough of it accumulated in one place, a being was born. When it was depleted, the being died.

"But it's hard to always remain centered in that place," Abuelo went on. "The simple act of living is filled with too many distractions. So what I need to do is show you how to settle into the heart of your medicine whenever you need to. And at a moment's notice."

Without any further preamble, Abuelo ran Jay through a series of exercises that were similar to Paupau's endless practice sessions. He had no trouble following them, but there were subtle differences. For one thing, under Abuelo's direction Jay could physically feel his *qi* as it woke in his chest, the energy flowing throughout him. For another, whenever Jay had a question, Abuelo would give him the answer, if he knew it. If he didn't, he would speculate with Jay about what the answer might logically be. There was none of Paupau's, "This is just the way it is." Or her enigmatic, "Someday you will understand why we do this."

Lupita had been just as helpful. Maybe it was a cousins thing.

"You're a quick study," Abuelo said as they worked. "I can feel the heart of your medicine growing stronger and more focused by the moment."

Jay could, too. The sound of shifting scales was a constant murmur in his mind. Deep in his chest, his *qi* was like a red-hot stream, radiating strength as it centered him.

"My grandmother had me doing exercises like these," he said, "only she never told me what they were for. And I sure never felt the same intensity in my *qi* before."

Abuelo gave him a considering look, but all he said was, "I suppose dragons have their own methods of passing on knowledge."

Then Abuelo showed him how to throw the fire.

"You don't have to do it the way I do," he said. "I just like the feeling of throwing something. With your medicine strong and centered, you can simply direct the path of the lightning with your mind."

But Jay liked the feeling of throwing, too, and soon the sky above the plateau was like a fireworks display. The lightning Jay threw was yellow dragon gold, but Abuelo's were all the colors of the rainbow.

It was fun, but finally, Abuelo called enough. Jay turned to him, grinning, his face flushed. The more fire he'd thrown into the sky, the stronger the flow of energy inside him had grown. His *qi*. The heart of his medicine. He felt as though he could have kept this up all night and not even begin to be tired.

"So can all of the cousins do this?" Jay asked.

Abuelo shook his head. "It has to be in your nature. Dragons are rare creatures, Jay. Your elemental spirit embraces all the elements. Fire and water, rock and air. You could make the earth shake, call up a wind or a rainstorm, light the sky with your lightning."

"Can I change into a dragon—you know, the way Lupita can become a jackalope?"

"You can, but it's probably not a great idea. While you and the dragon are one, it's still a formidable skin to wear. That big old lizard . . ." He spread his hands. "Without a lot of practice and discipline, the dragon nature can easily rise to the fore and if you don't keep a firm grip, it doesn't take much for it to rage out of control."

"I understand."

"And remember," Abuelo went on. "Your enemy will

have his own powerful medicines. So be careful when you confront him. The truth is, the only way you can be sure of a quick victory is if you ambush him."

"I don't want to kill him. I just want to send him away."

"You might not have a choice."

"People keep saying that, but we always have a choice."

Abuelo nodded. "Just as we can all die. Or the people around us can be hurt."

"Señora Elena says if I win this by killing El Tigre, the cousins will resent me and I'll have to prove myself over and over."

"She's right," Abuelo said. "But there are times when we have to act quickly and decisively, or we lose our chance for victory. Surprise is a great ally."

Jay shook his head. "No, I have to do this right, or not do it at all. I can't just sneak up behind him and kill him."

"He would."

"But I'm supposed to be better than him." Jay waited a moment, then added, "You could come with me."

"I don't think so."

"But—"

"Remember what I told you. However good my intentions, I always manage to screw it up. Without me at your side, you have a chance of things working out."

"But you're already involved. You helped me figure out the dragonfire."

"I did."

"So why help me that much?"

Abuelo shrugged. "You want to make a difference and maybe you won't screw it up. I've been away from the world long enough to think it might be possible. But not if I come with you."

"I'm still going to do this."

"I know you are. Many people are counting on you."

"I guess. But I'm doing this for me, too. I think I really do love the desert and the barrio and I want the people who live there to be safe under my protection. I could do this. I have to *know* I can do this."

Abuelo grinned. "Good for you. You've already learned the biggest lesson this situation could teach you."

Jay shook his head. Did people never stop with saying that kind of thing? But he couldn't help asking, "Any last advice?"

"Don't get too cocky. El Tigre hasn't survived as long as he has by being a pushover."

"I'll remember. And thanks for everything. I don't know what I would have done if I hadn't run into you up here and—"

Abuelo held up a hand, cutting him off.

"Don't thank me until you've actually succeeded," he said. "All I might have done is send you more quickly to your death."

- 8 -

Big fish eat small fish.
—CHINESE PROVERB

JAY HAD HOPED to see Lupita before he reached El Conquistador. But she wasn't in *el entre*. He couldn't find her when he stepped back across into the barrio, either. Both Tío's house and Rosalie's trailer were dark. The dogs were awake. They sat in a silent line by the fence and watched him as he walked past. He gave them a nod and continued down the dusty street. At the far end of the block, he tried calling Lupita's name—he kept his voice low, putting as much *intent* as he could into it—but it didn't make any difference.

He would have liked to have said good-bye to her. To Rosalie, too. To Rosalie and Tío and the friends he'd made through them and the band. And then there was Anna . . .

Considering how things had gone in the parking lot, he supposed they'd already said whatever good-byes they were going to, hadn't they?

He also wished he could have called his parents, but how could he explain what he was about to do? It wasn't just the upcoming confrontation with El Tigre and his *bandas*; when Jay tied himself to the barrio and the desert, he would also be giving up everything to do with his past life. Paupau would understand, but Jay was still too upset to want to talk to her.

The desert was the one thing he couldn't escape here, but he didn't mind. It called forth something deeper that resonated in him as nothing ever had before.

He could almost feel the land breathing underfoot. No, not breathing so much as radiating its presence with a pulse that felt like a heartbeat. He wasn't connected to it the way he supposed Señora Elena was, but he found himself walking in time to its slow rhythm all the same. He could understand the depth of its power, even from his place on the outside.

And although he couldn't tap into that medicine, its rhythm laid an odd calm over him, settling the ever present rustle of scales in his head.

As he neared Camino Presidio, the early dawn light came creeping above the peaks of the mountains where, in the other world, he'd left the stranger who'd called himself Abuelo. But here he was alone, walking down the street like a character in a Western, heading for the shoot-out. All he needed was a six-gun strapped to his hip.

He called up a tiny spark of dragonfire and flicked it at a candy wrapper lying in the dirt. The wrapper vanished in a burst of flame and turned to a smudge of ash.

Jay's lips twitched with a small, satisfied smile. He had his own built-in six-gun. He just hoped he wouldn't have to use it.

He was still a couple of blocks away from the pool hall when a dark-skinned man with glossy black hair fell into step beside him. The calm of the desert medicine kept Jay from starting at the man's sudden appearance; the *ping* of recognition told Jay the stranger was some kind of cousin. He must have come from *el entre*.

The stranger gave him a grin.

"<Are you really taking on El Tigre?>" he asked in Spanish.

Jay nodded. "<I'm going to try.>"

"<We weren't sure when we got Guadalupe's message— you know, like it was a joke or something? But you're the real deal, aren't you?>"

"Guadalupe?" Jay asked.

"<Yeah, Lupita. She talked to us. Hell, she's probably talked to everybody tonight, but you know how it is with the little cousins. Most of them talk the talk, but they won't actually do dick all. Though you can bet they'll show up to watch the show.>"

"<This is between El Tigre and me,>" he said.

"I can dig it," the stranger said, switching to English. "But you know . . ." He laid a closed fist against his chest. "I'm just here to tell you that *los cuervos* have got your back."

For a moment Jay wondered if the cousins had their own street gangs, but then he realized that the air above them was full of crows. Cousins.

"Thank you," he said.

"Give 'em hell," the stranger said.

He grinned again. He lifted his arms straight up, and when he jumped, the man was gone and a crow rose to join its circling companions.

Okay, that was cool, Jay thought. And now that he was paying attention, he felt dozens of little *pings*. There were cousins all around him. He couldn't see them, but he knew they were there. The little cousins. Birds and insects and rodents. They wouldn't be much help, but then, he didn't want them to be. If he was going to take over Señora Elena's responsibility for this little stretch of desert, he needed to do it on his own.

But it was comforting to have them as witness.

"We need to get going," Rosalie said.

Ramon nodded. He and the rest of Malo Malo had spent the last couple of hours setting up their gear on the flatbed trucks. Having hung around with the band for as long as she had, Rosalie knew enough about the stage setup that she could help with the basics—lugging amps and instruments, laying down cable—but fine-tuning was beyond her. She could make no sense out of the arrays of foot pedals or the thicket of wires that went into the soundboard, so at that point she'd pick an out-of-the-way spot to sit and wait, as she did now.

She wondered what kind of a turnout they'd get for an impromptu early morning gig deep in the barrio. The band had put up notices on MySpace and Facebook, and sent the information out through Twitter and to their regular e-mail list. Malo Malo had a loyal fan base, but most people were still asleep and it was a weekday.

"Do you think the *policía* will try to shut us down for playing without a permit?"

Rosalie turned to see Hector's boyfriend, Conrad, standing beside her. She scooted over a little on the bass drum case she was sitting on to give him room. It was funny, she thought, how she and the other boyfriends and girlfriends of the band referred to Malo Malo with a proprietary "us."

"I guess it depends on whether anybody complains," she said.

"That part of the barrio?" Ramon called over. "Nobody calls the cops about anything."

"It's the *bandas* we have to worry about," Chaco said from behind the drum kit. "Nobody has a shit down there without first checking if it's okay with El Tigre's lieutenants."

It was weird seeing Chaco setting up when it should have been Margarita. That especially hardened Rosalie's resolve about what had to be done.

"That's why Jay's going to take care of this," she said.

Chaco shook his head. "No offense, but I've met Jay. He's a nice guy, but come on."

"No," Anna said, surprising Rosalie. "He's lots more than that." She caught the look on Rosalie's face. "Well, he is," she said. "And he won't be alone."

Rosalie nodded, remembering what had happened earlier when they got to the junkyard that Billy's uncle owned. Car parts had been stacked high on the two flatbeds they were planning to borrow.

"Aw, man," Luis had said. "It's going to take us hours to move all that crap."

Ramon nodded. "So we better get started."

Except before they could, a handful of tall Indians had come walking out of the desert night. They wore jeans and T-shirts and old cowboy boots and their hair was tied back. None of them seemed much older than teenagers, but they walked with a confident grace that even Ramon couldn't match onstage. Their eyes were as dark as their hair, and seemed to swallow the light cast from the junkyard spots.

"Guadalupe asked us to give you a hand," one of them said.

As Hector started to make the sign of the cross, Rosalie smiled, knowing that Hector half believed the saint had spoken to the strangers. But she knew they weren't Indians. Lupita was a diminutive of Guadalupe, so the men must be her friends. Cousins. Desert spirits, like the little jackalope girl.

"Thank you," she told them.

The one who'd spoken vaulted easily onto the bed of one of the trucks.

"Where do you want this stuff?" he asked.

"Just over here," Billy said, pointing to an open stretch of parking lot behind the trucks.

The band members and their friends didn't even get to pitch in. In what seemed like only moments the strangers carried fenders and engine blocks and other car parts off the trucks without even breaking a sweat.

Rosalie and the others stood staring until the last piece had been removed.

"See you at the pool hall," one of them said.

Rosalie couldn't tell them apart. It might have been the first who'd spoken, it might be any of them.

"Yeah," one of the others said. "Play a kick-ass set!"

And then they melted back into the desert night as silently as they'd come. Rosalie thought she heard the sound of wings and exchanged glances with Ramon.

"Magic," he mouthed to her, and grinned.

Rosalie smiled now, remembering. The whole world was changing around them, but what surprised her the most was that it didn't bother her.

Hector stood up from where he was fiddling with the setup for his turntables and laptop. He looked at Rosalie.

"Do you really think those—what did you call them?"

"Cousins."

"Yeah," Hector went on. "You really think they'll show up? They were some bad-ass-looking dudes."

"And *strong*," Conrad said.

"They'll come," Anna told them. "And we're going to play a kick-ass set for them—if we can just get our own asses in gear."

She gave them all a fierce look, and everybody went back to work.

As the dawn light came over the peaks of the Hierro Madera Mountains, an old woman walked through the back alleys of the barrio, carrying a plastic lawn chair. Her progress was slow, but steady. But by the time the tops of the adobe buildings were catching the first rays of the sun, she had reached Camino Presidio. She opened her chair, set it down on the side of the street across from El Conquistador, and sat down. She didn't know how long she would have to wait, but she could be patient.

"You didn't come when it was Enrico going up against El Tigre," a voice said from beside her a few minutes later, "and he was your own brother. What makes this time different?"

Elena didn't bother to look at Rita. She kept her gaze on the doorway of the pool hall.

"This time I know it is happening," she finally said.

"I didn't make Enrico go," Rita said.

"I know. But you encouraged him."

Rita shook her head, but Elena was watching the pool hall.

"I wasn't so much encouraging him," Rita said, "as wondering why an old cousin of the powerful Salty Water Stream Clan hadn't already rid us of Flores. Especially when it was already her responsibility to do so."

Elena finally turned to look at her.

"You are misinformed," she said. "Any medicine this old lizard ever had came from the land, and Flores stole that from me. He took it piece by piece, so subtly I never realized until it was too late. Now I can feel the pain he inflicts upon these small desert acres, but I can do nothing to stop it."

"Yes, but—"

"And Enrico didn't even have that."

Rita stared at her for a long moment before she finally said, "I didn't know that."

"We all live with the burden of knowing too little, but in your case it got a brave—if foolish—young man killed."

"I—"

"I didn't know what Enrico planned until it was too late," Elena went on. "But I couldn't have stopped him. We can never stop these young men from throwing themselves into danger. But today, at least, I can bear witness to what will unfold."

"I thought—"

"Hush," Elena told her. She pointed upward to where a sky full of crows flew to vantage points on the tops of the surrounding buildings. "The crow boys are here. Jay must be on his way."

Some came in their animal shapes, some as five-fingered beings, but as Jay neared Camino Presidio, the cousins began to gather around the old adobe building that housed El Conquistador. Hawk uncles perched on nearby rooftops with a crowd of crow boys and a couple of old turkey vultures. On the windowsills below were smaller bird cousins: cactus wrens, flickers, doves, a lone phainopepla. Deer women stood in the shadow of an alley with squirrels and wood rats underfoot. Tarantulas and spiders and the little lizard girls watched from hidden places, while on the corner across the street from the pool hall, a gang of javelina boys were goofing around, pushing each other and laughing.

And others came—not cousins, but interested parties all the same. Ghosting in and out of *el entre* were the spirits of palo verde and mesquite and cacti, pale, insubstantial shapes that became more and more vague as the morning light grew.

There were rumors that Coyote Woman herself was on her way. That was always the talk when something big was in the air, but like the eagle cousins, she rarely came. Still, Old Man Tortoise made his slow progress down the street, and he hardly ever emerged from the desert. He was accompanied by two members of the cat tribes—a young bobcat and a tall mountain lion elder in a beaded buckskin dress whose features kept shifting between cat and woman.

There were dogs everywhere—both cousins and their natural kin—but there were always dogs wandering around the barrio. They wove in and around the motorcycles and low riders in front of the pool hall and the parking lot, relieving themselves on the wheels of more than one.

And the cousins kept coming, big and small, old and young. Everyone was aware of Señora Elena and Rita, but while they paid their respects with nods or a wave to Elena, none of them actually approached until the arrival of Malena Gracia, the matriarch of the Beaded Lizard Clan who'd come from south of Santo del Vado Viejo, across the border that only the five-fingered beings considered relevant. Like Elena she was an old woman and overweight, her tread slow as she walked down the street; like Elena, she'd brought a lawn chair as well.

"This is quite the turnout," she said after she settled down beside them. "Your little jackalope has been a busy girl."

"She's not mine to command," Elena said.

Malena shrugged. "You know what I mean. Is anybody taking bets?"

"On the outcome?"

Malena laughed. "We all know the outcome. I was thinking more on how long an untried young dragon will last against El Tigre."

"I don't gamble on people's lives," Elena told her.

Malena gave another shrug. "Well, I'm guessing seconds rather than minutes."

"Maybe Jay will surprise you," Rita said.

Malena turned to look at the snake woman, then gave a dismissive wave of her hand.

"Sure," she said. "And maybe the moon will step down from the sky and put an end to all this nonsense, but I'm not betting that'll happen, either."

She started to settle back into her chair, the plastic stretching, then lifted her head and looked around.

"What the hell?" she said.

Groups of five-fingered beings were drifting in from the various side streets. Teenagers, young adults in their twenties. None of them showed gang colors but many wore scarves or T-shirts decorated with skeletons.

"Malo Malo," Malena read off a T-shirt—*Bad Bad*. "What's that supposed to mean?"

"It's the name of a local band," Rita said.

Malena nodded. "I wonder who they're rooting for."

The crowd stood in small groups and looked around. Many pulled out cell phones and started texting.

"I don't think they're rooting for anybody," Rita said. "I think they're here for a show."

Malena gave her a blank look.

"All that Malo Malo gear?" Rita said. "These kids are expecting a concert."

"At this hour of the morning?" she said.

"Can you think of anything else that would get them out so early? And now," she added, "I hear a couple of trucks. If there *is* going to be a concert, I'm guessing that'll be the band."

Malena looked from Elena to Rita.

"Now whose idea was this?" she asked. "You know this isn't the time or place for a show. Somebody's going to get hurt."

"It's their barrio, too," Elena said. "So it's good that someone brought them here to bear witness."

"Except they think they're just here for a show," Rita said.

Elena shrugged. "In the end, it will be the same thing."

Inside the pool hall, Cruz turned away from the window.

"There's some old lady sitting on a lawn chair across the street," he said.

A couple of other *bandas* got up from where they were sitting and went over to have a look. A tall girl the guys called Sweetcheeks laughed.

"That's crazy old Elena," she said, then she called over

to where Maria was sitting by the bar. "Yo, Maria! Your mama's out there."

"I don't have a mother," Maria told her. "She's just my landlady."

"Man, there's all kinds of weird-looking people out there," another of the *bandas* said.

Cruz looked over to where El Tigre sat by the bar, drinking an espresso.

"You want us to get rid of them?" he asked.

Flores shook his head. "Why would I want that? The barrio is their home as much as it is ours."

"Yeah, but this is just weird."

"Now there's two old ladies sitting across the street," another one of the gang members said. "And isn't that Rita standing beside them?"

Flores didn't even bother to look up again.

"Just tell me when the China Boy shows," he said.

Cruz and the other gang members gave each other puzzled looks. But they knew better than to argue.

"Sure thing, boss," one of the *bandas* said. "Whatever you say."

Flores glanced at Maria. She had her own espresso in front of her, but she hadn't touched it. She'd looked up when Flores had spoken. Now she was back to focusing on some unseen distance.

"What about you, Maria?" Flores asked her. "You have some interest in the China Boy?"

She nodded, her face dark when she turned to him.

"He killed Alambra," she said. "Now I'm just waiting for your say-so that he can pay for it."

"You never cared for Alambra when he was alive, so why the interest now?"

"I still don't care about him," she replied, "but it doesn't matter what I think or don't. Alambra was a King. The China Boy owes us payback."

Flores laughed. "Maybe you'll get your chance," he said. "Keep that little blade of yours sharp and ready."

Maria grinned back at him, but the humor never reached her eyes.

"My blade's always sharp and ready," she said.

"Man, there's something going down," another of the *bandas* standing by the window said. "Now it looks like every kid in the barrio's showing up out there."

Cruz nodded. "And a hell of a lot of them wearing Malo Malo gear."

Around the pool hall various gang members got to their feet and started for the door.

"Everybody chill," Flores said. No one made another move. "I know you've all got this big hate on for Malo Malo, but right now nobody does a thing. We're just waiting on the China Boy—got it?"

The *bandas* wanted to ask why, but they knew better. They settled back in their chairs, on edge now, ready for anything.

Still standing by the window with Cruz, Sweetcheeks took out her cell and went online.

"The band's putting on a free concert," she said after a moment. "That's what all those kids are doing out there."

"Interesting," Flores said as if it was anything but.

He unfolded a newspaper and spread it out on the bar in front of him. Taking a sip of his espresso, he began to read the front page, just as he did every morning.

Lupita sat cross-legged on the roof of an adobe building across the street from the pool hall, surrounded by joking crow boys and an old turkey vulture. They'd arrived wearing their bird skins, but she'd had to climb up a drainpipe at the back of the building.

Now that she was here, she was having second and third thoughts about her part in this. There were so many people down on the streets—her own and the five-fingered beings—that it would be a miracle if no one got hurt. And inside the pool hall—how many *bandas* did El Tigre have in there?

The sound of truck motors drew her attention away from El Conquistador. North on Camino Presidio she saw two flatbeds approaching. She recognized the members of Malo Malo and their friends. There was no traffic this early, but she was still surprised when the drivers parked their trucks back-to-back, blocking the street. The Malo Malo fans surged forward. There were maybe a hundred of them—with a few cousins boosting their number—and they crowded close to the front of the makeshift stage.

Lupita watched the band haul a pair of generators from the truck beds and set them up to feed power to their equipment.

She turned her attention to the front door of El Conquistador, then back to the band. Any moment, El Tigre's gangbangers were going to come out to see what was going on. The two groups would be at each other in an instant.

She looked the other way down the street. Where was Jay?

As if in answer, a crow dropped from the morning sky, shifting into his man shape just before he touched the roof. He landed lightly on his feet. When he turned, Lupita recognized him. His name was Chico and he lived out in Crow Canyon, but he was often in the barrio.

"The dragon's on his way," Chico said. "I just talked to him."

"What's he like?" another of the crows asked.

"Not as big as I thought, but the dragon inside is full of fire."

The crow boys all grinned at each other.

They were actually looking forward to a fight between Flores and Jay, Lupita realized. Didn't they see how it could all go so wrong?

This was all Rita's fault.

No, that wasn't true. Rita might have convinced her to push Jay into this confrontation with El Tigre, but

Lupita herself was the one who'd agreed. And then she'd had the bright idea of gathering a bunch of cousins and five-fingered beings to watch the show.

She'd thought she was doing the right thing. She'd thought that this was what taking responsibility was all about. Making a change. Standing up to what was wrong. But when it all went wrong, it would be on her. She was going to be responsible for whatever happened when the gangbangers confronted the cousins and Malo Malo and their fans.

"This isn't how it was supposed to go," she said. "Somebody's going to get hurt."

Chico turned to her. "Damn straight, and his name is El Tigre. That dragon's going to shut him right down."

"But what if he doesn't? What if El Tigre wins and he sics his *bandas* on us and all those kids down there?"

"Too late to worry about that now," the old turkey vulture said in a rasping voice.

He pointed down the street. A couple of blocks north, Jay had stepped onto Camino Presidio. From the Malo Malo stage an electric guitar played a few bars from a spaghetti western soundtrack and all the crow boys laughed and pumped their fists.

When he turned onto Camino Presidio, Jay was surprised at all the people on the street. He got the little *ping* in his head from dozens and dozens of cousins, but there were also all kinds of teenagers, too. As he got closer, he saw that most of them were wearing Malo Malo gear. Then he noticed the two trucks parked back-to-back, blocking the street. And there were Malo Malo themselves, looking like they were about to play a concert. He spotted Rosalie, sitting on instrument cases at the back with the rest of the band's friends. There was Ramon right up front. Luis. Gilbert and Hector. A new drummer.

And Anna.

He started to turn away, but her gaze found his over the heads of the crowd at the front of the stage. She gave him a nervous smile and played a couple of lines of the theme from "A Fistful of Dollars," letting her guitar ring on the last note. He couldn't help but smile. He gave her a thumbs-up and she returned the gesture with both hands.

What was up with that? he wondered. The last time he'd seen her, she'd wanted to punch him in the face.

He'd have to figure it out later. If there *was* a later.

Because now he was here. There was no turning back. There was El Conquistador and he could feel the big-time *ping* of El Tigre inside. And then the door opened and they started to come out, the gangbangers with their tats and their colors. There were almost two dozen of them, male and female, mostly Mexican, but a few blacks, a couple of white guys, and one Asian. They carried baseball bats and chains and knives. A couple had handguns, held down along the sides of their legs. One of them had a machete.

They spread out in a line along the front of the pool room, and then Flores stepped outside with his lieutenant Cruz on one side and—

Jay blinked in surprise.

Maria was on the other. She gave him such a cold look it was hard for him to remember her as anything but this hard-ass *bandas* girl. It was as though they'd never talked outside Señora Elena's house yesterday.

"You go, dragon boy!" somebody yelled from the crowd.

"Yeah, kick some tiger ass!"

The crowd gave a half cheer until El Tigre looked up and down the street and everybody fell silent, realizing that if El Tigre killed Jay they'd have to face his displeasure.

Jay didn't blame them for being cautious. Maybe Abuelo was right. Maybe he should have snuck up and ambushed El Tigre instead of playing the big man, looking for a showdown on Main Street. Because who was he kidding? As his gaze met El Tigre's, he knew he didn't have the killer instinct to take Flores down.

But then the cool, hard look in El Tigre's eyes faded, and he smiled.

"Jay," he said. "I'm glad you came by so that we can have this chance to talk. I wasn't expecting an audience, but . . ." He gave an elegant shrug.

Jay wasn't fooled. He folded his arms and waited.

"Look," El Tigre said, "this unfortunate business with Alambra and the girl upsets me as much as it does you."

The muted sounds of instruments being tuned had been coming from the makeshift stage where Malo Malo was getting ready. It fell silent now. Jay could just imagine the angry look on Anna's face.

"I'm here to tell you," El Tigre went on, "that if you hadn't killed that idiot, I would have. You and I, we had a bargain, and I fully meant to uphold my side. I only hope we can put this behind us."

Now it was the *bandas'* turn to be upset. They couldn't have been surprised that El Tigre would punish anyone who disobeyed him, but it still didn't sit well with them.

"Why?" Jay asked.

El Tigre gave him a puzzled look.

"Why do you care?" Jay said. "Why does our having a truce, or it being broken, mean anything to you?"

"It's bad for business," El Tigre said. "It's just that simple. Crap like this goes on, it takes my attention away from making money. We had a bargain. One of my people screwed up, but I'm here to tell you that it's not going to happen again. We can make this truce work."

"No," Jay said. "It's over. What happened at the music hall is just going to happen again. Maybe not for a couple of months, maybe even longer. I don't know. But sooner or later another one of your gangbangers is going to hurt somebody else because you can't really control them. I don't think anybody can."

"You're making a—" El Tigre began, but Jay cut him off.

"A mistake? I don't think so. You're running with a bunch of sociopaths who don't care about anything except themselves. You can't reason with freaks like that. So it's time to shut this whole thing down."

El Tigre's eyes narrowed, though he kept the smile on his face.

"And you're here to do that?" he asked. "By yourself? Because don't think any of these cousins are here to help you. They've come to watch a show just as much as those kids came out to see one."

"I know. They're only here to witness."

El Tigre didn't say anything for a long moment. Finally, he asked, "Is this you talking, or is it the Yellow Dragon Clan?"

There it was, Jay thought. El Tigre's real worry was that he faced the whole clan, not just some kid with his dragon waking up inside him.

"Would it make a difference?" he asked.

Of course it did. But he was interested to see what Flores would say.

El Tigre shrugged. "Not really. I just want everything to be clear."

"This is between you and me," Jay told him.

"Good to know." He turned to his *bandas* and added,

"Who wants to get rid of this little piece of crap for me?"

Jay had been expecting as much. He centered himself, let his *qi* flow to the rhythm of the land thrumming underfoot. He called up the energy that had created fireworks in the sky in *el entre*.

He tried to watch all the gangbangers at once, but it was hard. He wouldn't use the dragonfire until they actually started their attack, but they were hesitating. He supposed they had a right to be nervous. Those who hadn't been at the dance hall would have heard in great detail what had happened to Alambra.

Then Maria took a step forward.

"Me," she said. "I'll do it."

Jay never saw where it came from, but suddenly her flick knife was open in her hand. Her gaze was fixed on Jay's, hard and dark.

"Well, now," El Tigre said. "Looks like the only one with any balls wasn't born with them."

He threw his head back and laughed.

In that moment of vulnerability, Maria turned, arm flashing, and the blade of her knife sliced through El Tigre's jugular. Blood sprayed everywhere. But El Tigre didn't fall. Instead, he . . . changed. He grew taller, broader. His dark skin was now covered with black fur. An enormous cat's head replaced his human features.

With one taloned paw, he struck Maria's chest with such force that she was slammed back against the wall of the pool hall five feet behind them. Her flick knife flew from her hand to clatter against the muffler of one of the choppers parked along the street. As she slid to the ground, her T-shirt blossomed with blood where El Tigre's claws had slashed her.

Jay stared, frozen in horror. It was like Margarita dying all over again. Her blood red against the white shirt. He saw her lips shape words that never came out. But he knew what she'd tried to say.

Guard her well.

Then her head slumped down against her chest.

Jay turned to El Tigre. Dragonfire flickered between his fingers. He had long enough to think: Flores isn't a tiger. He's a panther. A panther man with blood soaking the dark fur of his chest, turning it darker still.

Then he let the dragon wake up and a red film swallowed his sight.

"Okay, *that* I wasn't expecting," Señora Malena said.

In the lawn chair beside her, Elena gave a nod of agreement.

"Neither did I," she said.

Her gaze was locked on where her foster daughter lay crumpled against the wall of the pool hall.

"But she knew," Elena went on. "She knew all along."

Malena turned to her. "Knew what?"

Elena shook her head. "It doesn't matter."

But she'd read Maria's lips just as Jay did and she knew what they meant. *Guard Rosalie.* Which also meant guard her friends. Her family. This place where they all lived.

Elena turned to Rita.

"Fix this," she told the snake woman.

"I—"

"You made this mess. I can feel the dragon waking in that boy and while he might be many things, one of them isn't being prepared to control so much unbridled power. We need to bring the boy back into himself."

Rita glanced at the stage that Malo Malo had set up. She nodded.

"I think I know how," she said, and left the two old women in the doorway.

"That one," Malena began, then simply gave a shake of her head.

"She means well."

"So did my second husband, but he still managed to lose everything we owned on a rooster fight."

When Flores had dismissively referred to Margarita as "the girl," Rosalie and Hector were forced to restrain Anna. If they hadn't, she would have gone after El Tigre herself, then and there. But now the three of them and the rest of the band and their fans simply stood there, staring at the front of the pool hall. They'd been shocked enough by what Maria had done, but nothing could have prepared them for El Tigre's transformation into a literal giant cat man.

A giant cat man who was now turning his attention on Jay, who simply stood there in the middle of the street.

Except Rosalie didn't think Jay was just standing there. There was something going on. Flickering lights played around his fingers like miniature lightning bolts and he seemed taller, broader. That, and the flatbed of the truck was shivering.

"Do . . . do you feel it?" she asked Anna.

Anna shook her head.

"The truck," Rosalie said. "It feels like it's trembling— the way the stage did in the dance hall just . . . just before . . ."

Her words trailed off as she watched El Tigre stumble to sprawl facedown on the street. Blood pooled on the asphalt around his upper torso and he didn't move. The air was suddenly filled with a thick static charge. The gangbangers looked around. The ones with guns aimed their weapons at Jay. Rosalie couldn't see exactly what it was that Jay threw from each hand, but bright balls of light swallowed the guns. The men cried out in pain, dropping their weapons to the ground.

A crack appeared in the front wall of the pool hall, the adobe splitting, pieces falling off. The pressure made one of the windows pop, and glass sprayed onto the street. The man with the machete took a step forward.

Jay lifted both hands and pushed the air. The man flew back through the open door of the pool hall, landing somewhere inside with a huge crash. Then Jay stomped a foot on the street and more cracks appeared in the adobe walls of the pool hall.

"Oh, God," Anna said in a small voice. "He's really doing this. He's going to bring the place down just like he did the dance hall."

Before Rosalie could respond, a woman in a straw cowboy hat jumped up onto the stage. Rosalie had noticed her earlier, standing beside two old women in plastic lawn chairs.

"Unless we stop him," the woman said, "he's going to bring the whole barrio down. You've got to play something—loud and hard. We need to pull him back into himself."

Anna stared at her. "Who the hell are you?"

Out on the street, Jay stomped the ground again and the gangbangers' choppers started to fall over, crashing to the ground, one after the other. The *bandas* surged forward. But Jay seemed twice his normal size now. He threw more light from his hands. The fireballs exploded and the *bandas* scattered.

"Play something!" the woman cried. "Do it, or we'll lose him forever."

Rosalie didn't know why she trusted this stranger. She just knew that something really bad was happening with

Jay. And if there was anything they could do to stop it . . .

"Do it," Rosalie said. "Please."

Anna nodded, her gaze on Jay. She cranked up her guitar and played the opening bars of "El Barrio," one of Ramon's originals. She turned to face the band and gave a nod to Chaco behind the drum kit, stomping her foot so that he could pick up the beat. The bass drum came in, and then Ramon and Gilbert were at Ramon's mic with their trumpets.

"No!" Anna called to Chaco. "You've got the wrong beat."

Except he didn't, Rosalie thought. He wasn't playing to Anna's rhythm, but something from the morning air around them. It made everything feel solid and grounded. It was like he'd tuned into a heartbeat.

Anna picked up on it right away and changed what she was doing. The trumpets followed her lead. Luis turned up his bass and slipped into the pocket that Chaco had found. Once the trumpets were playing their part, Anna started to pick leads around them. Over by the turntables, Hector cued in a couple of samples from his laptop—the sound of an old truck starting up and the twittering of morning birds that he'd restructured into a trippy beat—then he lifted the arm on one of the turntables, brought it down on the vinyl and began to scratch a counter rhythm.

The woman in the cowboy hat pointed at Chaco.

"Slow it down!" she cried. "But gradually."

Chaco glanced at Ramon, then Anna. They both nodded in agreement. As he brought the beat down, the whole band echoed the slowing rhythm with him—guitar and bass, trumpets. They played single strokes, emphasizing each one. Hector killed the feed from the laptop and took the needle off the record.

Rosalie could feel her own heartbeat slow down with the music. Her gaze had strayed from the street. When she looked back now, Jay was no longer so large—at least not physically. But there still seemed something big about him. It was as though his presence filled all the space between the buildings.

"That's good," the woman in the cowboy hat said. "Now bring down the volume, too."

Like Rosalie, her attention was also on Jay. She had her back to the musicians so they didn't hear what she said, but with the flat of her hand, she kept motioning for them to continue to reduce the volume. They followed her direction until the sound coming from the stage was no more than a muted echo of the original thundering heartbeat.

In front of the stage, and up and down the street, the Malo Malo fans and cousins were caught in the spell. The monotonous rhythm the band now played in unison should have been boring. Instead, it filled an empty place inside them that they hadn't even known was there, connecting them to each other through its pulsing heartbeat. They bobbed their heads in time and smiles filled their faces. Here and there, some of the cousins began shuffling dances, stirring up the dust on the street. Up on the rooftops, the crow boys followed suit and happy cries of "Hey-ya, hey-ya!" came drifting down.

But whatever this connection was, it didn't have the same effect on the gangbangers. As Jay drew the fury of the dragon back into himself, their courage rose in direct proportion. They collected themselves from where they'd been scattered by Jay's fireballs. Picking up dropped weapons, they started toward him, Cruz in the lead.

"No," Jay said. "This stops here."

His voice was quiet, but it carried throughout the street. Everything stopped. The band, the movement of the kids and cousins. They all turned to where Jay stood over the body of El Tigre, facing the gangbangers. Even the crow boys fell still, standing on the edges of the rooftops, looking down.

Cruz shook his head. "The only thing you're going to stop is the blade of my knife."

Jay didn't say anything. The tiny lights began to flicker around his fingers again. The *bandas* shifted nervously, all except for Cruz.

"Throwing fireworks only works once, kid," Cruz said. "I know what's up. You can't pull the same scam twice and expect to get away with it."

Jay still didn't respond. That big presence Rosalie could sense in him swelled larger once more. She hoped he wasn't losing himself to the dragon again and gave the woman with the cowboy hat a nervous look. But the woman only smiled.

Before he'd allowed the dragon's red anger to swallow him, Jay had been pretty sure he was going to die. El Tigre had already killed Maria and it was pretty obvious he would be next. So he might as well make his own death count for something.

He no longer cared how much force he used or how many of El Tigre's men he took out before he died. El Tigre should have been finished when Maria had cut his throat. Instead, he'd changed into his animal shape as though the wound meant nothing, then simply swatted her aside, shattering her chest with one bone-crushing blow.

When El Tigre had turned to him, Jay had trouble focusing on anything except Maria. She'd probably known going in that she would fail. But she'd still been willing to try. That was true bravery. And even dying, even unable to use her voice, she'd mouthed her message to him.

Guard her well.

He wasn't sure if Maria had meant Rosalie, Señora Elena, or the desert itself from which the barrio had grown. That didn't matter, either. He'd have done his best for all of them. But he wasn't going to get the chance. The monstrous panther man that El Tigre had become was going to kill him first.

Knowing he didn't have a chance brought Jay an odd calm. He wouldn't call it bravery so much as an acceptance of the inevitable. He'd take his cue from Maria and go down fighting. Let the dragon level the pool hall and kill as many of the gangbangers as he could before El Tigre got him, too.

Except then the panther man pitched forward to lie still on the street, blood pooling on the dusty asphalt around the body.

And everything changed.

Whatever it had been that held him apart from the spirit of the land disappeared as suddenly as though someone had reached into his head and thrown a switch. The medicine flooded him, and he felt connected to everything in these small acres of desert. He knew every being that stood among the adobe buildings and cacti, every bird that flew its skies, every mesquite and saguaro and prickly pear, every stretch of dry dirt and scrub. And the connection kept expanding and deepening until it was all a huge noise in his head.

He knew everything, and nothing. From the Hierro Madera Mountains, through the barrio, to the far desert beyond. From the dry bed of the San Pedro River south to the border of Mexico. He could see and hear and smell it all at the same time and the barrage on his senses left him unable to pick out individual detail. It was one enormous rush of input.

He knew something was wrong.

He remembered the threat of El Tigre.

But El Tigre was dead, so what was the threat now?

He could remember letting the dragon wake up, but he had no idea if it had, or what it was doing.

He knew what Rita and Abuelo and even Lupita had said, but the dragon still seemed separate from him. He tried to find it in the overwhelming barrage of stimuli but it was hopeless.

He could remember Maria. He could almost see her body lying crumpled against the wall of the pool hall, chest crushed in, her T-shirt blossoming with blood. Or was he thinking of Margarita, murdered in the pool hall, the blood on *her* shirt? A thousand other images flickered through his mind in a headlong rush and he couldn't hold on to only one.

But he could see the blood.

Margarita's—no, Maria's. El Tigre had killed Maria.

The blood . . .

Like the red haze of anger that had loosed the dragon.

He could feel himself falling deeper into the bewildering, spinning morass of sensory input.

The dragon.

What was the dragon doing?

You know that you and the dragon are one and the same, right? he could hear Rita say in his memory. *It's part of who you are.*

Okay. Then what was *he* doing?

But it was too late to figure that out. He could no longer separate himself from everything else in the barrio. Every human, every cousin, every creature that *wasn't* a cousin, every plant, rock, arroyo, and dry riverbed—he was one and the same with them all now. He couldn't get away from the overwhelming press of them for long enough to focus on who he was, or what the dragon was doing. There was only the long fall into otherness.

Falling . . . falling . . . falling . . .

He tried to grab on to something—*anything*—that would allow him to get back into himself, but the spinning pressure of the thousand thousand others inside him ran rampant, all connected and there was no way to tell one from the other. No way to tell who he was, or where he was, or what he—

No, *the dragon*.

—was doing.

But it wouldn't be anything good. He remembered letting it wake up. And it—

No, *he*.

—had been seriously pissed. Right now it was probably destroying the barrio. And that meant *they* were going to show up soon—Paupau and the other dragons that had come with her after the dance hall was destroyed. They'd know he was out of control this time. They'd come to shut him down the way Lupita said the feathered serpents did.

He wasn't sure he even cared anymore. Because he couldn't live like this. If this was what it meant to be connected to everything in the barrio, he couldn't deal with it. He didn't see how anybody could.

But others had, hadn't they? Señora Elena had done

it. Even El Tigre, who shouldn't have been allowed to call himself that, since he wasn't even a tiger.

He supposed they were just stronger than him.

Because he was lost now and there was no way back.

Except . . . except . . .

The whisper of something pure crept through the chaos.

It was a singular sound and he knew he'd heard it before, but he couldn't remember where, or what it was. He focused hard on it, trying to hold on to its elusive sound. And then he recognized what it was.

An electric guitar . . . and trumpets?

Yes, trumpets.

Bass and drums, pounding a beat that the guitar and trumpets fought with for a moment, then joined.

A needle scratching on vinyl.

Malo Malo, he thought. This was one of Ramon's songs. The band must be playing somewhere.

Then he remembered seeing them on Camino Presidio, set up on the flatbeds of a couple of big trucks.

The music pulled him out of the morass. The quickened pulse of the music slowed and slowed until it was the same heartbeat that he'd first heard when he stepped out of *el entre*.

And as suddenly as he'd been lost, he was himself again.

Himself, but *more*. Still connected to it all, still a part of everything within this stretch of desert, but himself.

He could keep it as a background hum—the way he used to keep the rustle of scales in the back of his mind—or he could zoom in on one cacti, one adobe building, one person. . . .

He didn't know how he could have been so lost. Everything was in its place and he stood at the hub of the great wheel made of all their multiple presences. The medicine came up out of the ground right under him, from the wheel's hub, and filled him—not so much with power as with energy. The guardian of the barrio wasn't supposed to destroy things. He or she was here to keep everything connected. But he could destroy something if he needed to.

His eyes snapped open.

There was El Tigre. Still in the shape of some kind of panther man. Still dead.

There was the pool hall, its adobe cracked, the windows popped, shattered glass scattered on the pavement.

And there was Maria . . .

Movement distracted him. He saw the *bandas* gathering their courage. They were picking up weapons that the dragon must have knocked from their hands. Cruz was in front, the morning sun shining bright on the crown and devil's horns tattooed on his forehead. They were ready to start the cycle of violence all over again.

"No," Jay told them. "This stops here."

Cruz shook his head. "The only thing you're going to stop is the blade of my knife."

The morning chorus of birds could be heard from the next street over, oblivious to the drama playing out here. A block away, a young mother was nursing her newborn daughter. On the edge of town, a man paused as he opened his garage to take in the beauty of the sun coming over the mountains. At the lip of an arroyo, a roadrunner spread out its wings to capture the warmth.

Jay sighed. The morning was perfect. How could the *bandas* be so focused on shedding blood? It was so frustrating that they couldn't be made to see that their time here was done. Jay's annoyance with them made dragonfire flicker around his fingers.

Cruz wasn't impressed. "Throwing fireworks only works once, kid. I know what's up. You can't pull the same scam twice and expect to get away with it."

Jay met the gangbanger's gaze and held it for a long moment.

"You misunderstood me," he said. "I wasn't asking for the violence to stop. I'm telling you it *has* stopped. You're alone in your lust for it."

"What the hell are—"

"You think that knife of yours is thirsty for blood?" Jay broke in before Cruz could finish. "It's as tired of the violence as I am."

Jay remembered Abuelo telling him, *Dragons are rare creatures, Jay. Your elemental spirit embraces all the elements. Fire and water, rock and air.*

He called on air now. A wind, narrow and focused, plucked the knife from Cruz's hand and sent it clattering down the pavement.

Cruz took a step forward, stopping when Jay held up his hand.

"This is the way it's going to be," Jay said. "No more gangs. No more drugs. No more violence. If you want something to occupy your time . . ."

He made a sweeping motion with both arms and the long row of motorcycles and low riders parked in front of the pool hall literally fell to pieces. Metal crashed and clanged as it banged against other pieces and hit the pavement. Bolts and screws and nuts went rolling in all directions. The vehicles in the parking lot weren't spared.

"You can play with your rides," Jay said.

The other *bandas* started to edge away, but Cruz held his ground.

"You think you can clean up the barrio, man?" he said. "You think you're the first to try? They all try. The *policía*. The do-gooders. Nothing takes. You can't get rid of us. This is *our* place. *Our* home."

Jay shook his head. "I'm not cleaning it up. This place is already all it should be. It's just that somebody forgot to take out the trash."

Cruz snarled and lunged forward, taking a swing at Jay. But before his fist could connect, Jay called on a wind that picked the gangbanger up and flung him hard against the cracked adobe of the pool hall.

"When I said no more violence," Jay said, his voice still mild, but carrying to all parts of the street, "I didn't mean that I wouldn't enforce the rule."

He looked away from where Cruz lay, his gaze taking in one side of the street, then the other.

"Everybody clear on this?" he asked. "Anybody breaks these rules and I'll know. Don't think I won't. You even fart, and I'll know. And you don't get three strikes. Mess up once, and you're gone. Anybody have any questions?"

All the gangbangers had slipped away now except for Cruz, who was still trying to catch his breath.

"So no more fun?" a voice called from one of the rooftops.

Jay looked up to the crow boy standing there.

"You need to hurt people to have fun?" he asked.

The crow boy shook his head.

"Then you've got nothing to worry about, do you?"

Jay turned away and walked over to the pool hall. He ignored El Tigre's body, just as he ignored Cruz, but he was still aware of them, just as he was aware of everything on the wheel that was this piece of the desert. He knelt down by Maria's body and brushed the hair away from her eyes. Then he reached out with thumb and forefinger and gently pulled her lids down.

He realized that she hadn't done this just for the barrio, or to keep Rosalie safe. She'd done it as much for him as well. So that his guardianship wouldn't be tainted with El Tigre's death.

Would he have been able to take El Tigre? Before, he wasn't sure. The dragon part of him had power, but he had no fighting skills. But now . . . now he could snuff out even a creature as powerful as El Tigre without breaking a sweat.

Now, when it was too late to help Maria.

He became aware of Rosalie jumping down from the makeshift bandstand and approaching. Picking Maria up, he cradled her against his chest as he turned to face Rosalie.

"She . . . she's dead, isn't she . . . ?" Rosalie said.

Jay nodded.

Rosalie's eyes glistened. She reached out with a trembling hand, but Jay pulled back so that she couldn't touch Maria's body.

"No," he said. "You don't get to feel remorse now."

Rosalie gave him a surprised look. "What do you mean?"

But Jay had already stepped away into *el entre* and she was only speaking to the air.

Malena Gracia turned in her lawn chair to look at Señora Elena.

"You should have taken my bet," she said, "though I'm glad you didn't."

Elena shook her head. "I still don't—"

"Gamble on people's lives. I know. You already said that." Malena hesitated, then added, "Are you going to let him just take her body away like that?"

"Why would I stop him?"

"The question is, could anybody stop him?" Malena said. "But that's not what I meant. Shouldn't Maria be laid to rest here in Santo del Vado Viejo, with the rest of her kin?"

"She has no kin except for me, and I'm not dead yet."

Malena hesitated again, then said, "Maybe not, but you look like you're standing right at La Santa Muerte's door, ready to join this foster daughter of yours."

"I . . ." Elena sighed and fell silent.

Malena didn't press her. She looked across the street to where El Tigre's body lay, marveling again at how all it had taken to lay him low was one five-fingered being and the sharp blade of her knife. But the humans living in this barrio would never really know what she'd done. If they did, they'd make her a saint.

Her gaze shifted to the ruin of the *bandas'* motorcycles and low riders, all those fancy machines. That was something you didn't see often—a cousin who could talk to the elements and get them to do a favor like this for them. She was going to have to study up on the Yellow Dragon Clan, see what else they were capable of.

Elena shifted in her chair and the plastic creaked ominously in its aluminum frame.

"I didn't think it would be like this," she said finally.

Malena turned away from El Tigre's body to look at her. "Be like what?"

"That I would feel the way I do. Letting go of my

responsibilities . . . I thought I would feel only relief. That this great weight would be lifted."

"And it hasn't?" Malena asked.

"Yes and no. The truth is I never really thought it through."

"I don't understand."

"While Flores stole the potency of the medicine from me, he never took away the medicine itself. I could still feel the land and every being that lived in it. But that *is* gone now. It all went to Jay."

"You have *nothing*?"

"Only the memory of how it felt."

Malena reached out and took her hand. She looked again at El Tigre's body.

"That is a terrible price to have had to pay," she said.

A price she didn't think she would ever have had the courage to pay. Because how do you continue after such a loss? To be a part of everything and then to be trapped only within the confines of your own skin.

She thought that perhaps Maria had got the better part of the bargain.

Rita looked over the silent crowd as Jay stepped away into *el entre* carrying the body of Señora Elena's foster daughter in his arms. She knew the five-fingered beings who had come to see Malo Malo were stunned by what they'd witnessed, but the cousins were all oddly quiet as well. She didn't blame them. That trick with the choppers and low riders was something she'd never seen before, either. She turned to the band.

"You should play something," she said.

Ramon's only response was to put down his trumpet and jump to the ground, pushing through the silent crowd to where Rosalie stood.

"Like what?" Anna said.

Rita shrugged. "Do I look like a music director? You're the musicians. Do whatever it is that you do. But those people down there, they need something real to focus on. Give them that, and if they're lucky, they can probably convince themselves that none of this ever happened."

She turned to the edge of the stage but Anna caught her arm before she could leave.

Rita looked down at where Anna's hand gripped her upper arm until the guitarist let it go.

"Seriously," Anna said. "Who the hell are you?"

"Does it matter?"

Before Anna could reply, Rita jumped down and made her way through the crowd. When she reached El Tigre's corpse, she picked it up by the scruff of the neck as though the body had no weight. She tossed the body inside the pool hall, glanced at where Ramon was comforting Rosalie, then turned her attention to Cruz. He scrambled to his feet.

"Traitor," he said, and spat on the ground.

Rita could only shake her head. "Why? Because I drank beer and tequila in El Conquistador, shot a few games of pool? That was supposed to make me loyal to you?"

Cruz nodded.

"You're *serious*?"

When he nodded again, Rita laughed. A snake's tongue flickered from between her lips. Then for one moment she let the illusion of humanity fall and a rattlesnake's head took the place of her own.

Cruz stared at her.

"Did you ever really think I was one of you?" she asked.

"I . . . I . . ."

"Here's the deal, Cruz. The new boss in town seems to be antiviolence, so I can't hurt you the way I'd like to, but if I were you, I'd make tracks and put as much distance between Santo del Vado Viejo and wherever the hell you end up. You know, before he comes back and makes an exception for you."

"Why would—"

"You think he's never going to find out whose idea it was to make Maria one of your Queens?"

"It was supposed to be—"

Rita cut him off. "Doesn't make any difference what was supposed to happen. It's because of you that Maria got into *la vida loca*. You think he won't figure out who made her life a bigger misery until she finally held a knife to your gut and you had to back off? I don't know if even a continent is going to be big enough to put between the two of you."

"Bitch. You're going to tell him."

She shook her head. "I won't have to. The stink of what you've done lies all over the barrio. When he gets back and starts to sift through the history of this place, he's going to know."

"I'll—"

"You won't do dick, if you've got any kind of brains left in that tattooed head of yours. Now run along like a good little gangbanger. Chop-chop."

Cruz hesitated until she let the forked snake's tongue slip out between her lips again. Then he backed away until he could slip out of sight. Rita listened to his footsteps receding before she crossed the street to where the two old ladies from the lizard clans sat in their lawn chairs.

"I'm sorry about Maria," she told Señora Elena.

Elena nodded. "Thank you."

"I had no idea she had anything like that planned."

"Neither did I."

"Are you going to be okay? Do you need a hand getting home or anything? Because you're not looking so good."

"I will survive. It's what we're good at, isn't it? Whatever inconveniences the five-fingered beings bring into our world, we find a way to go on as we always have."

"I guess. Me, I'm going to find myself some breakfast.

Think I'll go gringo this morning. Bacon and eggs. Home fries. You want to join me?"

"Not today, thank you."

Rita nodded. She glanced at Malo Malo. The band was playing some old Sonoran *ranchero*, the guitarist leading the band; their lead singer was still trying to console his girlfriend. She saw Lupita approaching and gave her a wave before setting off down Camino Presidio.

She was feeling a little buzz from how everything had actually worked out for a change, and knew that talking to the little jackalope girl was only going to bring her down. As she walked, she wondered what Malo Malo was going to sing about now. With Jay on the job to clean up the barrio, they'd pretty much have to come up with a whole new repertoire.

"Why would he do that?" Rosalie said into Ramon's shoulder. "Why would he say that and then just disappear?"

Ramon held her close and stroked her hair.

"I don't know, Rosie. We were pretty harsh, the last time we saw him."

"It's not what you said, it's what you did," a familiar voice said.

Rosalie stepped back from Ramon to see Lupita standing nearby. There was something different about the little jackalope girl, but it took a moment to figure out what.

Then she realized that every other time she'd seen her, Lupita seemed to almost vibrate with restless energy. All of that was subdued now.

"What do you mean?" she asked. "What did we do?"

Lupita shook her head. "It's not my story to tell."

"I think I know what she means," Ramon said. "It's about Maria, right? She had something like this planned all along, but we just assumed she'd joined the enemy. We never gave her a chance to explain."

"You mean *I* didn't," Rosalie said. She turned to Lupita. "Is Jay coming back?"

"I don't know. He's awfully mad about what happened to Maria. Did you see how big his dragon is?"

Rosalie and Ramon shook their heads.

Lupita shrugged. "Well, at least he's got it under control. For now."

"Did Jay go back into that magic desert we were in last night?" Rosalie asked.

Lupita nodded.

"Can you take us there?"

"No. I mean, I could, but I won't. He wouldn't have left if he didn't want some privacy. We need to respect that."

"But—"

Lupita glanced at the stage; Anna was starting the band off on yet another traditional instrumental. The Malo Malo fans pressed up against the stage appeared restless. This wasn't what they'd come to hear.

"You should go play with your band," Lupita said, turning back to Ramon and Rosalie. "After all they've seen this morning, those kids could use something familiar and fun to bring them back down to earth."

"I guess," Ramon said. "But—"

"Go ahead," Rosalie told him. "I'll be okay here."

"I'll stay with her," Lupita said when Ramon still looked dubious.

The two girls watched Ramon make his way back through the crowd to the stage. The kids parted for him when they saw him coming. Some reached out and touched his arms and shoulders as he went by.

"He has something special," Lupita said.

Rosalie nodded. "But he never puts on airs."

"That's part of what makes him special. Malo Malo is going to go far."

"If it goes on at all," Rosalie said.

"Why wouldn't it?"

"Ramon always says that the band is like alchemy, a perfect mix. He doesn't want to be in a band where any member can go and just be replaced. It's always been everybody or nothing."

"And with Margarita gone . . ."

Rosalie nodded. "Yeah. I don't know what's going to happen."

Ramon was onstage now. He conferred for a moment with Anna and Hector, then Anna went over to the drum kit and said something to Chaco. He gave a nod and started a complicated rhythm on the snare, his gaze on Anna. She nodded, then turned to Ramon and the band jumped. The audience roared their approval.

"Well," Lupita said, "you could always tell him that if he lets the band fall apart, it's like he's letting the Kings win."

It was all Cruz could do to not break into a run. He felt like he had spiders crawling up and down his back until he finally rounded the corner of the pool hall. He stood there for a long moment, hand on the adobe wall, telling himself to calm down, just calm down, man. But it wasn't working. He took off again at a fast walk—fast enough to get his ass out of there, but not so fast that anybody watching might think he was running away like some little girl.

He should have been on his ride, a vintage 1966 BSA 650 Spitfire. He'd babied that machine ever since he'd picked it up as a wreck at a road show out in Linden and spent the next year rebuilding it to factory specs. But now it just lay in pieces in front of El Conquistador along with everybody else's rides.

Mother of God, what had happened back there?

Nobody was normal anymore. Flores. Rita. The Chink.

And Maria. Maria! He supposed they should have seen that coming—she'd been a stone-cold bitch from day one. Maybe it hadn't been the brightest move, jumping her into the Kings like that. Maybe they should have held out and got Sandro's pretty little niece Rosalie like they'd planned in the first place.

Except, would it have made any difference?

He kept going back to how the knife had just been yanked out of his hands.

And his bike. That sweet Spitfire.

Man, he'd never seen anything like what the Chink had done to their machines. The kid could probably have handled Flores as easily if Maria hadn't gone and cut his throat first.

There was serious payback due, but now wasn't the time. He had to think this through.

It wasn't like he was scared. He was just being cautious. And he was seriously pissed off. Especially with Rita.

Or whatever it was that Rita had become.

What the hell had happened? For a moment there he thought he'd seen a snake's head instead of her own. And that weird-ass tongue. He'd never noticed it before—but people were doing all kinds of crap to their bodies these days. Getting her tongue split like she had was just one more freaky thing that freaky chicks did.

He'd known all along there was something sketchy about her. He'd tried to talk to Flores about it, but hell, there was always something sketchy about him, too. Turns out he was right about the both of them because what the hell kind of monster had burst out of El Tigre's skin?

It was all too much like the fairy tales his *tío* had told him when he was a kid.

That's *exactly* what it was like.

The realization made the back of his neck feel like spiders were crawling all over it again.

But what else could it have been but—man, he didn't even want to think the word . . .

Brujería.

Maybe he wanted to ignore it, but the word whispered in his head all the same.

Magic.

Cruz wanted to believe that he didn't buy into magic. That he never had, never would. That it was all just bullshit, whether it was *los santos* like his *mamá* prayed to, or the Indian spirits that were supposed to haunt the desert and the mountains.

But he'd seen what he'd seen. Mother of God, *something* freaky was going down. And he didn't want to be any part of—

"Yo, Cruz!"

He jumped at the loud whisper that came from the alley he was passing. He reached for his knife, but it wasn't there anymore. Then he saw it was only Left Eye and he relaxed a little. Left Eye was pretty much a kid—sixteen, tops, Cruz figured—but he was lean and tough and always ready for a fight. He'd gotten his name after a drive-by when the bullet meant for his head glanced off his sunglasses, sending a shard of plastic right into the eye.

When he came out of the hospital, he wore a patch like he was some kind of Mexican pirate. A week later, two members of the Southside Posse were found dead in a ditch.

Left Eye looked up and down the street as he stepped out of the alleyway. He was carrying a baseball bat.

"What the hell happened back there?" he asked.

"No clue, man."

Left Eye slapped the bat against his free palm. "We've got to get the guys together. Inflict some damage."

"Yeah," Cruz started to say.

But then he remembered Rita's parting words.

I can't hurt you the way I'd like to, but if I were you, I'd make tracks and put as much distance between Santo del Vado Viejo and wherever the hell you end up.

He remembered the Chink's eyes staring right into him as his knife was plucked from his hand by . . . what? What had taken it?

Something the Chink had done.

The same thing that had trashed the long line of bikes and cars parked in front of El Conquistador.

Cruz didn't want that thing coming after him.

"Except we need to be smart about this," he said. "We need to find out just what the Chink and Rita are—"

"Rita? What's she got to do with this?"

Cruz shook his head. "Don't know. But she seems to be tight with the Chink and—"

She's got a forked tongue, he wanted to say, that matches the snake's head I thought I saw sitting on her shoulders.

But he finished with, "—we don't know who else is in

on this. I mean, you see what happened to our rides? Somebody had to set that up beforehand. A lot of somebodies, I'm thinking."

"But who'd do it? Not even those Malo Malo kids would be that stupid."

Cruz shrugged. "The 66ers? Maybe the Southside Posse?"

Left Eye's one good eye narrowed.

"Or maybe the cartel didn't like the job Flores was doing. Who the hell knows? But we need to figure out who and how many we're up against before we let them know that the Kings don't take crap from anybody."

Left Eye nodded. "So what do you want to do?"

Cruz looked down at the bat in Left Eye's hand. "I need to get me a stake. Let me borrow that."

"A stake for what?"

"To pay some rats to go sniffing around and figure out what's what. Whoever we're up against, they're going to know our faces."

"Yeah," Left Eye said, handing the bat over. "Good point. You need a hand?"

Cruz shook his head. "What I need you to do is hang around our people, see who knows what. But be careful. There's no way Maria was working on her own. We can't trust anybody."

"Aw, man. You really think there are other traitors?"

"Right now," Cruz told him, "the only ones I trust are you and me. Now get going."

Cruz waited until Left Eye took off, then headed for the liquor store a few blocks away. He wasn't worried about anybody seeing him with a baseball bat. People here were used to seeing the Presidio Kings walking through the barrio with weapons. Nobody was stupid enough to actually report it.

When he got to the liquor store, he took a quick look up and down the street, then went up the two steps and through the front door. The proprietor was a slender man with slicked-back hair and Elvis sideburns. And he was alone. He looked up at the sound of the door and Cruz smiled at the nervousness in the man's eyes. At least everybody hadn't gone loco. Some people still understood the Kings were still the real power in the barrio.

Cruz rested the bat on his shoulder.

"Give me your money," he said. "All of it."

"C'mon, man. I already paid you guys this week."

Cruz brought the bat down on the glass display in front of the cash register. Displays of jerky, matches, lighters, and candy fell with a shower of glass.

"Your head's next," Cruz said.

Jay stood on the plateau in *el entre* and gently laid Maria's body down. He heard a footstep behind him, but he didn't turn around.

"So," Abuelo said. "You're back. And I assume you won."

Jay turned to find Abuelo gazing curiously on Maria's body.

"Though not without casualties," Abuelo added.

"She wanted to see Aztlán," Jay said. "I never got to take her here when she was alive so I . . . I . . ." He started again. "She just wanted there to be peace in the barrio so she took my side. I hardly knew her, but she still wanted to save me from having to kill El Tigre. Did you know he's not even a tiger?"

Abuelo nodded, but he was regarding Maria's body with more interest now.

"*She* killed El Tigre?" he asked.

Jay nodded.

"But she's human."

"She took your advice and caught him by surprise. Like I should have done. Then she'd still be alive."

"Yes, and then you'd have won the cousins' fear instead of their respect."

"I don't know that it'd make that much difference. I didn't stick around long, but I can tell they're all afraid of me."

"Or simply cautious of the unknown," Abuelo said.

Jay shrugged. It didn't matter. Maria was still dead.

"Can you help her?" he asked.

Abuelo lifted his gaze to meet Jay's.

"What do you think I am?" he asked.

"I don't know. Some big power. Maybe one of what Lupita calls the thunders."

Abuelo shook his head. "If you compare me to the thunders, I'm the sound of a tiny pebble falling onto a rock."

"So you can't . . . nobody can . . ."

Abuelo stepped forward and laid his hand on Jay's shoulder.

"Some people call this desert the spiritlands," he said, "but the spirits of the dead don't usually linger here. They haunt their own world—usually the place where they died. We can't bring them back. Some have managed, but then they come back *wrong*."

"It's not fair. She should be alive."

"I don't believe in fate," Abuelo said, "but I know the wheel always turns as it is supposed to. We take many journeys. We face endless challenges. When the body dies, a new journey begins and who are we to say it is right or wrong? It's simply how the wheel turns."

Jay nodded and knelt by Maria's body. Abuelo crouched beside him.

"It's always harder on those who stay behind," he told Jay.

Jay nodded again. "Nothing's going like I expected. From the moment I got off the bus in Santo del Vado Viejo. Every good thing that happened to me just set me up for something bad. Every time I thought I was doing some good, somebody gets hurt."

"That's one way of looking at it."

Jay turned to him. "What's the other?"

Abuelo shrugged. "That people get hurt, yes, but many more are safe because of what you have done and will do. That what good things come to you should be cherished and remembered, seeing you through the times that are hard."

"You'd have to be really strong to live like that," Jay said. "I'm not that strong."

His gaze went back to Maria's still features. He'd never even considered a situation like this. Someone had given up her life for him.

"How's your head?" Abuelo asked.

Jay turned to him with a puzzled look. "What do you mean?"

"You've just had the weight of what? Thousands of other beings dumped into it."

"It was overwhelming at first," Jay said. "I was so lost in the wash of it. I didn't know what was me and what was everything else. But then I heard Anna's guitar and it brought me back."

"So the connections are gone?"

Jay shook his head. "No, they're all there—even over here—but it's like I've got a filter on it all. I have to think about making a specific connection, but I'm still aware of everything in the back of my head. It's just not all immediate and in my face." He shrugged. "I don't know how I got the hang of it so quickly. I guess it must be a yellow dragon thing—you know, all that training my grandmother made me do. Since we're supposed to be protectors, I guess we must have the ability hardwired into our genes, too."

"And you don't think that's strength?"

"Well, no. I mean, it's different, isn't it?"

Abuelo said nothing.

"Okay," Jay said. "I get it. It's just—oh, wait a minute."

He paused, head cocked. Then he stood up and vanished from the plateau.

"So what're you waiting for?" Cruz asked the proprietor of the liquor store.

Using the end of the bat, he tapped a piece of glass still attached to the counter. It fell, breaking into smaller pieces. The bat went back onto his shoulder.

"Well?" he said.

The man opened the register with shaking hands.

"Now you're just being an asshole," Cruz said. "You think I don't know you keep the real cash in your safe?"

"I—"

The man didn't finish. He looked past Cruz, his eyes widening. Before Cruz could turn, someone plucked the baseball bat from his hands.

"You got some kind of a death wish?" Cruz said as he turned.

But it was Jay Li standing there, and he wasn't intimidated. He took the bat in both hands and broke it in two.

Then before Cruz could move Jay brought the pieces down hard on Cruz's forearms. Bones snapped under the impact and Cruz cried out in pain. He backed into the counter, wanting to hold on to his arms, but he had nothing to hold on to them with.

Jay pointed one jagged end of the bat at his face.

"What did I say before?" he asked.

"Uh . . . uh . . . no more violence."

Jay nodded. "And what was going to happen if you ignored what I said?"

"Uh . . . I . . ."

Cruz couldn't remember, but he knew it wouldn't be good.

"I said you don't get three strikes," Jay told him. "Mess up, and you're gone."

"Right, right. I remember."

"So what do you do now?"

Cruz stared at the jagged end of the bat still pointing at his face.

"I . . . I don't know, man," he said. "What do I do?"

"You cross over to the north side of the San Pedro and you don't come back. And don't think I won't know if you try."

Cruz nodded. The rapid-fire drum of his pulse finally began to slow a little as Jay lowered the bat.

"You win," Cruz told him. "I'm gone."

"I know."

"But . . ."

Jay raised an eyebrow.

"You gotta know that they're going to be coming after you," Cruz said. "I mean, everybody. All the *bandas*, the cartels, hell, even the cops we've got in our pockets."

Jay nodded. "They're welcome to try. One at a time, or all at once. But guess what?"

Cruz shook his head.

"Tell them that they really don't want to get me pissed off."

Jay turned to the proprietor who was taking it all in with a look of amazement.

"I'm sorry this happened," Jay told him. "If I could compensate you, I would, but I don't have any money. I can only assure you that it won't happen again."

His gaze returned to Cruz. "You've got as long as it takes you to reasonably walk to the bridge. Don't make me come back for you. And don't think I don't know every-thing you've done. You don't want to see me again."

"Man, I need a doctor."

"They've got hospitals on the other side of the river," Jay told him.

And then he vanished.

"Mother of God," the proprietor said.

Cruz looked at him and the man took a quick step back.

Cruz shook his head. Like he could do anything with

two broken arms and that damned Chink on his ass whenever he turned around.

Cradling his arms against his chest as best he could, he went out the door. It didn't matter how careful he was. Every step shot a fierce jolt of pain up each arm.

It was going to be a long walk.

"Trouble?" Abuelo asked when Jay reappeared.

Jay looked down at the broken bat in his hands. He remembered the sound Cruz's bones had made as they snapped. He lifted his gaze to meet Abuelo's. Shaking his head, he dropped the splintered wood and returned to Maria's side.

"Nothing I couldn't handle," he said.

He sat cross-legged beside the body and explained what had happened.

"It's not going to end with that one kid," Abuelo said.

"I know. But it's what I have to do, right? I have to make the point until they get it and the people are safe. All the people—five-fingered beings and cousins. The land and everything on it."

"It's a big job."

Jay nodded. His gaze drifted back to Maria's features.

"If this were a story," he said, "there'd be some way I could bring her back. I could go on a quest for a magic jewel, or go look for her in the underworld."

"How do you know she'd even *want* to come back?" Abuelo asked.

Jay didn't say anything for a long moment.

"I guess I don't," he finally said.

"See, that's the thing," Abuelo said. "Everybody's got their own wheel. We can visit with them. Our stories can run together for a while. But the only wheel we can turn is our own."

"So what do I do?" Jay asked.

"We lay her to rest and carry on." Abuelo studied him for a moment before adding, "You've figured out how to talk to the elements now?"

Jay nodded again. "I guess being able to do that has a lot to do with the medicine I got from the desert."

"I think it's more a yellow dragon thing. But regardless, that means you can ask the stone to take her in. Her body will rest there, safe forever within its embrace."

Jay put a hand on Maria's cold brow.

"No," he said. "If we're going to bury her, I'll do it with my own hands."

Hours later Jay and Abuelo stood at the edge of the plateau, looking out at the mountains. Behind them, a stone cairn rose high over Maria's body.

"We should have said something over her body," Jay said. "Before we covered it."

"She's not here to hear you."

"But still . . ."

"Yeah, I know. Letting go is hard."

Jay fell silent again.

"I have to get back," Jay said after a while. "Are you sure you won't come? I could really use some guidance."

Abuelo shook his head. "Remember what I told you. If I go, it'll all fall to crap. That's just the way it is."

"But . . ."

"You don't have to be alone when you go back," Abuelo said.

"Who'd want to know me?" Jay said.

He wasn't being melodramatic. Maybe things were going to work out now in the southside barrios, but too many people had been hurt in the process. Maybe he had the same curse hanging over him that Abuelo thought hung over his own head. The problem was, Jay didn't have the option of bowing out the way Abuelo had.

He stepped out of *el entre* before Abuelo could respond.

The dark-haired man continued to look out over the mountains.

"Who?" he said. "Lots of people."

- 9 -

Everything works out in the end.
If it hasn't worked out, it's not the end.
—*ANONYMOUS*

IT TOOK ABOUT a week before the *bandas* finally got the message and cleared out of the barrios south of the San Pedro: Barrio Histórico. East Pueblo. Solona. South Presidio. All of them.

The lesson Cruz was forced to learn hadn't been passed on to his fellow *bandas* because he never saw them again. The gangbanger ditched his colors, crossed the San Pedro, and found a clinic where fake medical insurance papers held up long enough for him to get treatment. With casts on both arms, he caught a bus to LA and never returned.

It didn't matter. Wherever the *bandas* went about their business, Jay appeared and reminded them of his rules.

At a drug deal, he walked out of the shadows, destroyed the drugs with dragonfire and took the money, which he later passed on to victims of the gangbangers, playing the part of "the generous bandit" Malverde. He broke no more *bandas* bones, but he did personally walk them to the bridge and sent them north of the river with a strong wind at their back to keep them moving.

At a carjacking, he appeared in the backseat of the stolen Ford Taurus as the gangbangers were about to take off. He knocked their heads together, then reached forward and snatched the keys from the ignition. He vanished for a moment—stepping into *el entre*, then back out again—only to reappear on the street outside the car. When the *bandas* tried to get him, a strong wind blew them up against the adobe wall of a nearby grocery store and held them there while Jay explained their banishment. Then they, too, were walked across the Camino Presidio Bridge.

At a confrontation between members of the Kings and the Southside Posse, both sides were subdued and sent packing.

Any gang member who wore colors had them removed. Shirts and jackets were incinerated by dragonfire that never touched their skin. Scarves were snatched by the wind.

They didn't always see Jay, but his presence was felt from one end of his territory to the other. It didn't matter if the incident was large or small. Any deviation from his rules saw immediate reprisal and usually banishment.

Anyone who tried to return would find Jay waiting for them. Jay, or cousins like the crow boys who had taken to helping out where they could.

By the second week, the residents of the barrios could safely walk the streets. Their children could play in front of their houses without fear of a drive-by or the influence of the gangs. The shadow of the *bandas* no longer hung over them.

At nine o'clock on a Thursday night, Rosalie followed the last customers in La Maravilla to the door and locked it behind them.

"What are you doing?" Tío asked, coming out of the kitchen. "It's too early to close."

Rosalie sat down on a chair and shook her head.

"I'm too tired to work anymore," she said. "I still have my homework to do after we finish up in here and I don't think I've seen Ramon for more than a few minutes in over a week. You need to hire someone else, Tío. We can't go on like this."

"He'll be back. He's just seeing to the barrio."

Rosalie didn't have to ask who he meant. Tío firmly believed that Jay would return to them. Rosalie didn't. She remembered how he'd looked at her, standing there with Maria's body in his arms. And even if he wasn't mad at them, he was busy.

The stories went through the streets in whispers, how

something—no, some*one*—was clearing out the gang-bangers. They talked about it at school, in the stores, while filling their gas tanks, wherever the residents came together.

"He won't be back," Rosalie said. "I told you what Lupita said. These days he's like the big boss of the south-side barrios. Why would he still come to work here?"

Every night was busy now, but tonight had been par-ticularly hard. Paco was off sick, so not only did Rosalie and Ines have to wait on customers, they also had to bus the tables and take turns washing dishes. Tío didn't know it, but the only reason there were no customers at the moment was because at eight thirty, Rosalie had slipped out and put a CLOSED sign in the window.

"She's right, Papá," Ines said. "We have no life."

"I don't want him to think we've just forgotten him," Tío said. "I want him to know he can come back."

Rosalie wasn't sure if Tío actually understood what Jay had become. He hadn't been at El Conquistador that morn-ing. But even people who *had* been there didn't seem to re-tain what they'd seen. Rosalie had overheard kids at school talking about the great free Malo Malo gig, but there'd been no mention of a man turning into a panther, or dozens of motorcycles and cars falling to pieces.

She didn't know what had happened to El Tigre's body, but she had been there helping pack up the band's gear when a couple of trucks arrived and a gang of black-haired young men loaded up all the scrap metal into the back of them. She supposed they'd been cousins.

The peace in the southside barrios had even made the city news, but no one came forth to explain why.

"He's not going to come back," Rosalie said.

"But if he did . . ."

"You can give him a free meal," Ines said, "and tell him that you've hired someone new. For God's sake. It's not like he's the only cook available."

Ines didn't have a clue, but she had a point.

"We'll give it another couple of days," Tío said. "Whatever else he might be, he's also just a boy on his own."

"Papá, the weekend's coming. We can't *do* this on our own."

But Rosalie could see that his mind was made up. He turned and walked into the kitchen, and they soon heard the angry rattle of pots and pans. Rosalie reconsidered. Maybe Tío *did* understand what Jay had become and what he was doing. And he was probably right about being left on his own. But she didn't see how they could do anything about it.

"If he weren't my father," Ines said, "I would so quit on him right now."

Rosalie nodded. "Paco should be back tomorrow and maybe Anna or Ramon will lend us a hand."

Lupita had told Rosalie about the trailer in Solona that she shared. After work, Rosalie got Anna to drive her over. A beautiful girl with chestnut hair and large brown eyes answered the door. When Rosalie explained who they'd come to see, she called back into the trailer for Lupita.

"I kind of thought you'd be showing up sooner or later," Lupita said. "I expected it might have been sooner, but . . ." She shrugged.

"I was just trying to do what you said," Rosalie told her, "and respect his privacy."

"But now . . ."

"Oh, it's just my uncle. He's driving us crazy. He expects Jay to show up back at the restaurant any moment like nothing's changed. I know that's not going to happen, but I was hoping maybe Jay would go by and tell Tío himself."

"I don't think that's very likely," Lupita said.

"Have you seen Jay?" Anna asked.

Lupita hesitated a moment, then nodded. Rosalie caught the glint of moisture in the jackalope girl's eyes.

"What happened?" she asked. "Is he okay?"

"It depends," Lupita said. "For the barrios, for the people as a whole and the land we all live on, yes. Everything's fine. But for those of us who knew and cared for him . . ." She shook her head. "He's changed. He's all cold and dark now. He sees only his job, which he does very well."

Anna nodded. "Yeah, we hear the stories. The gangs are finished here."

354 ~~~ CHARLES DE LINT

"But he doesn't want any kind of personal relationship with anyone," Lupita went on.

Rosalie tried to replace the friendly, happy Jay she remembered with the one Lupita was describing, but she couldn't do it.

"Do you know where he is?" Rosalie asked.

"Seeing him won't do any good. He knows everything that goes on and if he doesn't want to see you, you won't find him. I only talked to him once, but it was like meeting a stranger. Everything that made him Jay is gone. There's only the dragon left."

"I thought they were one and the same," Anna said.

"They are. But you know how you have a different face for the different people in your life? Like there's your school face, and your band face, and the one your friends see? It's all you, but they're still different?"

Both girls nodded.

"He only wears the dragon face now," Lupita said. "Rita's seen him, too. She says it's because he doesn't want to be hurt anymore, because, like, who can hurt the dragon?"

"I need to apologize to him," Anna said.

"There's no point," Lupita said. "The dragon really doesn't care."

Rosalie pressed her hands against her chest but it didn't stop the wave of heartache she felt for Jay.

"There must be something we can do," she said.

Lupita shook her head.

"You know," she said, "if I'd known it was going to turn out like this, I don't think I'd ever have played the part I did in waking that damn dragon in him. I know it's a selfish thing to say, but I'd rather have my friend back."

Rosalie understood exactly what she meant.

"Doesn't this just suck?" Anna said. "I get exactly what I wanted, but I feel like shit. Those freakin' *bandas* screw everything up, even when they're gone."

Rosalie put her hand on Anna's arm.

"No, don't try to comfort me," Anna said. "Something had to be done about the 'bangers, sure, but I was the one who had to go all hard-line on some kid who never had a life before he got here, and now he still doesn't."

"It's not like you loved him," Lupita said.

Anna frowned at the jackalope girl. "I don't know what I felt. I just know I liked him a lot. But he also scared the shit out of me so I kept him at arm's length. But that wasn't enough, no. First I left him hanging, then I had to jump all over his ass, blaming him for everything that went wrong."

"You're still a drama queen," Lupita said. "Everything's not about you."

Rosalie could feel Anna's arm tense up. For a moment she thought Anna was going to deck the jackalope girl.

"You get a free ride on that," Anna said. "Don't let there be a next time."

Then she shook off Rosalie's hand and stalked away into the night.

Rosalie hesitated. She needed to go after Anna, but she could also see the tears welling in Lupita's eyes.

"She doesn't really mean that," she told the jackalope girl. "Well, she does, but she's got a short fuse about all of this because she really does blame herself. And she cares more for Jay than she lets on. She can be really fun and sweet when she's not, you know, all wound up."

"I . . . I should have kept my big mouth shut. . . ."

Rosalie stepped forward and gave Lupita a hug.

"I'm sorry we came over and upset you like this," she said into the girl's multicolored hair.

"It . . . it's okay. I don't even know why I'm crying."

"Because you care about him and you miss him, just like we all do."

Rosalie gave her another hug and stepped back.

"You're nice," Lupita said.

Rosalie ducked her head. "Yeah, well, if I was really nice I would have come by myself. I should have known that Anna would let her mouth run on before her brain caught up. She really does have a good heart, but . . ."

"I wasn't being much help."

"I wasn't going to say that. Don't beat yourself up about it. I'll come over again sometime and we can share the good things we remember about Jay, but right now I have to go catch up to Anna."

Lupita nodded. She waited until Rosalie was a couple of steps away before she called her back and told her the last place she'd seen Jay.

"The crow boys say he's still there," she added, "when he's not, you know, out saving the world."

"Thanks," Rosalie said.

She thought Anna would be halfway home, but she found her by the car, sitting on the curb, her face in her hands. She sat down and put her arm around her friend's shoulders.

"Are you going to be okay?" she asked.

Anna didn't answer. Instead, she said, "You know, she's right. I am a drama queen."

"No, you're not. You just feel things strongly. And it's not like you haven't had to deal with a lot of crap."

"And I'm such an asshole."

"You are an asshole," Rosalie agreed. "But you're not mean-spirited."

"I should go back and apologize to that kid."

"You can do that some other time. Right now I think she needs some space." Rosalie waited a moment, then asked, "Did you really mean what you said about Jay back there?"

Anna lifted her head and looked at the big cactus growing against the adobe wall of the house across the street.

"Do I love him? I don't know. Do I feel a little off balance and tongue-tied when he's around? Yeah. Could we have gone anywhere? Maybe, if I wasn't so stupid. But it's too late for any of that now, isn't it?"

"Lupita told me where Jay is—or at least where he spends a lot of time."

"Where? Can we—"

Rosalie put her hand on Anna's knee as she started to get up.

"We can check it out tomorrow," she said. "I don't care how safe the barrios are these days. It's still not a place I want to go in the middle of the night."

Jay couldn't remember who had warned him about the drug cartels, but El Tigre's bosses were quick in mounting an offensive. The same night that Rosalie and Anna went to call on Lupita, six black SUVs came up from Mexico, filled with gunmen. Jay had no idea how they got across the border with all those weapons. Money talked, he supposed.

He waited to confront them until they had left the freeway and were on a two-lane blacktop just south of the city. While they were still in the middle of the desert, he stepped out of *el entre* and waited. The first vehicle caught him with its headlights and slowed to a stop, the others following suit.

Before the gunmen could disembark from the SUVs, Jay called on the winds to help him again, and the vehicles fell to pieces, just as the gangbangers' had done in front of El Conquistador. He did the same with their weapons. Then he used his dragonfire to burn away their clothes, leaving the men themselves untouched. By now, he was so adept at this little trick that they didn't even feel the heat on their skin.

Naked, with a hundred small bruises and cuts, the men emerged from the wreck of their vehicles, hands cupping their genitalia. They might have been the cartel's elite, they might have only been gangbangers hired for the job—Jay didn't know or care. But whoever they were, they were cowed and helpless now.

"<Move away from what's left of your vehicles,>" Jay told them.

The men obeyed, moving gingerly onto the rocks and dirt at the side of the road.

"<Do you know who I am?">Jay asked.

The foremost man shook his head.

"<I'm the new rule around here,>" Jay told them. "<I'm letting you live so that you can go back and tell your bosses that the southside barrios are off-limits to them and the gangs. If they try to send anyone after me—it doesn't matter if it's one man, or a thousand—I'll know. And I will deal with them.>"

He threw a fireball at the wrecked cars and they were engulfed. Moments later, only ash remained on the blacktop. Hardened criminals though the men were, many made the sign of the cross.

"<Now go,>" Jay told them. "<Take my message to your bosses.>"

The foremost man hesitated, then said, "<Uh . . . Señor Brujo. How are we to return without clothes or cars?>"

"<You have legs,>" Jay said. "<Use them before I change my mind and deliver the message myself. In which case, I'd have no need of any of you, would I?>"

The men beat a hasty retreat, heading south along the blacktop. Jay wondered how far they'd get before someone would report a band of naked illegals to the authorities.

A lifetime ago, he would have thought that what he'd just done was the coolest thing ever. Now it was just another part of his job.

He stood there on the road, following them on the medicine wheel in his mind until he was satisfied that they were doing as they'd been told.

JAY

Back before the world changed, Rosalie took me to this abandoned shopping mall on the far east side of the city. I'd never seen anything like it. There was nothing there—at least not for anybody normal. It was all boarded up and covered with gang signs and graffiti. The parking lot was a dumping ground for junked cars and trucks, old fridges and stoves, and every kind of trash, all of it vying with the weeds, cacti, and scrub that had grown up through the pavement.

The *bandas* had shut the place down, she'd explained. There'd been so much vandalism and violence both inside the mall and out in the parking lot that the owners finally closed up and moved farther north. A chain-link fence had been erected, but that hadn't stopped people from getting in. Close to where we stood you could see holes cut in the fence. Farther on, where one of the access roads had originally led into the lot, somebody had obviously driven a vehicle right through.

"They call this the Ghost Mall," she said.

"What happened at the new place they built?" I asked.

"It's still there. It's out near those new subdivisions north of here."

"So why don't the *bandas* do the same thing there?"

"The people out there have the money to pay for their own *policía*."

"But—"

"This is the barrio," she said. "Nobody cares what happens here."

Rosalie told me that the gangs still partied and squatted in the mall itself—mostly the Southside Posse, but also the Kings and some of Los Primas Locos from the west side. It was also a place where they'd go to settle their differences, gladiator-style.

From where we stood outside the fence with her dogs, we could see a half-dozen motorcycles, a couple of low riders, and one pickup, jacked up on monster wheels. We didn't see any of the *bandas* themselves, but the vehicles told us they were there, probably inside the mall.

We didn't go in.

Rosalie never actually came out and said why she had brought me to see this place, but it wasn't hard to figure out. She wanted me to see the influence of the *bandas* at its worst. She wasn't on me as much as Tío about how the barrios needed to be cleaned up, but it seemed every day I'd be made aware in one subtle way or another. I'd felt guilty at the time that I couldn't help, but that was the old me, back before I figured out how to do the job I'd been sent to do. Before I assumed my place as a member of the Yellow Dragon Clan and accepted my responsibilities here.

I stand now in the same place that Rosalie and I did all those weeks ago. The mall looks as hopeless as it did then, but there are no more gangbangers. There are no more of them anywhere in the barrios I've taken under my protection. Its air of desolation suits my mood. It's not *el entre*, which reminds me of how I miss Lupita, and it's not the Barrio Histórico, where Anna and Rosalie live. I won't accidentally run into anybody I might know. I don't want to see any of them. No, that's not true. I just know it's safer if I stay away.

I don't see that I can afford having anybody I actually

care about in my life. Not anymore. Not after what happened to Margarita and Maria. I also don't want to treat anybody the way Paupau treated me. I don't want to use people. And I don't want to have to worry about them getting hurt just by being around me. I'm just going to concentrate on my job. I made the choice, so I'm going to man up and stick to it without any outside distractions.

I understand now why Señora Elena just sits there in her living room. It's easier when you don't have to pretend to be human. I don't even want to take in my own version of Maria to look after me. With the way everything I touch turns to crap, it doesn't take a genius to figure out how that would end up.

I need to be like Batman or Zorro—just show up when there's a problem and fix it. You don't see them hanging around with anybody when they're not on the job. I don't know how Paupau does it.

The cousins probably know where I am, but they know enough to not come calling. I thought maybe Lupita would. I ran into her during that first week when I was still banging *bandas'* heads together, wandering around *el entre* in my spare time.

She wasn't like she used to be. There was a wall between us now. Something in her eyes that I couldn't quite name. I'd almost say it was guilt, but what has she got to feel guilty about? It's more likely she's just scared of what I've become.

I haven't seen her since.

It's better this way.

I've seen Rita, too. It was the night I stopped a half-dozen bikers wearing 66 colors from coming into the Barrio Histórico. I guess they'd come to check out things for themselves, maybe claim the old Presidio Kings' territory for themselves. I was in a bad mood—I'd been thinking about Anna all day—so I was probably rougher on them than I needed to be. I broke a few arms, gave one guy a concussion, trashed all their bikes.

I stood there watching them flee, stumbling in the dirt of the dry riverbed, when I became aware of Rita standing nearby. On some level, I'd known she was there all along, but I'd been working on keeping a bit of a filter over things. I want to be a flesh-and-blood alarm system, just letting *bandas* business alert me. I don't need to know what Anna's doing, or where she's going. I don't need to know how busy it is at La Maravilla or that Tío's still keeping a room for me in his house. Lupita might be crying in her bedroom, but that isn't any of my business. None of it is.

Just the 'bangers. Just keeping everybody safe.

"Well, look at you," Rita said. "Once you commit, you go all the way."

My gaze stayed on the *bandas*, climbing up the crumbling side of the bank on the other side of the dry riverbed.

"I'm thinking I should deal with the problems north of the river," I said.

"That's Jesus Abarca's territory," Rita said.

I turned to look at her. "And he's, what? Their version of Señora Elena?"

She nodded.

"Well, he's not doing such a good job, is he?"

Rita hesitated for a moment, then she asked, "Didn't your grandmother teach you that you can't fix everything?"

"She didn't teach me anything that had any kind of clarity."

"Well, you don't move into somebody else's territory unless they ask you for help. Abarca is from an old desert fox clan, and sure you could take him, but you're going to tick off a lot of people if you do. All you'll really accomplish is to piss away the support you've built up among the cousins."

I turn my attention back to where the *bandas* disappeared. I can't *see* them on the other side of the river the way I can here. It's only when they come sneaking back into the south barrios.

"I look across this river," I say, "which I still think is a stupid thing to call it, since most of the time it isn't even a river, and all I see is a place where the *bandas* can hide out in between sneaking down here and causing trouble."

"And I'll tell you one last time, you can't fix everything.

That's not the way it works. Maybe you dragons can hold a big territory, but you need to be a part of it, too. The thinner you spread yourself, the less good you'll do."

"I don't know. . . ."

"Most people would appreciate the peace instead of constantly looking for more trouble."

"It's not that."

I don't quite know how to explain. The *bandas* are a problem I can understand. I know how to deal with them. But there are lots of other little things going on and I don't know if I'm supposed to handle them, too, or what. A guy arguing with his girlfriend. That could escalate, but do I step in right away, or do I wait till something actually happens, if it even does? Or what about kids fighting in a school yard? Or the guy that loses his job and comes home to his family all liquored up?

Where do I draw the line? I know where Paupau did. She only dealt with the problems that were brought to her. Except that seems so reactive. Why not deal with problems before somebody actually gets hurt?

Only that doesn't seem right, either. So a guy goes out and gets drunk. That doesn't mean he's going to beat on his family when he gets home. So a couple are fighting. That doesn't mean it's going to escalate beyond angry words.

It seems so much easier to just go across the river and take on a new bunch of gangbangers.

"You have to be part of the community," Rita said. "Do

you think Señora Elena just sat around in her house all day?"

That brought me back.

"Actually, I do," I said. "I know she's doing it right now."

"That's only because she's still learning to deal with being cut off from her connection to everything. Before that she was always out and around."

"She was just sitting in her living room when you took me by the other morning."

"That's because she was expecting you." I could hear the exasperation in her voice, see it in her face. "Otherwise she'd probably have been at the *taquería* with her cronies, having some tea."

"Yeah, well, I'm not her."

She shook her head. "Jay, you're hopeless. What happened to the kid I first met—you know, the one with all the personality?"

I shrugged. "I can't turn back the clock. This is what I am now."

"Now I understand why Lupita is so depressed."

"What's that supposed to mean?"

"Look at you," she said. "I wanted to get rid of El Tigre and the *bandas* and I knew you could do it. But I didn't think it would turn you into a humorless robot."

"You said something about Lupita."

"That's right. I convinced her to help me get you moving against El Tigre. I told her how it would be better for you and the barrio if you could connect with your dragon blood. That's why she helped. So think how she feels about how this all turned out."

"You wanted a yellow dragon. Don't complain now because you don't like what I am."

She gave me a weary shake of the head.

"Let me leave you with this," she said. "If you don't actually experience the world, if you can't appreciate it for its beauty and the joy that can come from your part in it, you're going to turn into something just as bad as El Tigre."

And then she stepped away into *el entre*.

I looked across the river and wondered about Jesus Abarca. Maybe I should give him a warning that if he didn't clean up his act, I'd have to do it for him.

Instead I did what I guess dragons do: found myself a lair in this old abandoned shopping mall. Except I don't have any treasure to guard. The only gold I have is part of the image of the dragon on my back.

I didn't realize what a good brooder I was until I started living in the Ghost Mall. My life's pretty much this simple routine: I eat at *taquerías* on the north side where I won't be recognized, paying for my meals with leftover money that I took from the *bandas*. Late at night, I'll often walk through the barrios, from East Pueblo through Barrio Histórica, from Solona down into South Presidio.

Sometimes I stop outside Tío's house. The dogs will come up the fence to look at me, but I don't talk to them, and I don't go in.

Other times I'll find myself outside of Anna's parents' house. If Anna's practicing, her music makes me ache. But the dragon doesn't care. The dragon doesn't care about anything except our responsibility to keep the barrios safe.

Mostly I just sit in the central court of the Ghost Mall. That leaves me plenty of time to feel sorry for myself.

One day, close to two weeks after that morning at El Conquistador, I sense the arrival of someone familiar. I'm aware of her as soon as she gets off the plane, and I track her as she makes her way through the city from the airport, across the dry San Pedro River, through the Barrio Histórico, through East Pueblo, all the way to the fence surrounding the Ghost Mall. She stands there for a long time, before she ducks through one of the holes in the chain link and picks her way around the junked cars and trash to the mall. Soon I can hear the sound of her shoes in the marble hallway, as well as being able to track her passage on the medicine wheel I've got in my head.

She finds me in the central court, sitting cross-legged on the rim of what was once a fountain. I don't say anything.

"<Why are you in this place?>" she finally asks me.

"What does it look like?" I say, refusing to speak Mandarin. "I'm being a dragon."

"A dragon doesn't hide in a place of squalor such as this."

"Yeah, well, things are different now from what it was like in the old country. It's time you got used to it."

"Shame on you. Such disrespect."

"Maybe I'd feel differently if you hadn't turned me into this thing I am now."

"The blood of the Yellow Dragon Clan is a gift. Can you not see all the good you have already done in this place?"

I shake my head. "Sure. It's good for the barrios, but what about me? I don't want to sound selfish, but when do I ever get a piece of my life to live for myself?"

"You have a duty to—"

I cut her off. "Yeah, yeah. I've heard all that a million times. But I've gotten rid of the problems here, so what am I supposed to do now? You ask why I live in this place, well, where the hell else would I live?"

"*In* the community, so that its residents can easily come to you with their problems."

It's funny. One of her looks used to have me shaking in my sneakers. Now I don't care.

"So *now* I'm supposed to interact with other people?" I say. "You spend the last six years making sure I don't have a friend, that I don't live any kind of a normal life, and now you say I'm supposed to be a part of the community? Just how does that work?"

"You seemed to be doing well enough before your confrontation with that drug lord and his gangsters."

"We've got gangs in Chicago," I say. "We've got gangsters and all kinds of crap. How come you don't deal with them the way I did here?"

"The place we protect is not in service to us," she says. "We are in service to it. When we are needed, we will know. Or someone will come forward and request our aid. It is not up to us to judge right or wrong, only to keep the peace."

"But—"

"Yes, there is evil in Chicago. There is evil everywhere. But so long as the peace is kept, people need to be allowed to make their own choices. We serve the emperor."

"There are no more emperors."

She nods. "In that you are mistaken. Now our emperors are the spirits of the places we have chosen to protect."

"Yeah, that sounds great, except *I'm* the spirit of this place now. So I guess my job is to protect myself."

She sighs. "You have done very well for yourself here, grandson. You took up the challenge you were given and you came forth wearing the mantle of one of the Yellow Dragon Clan. I am very proud of you. But you are not the emperor. Yellow dragons are never emperors. We serve; we do not rule."

"There is no spirit of this place," I tell her. "Not anymore. There's only a medicine wheel of power spinning in my head. There's only me."

"Then you are not looking deeply enough."

"Could you *please* just say something in plain language? Just for once."

"I am speaking as plainly as I can," she says. "I don't

have your connection to this place. I cannot find its spirit for you."

This is pointless. Nothing has changed. We might both be big scary dragons now, but we're not equal. At least not in her eyes. So far as she's concerned, I'm always going to be the student who has to figure this crap out on my own. And if that's the case . . .

"You should probably go," I tell her.

"James . . ."

"No, really. We don't have anything to say to each other. Not anymore. We probably never did. You call me 'grandson,' but I've always just been this—what? Apprentice, I guess. This kid you could manipulate."

I can see a flash of anger in her eyes, but I don't care.

"You *are* my grandson. You will always be—"

"The kid that you and your other dragon buddies were going to put down if you decided I wasn't using my magical superpowers properly."

"That's unfair."

"But it's true, isn't it?"

"We wield enormous power," she says. "Because of this there must be certain checks and balances."

"Or you could just explain things clearly so that a kid like me doesn't go off into the unknown without a clue."

"The journey into our power that we must take—alone— that has always been the way of the yellow dragons."

"Well, then all I can say is that the way of the yellow dragons is pretty messed up."

I can see the dragon fire in her eyes now. She stands taller, her mouth a tight, stern line.

"What are you going to do?" I ask. "Attack me?"

"You have no idea how much—"

"That'll go over well with the others, won't it?" I say, cutting her off again. "Maybe they'll come and put you down."

For a moment I think she's going to make me listen to whatever new BS she's got to say, but she surprises me. All she does is give me a brusque nod, then turns away.

I track her as she leaves the mall. I track her all the way back to the airport where she sits glowering at her gate.

I'm not proud of how I treated her. I guess it all just boiled over—seeing her, listening to those platitudes that I've already heard a million times before. I'm not proud, but I'm not ready to take any of it back.

Except . . . except . . .

I can't let go of this one thing she said.

Now our emperors are the spirits of the places we have chosen to protect.

In this case, that'd be Señora Elena. She had been the spirit of this desert and the barrios that have been built on its skin. She used to be connected to everything the way I am now, but I took that away from her. I am the spirit of this place now.

Except . . .

I remember Rita telling me how all Señora Elena does is sit in her house, trying to deal with the loss. I just have to think of her and I can see her on the wheel and know that's still true.

I remember Señora Elena telling me she was ready to give up the responsibility. She'd said she welcomed the opportunity.

But maybe she didn't realize exactly what that meant.

I do. Yeah, I've got the big medicine wheel spinning around in my head. And maybe I feel alone, or at least disassociated from all these pinpricks of spirits that I can find on every spoke of the wheel, but that's my own doing, isn't it? Because I decided that I can't be with my friends anymore. But for all my whining and complaining, the bottom line is I revel in this connection to everything.

It's got nothing to do with the duty put on me by my yellow dragon genes and everything to do with how amazing the connection is. This sense of belonging, seeing how every little thing affects everything else, big and small and in between. I don't care that I'm at the center of it all. I care about how everything connects and I get to see it. I get to be a part of it all.

If I had to give it up the way Señora Elena did . . .

I realize I have to go see her.

I lose Paupau just as I'm walking up to Señora Elena's door. Her plane must have left the runway. I knock on the door. There's no answer—not the first time I knock, nor the second or third—but I know Señora Elena is inside. So I open the door and walk in.

I go through the kitchen and see her sitting in her living room, still watched over by Jesus on his cross on one wall, Our Lady of Guadalupe on the other.

"I'm fine, I'm fine," she says without lifting her head.

"I can see that," I tell her.

She looks up at the sound of my voice.

"Oh, it's you," she says. "I thought you were one of the neighbors, checking up on me. They think I've suddenly become helpless."

"Maybe they're just worried because all you do is sit in here."

She shrugs it off. I know how she feels. I've never liked people fussing over me, either.

"You're doing a good job," she says instead, changing the subject. "You've done Maria proud."

Just hearing her name hurts.

I try to keep the dragon to the fore. The dragon doesn't worry about personal things. He just does his job. But there are buttons people can push, names that kick right through the walls the dragon keeps around us.

So now it's my turn to change the subject.

"There's something I want to try," I say. "I don't want to explain it exactly, in case it doesn't work, but . . ."

She raises an eyebrow.

"But I was hoping you'd give me permission to try."

I'm doing such a bad job of this.

"This affects me personally?" she asks.

I nod.

"I know you can talk to the elements," she says. "I know the medicine wheel I carried lies inside you now. What new abilities have you uncovered in yourself?"

"None. I just . . ."

I should just tell her, I think, but then she smiles.

"So long as you don't try to change who I am," she says, "or have some bit of medicine that's supposed to magically cheer me up, I give you my permission to try your mysterious experiment."

"You're very trusting."

She shrugs. "You are my heir, and really, what do I have to lose? But," she adds, "if it doesn't work, I want to know what it was that you were attempting to do."

"Sure."

I call up the medicine wheel in my head. Finding Señora Elena on it is a piece of cake—she's sitting right in front of me. But then it gets trickier.

I talk about the medicine wheel like it's got weight and substance, as though it's this big wagon wheel turning around in my head. But it's actually far more delicate and complex. Instead of sturdy wooden spokes, I have millions of little threads radiating from me, each of them connected to every being or place, every cousin and five-fingered being and stray dog in the barrio, every dry wash and plant and gust of wind. If I don't think about them, I have no problem dealing with their presence. It's like electricity running through a house—you only think about it when you flick a switch. Otherwise it's just there. Same here. If I want to find someone or something specific, the little search engine does its thing and immediately connects me to the right thread.

But what I'm looking for now is the *memory* of one of those threads, the one that was broken when El Tigre died and Señora Elena gave up her connection to the medicine wheel so that it would all come to me. The intricate spiderweb pattern suddenly becomes a bewildering chaos.

It takes me a long time to find that one elusive thread. I don't know what Señora Elena thinks of me just standing in front of her, all my attention focused on a place she can no longer go. I can't look at her. I have to center all my attention on what I'm doing.

Time goes by—I don't know how much—and I sift through the threads with meticulous patience. Then finally I sense an echo, follow the echo through to the memory, unravel the memory, and there it is.

I get a little rush of satisfaction, but it's quickly replaced by a growing frustration because I can't get a grip on it. Every time I get close, it slides away through my metaphorical fingers, slippery as mercury.

My frustration is making things worse and I'm afraid that I'm going to lose it again. So I use the part of me that's the dragon. The scales whisper in my mind and he surges forward, snagging the thread firmly between the points of two enormous claws. We admire it for a moment, then we fling it to where Señora Elena sits unknowing. The end of the thread entwines with the one that connects her to the hub where I am and—just like that—now there are two of us at the center of the medicine wheel.

I open eyes I hadn't realized I'd closed to see Señora Elena jerk upright in her chair as though she just got an electric shock. Her features darken with a flush, her eyes widen.

"What—what have you done?" she asks.

But she knows. I can tell by the grin on her face and the blossom of pleasure I feel through our connection on the medicine wheel.

"I saw my grandmother earlier today," I say. "She told me the usual bunch of stuff I didn't want to hear, but one thing stood out and made sense: I'm a yellow dragon. I'm not an emperor. I *serve* the emperor."

"I don't understand."

"Sure, you do. There are no more emperors. So now we serve the spirit of the place that we protect. I can't be both protector and emperor."

"You . . ."

I nod. "You're the spirit and I'm your protector."

"I . . . I didn't realize such a thing was possible."

"Neither did I. But it's cool, right? This is what you wanted, to be reconnected."

She gives me a slow nod.

"How can I ever repay you for this gift?" she says.

I shake my head. "You don't owe me anything. It's my duty to keep you safe, and I'm guessing, happy."

She leans back in her chair with a contented smile. I can feel her reestablish her own connections to the wheel and decide to leave her to it while I make us some tea. When I come back from the kitchen, a steaming mug in either hand, she's settled and calm, the way she was when Rita first brought me around to see her. But I already knew that through my own connection to the wheel, and through it, to her.

"Now what happens?" she asks.

"I don't know. I guess we'll work it out as we go along. You're the boss again, but this time you've got me to watch your back."

She nods. "Why are you living out at the East Pueblo Mall? It's an awful place."

"I don't know. It seemed to suit my mood."

Which is lighter now. The dark cloud hanging over me has thinned—probably because things are right in the dragon's world now. He has an emperor to serve.

"You could live here," Señora Elena says.

I'm at a loss.

"Oh, don't look at me like that. I might be old, but I can still take care of myself. I let Maria look after me for her sake, not mine. The girl needed someone to take care of after all she'd been through. I'm only offering you a place to live, and the cousins are already used to coming here with their problems."

Maria.

Señora Elena's happiness doesn't take that pain away.

"Come with me," I say, offering her my hand.

Our fingers clasp and I take her to *el entre*, to the plateau and the tall cairn of stones that mark Maria's grave. Señora Elena's eyes fill with tears.

"She was such a brave girl," she finally says. "I had no idea how brave."

"Yeah, she knew I'd screw it up. She knew I'd either freeze, or explode—neither of which would have solved anything—so she took it on herself to deal with El Tigre."

"She made the choice," Señora Elena says, her voice gentle. "You can't blame yourself."

"You mean I shouldn't, which isn't the same thing at all."

"I suppose it isn't."

"I just wish I could have had the chance to know her better."

"So do I."

I turn to look at her in surprise. "But—"

"I had no idea she'd planned to do this thing," Señora Elena says, "so how well did *I* truly know her?"

We fall silent. Standing there on the edge of the plateau, we listen to the wind, and pay our respects for a long time. After a while I start to talk. I tell Señora Elena about the man I met here, how he taught me about the dragonfire.

"He called himself Abuelo?" she asks.

I nod.

"I have heard stories of this man, or one very like him. They say he is the son of one of the thunders and a coyote woman. Meeting him can be a moment of either tremendous good luck or bad, depending on his mood."

"I guess I caught him in a good one."

She nods. "Or he saw a kinship in you. He is as displaced a being as you dragons are when you are away from your homelands."

"I suppose. . . ."

I look away across the mountains.

"Rita told me about this man named Jesus Abarca," I say after a few moments. "He's the northside barrio version of you, I guess."

Señora nods. "I know him. He is a good man."

"I was wondering if we should offer him some help with the *bandas* up there."

"I think we need to clean our own house first," she says.

"But the gangs are all gone."

"Yes. But we still have poverty. We still have all the things that brought the gangs into being in the first place." She smiles. "Do you know what would be a wonderful symbol of hope and change?"

I shake my head.

"If you finished high school."

"Oh, come on. You've got to be kidding. I'm this—whatever I am now. How is anything I might learn in school going to help me with the job I have right now?"

Señora Elena shrugs. "Consider it. Think of how it will look to the barrio children. The dragon thinks it's an important thing to do. They will want to look big in your eyes, so they will follow suit. Perhaps you see no use for education, but it will be of great help to them."

"How would they even know I'm the dragon?"

She laughs. "There are no secrets here. Haven't you figured that out yet?"

I think about what it would be like. Different from Chicago, at least. I wouldn't have to hide the dragon on my back, for one thing. Maybe I could even convince myself I was living a normal life.

"I'll think about it," I tell her.

"Please do. Maria thought it was important. You could do it to honor her."

"Way to play the guilt card."

Her only response is a smile.

When we get back to the barrio I have to go take care of a couple of gangbangers who still can't seem to get it through their heads that they're not welcome south of the San Pedro River. They're at Rosalie's school, by the stands at the baseball diamond, trying to move some dope. It doesn't take me long, even though one of them is stupid enough to pull a knife.

I send them packing and climb up into the stands. Sitting up there, I have a good view of the whole school yard and the low, rambling adobe building that's Cochise Vista High School. I watch some kids run laps on the oval, but my gaze keeps drifting back to the school building.

The medicine wheel tells me Rosalie's in there.

I know there's still unfinished business between us, but I don't know how to approach her, where to start with it.

I end up going back to the Ghost Mall. I thought that by connecting Señora Elena back to the wheel my life would get simpler. That everything would fall into place and make sense. But all it's done is given me more to work through.

I'm not in the same mood that first brought me to the Ghost Mall, but for all its ruin, it's still a good place to be on my own and think.

"Tell me again why this had to wait until after school," Anna said.

She and Rosalie were walking east on Camino Senita, heading into East Pueblo. Anna had two dogs, one leash in either hand. Rosalie dealt with five of them, somehow managing to keep them all from getting tangled. Oswaldo walked beside her, too well-behaved to need a leash.

"I've already missed enough days as it is," Rosalie told her, "and with it being so busy at the restaurant, I haven't had the chance to catch up."

"I said I'd come by and help."

"I know. And I appreciate it. But that doesn't mean I can just keep cutting classes. Leave it!"

The last was directed at little Pepito who was at the end of his leash, trying to investigate a dead bird.

"I get it," Anna said. "But you know me. Once I decide to do something—"

"You just do it."

Rosalie looked ahead toward the ruins of the abandoned East Pueblo Mall.

"God, this place is still so creepy," she said. "Even knowing the 'bangers won't be there."

Behind the chain-link fence, the parking lot shimmered in the heat and seemed to stretch into forever before it finally reached the boarded-up mall. It was slowly being reclaimed by the desert. Weeds and scrub and cacti grew out of the pavement. But three tall saguaros that had once stood sentinel by the front entrance were lying on their sides. It had taken sixty, maybe seventy years for them to reach that height, but thanks to the gangbangers they were now dead and browning.

Anna led the way to one of the holes in the fence, and Rosalie let the dogs off their leashes, one by one.

"Okay," she said to them. "Go wild."

And off they went, running in circles, Oswaldo in the lead. Rosalie draped the leashes around her neck.

"Do you think Jay's actually going to be here?" Anna asked.

"Who knows? You heard what Lupita said."

"Yeah, and it didn't sound promising. If he wanted to talk to us, he'd have come by already and that hasn't happened. Considering how harsh I've been, I don't blame him."

"Don't be so hard on yourself. At least he didn't bite your head off the last time you saw him."

"What was up with that?" Anna asked. "You guys were always so tight."

"It's got something to do with Maria."

Anna shook her head. "I don't get it. Why does he care? He hardly knew her. And how were we supposed to guess that she was planning something like that? What kid our age spends a couple of years going deep undercover? If I saw it in a movie, I'd never buy it."

Rosalie remembered what Lupita had said just after Jay disappeared with Maria's body.

It's not my story to tell.

"No, it was more than that," she said. "I wonder if we'll get to ask just what."

"Well, heads up," Anna said. "Looks like you might get that chance."

Rosalie looked ahead to where Anna was pointing. The dogs had all run to the front entrance of the mall, where they sat in that patient half circle they only did around Jay, but he wasn't there. The girls looked at each other and quickened their pace. They'd almost reached the dogs when there was motion in the mall entrance, and Jay stepped outside.

Rosalie stopped when she reached Oswaldo's side. Jay didn't look any different than he had when he'd still been working at La Maravilla and living with Tío, nothing like the scary guy she'd seen him become in front of El Conquistador. But where she could have once fallen into an easy conversation with him, now it felt as though they barely knew each other.

That morning at the pool hall lay between them, punctuated by the terse dismissal he'd given her just before he'd disappeared. The only thing that gave her hope was that she could tell by the way he stood and the look in his eyes that he felt the same way.

It took Anna to break the awkward silence.

"I owe you an apology," she told him. "Big time."

Rosalie glanced at her. Anna was dressed in jeans and sneakers with a yellow shirt tied at the midriff, her red-streaked black hair tied back in a ponytail. It was a casual look, but Rosalie had sat in her bedroom for twenty-five minutes until Anna had achieved it. She remembered wanting to tell her not to lead Jay on, but she'd stopped herself, not quite knowing why. But now she understood, and she was glad she hadn't said anything.

Jay's gaze locked on to Anna's.

"No, you don't," he said. "You were totally right. I should never have cut a deal with Flores. I could have stopped it all long before anybody got killed."

"Except you didn't know you could," Anna told him. "I get it. I know that now. I just had my mind made up and couldn't stop carrying on like some bitchy drama queen, as your friend Lupita never gets tired of telling me."

That brought the hint of a smile. He walked over to one of the dead saguaro and sat on the ledge of the container that had once held the giant cactus. He snapped his fingers and the dogs all flowed over to where he sat, flopping on the ground around his feet, except for Pepito, who jumped up onto his lap.

"Things really got messed up, didn't they?" he said, scratching Pepito behind the ears. "I wanted to come see you guys, but I didn't know what kind of a welcome I'd get. I sort of still don't know."

Anna nodded. "Yeah, life should come with some kind of freakin' instruction manual. But knowing us, we probably wouldn't read it, anyway. Well, Rosalie would, but she's our resident saint."

That got another smile. Anna closed the distance and sat down beside him. After a moment, Rosalie did the same.

"I'd ask how you were all doing," Jay said, "but I already know."

Anna lifted an eyebrow and he tapped his head with an index finger.

"I'm connected to everything now," he explained. "I can tell where anybody and anything is, what they're doing."

"Even what they're thinking?" Rosalie asked.

He shook his head.

Rosalie tried to imagine what that would feel like, but she couldn't.

"Is it weird?" she asked.

"Not really—at least not anymore. But when all those thousands of connections first came rushing in, I didn't think I'd ever get back to myself again. I thought I was going to drown in them." He turned his gaze to Anna. "It was your guitar . . . hearing the band's music that brought me back."

"I'm glad we could help," Anna said. "But it wasn't our idea. Rita told us to play and then she conducted us like we were an orchestra."

"It still worked."

"Yeah." She studied him for a moment. "So we're good?"

Jay nodded.

They fell silent, none of them sure of where to look or what to say next. It wasn't as awkward as when Rosalie and Anna had first arrived, but it wasn't a comfortable silence, the way it had been when they used to just hang out together.

"Tío's still got your room waiting," Rosalie finally said. "And your job at the restaurant. I keep telling him that you've got no reason to come back but . . ." She paused. "What can I say? It's Tío. Maybe if you get a chance you could drop by and tell him. I think he needs to hear it from you."

"How would you feel if I did come back?" Jay asked. "Would it bother you?"

Rosalie could only look at him.

"Why would you even want to?" Anna asked.

"Why wouldn't I?"

"Well, you're some big-deal dragon guy now, aren't you?"

Jay couldn't seem to look at them. He focused his attention on the scruffy little dog on his lap.

"Knowing you guys," he said. "Working in the restaurant with Tío and Rosalie, hanging out with the band . . . that was the first time I felt like a normal person since I was eleven years old." He held up a hand before either of them could speak. "I know, I know. I'm not normal. But I can't tell you how good it felt pretending that it was real."

"But it *was* real," Rosalie said. "I don't know exactly what it is you are now—you know, in this other life of yours—but you're still just Jay, too. This guy from Chicago who's funny and fun and we all really like. I'd love it if you came back." She waited a beat, then added, "Even if it does mean I'll have to listen to Tío telling me 'I told you so' for the next couple of weeks."

"She's right," Anna said. "Can't you be both?" She poked him with a finger, grinning when he looked up at her. "It'd be like having this secret identity—just like a superhero."

He had to smile.

"Except it's not very secret," Rosalie put in.

"Well, no," Anna agreed. "Everybody's heard the stories." She paused for a moment, then asked, "Did you really take out a whole army of cartel soldiers in this big gunfight south of the city?"

"No, I—is that what they're saying?"

Anna leaned closer to him. "Well," she said in a conspiratorial whisper, "you tell us, Mr. Connected-to-Everything."

There was a moment when Rosalie thought it could go either way. But Jay laughed, the good humor lighting up his whole face the way she remembered it used to. And then they were all laughing, and all the distances between them seemed to go away, just like that.

"I've really missed you guys," he said when they'd all caught their breath.

"Me too," Rosalie said.

Anna nodded. "I just wish I hadn't been such a—"

Jay put a finger against her lips.

"We're starting over again," he said. "Or at least putting aside the last couple of weeks."

Anna nodded. "Maybe," she said, her voice serious, "we could go back a little further than that. You know, to before I started giving you the cold shoulder."

He studied her for a long moment and Rosalie wished that she could do his vanishing trick and just be somewhere else so that they could be alone.

"I . . ." He had to clear his throat. "Yeah, I could do that."

Anna bumped her shoulder against his. "Look at you, Mr. Cool."

"I wasn't—"

"Joking," she told him. "You *are* cool."

He gave a slow nod. Rosalie couldn't figure out if he was agreeing, or just trying to work out whether or not she was teasing him again.

"Just to be clear here," he said, "and it's the last time I'll bring it up because we're all starting over and everything, but what changed your mind? Is it because the *bandas* are gone now?"

"God, no," Anna told him. "I mean, it's great that they are, but this is . . . I don't know. I guess I was following the movie in my own head instead of the one that was playing out in the real world. It was totally unfair."

"You read my journal, didn't you?" he said.

Anna ducked her head, a flush creeping up her neck.

"Only because I made her," Rosalie said. "But I was just so worried about you and I thought there might be a clue or something in it that would help me find you."

Jay nodded, but his gaze stayed on Anna.

"So I guess you know how I feel about you," he said.

"Yeah," Anna said. "But we're all into the starting over thing, so who knows how you feel now. I mean, if that's the way you want it to be."

"You know it's not."

"I guess. But I'm going to be honest with you. I'm not a hundred percent sure I know how I feel. But I can promise that this time I'll . . . you know . . . be a little more open-minded about everything. God, I wish I had a guitar. Everything makes more sense when I've got one in my hands."

Jay smiled. "Rock goddess."

"Superhero."

They grinned at each other.

"So what are you going to do now?" Rosalie asked. "Are you coming back with us?"

Jay nodded. "And I'm thinking of going back to school. Here, I mean. In Santo del Vado Viejo."

This was a day of surprises, Rosalie thought.

"Really?" she said.

Jay nodded. "Señora Elena thinks I should, and I guess she's right."

"That name sounds familiar. . . ."

"She's the real heart and spirit of the barrio—at least south of your fake river. El Tigre took the medicine from her and I gave it back."

"So you're not the big boss?" Anna said.

Jay laughed. "No, I'm just the muscle."

"You've missed a lot of your year," Rosalie said, ever practical, "but I can help you catch up."

"I don't want to be a bother."

"Are you kidding?" Anna said before Rosalie could respond. "She lives for this kind of thing."

Rosalie punched her arm.

"Some protection here!" Anna cried.

Laughing, they gathered the dogs and headed back to Tío's house.

Later that night Jay walked down to the Vulture Ridge trailhead. The night had cooled, but it was even cooler in *el entre*. Following a thread on the medicine wheel, he took the trail up into the mountains, heading for the canyon and the big slab of rock where Lupita had taken him the first time. When he got there, she was sitting cross-legged at the very edge of the rock, looking out at the desert. She didn't turn around, but he was sure she knew he was there.

"Hey, Lupita," he said. "It's been a while."

"Oh, listen," she said without turning around. "Some big cousin is talking to the little jackalope joke."

"Okay, I deserve that. And I keep telling you: not a joke."
She still wouldn't look at him.

"I'm sorry," Jay told her. "I'm as sorry as the whole world and the sky above and the stars beyond and the galaxies beyond them."

"That's pretty sorry," she said, finally facing him.

"Well, I am. I shouldn't have been ignoring you. It's just that the last time I saw you I got the feeling you didn't really want me to be there."

"You don't have to be sorry," she said. "I'm the one who should be sorry. I'm the one who got you to go off into the mountains where you could have been killed."

"What are you talking about? I seem to remember you suggesting I take off for some other desert where no one could ever find me."

"That was just me being clever."

Jay smiled. "You mean like reverse psychology?"

"I guess. But I should never have done it. The thunders could have killed you."

"So why did you?"

"Rita kind of talked me into it. And I knew you couldn't face El Tigre without getting some help at being a dragon. So I decided she was right."

"Makes sense to me." Jay waited a moment, then added, "I didn't meet any thunders."

"Then how did you learn to become such a fierce dragon?"

"I met some other guy who called himself Abuelo."

Her eyes widened. "Really? Ay-yi-yi. The mother cousins use him to scare their kids into being good."

Jay shrugged. "He seemed nice enough to me. A little distant, but if it hadn't been for him I'd have been even more untogether when the medicine wheel came into my head."

"That must have been so weird."

"Big-time."

"But you gave it back to Señora Elena, didn't you?"

Jay laughed. "You cousins really are a bunch of gossips, aren't you? But yeah, I did. Or I sort of did. We share it now. She's back to what she was before El Tigre showed up and I'm her backup—the one who makes sure that the things that are supposed to get done actually get done. Like getting rid of the *bandas* and keeping them away."

Lupita's features hadn't brightened, but now she grew serious again.

"I'm sorry about your friend Maria," she said.

"Yeah, me too."

"Did you tell Rosalie why she joined the Kings?" she asked.

"No. I made Maria a promise and I'm going to keep it."

"Do you still have to keep a promise when the person you made it to is dead?"

"I think so. And really, what good would it do if I did tell Rosalie? All it would do is really upset her."

"She might surprise you," Lupita said. "That girl's like the old bones of stone holding up the mountains. I think she deserves to know the sacrifice her friend made. If she never does, how can she properly mourn her?"

"I don't know. I promised Maria. . . ."

"Then promise me you'll at least think of it."

"Okay."

"Good." She clapped her hands. "So do you want to go tease the javelina boys?"

He smiled and shook his head. "Not tonight. I have to get up early tomorrow."

"Oh, pooh. You're no fun."

"What can I say?"

"You could say yes. You could sing 'Ai-yi-yi!' with me and then suggest we go dance with the aunts and uncles and twirl under the stars."

She gave him a hopeful look.

He shook his head.

"Well, you could at least walk me home," she said.

"That I can do."

Anna picked Rosalie and Jay up on Jay's first day at school. The girls sat in the front of the Valiant while he lounged across the backseat. He listened to them chatter for a couple of blocks, then sat up.

"I've got an idea," he said.

"You're not wearing your seat belt," Anna said.

"You're changing the subject."

"We don't have a subject yet except for you not wearing your seat belt. I don't want to get a ticket."

"Okay, I'll put on my seat belt," Jay told her.

"What's your idea?" Rosalie asked.

"We should have a big street party—a real fiesta," Jay said. "It'll be to celebrate the *bandas* being gone and we'll invite anybody who ever had to deal with their crap."

"That'll be everybody in the barrio," Anna said.

"Kind of my point."

Anna nodded, keeping her gaze on the street ahead. "That could be fun."

"And Malo Malo should totally be the headline band," Jay said.

"We're not playing anymore," Anna said. "Ramon says the band is done."

"Because of Margarita."

She nodded.

"But maybe this'd be the perfect opportunity for him to see how wrong he is in this," Rosalie said. "You guys sounded great with Chaco sitting in. It wasn't the same, but it was pretty amazing. Imagine how good it would sound if the rest of you actually had the chance to practice with him before a gig."

Anna nodded. "I really miss playing."

"So it's decided," Jay said. "When should it be?"

"You have to convince Ramon first," Anna said.

"No problem." Jay sat back. "Putting on my seat belt now."

Anna laughed. "Yeah, just as we're pulling into the school parking lot."

Everybody knew who he was. No one came up to Jay, but from collecting his schedule at the office to walking to his first class, whispers followed in his wake. It was so different from his old school, where he'd worked so hard to disappear into the woodwork. He wasn't sure he liked being the center of all this attention.

He had worried about having to vanish from class if some problem came up, but the morning passed without incident. No 'banger tried to sneak into the barrios to sell dope, jack a car, or throw up a few signs on newly cleaned walls. But at lunchtime the medicine wheel drew him to a few kids standing under a big old mesquite tree on the far side of the school yard. He looked around. He was waiting for Anna and Rosalie, but they hadn't come back from putting books in their lockers yet. No one was watching him.

He stepped into *el entre*, stepping out again right beside the kids.

"Jesus!" one said.

"No, my name's Jay."

The biggest of them stepped up. "What's your problem, man? You looking for trouble?"

"You're my problem. You're talking about starting up a gang and I'm here to tell you that if you keep it up, I'll be sending you out of the barrio. One-way trip, no return."

The kid laughed. "You don't look like much. You're the big deal supposed to be keeping us all safe? How're you going to keep us safe if you kick us out?"

"You misunderstand my job," Jay told him. "I'm only here to look after the people who live in the barrio—who want to be here. I couldn't care less what happens to you if I have to kick you out."

The kid shook his head. "You don't look so tough."

"I'm not," Jay told him. "Not really."

He held out his hand and woke a ball of dragonfire.

"You ever see how fast one of these things can burn up a person?" he asked.

The kids started to back away, all except for the biggest one.

"You don't scare me," he said, though his eyes said different.

"I'm not really trying to. I'm just explaining the rules that allow you the privilege of staying here."

"Man, the sooner I get out of this shithole the better."

"That's fine. But still no gangs."

"Screw you."

Jay nodded. "What's your name?"

"José Vargas."

"Are you related to Malo Malo's drummer?"

"She was a cousin. Why? What's it to you?"

"She'd be disappointed in you."

"Jesus, like I care."

"You should. Say good-bye to the barrio, José."

He grabbed the boy's arm and shifted them into *el entre*. When he let José go, the boy took a swing at him, but Jay dodged it with little effort. José took another swing and Jay asked the wind to push the kid away. José spun comically, arms windmilling to keep his balance.

"Enjoy your new home," Jay said. "Let me know if you change your mind."

Then he stepped out of *el entre*, just in time to meet the girls for lunch.

"Sorry," Anna said. "We got sidetracked in the bathroom."

Jay held up a hand. "Don't need to know more."

"So what've you been up to?" she asked. "You've got a bit of a glow happening there."

"Nothing. Just making new friends."

After school Jay went back to *el entre* to look in on José, but the kid started throwing rocks at him, so Jay left him there.

Rosalie had already told Ramon that she couldn't see him because she had too much homework. So did Jay, but he wanted to talk to Ramon before he started, and since Ramon wouldn't be coming by, Jay went to him. The medicine wheel led him to Ramon's backyard, where Ramon slouched in a lawn chair, his gaze on the night sky. He turned his head when he heard Jay's footsteps.

"Hey, dragon boy," he said.

"I'd say 'Hey, music boy' back," Jay said, "but you're not playing anymore, so . . ."

Ramon nodded then returned to watching the sky. Jay pulled over a plastic milk crate, turned it over, and sat down.

"Yeah," Ramon said. "It pretty much sucks. I haven't picked up an instrument since we finished that gig in front of the pool hall." He fell silent for a moment, then added, "No, that's not exactly true. It's just when I do pick up an instrument, there's nothing there anymore. No spark, no joy."

"Joy," Jay repeated.

"Okay, I know. I was totally the political animal and I wasn't exactly writing happy songs, but there was still a joy in what I was doing."

"Well, sure. If it had all been downer tunes you'd only have had a bunch of goths coming to your gigs."

"You're being hard on goths. They're not into depression. They're just not afraid of looking into the darkness."

"You know what I mean."

"Yeah. But the problem is, when I play now, it all sounds flat. I think I'm done. Maybe I'll start hanging out with the uncles, drinking mescal tea."

"Come on, man," Jay said. "The people need Malo Malo. You don't see me turning my back on my job, do you?"

"Actually, I think your job makes my job unnecessary."

"Good music's always necessary. I haven't solved all the problems down here. All I did was get rid of the gangs. The kids still need you to be their conscience. How else are they going to learn to develop their own? And you're their voice, man. You're the one who tells their stories."

Ramon shook his head. "With Margarita gone, it's not the same."

"Of course it isn't. But do you really think she'd want you guys to give up your music? Do you think that's the legacy she'd want to have?"

When Ramon didn't respond, Jay decided to take another tack.

"Remember that hike we went on?" he asked.

Ramon nodded.

"You told me then that it was important for us to follow our dreams. You said I should go for what I believed in because at least I would have tried."

"That sounds like something I would have said."

"You're not trying anymore."

"I told you. When I pick up an instrument—"

"That's when you're sitting back here," Jay broke in, "or in your room, right? On your own."

"Your point being?"

"You didn't try with the band."

"They feel the same way."

"Anna doesn't. I haven't talked to the others about it, but I know she doesn't."

"What are you saying?"

"You know what I'm saying," Jay said. "You need to get together with the others again. Find another drummer, or just work with Hector's beats."

"And if it doesn't happen?"

"At least you gave it a shot."

"I don't know. . . ."

"Okay," Jay said. "I've got one last card to play. Do you think Rosalie deserves to be with someone who doesn't have the courage to get off his ass and try?"

Ramon sat up. The light was dim, but Jay could feel the flash of anger.

"That's low, man," he said.

His voice was mild, but the fire stayed in his eyes. His hands gripped the arms of the lawn chair.

"Maybe," Jay said. "Probably. But I'm sticking with the question."

"What? You want me to break up with Rosalie?"

"God, no. I want you to play music again."

Then he told Ramon about the idea he had. Ramon didn't say anything for a long time. He stared across the yard. He looked past the old GMC truck his brother was rebuilding, past the cacti and creosote bushes, through the chain-link fence to the alley beyond. Jay didn't think he was actually seeing anything.

"And everybody else is on board with this?" Ramon finally asked.

"Don't you think that's something you should be asking them?"

Ramon turned to look at him.

"Man, this dragon business sits well on you. The kid I met back when wasn't half so decisive and sure of himself. There's steel in your backbone now, and no give."

Jay shook his head. "I would never try to make anybody do anything—except if they tried to bring the gangs back. That's nonnegotiable."

Ramon nodded. "You really think Rosalie's disappointed in me?"

"Are you kidding me? She adores you. What I was asking was if she deserved to be with someone—"

"Who doesn't have the courage to follow his dreams. Okay. I get it." He sighed. "You win. I'll give it a try. I can't promise anything. I don't even know if anyone besides Anna still wants to. But I'll try."

Jay checked in on José before he returned to his room at Tío's. The threads of the medicine wheel could have taken him right to where the boy was, but he chose to step into *el entre* some distance from where José sat on a rock, his arms wrapped around himself. He watched the boy for a while, then approached on silent feet until he was right behind him. He reached over José's head and dropped a bottle of water in the boy's lap.

"What the—"

José turned around, but Jay was already gone.

A few nights before the big free concert and fiesta that Malo Malo was headlining, Rosalie and Jay were sitting out in front of Rosalie's trailer. The sky was huge tonight—no clouds and the stars went on forever, even with the light pollution from the city. Occasionally, coyotes would start up their song somewhere in the desert and all the dogs would lift their heads for a moment before settling down again. The day's heat had died and a cool breeze was blowing in from the desert, carrying the scent of creosote.

"I think the concert should be a memorial for Maria as well as Margarita," Jay said.

Rosalie turned to look at him. "That can't happen. I know she killed El Tigre, but so far as most people are concerned she was still one of the Presidio Queens. Most people just think it was because of a falling out among the Kings."

"They'd be wrong."

"I know. I mean, probably. Oh, I don't know."

She sat back in her chair and stroked Oswaldo's head where the big mastiff was resting it on her lap. If he could have had his way he would have crawled right up on her the way Pepito was sprawled across Jay's knees, snoring softly.

"I made a promise not to tell you something," Jay said after a while, "but Lupita thinks it doesn't hold anymore because Maria's dead now."

He heard Rosalie's intake of breath.

"What do you think?" Jay asked. "Does it still hold?"

"Is this about why she became a Queen?"

"Yeah."

"Oh, my God. It has something to do with me?"

Jay sighed. He should have known. Once you started something like this, you had to take it to the end.

"Yeah," he said. "They were going to jump you. They wanted to get back at Tío because of the way he always speaks out against the gangs."

"I would *never* join a gang."

"You weren't going to get a choice."

Rosalie just looked at him, not getting it.

"Maria did what she did," he said, "so that they'd leave you alone."

"Tell me that's not true."

"I can't."

"Oh, God. That means . . . all this time . . ."

Rosalie put her face in her hands and started to cry.

Jay sat staring at her for a long moment, not knowing what to do. Finally, he put a protesting Pepito down and knelt by her chair, an arm across her shoulders. She burrowed her face against him, her whole body shaking. He patted her awkwardly on the back and wished Ramon was here because he didn't have a clue how to deal with this. He just knew he felt awful for having caused it. Lupita had been so wrong.

"I should never have told you," he said.

Rosalie kept crying, but she shook her head.

"I—I needed—to—to know. . . ."

Jay didn't think so. Not if it left her feeling like this.

The dogs were restless now, sensing her distress. Oswaldo had begun to growl, low in his chest. His gaze raked the yard, looking for the cause of Rosalie's upset. Little Pepito pressed himself against her leg, whimpering.

Jay came to a decision. He didn't know if it would help or make things worse, but he had nothing else.

He stood up, pulling her to her feet. She had to lean against him, unable to stand by herself, her shoulders still heaving.

"I'm going to show you something," he said.

And he took her to the plateau in *el entre*.

She stiffened in his arms, then slowly lifted her head and looked around. Jay didn't think she could see much through the blur of her tears, but she knew she was no longer in Tío's backyard. She stepped back, wiping her eyes on the sleeve of her shirt.

"What . . . where . . . ?"

She turned from the vast starlit view of the mountains.

She looked him in the face, then saw the tall cairn of stones that rose up beside them.

"This is where I brought her," Jay said. "It's a place she always wanted to see. She called it Aztlán."

"The promised land," Rosalie murmured.

She knelt down in front of the cairn and laid her hands on the stones.

"Oh, Maria," she began, then she could go no further.

She pressed her forehead against the stones and began to cry again, softer now. Jay sat beside her and put his arm around her shoulders once more, offering what comfort he could.

This hadn't been such a good idea, either, he realized.

It was a long time before Rosalie finally sat back. She wiped her eyes again, then turned to Jay.

"Thank you," she said.

"For what? Making you feel awful?"

Which was certainly how he felt for putting her through this.

She shook her head. "No. Thank you for giving me back my friend."

"I don't know what to do with him," Jay said to Lupita. "I left him here overnight, but . . ."

The two of them sat on top of a jut of red rock and watched José walking aimlessly through the arroyo below them, kicking at stones.

"He's just a wannabe gangbanger," Jay went on. "He hasn't actually done anything yet. But he seems pretty determined to get another gang started."

"Have you asked him why?"

Jay shook his head. "I can't get past the tough-guy mask he won't take off."

"He looks around fifteen."

Jay nodded. "Any ideas?"

"You have to get him to talk to you."

"Or maybe us?" Jay said.

Lupita grinned. "You're pretty chicken for a big, scary dragon."

"I just don't know where to go with this," Jay said. "I thought it was a good idea to take him somewhere to chill, but I didn't really think it through. I should have let it go until he actually did something."

"And then you'd banish him."

Jay sighed. "Yeah, that doesn't really work, either, does it?"

"You might not be able to save him. Some people don't want to be saved. They need to make their own mistakes, no matter how much it hurts them."

"I suppose. He's a cousin of Margarita's."

Lupita nodded. "Okay. And sometimes you have to go all tough love on them."

She stood up and brushed stone dust from her pants.

"Let's go see what he's got to say for himself," she said.

Jay was so used to Lupita in *el entre*, walking around

with her little horns and her floppy jackrabbit ears, that sometimes he forgot how other people reacted. José looked up when he heard them coming down into the arroyo and his eyes went so big Jay thought they might pop out of his head. And though he might be a wannabe 'banger, Lupita's appearance had him ready to bolt.

"Hang on!" Jay called to the boy as they approached him. "I just want to talk to you. Maybe we got off on the wrong foot."

José couldn't stop staring at Lupita.

"What . . . who's that?" he said.

Lupita grinned. "Oh, he's cute. Can I have him?"

"Not helping," Jay told her.

He stopped a few yards from where José stood, grabbing Lupita's arm to keep her beside him.

"Seriously, man," José said. "Did you spike that water you dropped on me last night? That *was* you, right?"

"I brought you the water," Jay said, "and it wasn't spiked. This is Lupita. She won't hurt you."

José nodded, though he didn't seem convinced.

"Is she the devil?" he asked.

Lupita giggled.

"Okay," José said. "I don't see the devil giggling. But, man." He gave his head a shake. "I don't know if I'm coming or going anymore."

"I know the feeling," Jay said. "So Lupita says I should have asked you why you want to start a gang."

José gave him a how-dumb-are-you look.

"You have to ask?" he said. "It's the only way to stay safe. You need your homeboys to watch your back."

"Against what?"

"Huh?"

"What kind of danger do you think you're in?" Jay asked. "The gangs are all gone from the south barrio."

"Yeah, and if we want to go across the river for a show or something? You don't think the 66ers are gonna be all over our asses?"

Lupita laughed.

"What's so funny?" José asked.

"Nothing. It's just you five-fingered beings make everything so hard on yourselves."

"Five-fingered what?"

"People," Jay said. "Humans."

José gave him another withering look. "You trying to tell me you're not human?"

"Have you really looked at Lupita?"

"Oh . . . yeah. But what about you?"

"You don't want to see my other face," Jay said.

Something in the tone of his voice kept José from making a smart remark.

"What are we going to do with him?" Jay asked Lupita.

She shrugged. "Let him do whatever he wants across the river. If he's stupid enough to still get mixed up with the *bandas* over there, is it really your responsibility?"

Jay shook his head. "That's Jesus Abarca's territory."

"So there you go."

"You can't tell me what I can or can't do," José said.

"Do you want to stay here?" Jay asked.

"No, but—"

"Then listen up. Do whatever you want when you're on the other side of the San Pedro. But if you bring gang business southside—and I mean *any* kind of gang business—you'll be seeing me again. But for only as long as it takes me to escort you to the border."

José shook his head. "What makes you think—"

"I think he needs a demonstration," Lupita said.

Dragonfire would be impressive, but Jay bent and picked up a rock.

"This is your head," he told José.

He asked the rock for a favor, and when he closed his hand the rock crumbled into dust. He opened his hand.

"And this is your head if you keep pissing me off," he said.

José paled.

"Yeah, it's real," Jay told him, "and yeah, I'm serious. Do we understand each other now?"

José gave a quick nod. "No gangs southside. Got it."

Jay crossed the distance between them, and José cringed.

"Relax," Jay said. "I'm just taking you home."

He returned the boy to the school yard. When he came

back to *el entre*, Lupita was still waiting for him.

"Ay-yi-yi," she said. "Aren't you the tough guy."

"I feel like an idiot saying stuff like that."

"But if it works . . ."

"I suppose. Are you coming to the street party?"

"I think all the cousins are coming. I just hope they don't get too rowdy, because then you'll have to go all tough guy on *them*."

She danced around, shadow-boxing with a fierce look on her face.

All Jay could do was laugh.

JAY

The night before the big fiesta street concert we're all out putting up decorations, setting up the stage and food tents, and getting the other last-minute preparations done. We don't get back to Tío's until past midnight and we're all tired so no one stays up long. Ramon and Rosalie go to her trailer, Anna crashes on the couch, and Tío and I go to our own rooms. Everybody else heads for home.

I lie down on my bed but I can't sleep. It's not only because I know Anna's on the couch, though that's part of it. Things are good between us. Not exactly where I'd like them to be—she's not my girlfriend yet or anything; I haven't even kissed her—but we're spending a lot of time together, getting to know each other better, and I have the feeling that if no new disaster comes along, it'll only be a matter of time.

Just lying here waiting to fall asleep makes me feel even more restless. Finally, I get up and step over into *el entre*. I figure I'll pay my respects to Maria—I haven't been out there for a couple of days. While I'm doing that I'll grab the chance to soak in some of the peace I always feel when I'm there. It makes me feel so grounded when I get back.

I shouldn't have thought of disasters—Rosalie's always telling me not to put negative thoughts out into the world because that just gives them substance. But I did, and wouldn't you know it, when I arrive on the plateau, someone else is there. I get that *ping* in my head that tells me it's a cousin. A powerful cousin, and nobody that I know.

She doesn't look like much from first glance. She's sitting cross-legged in front of Maria's cairn, a small woman with brown hair falling over her face as she plays a loose blues progression on an old beat-up small-bodied guitar. When she looks up, I see her violet eyes first, and then a moment later I see the spirit shape rising big into the sky behind her and I realize what she is.

"You're a dragon," I say. "Of the Yellow Dragon Clan."

The woman mutes the strings of her guitar.

"Yeah," she says. "Your grandma's really disappointed by that, too. White girl stealing away some Chinese kid's heritage and all."

"No, it's not that. I just didn't know it was possible."

"Yellow dragons come in all shapes and sizes and colors now. I know it wasn't always like that—used to be there was one emperor, one dragon protector. But the emperor's long gone and there are lots of us now. These days our protection is centered on a place, or it covers less conventional subjects."

"Say what?"

She shrugs. "You watch over the land on the other side of these borderlands. I protect the homeless."

"But . . . they're everywhere."

"Yeah, I know. It keeps me busy. It's like trying to carry water in a sieve, but I do the best I can. Mostly I travel around and set up operations that can help them help themselves."

Her fingers have gone back to the guitar again, noodling the way Anna does when she's talking, except the woman's playing a soft blues riff.

"What's your name?" I find myself asking.

"People call me Berlin."

What kind of a name is that? I want to ask and I guess she sees something in my face.

"It's not that complicated," Berlin says. "I used to walk

around with this great big wall inside me, keeping the world out. I managed to take it down after a while, but the name stuck."

"So why are you here?" I ask.

I can guess. I don't know what they think I've done, but the clan must have decided that I've become too dangerous so they've sent her to deal with me. Why else would a yellow dragon be here?

At least they didn't send Paupau.

I use the medicine wheel to check out the plateau, but the threads don't connect to anyone else—dragons, cousins, or even Abuelo. I suppose they don't think I'm much of a threat, because they only sent one of the clan to deal with me. But I won't go without a fight. I start to talk to the winds, to the stone under our feet, getting myself ready for her attack.

But she doesn't seem to be in any kind of hurry.

"It's about your grandma," Berlin says.

I sigh. So all of this is because I didn't give her the respect she expects from me. But the next thing Berlin says turns everything upside down.

"We're worried about her," she goes on.

"You're worried about Paupau? You're not here to . . ."

My voice trails off. Berlin's violet eyes study me for a moment, then she smiles and shakes her head.

"No, no," she says. "Everybody thinks you're doing a terrific job. They think you're already got the maturity of a dragon well into his second century. And I agree."

"Then what . . . ?"

"You know about dragons going rogue?" she asks.

I nod.

"It usually happens all at once," she says. "Something sets them off and they just snap."

Like I did when Margarita was killed.

I don't know if she can read my mind, or if it's showing on my face again.

"No, not like you when your friend was killed," she says. "You shut the rage down and got everybody out before the building collapsed."

"How do you *know* that?"

"I was here," she says. "I was with the others when we came to see what had happened."

"So it was like a cop has to go up in front of the police board if he discharges his weapon. You guys are the dragon equivalent of the police board."

She nods. "Kind of."

"Or like the feathered serpents down south."

"Yeah, more like that."

She has the decency to look a little embarrassed. She stops playing for a moment, then starts again in a different key.

"So what's this got to do with my grandmother?" I ask.

She mutes her strings and leans on the small body of her guitar.

"It's a little more rare," she says, "but sometimes a dragon starts to go off. It's a little something here, a little something else there, and the next thing you know you've got a rogue on the loose, tearing apart all the things she's supposed to be protecting."

"You think Paupau's going *rogue*?"

We might have had our differences, but the one thing that defines my grandmother is her control. I can't imagine her without it. For six years, I was witness to it every single day.

"We don't think it's gotten that far," Berlin says. "But the signs . . ."

"What signs?" I ask when she doesn't go on.

"Your grandma is the last of the Chinese yellow dragons," she says, then she pauses. "Well, technically, you are. But you know what I mean. Paupau is the last of the old-school ones. She's big on tradition."

"Tell me about it."

"But not so much anymore. She's made herself completely unavailable to those requesting her help. She spends her days sequestered in her apartment. At night, she wanders the streets waiting for someone to try to take advantage of the little old Chinese lady. And when they do, she . . . deals with them."

"Oh, crap. She hasn't killed anybody, has she?"

"Not yet. Until last night, she'd just been roughing them up—laying down the law, dragon style."

"What happened last night?"

"She put a man in a coma. She's so angry, but she won't say why."

But I know why.

"I think it's my fault," I tell Berlin. "I called home yesterday."

Both Rosalie and Anna had been after me for days, trying to convince me to call my parents.

"You're mad at your grandmother," Rosalie said. "I get it. Don't forget, I met her and she's a real piece of work. But your mother and father—"

"*How* can you not have called them since what happened at the dance hall?" Anna said. "They must be worried sick."

"I know. I'm just afraid that Paupau will pick up. I'm not ready to talk to her yet."

Anna shook her head. "Superhero," she said. "You've got to bite the bullet on this one and just do it. Take the chance."

Rosalie nodded in agreement. "You really do, Jay."

So that night I took my cell to the trailhead and punched the speed dial for my parents' restaurant. With the time difference, they should have just been closing up.

I was so nervous I actually had to sit down on the bench there. Some big, scary dragon I was. I found myself hoping that no one would pick up. I could tell the girls, hey, I tried but—

"Hello. You've reached the Dragon Garden."

All my nervousness drained away. Just hearing her voice made me feel happy and safe.

"Mom?"

"Jay! We've been so worried." I heard her call to my dad. "Jimmy, pick up the extension. It's Jay on the phone."

That's why my James became Jay. We already had a Jimmy in the family.

I had a good conversation with my parents. Scratch that. I had a *great* conversation with them. At least I did, until my mom said she'd go get Paupau so I could talk to her.

"Don't, Mom."

It was so quiet for a moment that I thought I'd lost the connection.

"Hello," I said.

"We're still here," Dad said.

I could hear the thoughtful frown in Mom's voice.

"Why don't you want to talk to her?" she asked.

I put it as diplomatically as possible.

"We're . . . we're having a difference of opinion. She doesn't think I should be allowed any free will, and I disagree."

"Is this dragon business?" Mom asked.

"Um, yeah."

Mom sighed. "Well, you won't get any argument from me on that. I never agreed all that ridiculous training."

When she said that, it made me wonder how much she

actually knew about what had been happening between Paupau and me.

"Why didn't you stop her?" I asked.

"It's like trying to move a mountain," Dad said. "Believe me, we tried. But this dragon business . . . it goes back forever—for generations in the Xú family. Your mother and Paupau have been arguing about it for years."

Mom added, "The only reason I agreed to your moving away without even finishing high school is that at least it would get you away from her for a while. Everything is always so serious with Paupau. I thought you should have a chance to be a seventeen-year-old, to find your own way, even if it meant my baby boy was moving so far away."

Even over the phone I felt embarrassed.

"I'm not a baby anymore, Mom."

She laughed. "You're my youngest. You'll always be my baby."

"I'm going to school here," I said to change the subject. "It's tough catching up this late in the year but I've got friends helping me."

"Good for you, son," Dad said.

We talked some more and it was all good until Mom finished with, "You know I'll have to tell Paupau you called."

Which meant I was giving her even more disrespect by not speaking to her.

"Yeah, I know," I said.

"I talked to my parents," I tell Berlin, "but I refused to talk to Paupau. We already had an argument the last time I saw her, so this was just going to make it worse. But I thought she'd only be mad at me. I never thought it would affect anybody else."

"So what *is* going on with the two of you?" Berlin asked.

"You have to ask? For six years she puts me through this insane exercise and meditation program, but she won't tell me why. At least not in any way that makes sense. She gives me riddles, not explanations. Then she just sends me out into the world where I'm supposed to find my destiny, but if I screw it up—and how do I not screw it up when I don't have a clue what's really what?—she and a bunch of her friends are going to come and kill me."

Berlin's quiet for a long moment.

"Yeah," she finally says. "That's been a source of disagreement for a lot of people in the clan. But you have to remember that she went through the same process herself. It's how the Chinese dragons have always done it."

"Tradition."

She gives me a humorless smile. "Pretty much."

"So did you have to go through that?"

She shakes her head. "But I wasn't any happier with the seven years I studied with a sensei in Japan learning meditation techniques, martial arts, kendo, and that kind of thing."

"Kendo?"

"Kind of the Japanese version of fencing."

"You don't look Japanese."

She shrugs. "I'm not. That's just the branch of the clan I hooked up with. They pulled me out of an orphanage—my parents were both dead. Dad was a junked-out musician, Mom a hooker. Not much life expectancy in either profession."

She says it like it's no big deal, but now I know why she chose the "emperor" she did.

"Anyway," she goes on, "life was tough in the dojo, but we always knew what we were doing and why, and we sure as hell didn't get sent out solo to wake up our dragons."

"So you see why I've got issues," I say.

She nods. "But I'm going to have to ask you to man up and try to make things right with her. Show her a little respect."

"Why should I?"

"Because you're a good kid and she needs it. Look, you don't have to kowtow to her like everything's okay and you don't have your issues, but surely you've got some good memories of her? Was it six years of hell, or just a tough boot camp that went on for way too long?"

"No, there were good times."

"Try to focus on them and not the crap that winds you up."

"But she was going to *kill* me."

Berlin shakes her head. "We'd have had to do something if you gone completely rogue, but killing you wasn't nearly the first option."

"I don't know. . . ."

"You don't have to go live with her or anything. You couldn't, anyway. You've got your own responsibilities now. But go talk to her."

"Or you guys are going to come down on her."

"We're just trying to stop this before it gets worse."

"The guy in the coma—what happens if he dies?"

She shrugs. "Then he dies. Look, these guys she's taking out, they're not exactly the cream of society, but she's hitting them way too harsh. She shouldn't even be dealing with that kind of thing. Our job is focusing on the big picture. We only deal with the little stuff if somebody specifically asks us to get involved, and even then it's our call."

For days now, I've been wrestling with questions about where I'm supposed to draw the line in terms of my responsibilities. I guess I couldn't get a clearer answer than that.

"So I talk to her and then I can go?" I say.

"That'll be up to you."

"But if I'm done with her, won't she just keep doing what she's doing?"

"I don't know," Berlin says. "Maybe it'll give her closure. At some point the sensei always has to let the student go."

"I guess."

"You won't know until you talk to her."

So I let her take me to Chicago. The cool thing is that she shows me how *el entre* can be used to bridge great distances. Like we only walked for an hour or so through an ever-changing landscape, but after that hour we were already on the outskirts of Chicago. The only bad moment was when we got a certain distance from the barrio and I felt the medicine wheel fade away.

I would have fallen if Berlin hadn't caught my arm.

"It's okay," she says. "It'll still be there waiting for you when you get back. It's always tough the first time."

I nodded, but as the emptiness filled me I finally really understood how Señora Elena must have felt.

"Can Paupau travel like this?" I ask now. "Because the last time she came to see me, she came by plane."

"She was showing you respect," Berlin says.

"I don't understand."

"Instead of just taking a walk through the otherworld and reaching you in an hour or so, she took the time to take the long way to see you. The way everybody else has to travel."

Great. Now I've got that to feel guilty about, too.

"Can you find your own way back later?" Berlin asks.

We're still in *el entre* but it's different here. All deep woods and granite-backed hills. But I remember the way we came.

"Sure," I say. "You're not going to audit my meeting or anything?"

She laughs. "I can see how it might seem like it, but we're not Big Brother always watching over each other. It's only when circumstances don't give us any other choice. We've all got our own lives."

"Will I see you again?"

"I don't have a phone or anything, but if you want to see me, just ask a homeless person where I am. They won't have a clue what you're talking about, but I'll know you're trying to contact me."

She puts a hand on my shoulder.

"Good luck, Jay," she says. "The clan thanks you for doing this."

"Pressure much?"

"You're going to do just fine," she tells me.

Then she's gone. I step out of *el entre* myself and go looking for Paupau.

The medicine wheel's not in my head anymore, but I find other threads—faint and delicate—that grow stronger when I concentrate on them. I realize that just as everything in the southside barrio is connected to me, all the yellow dragons are connected to each other, too.

It doesn't take me long to find Paupau.

She's in the waiting room of a hospital. I have a moment of panic thinking something's happened to one of the family, then I realize that she's here because of the guy she put into a coma.

Paupau going rogue?

Not likely. But she knows she screwed up.

She looks up at my arrival and I give her a low, formal bow. She looks smaller than I remember. Not exactly helpless—not by a long shot, really—but kind of shrunk into herself. Like for once she could actually use some outside help. I feel bad for her, but it makes this much easier.

"<All respect to you, Grandmother,>" I tell her in Mandarin. "<I hope you will forgive my unseemly behavior the last time we spoke.>"

She might know she screwed things up. She might look a little . . . well, diminished. But the iron is still there in her eyes as she studies me.

"<Why are you here?>" she asks.

"<Can't a grandson visit his grandmother?>"

"<Have you abandoned your territory?>"

"<It's not exactly mine,>" I say, "<but, no. Of course not.>"

"<Good.>"

She spends another moment studying me, then she says in English, "They sent you, didn't they?"

I don't play innocent.

"If by 'they' you mean a woman named Berlin, then yes. She asked me to look in on you."

"Hmm."

"And I, um, if I'm going to be honest, I have to admit I've been a little . . . frustrated about, you know. Us. Things that I was told and things I wasn't. Having to go out and somehow pull off this whole dragon thing without screwing everything up."

"I can remember feeling the same way, although I was somewhat older than you are now when the rebellion stirred in me."

I sit down in a chair beside her. "It did?"

"Of course. Though I always knew it was something you would have to do, I hadn't considered how painful it would be when you spread your own wings. I understand my own teacher a little better now."

"But why does it have to be this way?"

"It is tradition."

"Not for all the yellow dragons. Berlin told me it wasn't like that for her."

"Yes, but they aren't the royal dragons we are. Our ancestors protected the greatest emperors the world has known. There was a time when China was the center of civilization."

I nod. "But it's not that way anymore."

"No. So, then. All the more reason to keep tradition alive. What use is respect unless it is earned? How can one grow wise without first making mistakes?"

"Except a yellow dragon's mistakes can kill people. It can destroy—well, I don't know how much. Maybe a whole city."

"This," she says in a tone I remember from when she thought I was being particularly dense, "is why there are safeguards."

"Safeguards. Right."

"But you did well, Jay. The safeguards weren't needed for you."

"But if they had been?" I can't help but ask. "Would you really have killed me?"

"Killed you? Who has filled your head with such nonsense? I am a hard taskmaster, but I am not a monster."

"But—"

"If you had lost control of your dragon, I would have helped you subdue him and started your lessons all over again from the beginning. But if anyone had suggested that you be killed, they would have faced my wrath."

Wow. Didn't see that coming. But I believe her and I feel terrible.

"It is not an easy task that is set before us," she says, "but that is why we are as strong as we are. We must be, if we are to survive and prosper."

I give a slow nod. But then I have to ask her, "You know that we're one and the same with our dragons, don't you?"

"Of course."

"Then why do you always talk about them as though they're separate?"

"I find it easier to remember my humanity when I do so. The dragons are such mighty spirits. The power they wield can be seductive, so much so that we might consider that *we* are the emperors rather than the guardians."

Now it's my turn to study her. A lot of little things click into place, from Berlin first showing up on the plateau to my being here in this hospital with Paupau.

"There's nobody in a coma, is there?" I finally say.

"Of course there is," she says. "What else would you expect in an ICU?"

"But nobody you put in one."

"No."

"And you haven't been shirking your responsibilities and going out in the streets trying to bait muggers to attack you."

A hint of a smile flickers in the corner of her mouth.

"Why would I do such a thing?" she asks.

"So there was never any worry that you might go rogue."

She shakes her head and I realize I've been played.

"Why would you have Berlin come tell me all of that?"

"I wanted to see you. I wanted to tell you how proud I am of you."

"You couldn't have just come and told me that?"

"I tried," she says, "but you were not ready to hear it. You were too angry to listen to anything I might say."

"I guess I was."

"And now?"

"I still have issues."

"Good."

I have to shake my head. "How can that be good?"

"You are a yellow dragon of an old and noble clan. It is important that you stand up for yourself and know your own worth. It is your duty to protect your emperor, but only if that emperor is fair and just. You must have the strength of character to stand up to him if he is not. You cannot be intimidated by the grandeur of anything or anyone."

Then she repeats something that she always asked me when I complained that I wasn't strong enough to do something properly.

"Are you a yellow hamster?" she asks.

"No, Paupau. I am a yellow dragon."

She smiles. "Just so."

And then the iron leaves her eyes and she looks more like my mother than I'd ever tell either of them, so warm and loving.

"Your life in the desert," she asks. "Is it good?"

I nod. "Pretty much. And the parts that aren't, they're getting there."

"Then I am content."

I put my arms around her.

"I love you, Paupau," I say.

"I know. But not as much as I love you."

ACKNOWLEDGMENTS

◆ Special thanks to my wife, MaryAnn, whose help with reading and editing the manuscripts before anyone else sees them is part of this journey we've now been on for thirty-four years;

◆ to our pup, young Johnny Cash, who reminds me to get up from behind the desk and have a little fun, and our feline girl, Clare, who keeps me company, content to sleep away the day on a nearby bookcase while I am working;

◆ to Stu Jenks (check out his art at www.stujenks.com), Kin Jee, and Deborah Pela for their help with the background in this book;

♦ to Rodger Turner, friend and advisor in bookish things, and also Web master for my Web site and the indispensable www.sfsite.com;

♦ to my agent, Russ Galen, who's everything an agent should be, and much more;

♦ to my editor, Sharyn November, who always has faith that the story will be done and keeps me on my toes with her astute editorial pen;

♦ and last, but not least, to you, the readers, who receive these stories with such open hearts and minds. Your encouragement and enthusiasm nourish my muse and keep me writing every day.

Come visit my home page at www.charlesdelint.com. I'm also on Facebook, MySpace, and Twitter, so you can drop in and say hello to me there as well.

CHARLES DE LINT is widely credited as having pioneered the contemporary fantasy genre with his urban fantasy *Moonheart* (1984). He has been a seventeen-time finalist for the World Fantasy Award, winning in 2000 for his short story collection *Moonlight and Vines*; its stories are set in de Lint's popular fictional city of Newford, as is his novel *The Blue Girl* and selected stories in the collection *Waifs and Strays* (a World Fantasy Award Finalist).

He has received glowing reviews and numerous other awards for his work, including the singular honor of having eight books chosen for the reader-selected Modern Library "Top 100 Books of the Twentieth Century."

A professional musician for close to thirty years, specializing in traditional and contemporary Celtic and American roots music, he frequently performs with his wife, MaryAnn Harris, fellow musician, artist, and kindred spirit.

Charles de Lint and MaryAnn Harris live in Ottawa, Ontario, Canada, and their respective Web sites are www.charlesdelint.com and www.reclectica.com.